Me, The World,
and a Dog Named Steve

The Mini-Expeditions

Author
Wayne Cotes

Edited By
Denise Bohart Brown

Printed in the United States of America

ISBN: Softcover   978-1-63871-405-7
           Hardback   978-1-63871-406-4
           eBook   978-1-63871-407-1

Republished by: PageTurner Press and Media LLC
Publication Date: 08/11/2021

To order copies of this book, contact:

PageTurner Press and Media
Phone: 1-888-447-9651
info@pageturner.us
www.pageturner.us

To my family, who has stood by through the good times and the bad. Your support and unconditional love have meant the world to me. A special thanks to my mom and dad who taught me to love reading and set me on this path at a very early age.

A special thanks to my Mom who gave generously of her time to help me edit my writing. Hence the reason we're on Edition 5. I should have asked for her help sooner.

To those of you who were good enough to leave reviews, thank you. Good or bad, they help. This edition was done with your criticism in mind.

To the love of my life, thank you for putting up with me. For your encouragement and sense of humor and the hundred things you do every day.

To my friends who believed.

AUTHOR'S NOTE

Thank you for purchasing my book. As a still relatively new author, having anyone buy my book is exciting for me. I sincerely hope that you enjoy it. If you have comments or criticism, please either leave a review on Amazon or feel free to email me at wayne.cotes@yahoo.com. I will respond to every email.

I'm now on my fifth and final revision of "Me, the World, and a Dog Named Steve: The Mini-Expeditions." I listened to the critics and tried to cut down on the tedious details. I completely re-wrote the story "Mayan Treasure," took the proverbial knife to a few other stories in order to trim the fat, and added some new stories to fill the pages.

If you enjoyed these stories, please take time to read my other two "Me, the World, and a Dog Named Steve" adventures.

Semper Fi!

MEETING BOB

CHAPTER ONE

"What security does Hansen have with him?" the small man asked in heavily accented English. He was 5'5" tall and maybe 130 pounds soaking wet. He was only being brave because my hands were tied behind my back and my feet were bound to the chair I was sitting on. I knew the type; he was a coward at heart. I could practically smell the fear coming off of him.

"I don't know," I said through gritted teeth. "I told you, I only met the man earlier tonight." I actually didn't know what time it was. There were no windows for me to tell if the sun had risen yet. I suspected that I hadn't been unconscious for long. They had started questioning me as soon as I came to.

The little guy, Felipe is what the other three members of this little terrorist group called him, raised his hand and slapped me across the face. It stung but was hardly a devastating blow. He backhanded me for good measure. That hurt a bit more, but not by much. I was more disgusted then pained by blows. If a man was going to hit me, at least hit me with a closed fist.

"Pussy. You hit like a five-year-old," I spit in his direction. Either the spitting or the name calling made him angrier than he already was. This time, he swung from the back forty, his fist clenched in a tight little ball. He telegraphed the punch and as his hand came in, I tilted my head so his fist caught the top of my skull instead of my face. I heard the crunch of the bones in his hand. I'd have a knot where his punch landed but he came out on the short end of that little exchange.

Felipe whimpered and pulled his hand in close to his body. It was already starting to swell. "Word of advice kid, if you're going to be a terrorist, you need to toughen up some." Felipe didn't have a response to my sage words.

"We're not terrorists. We're environmental warriors. Your Neanderthal brain can't comprehend the difference but it's men like you who are the problem." This came from the only woman in the group. Her name was Laura. Dressed in all black, with her alabaster skin and raven hair, she looked like a disembodied head, standing in the shadows like she was. They had corrected me on the nature of their organization several times since they took me captive. If one of them was going to seriously hurt me, it was going to be Laura. She had killed before, or at least come close to it – of that I was sure. Like the smell of fear Felipe exuded, Laura stank of coldness and iron.

She didn't even glance at Felipe, who was still cradling his hand while trying to get some frozen vegetables out of the freezer of the old, run-down refrigerator in the kitchen of the building where they were holding me. "Look, Mr. Grey, it isn't you that we're after. Give us the information we want and when this is all said and done, we'll let you go." The tone of her voice was less than convincing.

"Lady, even if I knew the answers to the questions you're asking me, I wouldn't tell you," I said with more bravado than I felt. I was mentally prepared to be tortured, but only in so much as anyone could be ready. That conviction could dwindle fast, depending on what they planned on doing to me.

"Fine," she said, frustration finally tinging her otherwise robot-like voice. "If you have no information to give, then we don't need you any longer. Fred."

Fred lumbered up. There was no other way to describe how he walked. It was a slow, shuffling pace that nonetheless seemed to chew up distances. He wasn't particularly tall, but he was big – an intimidating combination of muscle and fat. He was the other one that worried me. Where Laura was cold and calculating, there was little going on behind

Fred's eyes. If ever you could say someone looked soulless, it would apply to Fred.

I tensed up and tried to scoot back the chair I was tied to. All I managed to do was almost tip over.

Fred was within a few feet of me when the fourth and final member of this group spoke up. "Hold on a minute, Fred. We may need Mr. Grey later. A hostage could be valuable if this doesn't go according to plan." I liked how they tried to be respectful by calling me Mr. Grey, like this was a business meeting instead of a kidnapping.

Dalton was the other ringleader of this little circus. He was more than Laura but neither of them liked sharing power with the other. If they weren't united in a common cause, they'd be at each other's throats. Their common cause, in this case, was the desired death of the multi-billionaire venture capitalist, Robert Hansen III, for "crimes against the environment." Based on their conversations since they had taken me hostage, they had held court, found him guilty, and meted out the sentence – all without affording Mr. Hansen the ability to defend himself against their accusations.

So, how did I get involved in this little foray into the darker side of environmental activism? I saved the man from getting his ass kicked in a bar fight and then drank his scotch. Apparently, that meant Mr. Hansen (or Bob, as I had taken to calling him, because it clearly irked him which I found amusing) and I were friends. This group jumped me, knocked me unconscious, and I woke up tied to this chair and being peppered with questions about Bob's security situation.

It had all started out as a normal vacation – the first real vacation I had taken in five years. All I had wanted to do was celebrate my retirement after 27 years as a police officer and 30 years as both an active duty Marine and a Sailor in the Navy Reserves. Some people, trouble always seems to find, no matter where they go. I am one of those people.

CHAPTER TWO

I had flown in to Managua, Nicaragua, and then taken a bus up to San Juan Del Sur where I planned to spend five days surfing, sunning, and eating. I had rented a small beach house near Playa Maderas with ready access to the ocean. I was on day three of my vacation and, if this house was still available, I was considering extending it another week.

After a morning of surfing, a few hours laying out on the beach, and a good whiskey while I watched the sunset, I was showered and changed and ready for a night out. My plan was to head to a bar that offered great food and ice cold beers. Major bonus: it was owned by a Marine, so I was all in.

When I arrived, my table wasn't quite ready, so I stepped up to the bar and ordered a beer. I was there maybe five minutes when an older gentleman also stepped up to the bar and ordered a whiskey, neat. I could tell by his accent that he was American. I asked anyway. "Are you from the States?"

He looked in my direction. His gaze was neither hostile nor friendly. "Yes," was his only reply. He turned back to the bartender and took his whiskey and placed a $20 bill on the bar and waived off getting any change back. He may not have been particularly friendly to me, but he left a good tip so he couldn't be all bad. Maybe he had come here just to have a drink and be left alone for a bit. I knew that feeling and respected his privacy.

I turned to look around the restaurant. The place was crowded. Not ten feet away from me was a table with about eight guys. It was hard to get an exact count as they kept coming and going and moving about. College students, based on the similar designs of their shirts, each of which depicted a roaring tiger and a university's name. The table was littered with empty beer bottles and pitchers. The whole table was loud and obviously drunk. I could smell trouble and these guys reeked of it.

I must have stared too long. "What are you looking at, old man?" one of them said belligerently.

"Just looking around, my friend," I replied in a calm voice, secretly hoping that my table was on the opposite side of the building from them.

"Well, look somewhere else."

I just smiled and nodded my head. It wasn't worth the trouble to stand my ground with the guy. I was confident I could take him in a straight-up fight (and maybe one or two of his buddies, too) depending on how quickly and aggressively I acted, but all eight of them was too much. Plus, at my age, I had aversion to pain, and a fight with that table was going to result in a world of hurt for me come morning. That, and I didn't want to end up in the local jail. I didn't know a lot about Nicaragua's penal system and I didn't care to find out the hard way.

I turned back around and took a sip of my beer. I kept an eye on the group via the mirror behind the bar as they polished off another pitcher and ordered a round of shots. I could see my own reflection as well. I was in good shape for a fifty-year-old man. My brown hair was cut short, military-style, with little gray showing. The same could not be said for my closely trimmed beard; it was peppered with white. Brown eyes with flakes of hazel sat above a nose that had been broken one too many times. The short-sleeved, button-down shirt I was wearing clung tight to the lean muscles of my arms. A lifetime of martial arts had left my muscles corded versus bulky. Wide shoulders, a narrow waist and long legs rounded off my 6'0" frame.

"Excuse me. Could you watch my drink? I need to use the restroom," asked the older man standing next to me. I hadn't paid much attention to him after my initial question, but now that I did, I could see in this setting he looked out of place. He was wearing a light blue polo shirt underneath a high-end sports coat. His silver hair was combed back and not a single hair was out of place. The expensive watch and the shoes that had to cost at least $600 completed the impression that he was a man of means. Most of those in the bar and restaurant were more casually dressed.

I smiled at him. "Not a problem," I said with a nod. "Bathrooms are on the other side of the restaurant."

"Thank you," he replied, setting his drink down next to mine and heading in the direction of the bathrooms. Unfortunately, the path he had to take went right by the rowdy group of college kids.

I saw the kid that had addressed me earlier turn away from the table, a full beer in hand, and right into the gentleman. The beer went up and in, spilling the contents all over the college student. "What the fuck, man?" the kid said loudly. A few of his friends turned their heads, but no one paid him any attention as the waitress set a tray full of shots down on the table. "You spilled my beer, asshole." The kid reached out and shoved the older man hard enough to knock him back a step.

Setting my beer down, I moved quickly to intervene. "Whoa there, big guy," I said, stepping in between the two of them. "Let me buy a round for the table."

"Fuck you, man," the kid said, turning his focus from the older man to me. "That asshole spilled my beer." He tried to move through me but my stance was set and I proved harder to push aside than he thought. "Get the fuck out of my way, dickhead," he ordered, his face coming with inches of my own. I could smell the reek of beer and rum coming off him.

The kid was itching for a fight. I glanced over at the table and his friends were still engaged in drinking their shots, chanting something as they raised their glasses in the air. I smiled at the kid and took a step back. The kid, thinking I was giving him some room, started to move forward and around me. My elbow came up – a short powerful strike that caught him on the underside of his chin and clicked his teeth together audibly. His eyes rolled back in his head and his knees buckled.

I moved forward and caught him. Not gracefully – the kid was heavier than I had thought, but I managed to guide him to a chair. I tapped one of his buddies on the shoulder to catch his attention. "Hey bro," I said when he looked in my direction, "your buddy here has had a bit too much to drink."

The guy looked at his friend and then pointed, covering his mouth to hide the laughter. "Dudes! Look at Billy. He's out, man." The rest of the group looked over and started laughing. I casually passed the knocked-out kid off to his buddy and then turned around to find the older man. He was standing where I had left him, but the look on his face was one of surprise.

I grabbed him by the arm and guided him toward the door. "We need to get out of here before that kid recovers. He's not going to be happy when he comes to and tells his buddies what really happened."

The man hesitated. "You knocked that man out," he said, concern in his voice.

"Yeah. Someone had to. He was looking for a fight and he had set his sights on you," I told him as we exited the restaurant. I glanced behind me to see the kid starting to regain consciousness. I increased my pace. "We really need to get out of here."

The man looked over his shoulder as well and nodded, keeping pace with me. I dropped my hand off his arm. Both of us continued walking down the street. I didn't have a destination in mind, I just wanted to put some distance between us and the restaurant.

"Thank you for what you did back there. The last time I was in a fight was fifty or more years ago." The man's voice was cultured, his tone perfect for public speaking.

I shrugged. "My pleasure. I can't stand bullies and that boy was a bully."

"I'm Robert Hansen." He stopped to introduce himself and stuck out his hand. I paused as well and shook it.

"Jerod Gray." We continued to walk down the street, our pace easing a little now that we were a few blocks from the restaurant.

"I'd buy you drink but I think I'm done with bars tonight. I have a bottle of scotch at my place if you care to join me," Robert offered.

"Depends on what you consider scotch," I said with a smile. It was a sixteen-year single malt that happened to be one of my favorites. "Absolutely," I told him, my smile widening. This evening wasn't turning out too bad, other than missing dinner.

We continued in silence for a few. "Do you go by Robert only, or do you have a nickname like Rob or Bob?" I inquired casually.

"I go by Robert. The only person who ever calls me Rob is my wife. I can't stand the name Bob," he said seriously.

I smiled again. "Bob it is, then," I thought to myself.

CHAPTER THREE

I was a little embarrassed at how easily I had been captured after leaving Bob's house. Granted, I'd had a little too much to drink. Nonetheless, it rankled that I had been taken by a group of amateurs. They had jumped me about two blocks from the large house that Bob was staying in. Laura and Felipe had approached me from the front with a map in hand under the ruse of asking me for directions. I had been happy to help and hadn't even heard Fred approach me from behind. He was the only one of the four with the brute strength to knock me out with one blow so I assumed it was him that hit me on the back of the head.

"Felipe, you stay back and make sure our guest doesn't get restless and try to escape. Fred, grab the bag," Dalton said. "Double check what gear you think you'll need. We leave in…" Dalton looked at his watch, "ten minutes."

"We don't know what kind of security Hansen has. We could be walking into a shit show," Laura said, the deflection of her voice not altering at all.

"It's a risk we'll have to take," Dalton said matter-of-factly.

Laura looked like she was going to argue, but stopped herself and just shrugged her shoulders.

Dalton and Laura went about checking their gear while Fred stood perfectly still in the middle of the room, a heavy-looking bag in his right hand. Felipe was still in the kitchen area holding a bag of frozen peas to his bruised and swollen hand. With everyone not paying any attention to me, I was able to start working on facilitating my escape.

A young Sailor attached to the Survival, Evasion, Resistance, and Escape School at the naval base in Coronado, California had shown me all the places she secreted items that might come in handy if she were ever taken hostage. She was impressively clever in where she hid things, and I had followed some of her advice and removed a razor blade from the waistline of my pants. It took me longer than I anticipated, but I finally managed to get the blade loose and went to work on the ropes binding my hands.

It took a few minutes to get the blade properly positioned so that it was cutting at the rope. I was pretty sure, based on the stinging feeling along my palm, that I had cut my hand as well. Small price to pay for a chance at freedom.

Working the razor blade like I was turned out to be slow going. My hand was at an awkward angle and I kept having to readjust the razor in relation to the rope in order to make it cut. While I worked, Dalton and Laura left the room, followed by Fred.

When I finally felt the ropes give, I glanced up at Felipe. He was still engrossed in nursing his hand. Quickly, I reached down and severed the ropes binding my feet. No sooner had I sat back up then Felipe glanced in my direction and gave me a suspicious look. I was concerned that he had seen me stick my hands back behind my back and that he would sound the alarm and bring the other three running.

I cleared my throat. "Can I get a glass of water please?" I asked, making my voice sound raspy.

Felipe shot me a baleful stare but grabbed a cup off the counter and filled it from the sink, wincing as he tried to use his damaged hand. He came to within a few feet of me and then tilted the cup upwards and poured out the contents. I gave him a blank look as the last of the water trickled out onto the floor. The corner of his lip twitched up in a condescending smile.

"God, you're a dick," I said with a sigh. "Will make it easier, though. If you were a nice guy, I'd have some qualms about what I'm about to do."

"And what do you think you are going to do, being tied up?" he asked sarcastically, and then he looked down at the ropes that had once bound my feet. Realization dawned on him and his eyes went wide and his mouth opened to sound the alarm.

I didn't give him a chance. My left fist shot out and caught him square in the solar plexus. His breath rushed out of his lungs. He tried to inhale but failed, and his face turned red and his eyes rolled wildly. I stood and grabbed him by the shirt and hit him two times solidly in the face and then dropped him, unconscious for the moment, to the ground.

I worked quickly, using the ropes they had bound me with to secure his hands and feet in such a manner that it left him hog-tied. He was just coming to when I shoved a rag in his mouth. "I hope you took some notes, Felipe. That's how a man hits another man. None of this pansy-ass slapping shit you did. Now, be quiet, or I might decide you're less danger to me dead." Felipe looked terrified but he didn't make any noise.

I made a hasty search of the room to find any weapons or tools I could use. There was little to choose from. I did find some heavy-duty zip ties, a metal pipe about two feet in length, and some duct tape. For a quick search, I wasn't entirely disappointed. A metal pipe made for an effective weapon in close quarters combat. Of course, against a gun it was less useful. While I hadn't seen any guns since coming to, I didn't rule them out. They were here to murder Bob, and a gun seemed like the simplest means to achieve that objective, plus the bag Fred had been carrying looked like it held a few.

I used one of the zip ties to secure the tape to my belt and shoved the rest in the cell phone pocket on my pants. I was almost to the door that led to the room that Fred, Dalton, and Laura had disappeared into when I heard a car start up. "Shit," I said to myself, and quickly crossed the short space to the door. No one was there and the car I had heard start was pulling away.

Dalton had said ten minutes and it hadn't been ten minutes yet. I needed to get to Bob's place. Problem was, I didn't even know where I was at.

CHAPTER FOUR

"Wake up, Felipe," I said politely, as I poured a glass of water on his face. He came to sputtering, the water having trickled into his mouth. I pulled the rag out. It took him a moment to orient himself to his surroundings and once he did, his eyes rolled wildly in terror.

"Here's the deal, numbnuts. I need you to tell me where I am and how to get to Hansen's place via the quickest route. Do so, and I won't feel compelled to start breaking things. I usually start with fingers and work my way from there." I grabbed a hold of one of his fingers and exerted a little pressure. He tried pulling away but with his hands and feet trussed up, he did little more than scoot an inch. "Now, where am I?"

I had known Felipe was a coward. He started talking right away and within a few minutes, I had the information I needed and I didn't have to break a finger to get it. I also managed to extract where my cell phone was located and attempted to call the police. While I got through, my Spanish was horrible and the man on the other side of the call didn't speak English. I gave up after a few minutes and hung up wondering if the police here could trace a call back to a cell phone like they did in the States. I hadn't bothered to get Bob's number or I would have called him.

The only transportation to be had at the little shack where I had been temporarily kept as a prisoner was a small, 70's model motorcycle with a 75cc engine. I had grown up on a farm and as a kid I'd had a similar bike, but that was years ago and even then, I had never been very good at riding. My inability to ride a motorcycle was a constant source of amusement for my second ex-wife. She was an avid rider but claimed she didn't have the patience to teach me, despite having a certification as a police motorcycle instructor for the department where she worked.

I wasted precious minutes finding the key, and then another few getting it started. I estimated that by the time I was on my way, Laura, Dalton, and Fred were probably already at Bob's and preparing to carry out their plan to murder him. As I gunned the engine and shifted roughly to second gear, I was praying I wasn't too late.

CHAPTER FIVE

I was two blocks away from Bob's place when the area around me was suddenly lit with flashing red and blue lights. I glanced behind me. A police officer in a newer model sedan was right behind. "Shit!" I said emphatically. I didn't have time for this. I considered for a moment just to gun it and make a break for Bob's. If the police decided to chase me, it may create enough of a scene to cause Laura and Dalton to cancel their plans. I twisted hard on the throttle and the little 75cc engine shot me forward.

One tiny flaw in my hastily and ill-conceived scheme – I had never been good at riding a motorcycle. I banked a hard left onto the street Bob's house was located on. Midway through the turn, I hit a pothole and lost control of the bike. I knew the moment I was going to crash. I had time to wish that I had brought the tough, bull-hide leather jacket that I had taken with me all over the world. It would have at least protected me from some of the road rash that was coming my way.

I fought to get the bike righted. I almost had it, too, but I hit a curb, causing the motorcycle to come to a sudden stop. I cursed Newton's First Law of Motion that stated that an object at rest remains at rest, and an object in motion remains in motion, unless acted upon by an unbalanced force. I was really concerned about the object in motion part. While the bike stopped, I did not. I flew over the handlebars and hit the ground at about 20 mph. I felt ribs crack as I rag-dolled it across Bob's front lawn.

I flopped to a halt about thirty feet from the now wrecked bike. I heard the police car screech to a halt and someone yelling in Spanish. I didn't try to do anything, I just laid there on my back, fighting the pain of breathing and staring up at the stars. Despite the pain I was in, I had to admit, it was a beautiful night.

CHAPTER SIX

"The papers are all done and your attorney should have you out of here with all charges dropped by 3:00 p.m. today," Bob told me from the other side of the bars in the visitor's area of the jail that I had called home for the past week.

After the accident, the police officers on scene had summoned the ambulance that transported me to the hospital for a short stay. I had received sixteen stitches, including four to a laceration on my cheek, four to a cut on my knee and the remainder to a nice gouge along my right elbow. More scars to add to an already scarred body.

"The three yahoos that planned to kill you?" I asked, referring to Laura, Dalton, and Fred. Felipe had been picked up at the small house where I had left him. I was tired and I ached all over and the tone of my voice was less than pleasant.

"They were caught at the Honduras-Nicaraguan border and apparently admitted their plans during their interrogation," Bob answered.

I thought about the interrogation that I had been submitted to. Not all of the bruises on my body were from my motorcycle accident. I had told them what I knew, which wasn't much. Part of me wanted to defy the investigators who "questioned" me, to spit in their faces. In the end, though, I hadn't done anything wrong outside of speeding, riding with no lights, and my very brief attempt to flee, which wasn't even a real pursuit. I was already almost at Bob's and all I wanted to do was attract enough attention to bring enough cops to the scene to scare Laura, Dalton, and Fred away. My plan had worked. I should be proud, but what I really wanted was to be in a decent bed in a place where I didn't have a dozen roommates.

"Good." That was all I could think to say.

Bob looked down at his hands and was quiet for a moment. When he looked back up, he looked thoughtful. "I have a proposition for you."

I gave him a wry smile. "As tempting as it is, no. I won't sleep with you for a million dollars."

I saw the corner of Bob's lip twitch up so I knew he thought the joke was at least a little funny. "Not that kind of proposition. I'd like to offer you some employment."

I was intrigued, but I had been working for the better part of 35 years and had just retired to enjoy the fruits of that labor. I didn't want to sit a desk or work a 9-to-5 anymore. Still, I asked. "What's the job?"

"I collect artifacts with a goal toward preserving them and, where possible, returning them to their rightful owners. There have been times when the artifacts I want to acquire are in the hands of people with little to no scruples. I've employed private investigation and security firms to assist me with this hobby with mixed results. Twice in the past week you have saved me from harm. You are quick on your feet during situations where others would most likely freeze, and I thought you may have the skillset necessary for the kind of work I'd be asking you to do." He took a moment to pause and draw a breath.

"You wouldn't have to work full-time, just when needed, but I can offer you a salary of $50,000 a year, plus bonuses paid based on the job itself. I can also offer benefits to include medical and dental, life insurance, and a generous expense account."

The attorney I had hired had told me exactly who Robert Hansen III was. He wasn't just a tourist in this part of the world. His company, Hansen Investments, owned several large coffee plantations in this area, as well as a gold mine and a factory that made wire insulation. In fact, Hansen Investments owned companies all over the world. He was a venture capitalist with a personal net worth of over $2 billion. He could easily afford the salary he was offering.

"$60,000 in salary, and I get to call you Bob," I said with a smile.

"If you call me Bob, I'm only paying you $45,000," he replied with a slight frown.

"Deal," I said, my smile growing wider. My retirement was enough for me to live on comfortably. It was worth the $5000 off his initial offer.

"I may come to regret this," he grumbled.

I smiled. It was the first real smile I'd had in several days.

BLOODCLOT

CHAPTER ONE

" Good evening. I have a room reservation for Dr. Jerod Grey," I told the lady behind the counter as I laid down my driver's license and credit card. The title of doctor was a real thing. I had earned my Doctorate in Education with a focus on educational leadership through a university in Southern California.

The lady looked tired and bored. I didn't blame her, it was 2:00 a.m. and I had just rolled in. I'd had a late start getting on the road and it had taken me almost six and a half hours to drive from Colorado Springs, where I had been visiting my mom, to Cortez, Colorado, where I planned on staying for a bit to explore Mesa Verde National Park.

I had lived here for a short while back at the start of high school. It had been a short stay, less than a year. My dad had been in construction and we moved around to follow the work. Cortez had just been a minor stop along the way. I didn't have such fond memories of the high school there, but outside of that, it had been one of the most fun places we had lived, and I had spent weekends and the summer exploring the mountains behind the house where we lived. We had also visited Mesa Verde once and I had been fascinated by the cliff dwellings and had always wanted to return. The park had been established in 1906 and occupied over 52,000 acres. With more than 5000 sites and 600 cliff dwellings, it was the largest archeological preserve in the United States and worth spending a few days exploring, particularly now that I was fully retired.

"Dr. Grey, you'll be staying in room 115," the hotel clerk said, as she pushed a key across the counter along with a map to where my room was at. I could have done without the map. It wasn't a big motel, but they had rooms with kitchens, and I preferred to cook for myself rather than eat out all the time.

The name tag pinned to her shirt said her name was Sarah. She looked older than my fifty years, but then I had been blessed with good genes. My mom, who was now into her seventies, could easily pass for my older sister. It also helped that I stayed in shape. I'd never have six-pack abs but at least my stomach wasn't hanging over my belt.

"Thank you, Sarah," I replied as I picked up my key and the map and headed out the door of the lobby. She looked surprised at my use of her name, but it earned me a smile. My Jeep was parked just a short walk away. Opening the door, I grabbed my canvas backpack and the messenger satchel that sat next to it.

There were four things I never left for a trip without: the backpack, the satchel, a faded, bull-hide leather jacket I always wore, and a pair of hiking boots that were good for anything from hiking all day to a casual dinner date. With the backpack and satchel, I could carry everything I needed – as long as I had the chance to do some laundry along the way. I generally only carried five days' worth of clothes with me. Not that I needed a reason, but doing laundry had been a good excuse to stop by Mom's for a few days while I was on what I hoped was the first of many road trips, now that I was retired. Plus, she enjoyed the company.

The motel room was larger than I expected, with a full kitchen and a small living room with a couch and comfortable-looking chair. The mattress on the bed looked thin and hard. Probably would torture my back but hey, that's what ibuprofen was for. I had spent 27 years as a police officer and 30 in the military, both as an active duty Marine and a Navy Reservist. The combination of the gun belt I wore as a police officer and the heavy body armor and Kevlar helmets I wore on deployment with the Marines and Navy had done a number on my back. 1600 mg of ibuprofen a day and regular trips to the VA Hospital for physical therapy were what kept me running.

I set my backpack and satchel on the chair and then rifled through the backpack until I had my shaving kit. A quick shower and I'd be ready for bed. I had a full day planned for tomorrow and I didn't want to waste any of it, despite the late hour I had gotten in.

CHAPTER TWO

My eyes popped open and somewhere in the back of my head I started the countdown to when my alarm would go off. "Three, two, one." I reached over to turn it off before it even got through one annoying cycle. I had an uncanny knack for telling time on my internal clock.

I popped out of bed and immediately regretted it as my back reminded me that I needed to go a bit slower. I grabbed the bottle of ibuprofen off the nightstand and quickly swallowed four without even water to wash it down. I hadn't been to the store yet to pick up any groceries, so breakfast was out of the question. My plan was to stop and refuel the Jeep at one of the local gas stations with a convenience store attached and grab a cup of coffee and something to eat there. When my day was done, I'd swing by the local market and pick up food for the next few days.

A quick shower just to freshen up and I was out the door, grabbing my messenger bag as I went. The satchel had a canteen of water, a few power bars, and several other little odds and ends that could come in handy if I ever ended up getting lost in the wilderness. It also held my gun. Even as a retired police officer, I was eligible to carry a concealed handgun in most of the fifty states. There were exceptions, of course – federal buildings, capital buildings, and, of course, national parks –

but I'd rather have it and not need it, than I would to need it and not have it.

My Jeep was a 2008 four-door Wrangler with a two-inch lift, 35" tires, and all the bells and whistles including a snorkel, winch, and heavier duty axles than what had come stock. It wasn't built with the intent of doing serious rock crawling, but it was enough to get me into the back country and out again without too much worry. It was still early enough in the spring that I had left the doors on but if the weather warmed up today, I could pull the back and side windows off the frameless top I had installed, and at least enjoy the weather that way.

I pulled into the gas station just a little past seven in the morning. Swiping my debit card and setting up the pump and nozzle so that I didn't have to hold it, I headed inside to pour myself a cup of coffee and hopefully find something for breakfast that was filling enough to see me through the day, if I ate a few snacks to supplement it.

A young boy sitting on a camping stool about five feet away from the front door caught my attention. He was about ten years old, with sandy brown hair and freckles across his nose and cheeks. Next to him sat a large box with the words "Puppies for Sale" handwritten on the front.

I stopped to look. Five little puppies jumped up the side, clambering for my attention. One sat off to the side gnawing on a stick she had found somewhere. She had one ear that was solid black and flopped over and the other that was white with a little blue in it that stood straight up. She spared me only a glimpse to make sure I wasn't going to steal her toy before going back to doing what she was doing. They were beautiful-looking pups with blue merle coats and bodies still round with baby fat. "What do we have here?" I asked.

"Puppies, sir," the boy said, stating the obvious.

"Unless I'm mistaken, these are blue heeler pups." After leaving Cortez, my family had ended up living on a farm just outside of Colorado Springs near a little place called Ellicott. Geographically, it had been no more than a blink of the eye along Highway 94, but it had been a great place to live and go to school. It had also been hard work as my dad dabbled for a bit in cattle ranching. We used herd dogs to help and those dogs had all been Australian Cattle Dogs. They were called heelers as a nickname due to their tendency to nip at the heels of livestock. They were some of the best dogs I had ever had. They could come in blue merle or with a red coat.

"You're not mistaken, sir." The kid was polite. "They're pure bred even if they don't have papers. My dad says they make great stock dogs."

I reached down and played with the five that were eager for attention. Their coats were soft under my hands as I petted them. For their part, they were puppies. They gnawed at my fingers, rolled around, and knocked each over as they vied for my attention. All but the one who was content to gnaw on the stick she had.

"How much?" I inquired.

"$20 a pup, sir."

"I'll think about it. You going to be here this afternoon?" I asked.

"I'll be here until they're sold sir, or my dad comes to pick me up. Whichever comes first," the boy replied.

I nodded my head as I stood up, reluctant to leave the puppies. It had been a few years since I had a dog. I thought about my lifestyle, the travelling I wanted to do, and how a dog would fit into that. "Maybe I'll stop back by this afternoon then." I took one last glimpse at the puppy gnawing on the stick and then went inside the store.

CHAPTER THREE

It had been a long day of hiking and exploring Mesa Verde National Park. I had spent an extensive amount of time at the Balcony House and the Cliff Palace, one of the best-known cliff dwellings in Mesa Verde. I was happy with the knowledge I had gained and the pictures I had taken.

Before I headed back to my hotel, I stopped at the grocery store to pick up food and was driving back when I spotted the gas station. It was around 4:00 p.m., but the boy with the puppies was still sitting there, just to the right of the entrance. I decided to stop in again and look at the puppies.

"You're back, mister," the boy stated casually as I walked up. I was surprised he remembered me.

"I am. How were sales today?" I asked.

"Pretty good. I have only one puppy left."

I looked in the large box and saw the one female pup who had been more interested in her stick than she had in me. Now though, she seemed lonely and was begging for attention. As soon as I reached down to scratch her behind the ears, she started licking and wrestling with my hand. It was cute and I was inclined to pick her up. She immediately went for my face, her tongue and tail moving a hundred miles an hour.

She wiggled in my arms quite a bit, and out of concern for dropping her in her fevered excitement at someone paying attention to her, I slowly dropped to both knees and set her on the ground. It quickly became apparent that she was undeterred in her desire to lick my face. Even given the disparity in weight between a 200-pound man and a little puppy, she was winning. I was bowled over onto my back by her enthusiasm and she crawled up my chest to pin my head between her small paws.

"Looks like she has made her choice, mister," the boy stated, in between my laughs.

"Looks like she has," I said, as I was finally able to sit up, a smile on my face. The puppy settled into my lap, happily gnawing on the fingers of my left hand.

"That will be $20," the boy said, holding out his hand.

With some struggle, I was able to pull my wallet out while I still sat on the ground and handed the boy a $20 bill.

"What are you going to name her?" the boy inquired.

I thought about it a moment. "I think I'll call her Steve." It seemed to fit the little bundle of energy in my lap and it made me laugh. A girl dog named Steve was humorous in my book.

The boy looked at me and shook his head. "Steve is no name for a dog, mister."

I disagreed but I didn't tell the boy that.

CHAPTER FOUR

Steve whined from the side of the bed that she was sleeping on. It was loud enough to wake me, at least partially. I wasn't a hard sleeper necessarily, but I didn't wake easy either. I rolled over to absently stroke her back, thinking she just needed some attention, but she whined again. I decided to take her out for a quick walk. She was a puppy, after all, and her bladder control wasn't quite there yet as was evidenced by the wet spot I had stepped on earlier in the night.

"Ok girl, we'll go for a quick walk," I said to her, sleep making my words muffled.

I had stopped by a local pet store before returning to the motel and bought her a few items: a leash, a harness, and a collar, as well as a few small tennis balls and, of course, cleaning supplies. She loved the balls and we had spent half our evening with me rolling them on the bed and her chasing them. The collar had a tag with her name and my telephone number on it. The tag clicked against the collar as she came closer to me.

Lifting her off the bed, I just hooked the retractable leash to the collar and hoped that she didn't pull hard enough on it to choke herself. It was the prime reason I had also bought a harness for her. She wasn't my first dog.

Opening the door to the motel room, I walked out into the cool night air. My internal clock said it was almost 1:00 a.m. I didn't really care, so long as Steve did her business quickly. We walked down the sidewalk toward a grassy area and once there, I gave her free reign, allowing the leash to extend to its maximum length. She immediately started sniffing around.

Steve had done what we came out to do and I was about to call her to me when I heard a disembodied voice say, "The cave is there. It was found by a couple of local kids last summer. I questioned both and it sounds legit. The way they described it, it matched up with the notebook you have. If the cave exists, then maybe that old codger we stole it from was right and the blood clot thing is there. We could make a fortune."

The voice was male. Deep, but he was talking quietly like he knew his voice usually carried. Even whispering, he was clearly audible. I didn't hear a reply, so I assumed that whomever it was, was talking on the phone.

I paused, questioning for a moment whether or not I had heard correctly. My first instinct was to call the police. What did I have to offer them, though?

I looked at the side of the motel and there were four windows that the voice could have come from, but there was nothing to distinguish one from the other. No lights on, curtains were all drawn, no way for me to tell where the voice had originated. Additionally, it didn't sound like the man here at the motel had whatever notebook he was referring to. Even if I could pinpoint the sources of the voice, I had nothing to give them. If anything, I'd sound like the crazy one, particularly if I brought up the "blood clot." What the hell was that a reference to?

"I know we looked for it before and ended up wasting a whole summer," the voice said, speaking again. "Quit being a bitch and meet me at the place where we get the waffles. Berry's or whatever it's called." There was a pause as I imagined the person on the other end of the phone replied. "6:00 a.m. I need some sleep."

That last statement almost earned him an "amen, brother." I finally glanced at my watch. Just a little past 1:00 a.m. like I had thought. Steve had wandered back over to me and was now laying on top of my boot, chewing on the boot lace. She had already left teeth marks on the leather hiking boots, which was going to force me to get another pair when I arrived back home. I didn't need her chewing through a boot lace, too.

Reaching down to pick her up, I heard the deep voice confirm that he and whomever he was talking to was going to meet at 6:00 a.m. at a place possibly called Berry's. I could try to look it up on my phone, or I could ask the receptionist at the front desk. I decided to go with asking the receptionist. Cortez was not a big town and she most likely knew every restaurant, not only in Cortez, but in the surrounding towns of Mancos, Dolores, and Durango, too. Also, the GPS on my phone had gotten me lost a time or two so I didn't really trust it.

I turned and headed back to my room. I didn't know who the embodied voice belonged to, but in my head, I had already started calling him "Bull." I'd be up early. Early enough to see who checked out before 6:00 a.m. I was hoping the body would match the voice and there would be three little old ladies and one big bubba of a guy checked into those four rooms at the end. That would make my life easier. That last thought was followed by, "When has that ever happened?"

CHAPTER FIVE

I was in the motel lobby at 5:00 a.m. and to my good fortune, Sarah was still working. Before coming over to the office, I had stopped and obtained the room numbers for the four rooms in question. My hope was that with a little flattery, a fat tip, and a bit of flirtation, I might convince Sarah to divulge some details on who was staying in any of those rooms.

Steve followed along on her leash, the lead shortened to keep her close to me. People fawned over puppies and Sarah was no different. I let her take her time petting Steve and Steve didn't mind the attention. When the fawning had come to its natural conclusion, I got down to some subtle prying.

I shouldn't have even bothered. While Sarah was happy to take my tip, she was unwilling to share any guest information unless I was a police officer and had a search warrant for that information. While I had been a police officer for 27 years, I was retired now, and with no way to get a search warrant, I was left to do it the old-fashioned way.

I went to the Jeep and maneuvered it around so I could see both sides of the hotel. To do so, I had to occupy a parking stall in the lot of the business next door. Normally, that wouldn't make me uneasy, but this place had several cameras and a lone vehicle sitting in an empty lot would attract the attention of whomever was monitoring those cameras. Hopefully, the cameras were there more for show than to serve any practical purpose. I wasn't interested in being contacted by the police or an over-eager security guard. Before I settled in, I pulled out a set of binoculars, just in case I needed a closer look at something.

On the seat next to me, Steve gnawed on a rawhide chew stick with single-minded purpose. Her tail would wag any time I reached over to pat her back. She didn't show any signs of food aggression, which was good. Not that I planned on having any other dogs, but if I did, I didn't want the two of them fighting over the food bowl.

A family with a husband, wife, and toddler walked out of the top left (from my point of view) motel room. The mom was carrying the baby and dad was carrying everything else. His hands were full as he tried to get everything to the car in one trip.

The next hotel room was also on the left-hand side. This was a larger man. Burly, with obvious muscle but also a lot of fat. He was over six feet in height and had to weigh close to 300 pounds. His light brown hair looked greasy and was slicked back away from his face, exposing a receding hairline. He was wearing a t-shirt with what looked to be a woodchuck on it, blue jeans, and cowboy boots that had seen a few miles.

I picked up the binoculars and after a moment to adjust to zoom and clarity, the man came into sharp view. No other distinguishing characteristics other than a thin, blond beard that wasn't visible with the naked eye from where I was positioned. There was also the hint of a tattoo peeking out from cuff of his t-shirt on his left arm. It could just as easily be a large mole or scar. I had no way of telling.

Putting down the binoculars, I looked at the clock on the Jeep. It was a quarter to six. About the right time. I glanced at the other side of the hotel and there was no sign of any movement. Making a note of the cars in the parking lot in the event I had to backtrack, I shifted the Jeep into gear and backed out of the parking spot I was in.

By the time I had pulled up to the motel driveway, the man was in his vehicle, a large full-ton pickup truck with Colorado farm tags. He pulled the dually out of the parking lot and onto Highway 491 toward the middle of town. I followed at a discreet distance. Doing a tail was easy on such a large vehicle.

The big guy pulled into the same gas station and convenience store where I had found Steve, and after getting the pump started, he went inside. I followed a few minutes later.

I knew as soon as he poured a cup of coffee and grabbed enough snacks to feed a small army that this wasn't a man who intended to stop by a restaurant any time soon so that he could eat some waffles. My suspicions that I had followed the wrong person were confirmed a minute later when the big man greeted the cashier and his voice was not near deep enough.

Immediately I left the store. Steve whined as I got in the truck. She was sitting up in her seat, her light-colored ear up and her eyes wide and bright. She seemed excited and I thought maybe she was picking up on my tension over the wrong call I had made. Or, maybe she was more astute than I was giving her credit for. I was a touch excited. The thrill of the chase had stirred the old cop's blood running through my veins.

It was now slightly past 6:00 a.m. I could either return to the motel to see if I could pick up a trail on Bull, or I could try to find this "Berry" place and hope that I would recognize one of the cars that had been in the motel parking lot. It didn't take me long to decide I was going to try and find Berry's place. The man had been forceful about meeting at 6:00 a.m. I didn't think he'd miss it and that meant he had already left the motel.

I continued up the 491 to where it split and turned right onto West Main Street. I would have missed the small restaurant just to my left on North Elm if I hadn't glanced down the street at the right moment. It wasn't called Berry's, but it was close enough that I thought I'd check it out.

Pulling into the parking lot, I checked the cars to see if there were any parked there now that I would have recognized from the motel. Nothing jumped out.

I backed into a parking space and after shutting down the Jeep, grabbed Steve out of her seat and put her on a leash to give her a quick walk before I went into eat. I toyed briefly with the idea of simply walking into the restaurant with her, but I knew there were rules against doing so unless she was a service animal. At eight weeks old, best I could do was weakly claim she was in training. She'd be fine in the car. I'd crack a window and it was still cool outside with the sun just barely lighting up the horizon.

I used our quick walk to see who was inside the restaurant. There were only four tables occupied. One was a family of four, one a man sitting at the counter by himself. Either of the last two tables is where my guy could be sitting, depending on who he had been speaking to on the phone earlier this morning.

The first of the tables that interested me contained a man and a woman, both in their late twenties to early thirties. Based on the tension between the two, they either were, or had been dating, and it had ended badly or was about to. The woman was attractive. Blond hair that looked natural, pulled back and done in a French braid that fell to about her shoulder blades. Ten years ago, I would have expected to see her on the cheerleading squad for a big college, and the intervening years hadn't been unkind to her.

The man sitting across from her was cut from the same cloth. I pegged him as the college quarterback. I couldn't judge his height, but he looked to be taller than me and bigger across the shoulders and back. His features were such that he could be Native American or Hispanic, dark hair and dark eyes set over a strong, proud nose.

He had peaked in college, though. Some of the muscle that layered his frame had gone soft; he was still wearing a class ring and hanging on the back of his chair was a letterman's jacket. Clear indications that college had been the highlight of his life. His face was set in a hard frown as he argued with the woman, his hands making sharp, angry gestures as he laid out whatever points he was making. He must have raised his voice because the waitress looked at him nervously and some of the other customers also paused to glance in his direction.

I put Steve up into the Jeep and grabbed her a chew toy to keep her busy while I went into the restaurant. I knew as soon as I heard the man's voice that I had the right guy. Bull. Given the man's size, the nickname fit. I sat at a table near the two of them that afforded me a good view and, after ordering a cup of coffee, black, from the one waitress on duty, tried to listen in on their conversation.

"I'm telling you, Rachel, this is it. I just need the notebook," Bull said, trying to whisper and failing. "If this really is the cave, we could be rich. Enough so that you wouldn't have to work at the bank anymore. We could go to Europe like you always wanted." There was a note of pleading in his voice tinged with desperation. He reached out and put his meaty hand over her much smaller one.

Rachel's head had been down but when he put his hand over hers, it snapped back up and her eyes flared wide as she snatched her hand back and held it to her chest like it had been physically hurt. "Don't touch me. You lost that right years ago."

I saw the tension in Bull's body – the tightening of the jaw and flexing of the muscles in his forearms as his fist clenched and unclenched. "Just give me the notebook and I'll leave you alone." There was menace in the tone of his voice.

"I don't have it," she said. The strength that had been in her voice a few seconds ago was gone and in its place was fear. I still didn't doubt my earlier assessment that Bull and Rachel had been a couple at some point and that it had ended badly. It was clear now that the relationship had been in the past. I was also convinced that it had been abusive. Maybe it hadn't started out that way, but I would have put money on that's how it ended.

"Where is it?" he asked, his voice still ominous.

Rachel looked like she was about to say something and then changed her mind, her lips clamping shut.

"Rachel!" Bull said, his large fist raising up. "Tell me!" That meaty hand slammed into the table with enough force that the silverware rattled, and water sloshed out of a cup.

"Excuse me, sir?" I said calmly. It was a gamble getting involved in a domestic dispute, particularly one that was rooted in violence and abuse. I could make things better in the moment only to make matters much worse later down the road. In truth, though, I had interjected myself the moment I heard a nameless, faceless voice mention the notebook at the motel at one-something in the morning. I might as well go all in. "You're frightening the other customers." I took a sip of my coffee.

Bull glared in my direction. "Mind your own business, old man."

I sighed. What was it with people calling me old man? "I'd like to. In fact, I'd like nothing more than to simply sit here and enjoy a nice breakfast, but here you are, yelling and carrying on. Threatening that young lady. Basically, being an asshole and assholes upset my digestion. Kind of spoils breakfast." I set my coffee cup down and leaned forward, my elbows on the table. "By the way, junior, I'm not old, I'm well-seasoned."

My voice wasn't threatening, but it carried with it the weight of experience. For most of my adult life, I had been leading men and women. As a Marine, as a police officer and member of the SWAT team, and as a Senior Chief in the Navy reserves, in combat and out. I held the bodies of men and women as they bled out, pleading with them to hang on just a moment longer. I had taken lives. There was an edge to men like me that other men recognized and, if they were smart, steered clear of. Bull wasn't that smart.

He pushed his chair back violently and stood up in the same motion. He was bigger than I had thought. 6'4" or 6'5" and with him now standing, I got the full picture of just how immense he was. I let out another sigh. I didn't doubt my capabilities. I had been studying martial arts since I was fourteen years old, but one punch from a man that big was going to hurt and I avoided pain where I could.

"I see." I let a slight smirk twitch the corner of my lips up as I stood up.

"John!" Rachel said from behind the behemoth standing before me with nothing more than a table and air between us. So, the man had a name. I preferred Bull, it seemed more fitting.

"John, now don't you do anything stupid in here. Your daddy will have a fit." The waitress spoke almost on top of Rachel. She had the phone in her hand, and I was hoping she was calling the police.

John hesitated, fear flashing across his face at the mention of his father, but only for a moment – then he was lumbering forward.

My brain started calculating all the possibilities. I quickly identified any improvised weapons – the napkin holder as a blunt impact weapon, the butter knife or fork that were laid out as the place setting for my table, my hot coffee that could be a temporary distraction if thrown in the face – all of those things and more raced through my head. How much room did I have to move back, how many feet was it to the door if I had to make a quick exit?

There was also the trick of not being the instigator, at least of the physical aspect of this fight. John had to throw the first blow. After that, I was reacting in self-defense. I brought my hands up, palms facing toward John. If there were cameras in the diner, it would appear I was trying to calm him down. On a more practical note, it brought my hands to a spot where I could defend myself against any punches thrown.

John lumbered to within a few feet of me. His fists clenched tightly as they hung along the sides of his body. Neither of us said anything and the tension mounted. Behind him, Rachel begged him to stop and just to sit down. "John, please. I have the notebook. I'll give it to you but you have to leave."

That caught the big man's attention. He turned his head and torso to look back at Rachel. She pulled a worn and beaten leather-covered notebook out of the handbag she was carrying and dropped it on the table. It wasn't what I had been expecting. For some reason I was convinced it was going to be a stack of loose-leaf papers, yellowed with age and bound together with twine. It was more of a journal. A supple leather cover dyed a dark maroon held dog-eared and worn pages. The journal had been around for years, probably several decades, but it was still relatively new in the grand scheme of things.

The minute the journal was out, John forgot all about me. He took the few steps back to the table and picked the journal up. After thumbing through a few pages, he let his hands drop to his sides, the journal now tucked between his arm and his body. He seemed about to say something to the girl, but she shook her head no as her chin sunk to her chest and tears started to flow from her eyes.

Anger, or maybe embarrassment, caused his face to flush red. He took a long step forward and then he was past her and headed to the door. When it finally closed behind him, the restaurant let out a collective sigh of relief as the tension drained from the room.

I took a few steps so that I was standing in front of her table. "Rachel, I'm Dr. Jerod Grey. I'd like to ask you a few questions about what just happened here." Sometimes using the title helped. It conveyed to the person I was talking to that I was someone in a position of authority and trust.

She looked up, using the back of her hand to wipe away the tears. She nodded her head and indicated the chair that John had occupied less than a minute ago.

CHAPTER SIX

I climbed back in the Jeep, taking a few moments to pet Steve who was so excited to see me that her whole body wiggled back and forth as she wagged her tail. It had taken a little coaxing and a few cups of coffee, but Rachel had finally told me the story about the journal, how she and John had come to be in possession of it, and how they had spent their last summer together before college.

The journal had come from an old man who lived just a few miles outside of town. Several years before the man had purchased the property, there had been a murder-suicide there and the myth was that the chalk outlines were still visible on the floor. Rachel, John, and a few of their friends had been drinking and thought it would be a good idea to break into the house just to see if the rumor was true. There hadn't been a plan to steal anything, but John grabbed the journal to prove that they had been there – just in case someone questioned his integrity on the matter.

I had suppressed a chuckle at that statement. It reconfirmed my working theory that John wasn't that bright. By swiping the journal, he had turned a criminal trespass (a misdemeanor) into a burglary (a felony,) and waving the journal about in order to convince people that he had committed said burglary seemed like a stupid thing to do. Right up John's alley.

The journal had contained notes and drawings leading Rachel to believe that the old man had probably been one of the archaeologists who worked with the National Park Service at Mesa Verde. One section contained information about a cave that the man had been searching for and the word "blood clot" was underlined multiple times. John had been convinced that the term referred to a ruby and that if they could find the cave, they could find the ruby.

Rachel had never been convinced that there was a treasure, but she thought the idea of searching for it would be fun. They spent the summer before college camping out for days at a time and combing the area for the mysterious cave. As the days stretched into weeks without the cave being located, John's obsession grew, as did his frustration.

"That was the first time he hit me," she had told me in a voice barely above a whisper. "I knew he had a rough time growing up and that his dad used to beat his mom, but he swore he would never be like that." Despite the intervening years, the pain of that betrayal was still there.

When it happened again, she left him. She went off to college in one part of the state and John in another. Rachel hadn't ever intended to move back to Cortez. A failed marriage, an outsourced job, and a sick mother all seemed to conspire to bring her back here. She worked at the bank now. Her mother was doing better and helped Rachel take care of her son during the day while Rachel was at work. She had heard John had been injured playing football and never got back to 100%. He ran a vehicle repair garage for his father now.

Since moving back, she had run into John maybe half a dozen times. He'd never inquired about the journal until just recently. A couple of local kids had apparently found a cave that matched the description in the journal.

"Do you know the kids?" I had asked.

She shook her head no, but she also told me that she could probably find out. "It's a small town," she told me. I thanked her for her time and left her with my business card.

It took me a moment to get Steve settled and back to chewing on one of several rawhide sticks that she had amassed in the front passenger seat of the Jeep. My next stop was going to be the large retail store I had passed on my way into town. I carried most of what I needed for camping in the back of the Jeep, but my long road trip had depleted my supplies and I needed to restock. After that, I was going to try and locate the man whose house Rachel and John had broken into all those years ago. Rachel had given me a good idea as to its location and the man's name: Dr. Darryl Henderson.

CHAPTER SEVEN

I knocked on the heavy wooden door and then stepped back so that I could be easily seen if someone chose to look through the peephole. It took a few minutes, but the door opened and a wizened old man peered up at me through thick glasses. He was dressed in a robe, white t-shirt and sweatpants that looked about one size too big for him. His gray hair had thinned to the point where shaving it all off would look better than the few straggly hairs that were left.

"Can I help you?" he asked. His voice was something you'd hear in a lecture hall, a clear baritone that would carry to a hundred students.

I extended my hand, a business card between my fingers. "I'm hoping we can help each other, sir. Dr. Henderson, my name is Dr. Jerod Grey. I have some information about a journal that was stolen from your house about ten years ago."

The man seemed surprised and then suspicious. "Do you have it?"

I shook my head no. "No, sir, I don't. But I know who does and perhaps with your assistance, I can get it back for you." My hand was still extended; he hadn't reached for the card yet.

Dr. Henderson looked like he was about to take the card and then his hand hesitated. Disappointment clouded his face and he slowly shook his head no. "I'm sorry, Dr. Grey. That was a long while ago and it was frivolous work. A hobby that became an obsession for me. Without realizing it, the people who broke into my house that day did me a favor. Losing that journal broke the spell that finding Blood Clot's cave had on me.

He said "blood clot" differently than John and Rachel had. Like it was a person instead of an object. It piqued my curiosity. "Sir, if it wouldn't be too much trouble, I'd like to hear about Blood Clot. Maybe over lunch and a beer?"

The old man thought about it a moment. I was prepared for him to say no but then he reached up and took my card from my hand. "You know, Dr. Grey, I'd like that. There's a sport bar downtown called Markey's. I'll meet you there at about noon. They have cold beer and good burgers."

I smiled. "Sounds good, sir. See you at noon."

Returning to the car, I looked at my watch and, with a few hours to kill, decided to take Steve to the dog park, hoping there were other dogs there for her to socialize with. Pulling back onto the black top from the narrow dirt road that led to Dr. Henderson's house, I saw a black and white squad car parked off to the side of the road about a quarter mile in the opposite direction I was headed.

I didn't initially pay the law enforcement vehicle any real attention until it kicked on its lights and peeled away from the dirt turnout where it had been parked. Pulling off to the right-hand side of the road and coming to a stop, I fully expected the cop to pass me by on his or her way to a hot call, so it surprised me when he pulled in behind me.

I took the Jeep out of gear, set the parking brake, and rolled down both my front windows so that it didn't matter which side he approached me from. I glanced in the side mirrors and saw the man clearly for the first time.

He was young, maybe mid-twenties. A deputy, based on his cowboy hat, jeans, and white uniform shirt. He approached with the swagger of a man who had been working as a cop long enough that he felt competent in the performance of his duties but not so long that a healthy dose of cynicism had been added on top of the competence. Old cops had an air of bored indifference about them. They could think of a dozen places they'd rather be besides riding a squad car on patrol, but they'd go about their duties with the same dogged efficiency that they'd apply to any home project. The rookie approaching my passenger side window didn't have that yet.

In the mirror I saw him take a glance in the back seat before he stepped up to the passenger side window. "License, registration, and proof of insurance."

I reached up and removed the registration and insurance card from the visor and then carefully removed my wallet from my back pocket to hand him my driver's license. "Is there a problem, Deputy?"

He collected my documents and looked them over. "I'll be back with you in a moment."

An uneasy feeling came over me. I hadn't done anything wrong to my knowledge. Could be something as simple as a taillight out, but with the Deputy not being forthcoming, I didn't think it was that easy.

This time when the Deputy approached, he approached on the driver's side of the Jeep. Pulling open the driver's door, he asked me to place my hands behind my back and to face away from him. Not knowing what was going on, I complied as he put handcuffs on. I didn't want to escalate the situation by being argumentative, but I was becoming increasingly convinced that whatever was transpiring was not on the up and up.

The Deputy removed me from the car and took me back to his patrol vehicle. There he searched me, removing everything from my pants pockets including my wallet, which he held onto as he had me have a seat in the caged part of the squad car, and then he got in the front seat.

"Hey, what's going on here? I haven't done anything," I told him.

"Save it for the judge. You were in an altercation earlier today," he said gruffly as he started to rifle through my wallet.

"Altercation? I didn't even raise my voice," I growled back, knowing this had to have something to do with John. Now I was starting to get mad.

"He swore out a statement to the city police," the Deputy told me. "Said you beat him pretty bad."

"There wasn't a mark on that kid when he left. There were cameras at the restaurant. They'll show you what happened," I said incredulously.

"Not my case. I was just told to keep an eye open for a man matching your description driving a Jeep." He paused in his search of my wallet. "You're retired?" he asked, looking at my police ID.

I nodded as I sat back on the hard plastic seat of the squad car. "27 years," I said quietly. "You can call a friend of mine. He works in the area with the Bureau of Indian Affairs. He'll confirm who I am."

"What's your friend's name?" he asked.

"Nez. Eugene Nez."

* * * * *

Now that the handcuffs were off, I rubbed my wrists. They hadn't been put on particularly tight, but handcuffs were not meant for comfort. We were now standing outside his squad car. He had turned off the overhead lights but left the rear deck flashers on to warn traffic. Not that there was any other cars on the road where we were at.

"You've stepped into a steaming pile of shit here, Lieutenant." The Deputy's name was March Chacon. He was a good kid overall, with three years working in Montezuma County. "John Bass is the son of Bruce Bass, the richest man in the county. I won't say that the city police or the mayor are in his hip pocket, but they don't buck him on a whole lot of things either."

I nodded my head in understanding. The kid hadn't liked that I stood up to him and he told daddy. The City PD may have known he was full of shit, but they were going to go quietly about doing what was expected. The phone call to Nez had helped. Nez was not only well known in the area, he was respected. I had known him from my days in the Navy and there wasn't anyone more loyal or more honest than Eugene Nez.

"Is there a place I can rent a car?" The local law enforcement types would be looking for my Jeep. If I could switch that out for a rental, I could probably get around without being hassled. At this time of year, Cortez would have plenty of tourists and picking out one guy wouldn't be so easy. The Jeep, on the other hand, would stand out.

"Sure. You can park your Jeep at my place for now. I have an old barn we can put it in and then I'll give you a ride to the rental place."

I nodded my head in thanks. March was a good deputy, trying to do the right thing in a rough place.

CHAPTER EIGHT

I had grabbed what I needed out of the Jeep and made sure Steve was comfortable before taking the rental back into town. I would have preferred a vehicle that stood out less than the bright, red sedan the rental company had on the lot. It would do, though.

I met Dr. Henderson at the bar and grill. He hadn't been idle in the few hours since we first met. He had found and interviewed the two kids who had rediscovered the cave. "It's going to be right in here," he told me, as he circled a spot on a map. "Has to be."

"What exactly is it that I'm looking for?" I inquired.

"It's a cave. Inside the cave is supposed to be the oldest known painting of the story of Blood Clot, a mythical hero of the Ute tribe." He was clearly excited and I asked him to tell me the story.

"Long ago, an old man lived in a tipi with his wife. Every day he went out to hunt but game was sparse and he and his wife were going hungry. One day the man discovered some buffalo tracks and followed them to where the animal had stopped. There he found only a big clot of blood which he collected and took home to his wife.

"He gave the clot of blood to his wife and told her to boil it. When the blood clot was about to boil, the man and woman heard cries coming from the pot. They looked inside and found a boy child.

The couple pulled the child from the pot, washed him and wrapped him in a warm blanket.

"Over the course of the night, the baby grew larger and by morning, he was able to crawl. By the second day, the boy had learned to walk and by the third, he was walking with ease. The couple called the boy Blood Clot and treated him as their own son.

"Soon the boy started to hunt and the old man made him a small bow. The boy at first brought home a small creature and birds but soon, he needed a larger bow. He would never bring the game home himself, but instead would send the old man to get it.

"One day he brought home a cotton-tail rabbit. *'Look father, I have slain and animal with a white short tail.'* The next day, the boy said, *'Look father, I have slain an animal with a stripe on its back that lived in a whole in the ground.'* The boy had killed a badger and the old man brought it home and cooked it.

"The day after, Blood Clot told his father, *'I have killed an animal with black ears and a black tail.'* The boy had slain a female deer and the old man brought it home and cooked it and they were happy.

"The old man gave the boy a large hunting bow and the boy brought down a mountain lion and the day after that, a mountain goat. The old man looked upon his adopted son with pride, *'Look mother, each day he kills a different animal,'* and the couple was content and well-fed.

"One day, after slaying a beaver, Blood Clot went to his parents and told them, *'I must leave and seek a village. Tonight, when I hunt, you must stay in your tipi and latch the entry shut so that the wind does not blow it open. You are to stay there until I call you out.'*

"The couple listened to their son and that night, the wind howled and the couple became scared that their son was out in such dreadful weather. The old man started to go out but his wife stopped him, *'Remember what Blood Clot said, we are to stay here. Have faith husband.'* And the old man stayed.

"That morning, Blood Clot called to them. *'Come out and see what I have brought.'* The couple exited their tipi and found buffalo laying all around. *'Dry the meat and hides and the meat will last you a long time.'*

"Blood Clot asked his mother to make him lunch which she did, giving him pemmican. The cried and asked him to return but that day, he travelled.

"A few days later, Blood Clot came upon a village and there he met with the village Chief. The Chief gathered the whole tribe around and asked the boy to introduce himself and to tell them what tribe he belonged to. Blood Clot said, '*I do not know what tribe I belong to.*'

"The Chief asked the gathered people, '*Does anyone know to which tribe this young man belongs.*' People named the tribes – Elk, Otter, Beavers and others but none of them felt right. Then the Chief said, '*I think he must belong to the tribe of the buffalo.*' That felt right and Blood Clot immediately knew that is where he belonged.

"Blood Clot stayed with the tribe and married the Chief's daughter. Like he had with his parents, Blood Clot went out at night and hunted and would send someone from the village out to bring back his kill, but hunting had been poor and the tribe was hungry and winter was setting in.

"Blood Clot told the Chief, '*The tribe must lock themselves in their tipis tonight and no matter what they hear, they are not to come out until I call for them.*' The Chief understood and passed the word onto his people.

"That night, the wind howled fiercely and many of the villagers were terrified. The Chief's daughter was frightened for Blood Clot and against his wishes, she opened the door to the tipi and went out into the storm to find her husband.

"She found Blood Clot just outside their tipi and he told her, '*You were not supposed to come out until I called for you.*' With that, Blood Clot jumped on his horse and galloped away, turning into a buffalo as he did so. His wife cried and tried to chase him, but in vain and from that point onward, Blood Clot ran with the buffalo." Dr. Henderson finished the story and then took a long drink of his beer.

"Quite a tale," I told him with a smile. "And this cave is supposed to contain a painting of the story?"

The Doctor nodded his head vigorously as he put down his beer and wiped his mouth free of the foam. "Oh yes. If I had my journal, I would show you. The art there is quite remarkable. The cave was first found in 1968 by a group of hikers. It was rediscovered again in 1972 by a couple who were documenting their trip with a Polaroid camera. I have two of the pictures that they took in the journal."

It was my turn to nod. "Ok, then. I'll leave bright and early tomorrow." We finished our meal and paid the bill. It was going to be a long day hiking for me so I planned to relax the rest of the day and go to bed early.

CHAPTER NINE

Steve and I made our way across a landscape of sagebrush, pinyon, pine, Indian paintbrush, juniper, and yucca, following the established trail that would put me closest to the small geographical area where the cave was supposed to be. There were others up this early, hiking the trails before the summer sun made the temperature uncomfortable. Steve, being a puppy, alternated between running beside me and riding on top of my canvas backpack. I thought she might wiggle around too much to make the top of my pack a viable spot for her, but other than her incessant need to lick my face, she seemed content there.

It was three hours in when I found the bend in the trail that meant it was time to go off the established route and into the bush. The sun had climbed above the horizon and was beating down on us mercilessly. The broad-brimmed hiking hat that I picked up at the store was keeping most of the sun from my head and face and provided Steve a place out of the sun as well.

We took a break at mid-day, sitting in the shade of a tree while I ate a quick lunch consisting of jerky and a trail mix of dried fruit and nuts. I shared bits of the jerky with Steve and made sure she stayed hydrated. When we were done, we continued with our hike.

I paused and pulled out the map I had been using. I had already covered quite a bit of ground and the sun had been on the decline for some time. I estimated I had another two hours of light before I'd have to give up my search for the day and find a place to camp.

Looking at the contours on the map, there was a small canyon about a quarter of a mile from my current position that I thought might be a good place to check. The kids Dr. Henderson had interviewed hadn't mentioned a canyon, but they were fourteen or fifteen years old. I had been that age once and it was amazing how little details like that had often slipped my mind.

Folding the map and putting it away, I picked up Steve and set her on the top part of my pack and continued with my search. I was at the canyon's rim within ten minutes. It took me another five to find the easiest route down to the canyon floor, and not long after that, I was making my way along the bottom. Once I was down at the canyon floor, I set Steve down to burn off some energy. She was happily sniffing at holes in the ground and chasing grasshoppers as we walked.

The canyon was about half a mile long and at its narrowest point toward the western end, looked to be about ten feet across. The narrow parts of the canyon also had the steepest sides. Here and there, I saw signs that the canyon had been subject to flash floods over the centuries. I had checked the weather before coming out here and there had been a slight chance of rain later this evening, but nothing significant. Nonetheless, I didn't want to be down here when the sun set.

"Alright Steve, let's make our way back topside and then find a good place to camp for the night." Excitedly, she bounded over to me and then attacked a loose shoelace on my hiking boots. I laughed at her antics and proceeded to make my way back out of the canyon.

CHAPTER TEN

I found a nice, sandy spot beneath a Douglas fir tree that would make for a comfortable spot to sleep. No fire. The semi-arid zone where Mesa Verde was located would make it prone to wildfires if a spark landed on something dry. The weather was nice enough and I didn't want to take the risk for a little comfort. I did have a small, single burner propane stove that I used to heat up the packages of dried food I had brought with me. After dinner, I smoked a cigar, sipped whiskey from the bottle I had brought and played with Steve in the light of a small electric lantern until my eyes started to get heavy.

The sun breaking over the horizon woke me from a sound sleep. I stretched, trying to ease some of the tension in my back before getting up and preparing breakfast. The movement woke Steve who had been sleeping next to me. Being awake, she found it necessary to wiggle her way onto my chest so she could get right up to my face, tongue going a hundred miles an hour. I finally had to pick her up off my chest and set her on the ground where she wandered off to take care of her morning business.

Breakfast was a quick affair consisting of oatmeal and coffee and within an hour of waking up, Steve and I were once again walking along the canyon floor. I almost walked right by the entrance to the cave. It was close to the ground, not much taller than a foot or so high, and almost completely hidden behind a rock formation.

I took some time looking at the surrounding area for any evidence that the cave was being used as a den for any animal. I wasn't a tracker, but I had picked up a thing or two in my time as both a police officer and while I was in the military. Not seeing any indication of habitation, I took off my pack and, pulling out a flashlight, set out to explore the cave.

Years of sediment had settled around the cave's mouth but further in, it became impressively larger so that I was able to stand without difficulty. I scanned the cave walls and was awed by what I saw.

They were less paintings than they were petroglyphs with colors of brown, deep reds, and grays used to highlight various animals or provide a hue to Blood Clot's skin. The rock carvings were detailed and while there was obviously some wear from the passage of time, they were remarkably well-preserved. I could see where a one-dimensional view provided by the only known photographs of the cave would leave one with the impression they were paintings verses rock carvings, though this was speculation, as I hadn't seen the pictures personally.

I pulled out my GPS device with the intent of marking the spot with a waypoint. I should have known better. There was no way the device was going to transmit through hundreds of feet of rock. I'd have to mark the waypoint at the entrance.

Getting back down on my stomach, I wiggled back out the cave entrance. I was almost through and about to stand up when I felt a sharp pain in the back of my head. My brain had just enough to time to ask, "What the hell?" and then darkness overtook me.

* * * * *

I came to with my head pounding. I didn't have to reach up to the back of my head to feel the knot that had grown there. Not that I could anyway, as my hands were tied behind my back. My feet were likewise tied with thin, cotton rope.

I squashed my first instinct to fight against the bonds and instead, spent a moment looking around. I spotted John Bass by the entrance to the cave. He was sweating in the hot sun, leaving his black hair lying flat against his skull. He made several attempts to get down on his hands and knees as if to enter the cave, but he stopped each time, clearly nervous that his bulk wouldn't fit through the narrow opening.

With him distracted, I used the time to test my bonds. The ropes holding my feet were loose but the ones on my hands were tight. I tried to get to the razor blade I kept secreted in my waistband, but with the way I was propped up against a rock, I couldn't. The movement of my hands did attract some attention, though. Steve, thinking I was trying to play with her, started biting on the ropes. I was hoping her sharp, little puppy teeth would cut through the thin strands – I just had to keep her interested long enough to do so. With her behind me, I thought John wouldn't be able to see her.

"There's no ruby in there, John," I said. Speaking caused the pain in my head to increase slightly and made me wince.

The sound of my voice startled him and he spun around, his dark eyes wide with surprise until he realized it was me speaking and then his face grew angry.

"There has to be," he growled.

I shook my head no. "Blood Clot refers to a person. A Ute Indian myth about a great hunter, not a gem or a treasure. There's nothing in that cave but rock carvings."

John looked baffled for a moment and then he shook his head to clear the unwanted thoughts. "There has to be. I've been searching for it for years."

"You can look for yourself. I'm obviously not going anywhere," I said, using my chin to point to the rope binding my ankles together. He gave me a smug look and then tried again to muster the courage to squeeze through the tight opening.

This time he went for it and for a moment, I thought he would become wedged into the entrance. I could see the brief panic in his movements as he fought to pull himself through and into the larger cave beyond. Inch by inch he moved forward until his shoulders were past the narrowest part and then he disappeared all the way into the cave.

Quickly, I tested the bonds on my hands again and managed to loosen them considerably. Steve, annoyed that I was interrupting her play time with the rope, started gnawing on my fingers, letting loose a little growl in the process. Normally I'd find the whole thing amusing, but I didn't know how long I would have until John decided to come back out of the cave. With my hands and legs tied, I was at a distinct disadvantage.

A minute passed and I had loosened up the ropes sufficiently to access the razor blade. A few minutes later and I was free. Able to stand now, I involuntarily reached up and felt the knot on the back of my head. There was a little dried and crusted blood, but otherwise the skull seemed intact. A hard blow, but I hadn't even been left with the symptoms of a concussion – not counting the pounding headache.

I was going to grab my pack and go. That would have been the smart thing to do. But this man had hit me over the head and then tied me up. I couldn't let that go. I set the bag where I could grab it in a hurry if I needed to and then found a rock to sit on until John had satisfied himself that there was no ruby in the cave. I didn't have to wait long.

* * * * *

John had wiggled his way past the entrance. There was a moment when his shoulders got stuck in the cave's mouth, sending him into a near panic as he scrambled and strained to get through. It was only a matter of inches and once inside the cave, he lay there panting as he tried to get his wind back.

His heart still beating hard, he leveraged himself up to his knees and switched on his flashlight. His eyes hardly saw the petroglyphs decorating the walls; he was looking for the ruby. The cave floor was bare and there were no tunnels off the main chamber. Nothing and nowhere to hide a ruby. He kept looking, though, digging here and there, hoping to find it buried somewhere, anywhere.

Reality finally hit him and he collapsed to his knees, a single tear escaping his eye. That ruby was supposed to be his ticket out of this town, his escape from his oppressive father, and his way back to Rachel and the life he dreamed he would have back when he was in high school. All his hopes and dreams shattered in that moment.

* * * * *

The man who exited the cave didn't look like the angry man that went in. This man was a shadow. His shoulders were slumped and his head hung so low his chin rested on his chest. He didn't even see me sitting there, watching him cautiously. He seemed smaller somehow, deflated. Dr. Henderson's journal was visible in a cargo pocket of John's pants.

I no longer felt anger toward John. I felt sorry for him. This had been about more than money to him, it represented an ideal – one that had crashed in around him. "I'm sorry," I said, even as a part of me shouted that he had brought a lot of this on himself.

He looked up at the sound of my voice, his eyes red-rimmed and puffy. He had been crying. "You can go now," he told me quietly.

A dozen smart-ass remarks popped in my head. In the end, though, I decided to walk away. Grabbing my bag, I spent a moment setting the waypoint into my GPS. After, I walked up to John and removed the journal from his pocket. He didn't stop me or even so much as look in my direction. I thought about saying something more but decided against it. Calling Steve to me, we I started the long hike back to our car.

CHAPTER ELEVEN

D r. Henderson raised his mug. "Thank you," he said, emotion choking his voice. "Your finding the cave allows me to finally finish my life's work. I can't tell you what that means to me."

I lifted my mug and touched it to his. "Glad to have been of help, Doctor." In the background was the buzz of the dinner crowd at Marky's Bar and Grill.

"Darryl. Please, call me Darryl," he said.

I tipped my head in his direction. "Darryl," I replied with a smile. "What happens now?" I asked.

"That will be up to the Tribal Council and the National Park Service regarding the ultimate disposition of the cave and the petroglyphs. It's the Utes' heritage and the Park Service's property. I did get tentative approval to explore the cave and document my findings." He sounded excited and I could hardly blame him. This was something he had been searching for over the course of two or more decades.

"What about after you've explored the cave?" I inquired.

Dr. Henderson looked thoughtful as he set his mug down on the table. When he looked back up again, he gave me a crooked smile. "Maybe I'll write a book."

THE SILVER ROD OF
SULTAN KEDAFU

CHAPTER ONE

I stepped off the plane and onto the sweltering blacktop of the Ambouli International Airport in Djibouti City, Djibouti, Africa. It was the height of summer. Sweat immediately beaded up on my forehead and started running in little rivulets down my back. There were places in the world that were supposedly hotter, but I was having a difficult time imagining that to be the case.

I pulled on the broad-brimmed hat that I had brought with me. I had traded in the normal leather hiking boots I generally wore for lighter weight and better-ventilated boots. I still had the bull-hide leather jacket, but I threw it over the top of my canvas messenger bag, trusting to the long-sleeved khaki shirt I was wearing to keep the sun from frying me where I stood.

A hot wind blew in from the interior of the little country located on the Horn of Africa that did nothing to cool the temperature. It was akin to standing in the path of an industrial-sized hair dryer. I worried about Steve. She was in a crate in the belly of the aircraft and it would not be long before the temperature inside the plane would climb to a point that was unbearable. The crew of the Ethiopian-based airline had tried reassuring me that my dog would be fine, but it didn't stop me from worrying. If I'd had a choice, I wouldn't have brought her along on this trip, but there hadn't been anyone to watch her for me back in the States. I had even tried reaching out to friends I hadn't talked to since my days as a police officer.

Beside the guarantees of the crew, I did have one other thing going for Steve and me – we had an in with customs, and there weren't supposed to be any delays in getting us through quickly. Djibouti's policies on bringing pets into the country were easy enough to comply with. If your pet was under six months, no vaccination records were required. They'd vaccinate them after landing. Over six months, and you had to have a vaccination record issued at least a year prior to travel. Steve was now just under six months old but I also had her records with me. My contact and I had agreed that this would smooth the process.

I scanned the small group of people standing near the tarmac-side entrance to the airport and received a welcoming wave from a dark-skinned man with black, close-cropped, curly hair. If not for the little bit of gray at his temples, he could have easily passed for a man in his early twenties – his skin was that smooth and unblemished by the passage of time. He looked no older than the last time I had seen him, and that had been almost a decade ago.

Mohamed Kamil and I had struck up a friendship during one of two stints I did right here in Djibouti City, at Camp Lemonnier, while I was serving in the Navy reserves. He had been a part of the Djiboutian Navy and we had worked closely together. Like me, he had since retired. He now worked for Jean-Luc Duval, a French archeologist in the employ of my good friend, Robert "Bob" Hansen, the multi-billionaire venture capitalist who had requested I fly out here to provide "technical assistance" at an archeological site several hours north of the city.

I approached Mohamed; he took my hand in his own and pulled me close for a quick embrace. "As-salamu alakim," he said, loud enough to be heard over both the din of the crowd fighting to get into the cooler interior of the airport and the jet engines warming up on the tarmac.

"Wa alakim assalaam," I said, smiling as I returned the traditional Arabic greeting.

"I hope your flight was well. I had your pet and the case you brought with you moved to our vehicles. One of my men will make sure your dog is given water," Mohamed said in heavily accented English. He spoke the language fluently, along with French and Arabic, but his accent could make it difficult to understand him, unless you had worked with him for an extended period.

"Thank you," I replied gratefully. I still wanted to put eyes on Steve. I had been able to take her out of the crate for some exercise during a long layover in Ethiopia, and while it was only a short flight from there to here, Steve was still just a puppy. As thoughtful as Mohamed's actions were, his men wouldn't be able to tell if Steve was doing ok, as they had no baseline for how she had been just a few hours prior.

I quickly explained my concerns and Mohamed was more than understanding. "Of course, my friend. Of course. Let us proceed through customs."

Following Mohamed, I entered the cool interior of the airport. I was prepared to stand in line with everyone else, but Mohamed led me to an office where a Djiboutian Lieutenant Colonel was sitting behind a scratched and dented metal desk. There was a quick exchange of words between the two. The tone wasn't unfriendly, but I could tell it was all business with no small talk.

The Lieutenant Colonel requested my passport and I handed it over. A stamp and a picture from a small camera mounted to the desk, and Mohamed and I were heading toward the main entrance of the airport. A few minutes after that and we were climbing into the backseat of a Toyota Land Cruiser.

"Mr. Hansen has friends in very high places here in Djibouti. He has invested heavily in the infrastructure for our city and many of the jobs created by such investments go to Djiboutians. That makes him popular among both the political elite and the common people," Mohamed offered as a quick explanation for why we flew through customs.

I took a moment to check on Steve and pull her out of her crate. She seemed no worse for wear and was more than happy to see me, if her tail wagging and stubborn attempts to lick my face were any indication. It took me a moment to get her settled down and then we were off.

The air conditioning in the vehicle worked well and made the ride more comfortable, despite the heat of the sun beating down on the windows. Mohamed and I engaged in small talk, catching up on the last ten years. Outside of a brief introduction, the driver remained quiet.

After a time, the conversation died down and we both sat in silence, looking out the windows at the barren landscape. Steve wrestled with my hand for a bit, but slowly settled in and went to sleep, her head on my lap. Bob had given me some details about why I was here, but had been vague on others. He had simply said that Jean-Luc required some technical assistance and then refused to elaborate further. "Your cover is that you're doing an audit for Hansen Investments. Jean-Luc will fill you in on the rest when you get there," he had told me.

I trusted Bob, but I wasn't big on mysterious trips, at least not to Djibouti. Had it been Fiji, maybe I'd be less apprehensive.

CHAPTER TWO

The camp turned out to be more elaborate than I had anticipated. I had pictured tents without environmental controls pitched in the barren wasteland that was northern Djibouti. Instead, I found an enclave of shipping containers stacked two high that formed a square around a large central courtyard area. A man wearing a blue polo shirt, faded orange corduroy pants, and flip flops opened a chain link fence and let us through one of the courtyard's two entry points. A tall, central pole held camo netting that stretched to the surrounding containers, casting the whole area with shade.

The driver parked off to one side near two other SUVs.

"Welcome to home base," Mohamed said with a wide smile, clearly proud of the compound. "We house thirty personnel here, including our laborers, security and the few researchers we have. Dr. Duval's office is over there," he told me, pointing to a single stack container.

The Navy had used the same concept at Camp Lemonnier. The Soldiers, Sailors, Marines, and Airmen that called the base home lived primarily in Containerized Living Units, or CLUs. The CLUs were big enough to house up to eight people. It could get cramped, but it was better than some of the places the military had housed me. Just as long as they had air conditioning.

These CLUs all did. Power was derived from two large diesel generators in a fenced off area just outside the compound. In addition to the generators, I had seen two tanker trucks that held water and a third tanker that held fuel. I did quick calculations in my head and estimated that new trucks had to come out every week to keep the camp supplied with fresh water and power.

When the SUV had come to a stop, I picked up Steve and got out, putting her on the ground. After being cooped up for so long, she had excess energy to burn. Normally, I wouldn't let her run free in a place I wasn't familiar with, but I saw no one in the courtyard besides Mohamed, the driver, and me. There had been the man at the gate who let us in but he had disappeared – my guess was into the air-conditioned interior of one of the CLUs.

"This is quite the operation you have here, Mohamed," I said, as I took in the lay of the land.

"Mr. Hansen has been quite generous. There is not a strong archeological presence in Djibouti despite calls from the international community for the government to preserve the heritage and artifacts of the Afar and Somali people who call this country home. If not for people like Mr. Hansen and Dr. Duval, we wouldn't have the few items we do." The passion for his job came out in the tone of his voice and the rapid movement of his hands as he talked. He had always been proud of his country and its history.

"Robert is committed to preserving and protecting ancient relics," I said. I never called him Bob in public.

I went around to the back of the Toyota and grabbed my backpack and messenger bag along with the hard, plastic case I had brought. "I'll come back and get Steve's crate here in a minute, if you can show me where I can put my gear for now."

"Of course, my friend, of course. Please, follow me. Dr. Duval and his assistant are in the field but will be back for dinner. I will show you where you can shower and rest for now."

I called Steve to heel. It was something we were still working on. She had learned come, sit, lay down, and stay easy enough but heel was coming more slowly. I had to call her again and then have her sit for a minute before she'd follow me without running off.

The CLU Mohamed showed me to was typical for its type. There was a single twin-sized bed up against one wall, a small desk, and a wooden wall locker. A door to my right led to what I assumed was the bathroom. Other than the furniture being of slightly better quality, with its tan vinyl floors and metal walls, the room wasn't any different than the CLUs I had lived in the last time I was here with the Navy.

I thanked Mohamed and then shut the door and sat down on the bed. For the first time in two days, I was completely by myself. No crowded gate waiting areas or airports full of people. There was a small whine from the floor next to the bed. I looked down at Steve who was trying her hardest to jump on the bed with me. It was too high for her small body to make it. Leaning down, I picked her up and sat her on the bed next to me. "Well, not completely alone." She gave me a small bark and then laid down.

The room was comfortably cold. I leaned back on the bed and laid my head on the pillow. I was asleep moments later.

CHAPTER THREE

"D r. Duval, it's a pleasure to meet you." I shook the smaller man's hand before sitting in the padded, metal chair on the other side of the cluttered folding table he was using as a desk. A laptop computer covered in dust sat off to one side. An equally dust-covered desk lamp was opposite the computer.

Jean-Luc Duval was a good six inches shorter than I was, and with his slender build and youthful appearance, it was hard for me to picture that he was a tenured college professor with nearly twenty years of archeological experience both in the lab and the field. His dark brown hair was swept back away from his face and held in place by some sort of gel or oil. Considering my own hair had been cut close, military-style, for over thirty years of my life, I had never grasped the idea of haircare products outside of shampoo.

The archeologist's face and hands were freshly scrubbed, but dirt had left smudges on his beige shirt. He had been at the dig site for most of the day, having been back for only the past hour.

The nap I had taken had done wonders to revive me. I was still tired but refreshed enough to hold a reasonable conversation, so when Mohamed had knocked on the door to my CLU to tell me that Jean-Luc had returned and wished to meet, I had requested half an hour for me to shower and put on fresh clothes.

"Dr. Grey, a pleasure to meet you, as well." He showed me the courtesy of remaining standing until I had sat. "Monsieur Hansen says that you have a particular set of talents that may be of benefit to us here." He spoke with a cultured voice and a noticeable French accent.

"Mr. Hansen was vague in describing any difficulties you were having, so I'm unsure how my skills will help. While I'm a big supporter of archeology, my degrees are in psychology and education, not in any anthropological field. I'd be next to useless on a dig," I said, with a slight smile, crossing my legs as I made myself as comfortable as I could in the metal chair.

Bob had told me a great deal about Jean-Luc Duval, the finds he and his team had made out here, and the long-term intentions Hansen Investments and the Duval team had, but little about any troubles they were having. "I don't want to bias you one way or the other," he had told me any time I pressed too hard for details.

Jean-Luc steepled his hands and brought them up to his face while he thought about what he was going to say next. I waited patiently while he contemplated, knowing that when he was ready, he would speak. A few seconds turned into a few minutes and the silence between the two of us was starting to become awkward when he finally leaned forward and spoke.

"There is a thief amongst us, Dr. Grey, and I need you to find who that thief is."

It was my turn to think.

CHAPTER FOUR

Dinner was a pleasant affair. The food they served was basic but tasted good, a chicken chili over brown rice served with a cucumber salad and a dinner roll. Drinks were limited to water, flavored electrolyte drinks, and coffee. I was still tired from the long trip here and I had some work to do tonight so I drank a cup of coffee along with a couple of glasses of water.

That evening, I met most of the people who were on station at basecamp. Absent was Jean-Luc's assistant, Caterina Toscanos, his site manager Alfred Doyle, and one of the researchers, Ellen Cole.

While Jean-Luc had been amiable to Steve's presence, I didn't want to push the issue by bringing her with me to the common room where the crew and staff ate their meals. I had left her in my CLU with her own food, and she had been happily eating when I left.

After finishing my meal and engaging in small talk with a couple of the camp's residents, I returned to my CLU and I grabbed the case that I had brought with me, put Steve on her leash and we walked outside. Even with the sun having set, the evening was hot, the temperature still over 100 degrees. I made my way to the lab where the artifacts collected by Jean-Luc and his people were stored.

Bob had told me that the room was accessible only by an access card and a pin number. The two-part authentication was there to deter theft. With a heavy steel door and no other entrances into the room, the thief had to have access via the card and pin. That limited my list of suspects. Now that I knew why I was here, the contents of the case and the directions it had come with made far more sense.

In most cases, the stolen items had little value except to a few specialized collectors looking for something unique to add to their galleries. Most of those dealt in the black market. Preserving finds such as the site Jean-Luc was working on, or the sites at Asa Koma and Handoga, were not the priority of the Djiboutian government. At the site at Asa Koma, near an inland lake on the Gobaad Plain, they discovered pottery dating to before 2,000 BC. In Handoga, there were ancient ruins and engravings discovered in 1970 that dated to 3,000 to 4,000 BC. An archaeologist might find such things fascinating, but to a government official, a shard of pottery or a few rocks piled up together to form a rudimentary wall held little interest.

There was one item in the lab that was of significant value. The artifact, about three feet in length and made of solid silver, was thought to be the symbol of the Sultan Kedafu when he established the Mudaito Dynasty in 1734. In the legends of the Afar it was said to have magical powers. The greater mystery, in my opinion, was how that rod came to be at a site that predated it by nearly 5,000 years. It was a question best left to those with the expertise to speculate on such matters, men like Jean-Luc Duval. My job was to catch a thief and to catch them before they made off with the rod.

Using the common access card given to me by Bob, I scanned it and when the keypad turned green, typed in my personal identification number. I heard a click as soon as the door's lock released and pushed my way in, Steve following behind me despite her having found something more interesting to go after just outside the door. She had buried her nose in the dirt and let out a huff. The resulting blow back of dust had left her face covered in red dirt.

Once inside, I shut the door and then deactivated the alarm. The alarm wasn't monitored by an outside entity, but if it was triggered, it would make an annoyingly loud noise.

While Mohamed and Jean-Luc knew of my reason for being here, no one else did. I had the cover story of being an auditor employed by Hansen Investments to ensure the money being funneled to this dig was being spent wisely. Regardless, no one had asked me. They assumed that being a doctor, and being at this site, automatically meant I was an archeologist. I didn't encourage them in that line of thought, but I also didn't correct them.

I set the case down and then, after a quick look around to make sure that there was nothing she could get into, took Steve off her leash to run around while I worked.

Opening the case, I pulled out a laptop, a black box, several cables, and an electric screwdriver. Using the screwdriver, I removed the panel from the inside part of the access keypad. I had to look at the directions that one of Bob's IT types had written out for me and taped to the inside lid of the case. Taking one of the cables that had two alligator clips, I put one clip on a blue wire and the other on a green wire and then plugged that into a port on the black box. Hitting the power button on the computer, I gave it a minute to start. While I waited for the computer to boot, I plugged a second cable into the black box in the port indicated by the directions and ran that cable to a USB port on the computer.

The little black box would extract the data from the keypad and download that onto the computer. From there, I'd be able to use a program to translate that data to a readable format that would tell me when the building was accessed and by whom. I knew the dates and approximate times of the previous thefts and could cross-reference the data to further narrow my list of suspects. Better yet, the keypad had a feature that no one, including Jean-Luc, knew of – once a code was entered, a tiny camera snapped a photo of the person entering the code. A person could always claim someone used their card without their authorization. Much harder to argue with a picture.

CHAPTER FIVE

The small storage drive built into the alarm pad only held data for about a month before it dumped it to make room for more. Not a problem in this case as the thefts had occurred within the past two weeks. Less than five minutes later the data was downloaded to the computer.

Impatient for a suspect, I double-clicked on the program and scrolled through the data until I got to the date of the thefts. Only three entrances that day, but the data for whose cards had been used didn't show up. I'd have to reach out to Bob's IT guy to find a fix. That I could do from the room via the satellite phone I had.

I looked at the pictures attached to the entries. The first one was in the morning and showed an unknown female entering the room. As I had met everyone but Jean-Luc's assistant and one of the researchers, I assumed it had to be one of those two. The second picture was later in the evening. The light above the door was out, casting the person in shadow. Something about the vague shape of the face, the outline of the hand as it touched the face, and the hair made me automatically think it was a woman. I couldn't tell who, though. The last entrance was Mohamed. Easy enough to see with the light above the door now working.

The absence of light in the second picture and its presence in the last cast suspicion. She could have disabled the light, but that would have required her to know that the camera existed. Not something that was widely known, according to the IT guy.

I put everything back in the case and was about to collect Steve and head back to my CLU when I heard the telltale beep of someone swiping their access card on the keypad. I sighed. It was going to be difficult to explain my presence in the lab without blowing my cover. I said a brief prayer to whomever was listening that it was either Jean-Luc or Mohamed. I wasn't that lucky.

It was a woman. She was 5'7" or 5'8", slender, with long legs. The heavy canvas pants and baggy blue blouse she wore didn't conceal her shapely body. She had long, dark hair pulled back in a ponytail that hung almost to the middle of her back. Her large brown eyes widened even more at seeing me standing in the lab.

"Chi sei e perche' sei qui?" she said in a language I didn't understand, and in a tone that was a cross between anger and fear.

"Ummm, do you speak English?" I asked her.

"Sí. I do. Who are you and why are you here?" she demanded. Some of the fear was subsiding from her voice.

"My name is Jerod Grey." I started to reach for the Hansen Investment employee identification badge I had in my back pocket, thinking I could explain my way out of this by saying I was here to check on the operation and its security. The woman's hand darted out and came back with dirt-covered trowel pointed threateningly in my direction. Right-handed, she adjusted her stance so that she was leading with the right foot. With the way she held herself, the perfect balance of her stance and the manner in which she presented the trowel left me with the unmistakable impression that she had some training.

"I'm just reaching for my ID," I said calmly, my hands held out away from my body. "May I?" I asked.

She mulled it over for a second and then gave me a curt nod. "Slowly," she said, in accented English.

It was my turn to nod and I slowly removed my ID and held it up for her examination. "I work for Hansen Investments. I'm just here to conduct a site survey and see that Mr. Hansen's money is being spent wisely," I said as calmly as I could with the trowel aimed in my direction. The point appeared very, very sharp.

She held the stance for a moment more than visibly relaxed. "I am Dr. Caterina Toscanos, Dr. Duval's assistant. I heard you were coming and I apologize for my reaction. We've had some thefts and you startled me." She spoke quickly, making it difficult for me to understand her fully, but I understood enough. Setting the trowel down, she turned and walked to one of the tables near the back of the lab. With her back turned toward me, she asked how long I planned to be here and expressed her desire to speak with me more about their operation.

While she spoke, I looked around for Steve. To my chagrin, I couldn't see her right away. "That would be nice," I said distractedly. I didn't want Dr. Toscanos to be startled a second time and was about to let her know Steve was here with me when I saw the doctor reach up and touch her hair. In that instance, with limited light at the back of the lab casting most of her face in shadow, I knew that she was the woman from the picture. I cleared my throat and she turned around.

She must have seen the change in my face because her large brown eyes turned wary and she bladed her stance, again lending credence that she had some formal training in martial arts.

"I'm afraid I haven't been completely honest with you, Dr. Toscanos. I do work for Mr. Hansen but I'm not here regarding how his money is being spent. I'm here to investigate the thefts and I think you may know something about that." I stood relaxed and waiting. There was no sense in wasting precious energy being tense for a fight that hadn't even commenced yet.

"I know nothing about the thefts, Mr. Grey." Her voice had a hard edge to it.

"It was the way you touched your hair. You did the same in the picture I have of you entering this room the night the last theft occurred."

"Merda!" she exclaimed in what I now suspected was Italian.

She turned quickly around and grabbed two things off the table behind her. The first was in her left hand and was a leather case about three feet in length. I was sure that was the silver rod. The other was a rock about the same size as a baseball. She threw the rock with enough force and accuracy that it forced me to dodge hard to my right in a near dive. Lucky for me I did, too. The rock hit the metal door and shattered into a thousand tiny projectiles. I raised my hands in time to prevent most from hitting my face but I still ended up with a half-dozen tiny lacerations along my left cheek and jawline. "Shit," I said, echoing Caterina's earlier declaration.

I started to recover back to my feet but I underestimated how quickly the woman could close the space between us. I was barely on my knees when I had to block a vicious left front kick to my face. She had no sooner planted that foot back on the ground when she was launching a roundhouse kick. That strike I only partially blocked and ended up rolling to my right to absorb some of the impact. Not that the roll helped significantly. My left ear was burning, and I could already feel the swelling starting along my cheekbone.

While the roll didn't help take away all of the sting from her kick, it did put enough space in between us that I was able to get to my feet. She was fast and her technique was nearly flawless, but I was bigger and stronger and at the end of the day, all other things being equal, that gave me the advantage.

That sentiment echoed hollowly in my ears a moment later. While I hadn't forgotten the fact that Caterina was holding a three-foot-long baton made of silver, I had mistakenly discounted it. It was a priceless artifact and it didn't enter my mind that someone would use a priceless artifact to beat me with.

The first blow I caught with my forearm. Fortunately my arm didn't break, but it did go numb from about the elbow down. The second one caught me along the jawline. I stumbled as blackness clouded my vision. I tried to fight it and, for a second, my vision returned, only to see Caterina had the rod raised to bash me again in the head.

I was going to let the darkness take me, that way I wouldn't have to feel another blow, but then I heard a growl from somewhere behind Caterina. That caused the woman to pause in her strike and glance nervously behind her. "Merda!" she yelled as she jumped back. As she did so, she spun around in a circle and I could see Steve had the cuff of her pants clenched tightly between her teeth.

I started to get up, concerned that Caterina would hurt my dog, but the blow to my head had done a bit more damage than I thought and I ended up sitting down hard on the floor of the lab. I watched, unable to do anything, as the thief took a swing at Steve with the rod. Steve was nimble enough to dodge the blow, even being only a puppy. Australian Cattle Dogs were called heelers for a reason. Born and bred to herd cattle, they did so by nipping at a cow's heels. Not only was the instinct there, but so was the instinct to dodge an annoyed cow's kicks when the heeler nipped a bit too hard. Steve danced back out of range and growled deep from her chest.

Caterina gave the dog a wary glance and then darted for the door. Steve started to go after her. "Steve! Stay!" I managed to get out, even though yelling made my head hurt worse. Steve froze in place and Caterina made the door, the rod still in hand.

It was a few minutes before I was able to get up. I half stumbled, half walked outside, yelling to rouse the alarm. It took a second but lights started coming on in other CLUs. Mohamed was the first to get to me. I tried to explain to him what had happened but I was having a hard time organizing my thoughts. When I was finally able to get out that Caterina had stolen the rod, he told Jean-Luc who I then saw sprinting toward the gate, yelling for someone to bring a vehicle.

I'm not sure what happened immediately after that. I recalled telling Mohamed that I had taken a hard blow to the head and then the blackness finally caught up to me.

CHAPTER SIX

It took me a few days to recover. The base camp for the dig site didn't have a fully staffed medical office, or facility, or whatever but they did have a retired combat medic who was, in my opinion, almost as good as a doctor. There were no fractures to my skull or brain bleeds. After a day of bed rest, he declared me fit for travel.

I had been putting off calling Bob, but the times were right. Late afternoon here was early morning in New York where Bob's office was located. I pulled the satellite phone out of the case and placed the call to Bob's private office number. It rang twice and he picked up.

"What happened?" he asked without preamble.

"I got my ass kicked," I replied grumpily.

"According to a report filed by Jean-Luc, Caterina Toscanos was the culprit."

"And she made off with the rod," I added, a little embarrassed that I had failed to stop her.

"You wouldn't be the first to fail to capture her," he told me. "Her real name is Alexandria Hamilton. She's a British national wanted by Interpol and the law enforcement agencies of Britain, France, Italy, Ukraine, and Russia. Her thefts total over $23 million. She pulled off the heist of that armored truck carrying three original Da Vinci paintings in Moscow last year. She's good. Better than good actually. She's one of the best." His voice held a faint note of admiration.

I didn't blame Bob; I could appreciate the skill necessary to become one of the world's best thieves, even if I didn't care for how that skill was applied. "Did you say she was a British national?"

"Yes. Why?"

"She spoke Italian with a perfect Italian accent. She never broke her cover. Not even when we were fighting." My esteem for her discipline and skill went up just a smidge.

"Interesting." He was quiet for a moment.

"Why the baton?" I inquired. If she was one of the best, then the baton seemed a bit below her normal target range.

"I don't know, but I aim to find out. I'll let you know when I do," Bob said seriously. "Where are you headed from there?"

"Back to the States. I parked my Jeep in the long-term lot at the Billings Logan International Airport and I still have plans to hike Glacier National Park."

"Take a few days and stay at a nice resort along the way. My treat," he said.

I thought about the Sapphire Preferred credit card issued to me by Hansen Investments. I didn't know what the limit was on it, but last minute travel halfway across the world didn't come cheap and Bob never blinked at the costs. The benefits of being a multi-billionaire, I suppose.

"I'll think about it," I said after a moment.

There was an acknowledging grunt on the other end of the phone. "Take care, Jerod."

"You too, Bob," I said, a smile etching my voice.

"You know I hate it when you call me that," he replied grumpily.

"I know." I hung up, powered down the phone and stored it back in the case. Mohamed would give me a ride back to Djibouti City in the morning. I didn't look forward to putting Steve back in a crate for the long flight home but she seemed to have weathered it well on the trip out here. I reached out and scratched her back as she laid on the bed, gnawing the fuzz off one of the small tennis balls she had.

She paused and looked up at me with her bright eyes and her tongue out. I smiled back at her. She had saved me from taking more damage. She was proving to be the best partner I had ever worked with.

GHOST SHIP

CHAPTER ONE

S teve and I had spent a week hiking the Grand Canyon and then headed to Texas to spend a little time with my sister and her family before continuing east along I-20 into Atlanta. It was to be a quick stop in Atlanta to meet up with one of my closest friends, Anna Smith, and her boyfriend. The boyfriend's name escaped me at the moment, and unless she told me that whomever she was dating at the time had proposed to her, I wasn't likely to waste my limited brain storage capacity trying to remember the man's name.

Anna and I had known each other since my days in the Navy. She still served and was eligible for Master Chief this year – the pinnacle of the enlisted ranks. She was a Gunners Mate by trade, specializing in small arms and crew-served weapons. There was something sexy about a woman who could field strip an M-2HB heavy machinegun, and if the zombie apocalypse ever did occur, Anna would be one of the first people I'd select for my team.

From Atlanta, Anna, the boyfriend and I went up along the eastern seaboard to Nags Head, North Carolina. There we met up with her dad, Mark, and her younger brother, Max. All of us had planned a vacation. For me that meant hang gliding, kayaking the Outer Banks, taking the Jeep out along the beach in Carova, and spending five days in one centralized location – something I rarely did these days.

The motel we had chosen wouldn't top the list for luxury, but the beds were comfortable, the rooms clean, and the showers had plenty of hot water. That's really all that was needed. Steve and I took a room to ourselves and were sitting on a bench just outside of it. I distractedly threw a small tennis ball for her while I sipped on a beer. It was a perfect night and I could hear the waves crashing ashore.

Anna and her boyfriend had been fighting so I wasn't surprised when she came out of their room alone and came to sit on the bench next to me. She was an attractive woman. She had chestnut hair that was thick and curly and always seemed just one hair tie away from being unruly. When it wasn't pulled up into a messy bun like it was now, it fell in waves to the middle of her back. Her brown eyes were similar to mine, with flakes of hazel and gold. When she was upset, though, they turned fully hazel like they were now.

"Problems in paradise?" I asked as she sat down. I pulled a beer from the case and popped the top on it, handing her the now-open bottle. She took it absently.

"He can be such a butthole sometimes," she said, with a hint of bitterness in her voice.

"He's a man. Being a butthole comes with the territory," I said back to her, using her term.

"You're not usually one," she said with a sigh.

"There are a number of women in this world that would disagree with you," I replied with a chuckle. "The biggest difference between you and them is that we never dated."

She was quiet for a time as I threw the ball for Steve. I was beginning to wonder if this dog ever got tired. She was thirty weeks old now and was starting to lose some of that puppy awkwardness. Anna looked on the verge of saying something when my phone rang. I glanced at the caller ID, it was Bob.

I started to put the phone down, thinking I'd call him back in a bit, but Anna told me to go ahead and answer it. I hit the send button and put the phone up to my ear. "Hello."

"Where are you?" Bob inquired, not bothering with social niceties like hello.

"I'm good, Bob. How are you?" I said with a large dose of sarcasm.

"I hate it when you call me that," he said, resignation in his voice.

"I know. Why do you think I do it?" The sarcasm had been edged out by the humor in my voice.

"It's annoying," he said grumpily. "So, how are you Jerod?"

"I'm good. Thanks. How are you?"

"Good. Where are you? I have a job I need you for." I could hear the impatience in his voice.

"Nag's Head, North Carolina," I told him.

He was quiet for a moment and then asked, "How quick can you get to an airport?"

"About an hour, hour and a half. Norfolk International is around seventy miles from here."

"There will be a helicopter on standby for you when you arrive."

"A helicopter to where?" I asked.

"The *Rosa del Milenio*. She's a research ship for Belfast Pharmaceuticals sitting about thirty miles off the coast of North Carolina," he told me.

"How convenient. Let me guess, you own Belfast Pharmaceuticals," I mumbled. Bob had known where I was, or at least knew where I was going, and had set all the balls in motion before he ever dialed my number.

"What's that?" he inquired.

"Nothing," I replied. "What's this regarding?"

"I'll tell you when you arrive." He hung up the phone without a goodbye.

"Dick," I muttered.

Anna punched me in the arm. "Jerod Grey! Language!" Anna didn't cuss, at least not where people could usually hear her, and she had little patience for those who did. Curse words were generally met with mild violence, like the punch to my arm.

I flashed her a smile and then looked down. "I have to go. Work." That was all the explanation I was willing to offer and Anna had served in the military long enough she didn't push for more. She knew I what my work entailed even if I wasn't sure how to explain to people what I did for Bob. I was part problem-solver and part adventurer for hire. Since meeting him in Nicaragua, he had kept me busy. The pay was good, as were the benefits and perks. No one I knew had a Sapphire Reserve credit card paid for by their company, but no one else I knew got calls in the middle of the night with instructions to hitch a ride on a helicopter and fly out to an awaiting ship – and with no up-front explanation of the reason.

"Seriously?" She asked. "We are supposed to be on vacation."

I sighed. "I know." I didn't have an argument, but this was the way it had always been for me. I prioritized my work before other things, including personal relationships. It contributed largely to my perpetual state of singleness.

"Fine. Go." I could hear the hurt in her voice, even though she tried to cover it.

"Sorry." It was all I could think to say. I got up, gave her a quick peck on the top of her head and returned to my room to pack. Steve trailed along behind me, the tennis ball still in her mouth.

It didn't take me long. Everything I needed fit into the canvas backpack and matching messenger bag that I took everywhere with me. Steve and I were out the door and on the road fifteen minutes later. I was halfway to Norfolk when I realized that I had been the one to drive Anna and her boyfriend up from Atlanta. "Dammit!" I cursed to myself.

This is when the credit card came in handy. They'd have a nice rental parked in the motel lot near their room come morning.

CHAPTER TWO

Steve's first helicopter ride. She bore it stoically but didn't look happy about it. It was an AS365 N2 Dauphin helicopter built by Airbus – quite plush, as far as helicopters went. The interior was quiet enough that I didn't require hearing protection, but I wore a headset anyway so that I could communicate with the pilot more easily. There was a wall that separated the cabin from the cockpit that prevented us from simply talking face to face.

The pilot had pointed out the lights of the *Rosa del Milenio* making way on the rocky waters below us. From this height, the illuminated helideck of the ship looked entirely too small for the Dauphin to land on. This wasn't my first ride in the helicopter. I had been an avionics technician on the CH-53s during my days in the Marine Corps, earned my aircrew wings, and rode as a door gunner on the heavy lift Sikorsky Sea Stallions. The CH-53 was about twice the size of the Dauphin and I had seen Marine Corps pilots land those beasts in some tight spots so I was sure my current pilot would be fine. Logically, anyway. Landing in a helicopter was more akin to a controlled fall out of the sky, so my survival instincts kicked in regardless of my reasoned thoughts.

The pilot's voice sounded in the headset, advising me that we were cleared for landing and would be going in. I acknowledged and the helicopter banked sharply to the left as it lined up for its approach.

We were touching down on the deck less than ten minutes later. The pilot gave me the green light to open the door and disembark. He was only landing long enough to let Steve and me off. We had just cleared the rotor wash and the Dauphin was back in the air and headed back toward land.

There was a wind kicking up that created eight-foot swells on the water, with occasional waves that exceeded ten feet and sent saltwater spraying across the aft part of the ship. A final salute to the pilot and Steve and I were headed toward the hatchway that led to the interior part of the ship. One of the ship's crew was standing just inside the open door waving me over.

"Dr. Grey?" he asked as I came closer. He had an accent, but I couldn't quite place it. Spain, or perhaps Portugal, was my best guess.

"Yes," I answered simply. The *Rosa del Milenio* was 313 feet in length and had a crew of fifty, plus up to sixty scientists on board at any given time. Built by Freire Shipyard out of Vigo, Spain, and just recently commissioned, she was one of the most advanced research vessels on the water.

"This way, sir. Mr. Hansen is waiting for you in the ready room," the man told me as I entered a long corridor. The ship still smelled brand new.

"Bo... Mr. Hansen is here?" I had almost slipped and called him Bob in front of someone else. While I liked to tease the man, I wasn't going to be disrespectful in front of his subordinates. The man simply nodded in response to my question. "Well, this must be important then," I said under my breath.

The man looked back as he escorted me down the hallway, having heard me but not understanding what I said. I shook my head and indicated to him that it was just a thought to myself.

The ready room felt like it was at the heart of the ship. It reminded me of the ready rooms for pilots I had seen when I did tours of retired carriers such as the *USS Hornet* in Alameda, or the *USS Midway* in San Diego. Rows of chairs with small writing surfaces sat in three sections facing a podium and large screen.

Bob stood by the podium. He wasn't particularly tall, standing only about 5'6". He was older than me by around ten years, putting him in his early to mid-sixties. He was wearing a gray and white flannel shirt under a dark blue, thin down vest and black chinos that looked as if they had been tailored to fit him perfectly. His silver hair was combed back and impeccably styled. While the outfit looked casual enough, I had no doubt it probably cost more than all the clothes I had brought with me.

Bob smiled as I walked through the door, Steve trailing behind me, still attached to her leash. She was doing much better at heeling, but we still had some work to do before I completely trusted her off her leash in an unfamiliar area. "Jerod, good to see you."

I returned the smile. "Likewise, Bob." I crossed the room and shook his extended hand.

His smile turned into a frown. "I dislike when you call me that."

I smiled wider and he released my hand and shook his head in resignation. "Have a seat and I'll fill you in on why you are here." He indicated a chair right in front of the podium.

Dutifully, I took a seat and had Steve lay down next to me. Bob pulled out a remote and clicked a button and the screen came to life with a black and white picture of an old, four-masted schooner.

"This is the *Governor Parr*. She was built in 1918 by W.R. Huntley and Sons out of Parrsboro, Nova Scotia for Archie Davidson and Captain Angus Richards. On October 3, 1923, she was caught in a storm while running lumber from Nova Scotia to Buenos Aries. Captain Richards and another sailor lost their lives but the rest of the crew was rescued by the SS Schodack."

Bob hit the button on the remote and the next slide, also of the *Governor Parr*, appeared on the screen. In this photo the ship was clearly derelict, having lost her mizzen mast. "Several attempts to tow the *Governor Parr* to shore so that it didn't pose a hazard to navigation failed. The last attempt was made by the US Coast Guard ship *Tampa* on January 1, 1924, when she tried to tow the Parr to a port at Halifax, Nova Scotia. On January 2nd, the *Tampa* had to cut her loose when a strong gale threatened to bring down both ships.

"For years after, she was sighted multiple times in the Atlantic, anywhere between Nova Scotia and the Canary Islands. The *Governor Parr* was last sighted on February 13, 1931, off the coast of Nova Scotia.

She was presumed sunk after that. At least until two days ago." Bob hit the remote and another photo came up, this one taken from the air. It was a bit fuzzy but you could still make out the ship.

"A cargo plane flying between the US and Europe spotted the ship and went in for a closer view and snapped the photo – which is why it isn't that great. Still, my IT guys were able to conduct some analysis and determined it was a four-masted schooner of the same design as the *Governor Parr*," Bob added.

I interrupted him. "What was the *Parr* carrying when she was wrecked in the storm?" I inquired.

"Unknown, we think her hold may have been empty but we can't be sure," he answered, though he looked put out by the interruption. I motioned for him to continue.

"Captain Richards had charge of a ship before the *Parr*. Between 1901 and 1902 he was master of the *Kipling* that plied the same basic route as the *Parr*. That vessel went down off the coast of Maine in January of 1906."

"Richards didn't seem to have much luck as far as captaining ships went did he?" I said with heavy sarcasm.

Bob gave me a deadpan look, his face not even showing the hint of a smile. I sighed. "Please, continue."

"Allegedly, Captain Richards had a bust on the *Kipling*. It was a bust that had been kept at the Duomo di Siena, a medieval church in Siena, Italy, and was removed in 1600 following protests over its display."

Bob paused here. It took me a moment to understand why, but I finally realized that he was waiting on me to ask why it had been removed. I humored him, even though I really just wanted to go to sleep. It had been late when he called, and even later when I arrived at the Norfolk airport and subsequently the ship.

"The bust was of Pope John Anglicus of Mainz, also known as Pope Joan, the Catholic Church's one and only female Pope."

I knew a little of my Catholic history from Catechism as a child. "The Catholic Church has never had a female Pope," I told him.

"That's the common belief. She was supposedly Pope from 855 to 857. She had entered the Vatican in the disguise of a man, following her lover there. She was apparently an exceptional student and quickly had no peers in her academic fields of study. She rose quickly through the ranks and was confirmed as Pope following the death of Leo IV. She was later found to be a woman when she gave birth in a very public way, during a procession through Rome to be more precise, and was stoned to death as a result of her duplicity. Following her death, the Church tried to eradicate all evidence that she had ever served."

I rubbed my eyes and glanced down at Steve. She was already fast asleep on the floor. I was a bit jealous. "Bob, this all very fascinating, but why am I here?"

"My researchers believe that the coordinates to where the *Kipling* went down were held onto by Captain Richards and were onboard the *Parr* when he died. While the captain's log was recovered, those documents pertaining to the location of the *Kipling* were not. I've searched all over for them. I was able to locate the original captain's log for the *Kipling* but it doesn't list the coordinates where she went down. If this is the *Parr*, I need you to board her and see if you can recover those documents." He paused here a moment to give me a second for his request to sink in.

"Can't we just come alongside her and embark the ship? That's if we find her. This a big ocean and she's obviously been traversing it for a very long time," I stated.

"I'm concerned the *Rosa* will damage her if we come alongside. If she goes down, whatever chance we have of recovering those documents will be lost forever. The water here is too deep for a salvage dive."

I thought about it for a moment, my mind trying to work out the operation. I was failing. "Ok. I need some sleep before I try and puzzle out the logistics of all this."

Bob nodded. "I'll summon the steward and have him show you to your cabin. Breakfast is served from 5:30 to 7:00 a.m."

I looked at my watch. It was closing in on 2:00 a.m. "What time is lunch?" I asked with a smile.

"11:00 to 1:00. I'll see you when you wake up. The galley has coffee and snacks available all day."

I nodded and then stood up to gather my things. The steward arrived a few minutes later and led me to a cabin. I should have taken Steve out one more time for a walk around the deck before laying down, but the bed looked too inviting.

CHAPTER THREE

After that first night on board the *Rosa del Milenio,* Steve and I managed to get on a schedule that reduced the number of accidents she had to zero, which I was thankful for. I generally tended to find her "accidents" by stepping in them as I fumbled for the light switch in our cabin. I had also procured some more paper towels and some plastic bags from the ship's stores so that I could clean up after her when we made our rounds on the ship's main deck. We had been aboard the *Rosa* for four days now and in that time, everyone had taken the time to come introduce themselves to Steve. I was an afterthought.

Bob had given me the parameters for the operation. The *Rosa* was to get within 100 yards of the *Parr* and drop a seven meter boat into the water, and then a small crew, including myself, would come alongside the *Parr* and I would board, search the ship, recover anything of relevance or value, and then disembark – hopefully without doing any damage to the vessel that would cause it to sink.

It sounded easy enough on the surface, but I had my reservations. The ship had been floating around the ocean for ninety years and I didn't expect it to be stable. To mitigate some of the risk, I'd be going aboard with SCUBA gear. I wasn't an avid diver, but I was certified and knew just enough that I was hoping it would give me a fighting chance to escape if the ship went down while I was conducting my search.

Now all we had to do was find the *Governor Parr*. That was proving to be easier said than done. The cargo plane that had originally taken the picture had provided us with coordinates, but they were now several days old and when the *Rosa* arrived on station, the *Parr* was long gone. It had given us a starting point, though, and we had spent the last two days conducting an expanding square search pattern, attempting to find the ghost ship.

I spent my days working on Steve's obedience training and, when we weren't doing that, we were playing. It wasn't quite the vacation that I had in mind with Anna and her family, but it was still a good time to relax. It helped that the *Rosa* had a crew lounge with a full bar.

CHAPTER FOUR

There was a loud knock on my door that startled both Steve and me awake. I was discovering that my pup liked her beauty sleep and became grumpy when it was interrupted. With me that usually meant she was going to be stubborn and refuse to adhere to any of her training. For whoever it was beating on my door, it earned them a deep growl.

"What?" I barked at the door.

Someone tried the doorknob only to find that I had locked the door. Bob's muffled voice came from the other side. "It's locked," he barked back.

"No shit." I grumbled before getting up and walking to the door.

I was wearing a pair of shorts but no shirt. Bob had seen the scars that covered my upper body. I had been shot, stabbed, and blown up by an improvised explosive device. The scars were a road map of the self-induced abuse I had put myself through during my fifty or so years. While I exercised regularly, between the police department and the military, I had lived a violent life and it showed. It wasn't just the scars, though. My back ached constantly, my hips just a little less so, and I had tendonitis in my elbows and knees. I was a living, breathing poster child for what not to do with your life.

I unlocked the door and swung it open. "This better be good." I said with a growl of my own.

Bob stood in the doorway, his shirt and pants wrinkle-free and his hair perfectly combed. He looked like he had been awake for some time. By contrast, I hadn't trimmed my beard in days and I was in dire need of a haircut. He earned almost immediate redemption by handing me a cup of coffee. "I hadn't forgotten how grumpy you are when you're awakened out of a sound sleep," he said.

I took a sip to test the temperature. It was still piping hot. I took another sip, preferring to deal with the scalding heat then do without, and then stepped out of the doorway for Bob to enter.

"We found her," he said with a wide grin. "The *Governor Parr* is 500 yards off of our starboard bow."

Nervous excitement hit my system, forcing me the rest of the way awake. "What time is it?" I asked. My watch was on the small desk in the cabin.

"2:11 a.m.," Bob answered after glancing at his watch.

"Give me thirty to shower and take Steve for a walk and I'll meet you on the bow of the ship. I'm up now, might as well get a look at her."

Bob nodded and shut the door as he left. I rubbed my hand over my face and then took another sip of the coffee. There wasn't much that could be done at night. Any approach we made would be done once the sun rose. But, like I had told Bob, I was up now.

* * * * *

The *Governor Parr* now sat just a few hundred yards off the bow of the *Rosa del Milenio*. In length, she was only 100 feet shy of the research vessel. The sea was calmer than it had been since I had arrived on board, almost like glass. In the light of the half-moon, the ghost ship looked eerie. The mizzen mast was completely gone and the remaining three masts had toppled over the course of the past ninety years. There was no sign of any sails. Here and there I could make out holes in the hull, but all of them were above the water line. Nonetheless, she was listing to port, indicating that there was some flooding in the lower decks of the ship. I couldn't help but be a little in awe of the fact that this ship still floated. You had to admire such craftsmanship.

"Isn't she beautiful?" Bob said from beside me.

"Yes," I replied, "And a little frightening." There was an almost palpable feeling of malice coming from the ship. I had read some more of the *Governor Parr's* history in the days I had been on board the *Rosa*. Every attempt to remove her from the sea had been met with failure. This was going to be dangerous, of that I had no doubt.

Bob and I were quiet for a bit while we watched the distant ship. Steve lay quietly at my feet, gnawing on the fuzzy part of a small tennis ball I had given her. It wouldn't be long and she'd be able to fit a regular tennis ball in her mouth.

"Let's get ready," I said, pushing myself off the rail and heading for the back of the ship where we would launch the inflatable boat. We'd be getting underway with a coxswain, a crewman, and a rescue diver. We had toyed with the idea of a lifeline, but I had more concern that it would get tangled in the wreckage of the ship than I had about me being able to find my way out or them pulling me free.

I spent the next few hours getting everything ready for the boarding of the *Governor Parr*. The SCUBA tank I was using only held about thirty minutes of air and weighed about twenty pounds. I was hoping I wouldn't need it at all, but if I did, this wasn't going to be a pleasure dive and I didn't want my load to be too heavy.

The rest of my gear was pretty standard: a wetsuit, a dive knife, a small hatchet, a hammer, a flashlight, and a small, waterproof camera. What I couldn't carry out with me, I'd take a picture of and Bob could have his team analyze those photos later. There wasn't expected to be anything on the ship of any real value. Some of the instruments used in navigation like an old sextant, chronometer, or a Bygrave Position-line slide rule could bring in a little money, depending on their condition, but I wasn't there to recover antiques.

With my gear, and the gear of the crew, stowed for getting underway, I went to the galley and had breakfast. By the time I was done, it was almost time to launch.

CHAPTER FIVE

The boat pilot, or coxswain as we had called them in the Navy, gave the inflatable boat a little throttle and brought it in gently so that the nose of our boat came in at a 45-degree angle to the *Governor Parr*, our sponson barely kissing the hull of the larger vessel. I had been a tactical boat operator when I was in the Navy and I admired skill when I saw it. The coxswain made it look easy.

I was in the bow of the boat with the rescue diver. The top of the hull was still ten feet above my head. With the help of the diver, I grabbed a grappling hook with knots spaced about every two feet. It wasn't a long throw and I made it over on my first go. Slowly I pulled it back, waiting for the hooks to set. It caught a few seconds later.

Giving it a sharper tug, I made sure it was set and then took a firm hold and slowly put my weight against the line. It shifted some as the hooks dug in a little more, but it was holding. I smiled at the diver and leaned a little more on the rope. There was a loud crack; suddenly nothing was supporting my weight and I fell back, my shoulder blades hitting the front of the partially enclosed cabin with enough force that I knew I'd be sore tomorrow.

The grappling hook brought with it a large chunk of wood that bowled through the rail of the hull and hit my rescue diver, knocking him down onto the deck. He was cussing as he pushed the rotted beam off him.

"You hurt?" I asked him as I picked myself up. He gave me the thumbs up but he was rubbing his left shoulder.

I looked up at the hull of the ship. While the grappling hook hadn't held, the one thing it had done was pull a enough of the rail down so that I didn't have as far to climb up onto the deck of the ship. It appeared easier than it was, however, with the air tank and other gear I was wearing. I managed to jump high enough for my fingers to find purchase, but algae covered the hull and I couldn't find anywhere for my feet to gain any traction. It took me two more tries before I lay on the deck of the *Governor Parr* trying to catch my breath. Off in the distance I could see that a crowd had gathered on the starboard side of the *Rosa* and was watching me with interest. Bob waved and I half-heartedly waved back.

From where I was lying, I surveyed my surroundings. The deck was littered with debris and everything was covered in green algae. It was going to be slick and I was going to have to pay careful attention to my footing. Near the front of the ship I saw a hatchway that led to the decks below. There should be another hatch nearer my location, but because of where I came onboard, I couldn't see it.

Carefully, I came to my feet and then crept across the deck, checking the strength of the boards before putting my full weight on them. As I made my way toward the front of the deck cabin that had been blocking my view, the hatch became visible. Being closer to the aft of the ship, I was hoping the captain's quarters were not far.

I took a step and tested the boards ahead of me. They were spongy but holding. I transferred more weight to my forward foot. The boards creaked but took the increased pressure. My weight now evenly distributed between my left and right feet, I started shifting the load to my lead foot. The boards gave way. I tried to jump back but the deck all around me crumbled. I didn't have time to think up a cuss word and I was falling.

I dropped roughly ten feet to the floor of the next deck. I tried to roll to absorb some of the shock of landing, but was thrown off balance by the air tank on my back. All I really managed to do was face plant, the algae-covered deck doing little to cushion the blow. I felt my knee pop, causing a dull pain to spread through my leg. Now I could cuss and did so with gusto.

I was about to push myself up when the boards under me creaked loudly and then gave way as well. This fall wasn't as far, but it was into water. I managed to clamp my mouth shut as I hit with a splash and avoided sucking in any of the salty sea.

When I resurfaced, there was enough light coming through the holes I had created in the floors above me that I could make out my immediate surroundings. I was in one of the ship's holds. Broken pieces of wood and debris floated throughout the area. I didn't immediately see a way back up. With this much water in the hold, though, I did see why the *Governor Parr* was listing so badly.

I tried to touch the deck with my feet but the water was too deep. At least with my dive equipment, I was neutrally buoyant and the weight of the tank wasn't further taxing me. I broke out the flashlight and the intense white beam penetrated the darkness surrounding the little pool of light created when I fell through the ship. Near the front of the ship, I saw what could be a ladder well leading up and started swimming that direction. Due to the list of the ship, my feet eventually found solid "ground" to stand on but I stayed in the deeper water, not willing to risk punching through the hull below the waterline.

What I had seen did turn out to be a ladder well leading up to the next deck. Unfortunately, the stairs were in such a state of disrepair that they were unusable. I changed course and made my way along the outboard part of the ship, eventually coming to another set of stairs. These were in a little better condition and, going slowly, I was able to make it to the second deck.

Two more near falls through the floor and I came across what I hoped was the captain's quarters. I tried opening the closed door but found it was wedged tight, but, like everything else on this ship, it was rotted through, and it didn't take much work for me to break enough of the door away with the hatchet to slip inside.

The room was much of what I had expected. Even given the poor condition of the cabin, I could see where a narrow bunk had once been. There was also an old table where I pictured the captain took his meals, and a large desk where he worked on the charts or other paperwork associated with hauling cargo between ports. Those same charts, logs and papers were situated on shelves above the desk.

I collected what I could, putting them carefully in a waterproof bag I brought along specifically for that purpose. Some of the documents crumbled as soon as I touched them. Others, like the charts and books, were better preserved, the charts covered in a wax-like coating that helped to protect them from the elements – not that they were in anything near good condition. There were few materials made back in the 1920's that could hold off the effects of saltwater for too long.

Some of the documents I handled as gently as I could and snapped photos of their contents for Bob's team to analyze later. I was sliding the last of the logbooks into the bag when there was a sudden lurch and the *Parr* tilted more to the portside. I fought to keep my feet, grabbing hold of the edge of the desk only to have it crumble beneath my fingers. The dive shoes I was wearing weren't finding purchase on the algae-slick boards of the deck.

Quickly, I pulled out the hatchet and swung it with significant force at the center of the desk. It bit deep and provided me with a handhold that I could use to regain my balance. "Angry bitch, aren't you?" I said to the ship. I had found her secrets and now she was telling me in no uncertain terms to get out.

There was ambient light coming from the portholes in the captain's cabin, but I used my flashlight to glance around. Water was creeping into the cabin where before, it had been relatively dry, or at least as dry as a ninety-plus-year-old ship could be after floating around the Atlantic for so long.

The angle of the ship had changed enough that I was going to have a difficult time crossing the distance from the desk to the door, and then from the door to the ladder well leading to the main deck. I could use the hatchet kind of like the ice tools used when scaling glaciers on mountains. I only had the one, though. I could substitute the hammer for the second tool, but I didn't figure it would work as well as the hatchet.

I was about to give it a shot when the shelf behind the desk caught my attention. Initially, I thought it had pulled away from the wall a few inches. Ready to move on and get off this ship before she became any angrier, I turned away and pulled out the hammer. Something wasn't right about the way the shelf sat, though. I looked again.

What I had originally thought was just the shelf coming loose revealed itself to be a door. "Clever," I said to myself. The Captain had a secret compartment. The shifting of the *Parr* must have triggered the latch, causing it to swing partially open.

I pulled the door to the compartment open and then fumbled for a few items that fell out, including a small gold idol. The idol I managed to catch, but I missed a couple of other curios that hit the floor and tumbled into the water. I slipped the idol into my bag and checked behind the shelf for any additional items.

I shouldn't have been surprised at what I found. Captain Richards had allegedly acquired a bust of the Catholic Church's only female Pope; it wasn't inconceivable that he had picked up a lot of other knick-knacks of historical value along the way. I was able to recover old coins, figurines in stone, jade, and precious metals, a few old scrolls and a leather-bound journal. There was a vase as well, but I was concerned I wouldn't be able transport it without breaking it so I left it be, but I managed to get a photo of it, even if the angle of that picture was going to be off due to my precarious grip.

I had just slipped the last of the items I could recover into the bag when the ship lurched again. Unable to hold onto the hatchet, I hit the water filling the port side with a splash, managing to take a quick breath before I was completely submerged.

I was hoping to hit the bulkhead and push myself back up to the surface. My plan only half worked. I did hit the bulkhead, but instead of being able to launch myself back up to the surface, I broke through the rotting wood going all the way to my waist where the air tank and bag I was carrying snagged and held me in place. Panic gripped me.

I struggled futilely, trying to work my way out of the hole I was in, both literally and figuratively, burning through what precious little air I had been able to take in when I fell. It took a second for the panic to subside and for me to start thinking more clearly. I had the air tank. Pulling the regulator and mask to my face, I engaged the air and sucked in a big lungful through my mouth. I then tilted my head back, lifted the bottom of my mask to break the seal and exhaled hard to clear the mask.

No longer fighting for air, I could take a minute to survey the predicament I was in and puzzle a way out of it. The ship was going to sink, of that I was sure. I needed to be out when it did or it would suck me down past the limits of my body to endure the pressure of the sea.

I had lost the hatchet but I still had the hammer. It was slower going than I had anticipated. The water added resistance to the swing of the hammer, not allowing me to generate as much power as normal. Still, I chipped away at the boards in front of me until I had enough space to lift my knees through. I was out of the hole, now I needed to get off the ship. I watched the air bubbles that escaped the mask from my breathing and followed them up.

CHAPTER SIX

Robert Hansen paced the deck of the *Rosa del Melinio* impatiently. Jerod had been on the *Governor Parr* for approximately twenty minutes now. That wasn't long, but after the ship had shifted the first time, it was long enough in Robert's opinion. When the *Parr* shifted again, this time going over on its port side almost entirely, Robert cursed while other members of the crew and scientific staff aboard the *Rosa* gasped in worry. Beside him, Steve's bark was high-pitched, almost a whine.

Robert hadn't known what to do with the puppy. She had been glued to the spot where Jerod had climbed down a Jacob's ladder and onto the waiting boat. She clearly wasn't going to move until Jerod returned and for a moment, Robert thought to himself – what if his friend didn't return?

"Have the rescue diver prepare to go in," Robert ordered one of the crewman nearby. Robert had been commanding board rooms and courtrooms for the better part of forty years and his voice rang with a tone that brooked no argument. The crewman jumped to obey.

The *Parr* shifted again, this time the bow dipping fully below the water and the aft raising an equivalent amount. The ship started to sink more quickly.

I had regained the second deck when the ship lurched yet again, the aft going almost vertical. In my desperation to get out, I had thrown caution to the wind and was half running, half leaping to clear the stairs that lead to the main deck. My plan was simple: make the main deck and jump over the nearest side and hope that I didn't get caught in the vortex created as the ship sunk under the water and started its journey to the bottom of the ocean.

I barely caught the edge of a stair as the aft went upright. I managed to get a second hand on the stair, dropping the hammer in the process, and tried to pull myself up, but with the extra weight of the tank and the bag it wasn't easy. Inch by agonizing inch, I pulled myself up as my arms shook with the exertion. I reached a point where I could get my elbows over the board and then a foot.

There was a crack that reverberated through the ship. It wasn't heard so much as felt deep in my bones. For a moment, I thought the board I was clinging to had given way, then I was falling again. I found out later that the ship broke in half.

The aft part of the ship hit the water with tremendous impact. I felt ribs crack and my right arm went numb, the Parr meeting out punishment in her death throes. The aft part of the ship immediately started to fill with water, pushing me with force toward the rear bulkhead. I couldn't stop my momentum but I saw a possible way out before the ship sunk beneath the waves forever. I turned on my side and tucked into a ball so that the tank was facing in the direction the water was pushing me.

I crashed through the bulkhead, pain shooting through my back as the tank bruised my spinal cord. I gritted my teeth and was happy to find out that my legs responded to the urgent messages being sent my brain. I kicked once, twice, and then for good measure a third time before I angled up toward the surface. I came up about thirty feet from where the *Governor Parr* was just sinking beneath the surface. In the distance, I heard people yelling and cheering. I floated lazily on my back, my body too exhausted to move further.

CHAPTER SEVEN

B ob sat down in the seat across from me pushing one of the two cups of coffee he was carrying in my direction. "What? No breakfast?" I asked teasingly. Not that I was eating much. The broken rib I had suffered while on board the *Governor Parr* hurt every time I swallowed. Hell, it hurt every time I breathed, swallowing just made it hurt more. I had fixed myself a piece of toast that I was eating with my left hand. My right arm was slung across my chest – a temporary cast, compliments of the ship's medical officer, going from hand to shoulder. Add to that a dozen bruises and cuts that I had no idea how they had occurred except in the most general sense. The one plus to my bruised and battered body? I was on a research ship with some of the brightest minds in medicine on board.

"How are you feeling?" Bob asked.

"Peachy," I replied, setting down my toast and picking up the coffee for a sip.

"The journal you grabbed from the hidden compartment held the coordinates for the *Kipling*. I'll have a salvage team look into it. The rest of the items were of some value as well. I'll have them boxed up and shipped to you when we get back to land," Bob told me.

"What am I going to do with them?" I asked, curious.

"Put them up in your house."

"Have you been to my apartment? I barely have room for Steve and me. Why do you think I spend all my time traveling?" I told him, taking another sip of the coffee before picking up the toast again.

"You'll have a lot more room in your new place," Bob stated in a matter of fact manner.

"What new place?" Now I was suspicious.

"I have a house in the San Francisco Bay Area. Marin County, near San Rafael. I originally bought it as a vacation home. It has been completely remodeled and it's fully furnished. All you have to do is move in. Rent-free, until I can decide what to do with it," he told me.

"I can't do that, Robert." It was a very generous offer. Too generous.

"You'd be helping me out, Jerod. It sits on five acres, fairly secluded, and some kids have discovered it is unoccupied. They've been having parties there and it's costing me a small fortunate to clean and repair every time they do. The sheriff's office is threatening to file a nuisance abatement case against me," he told me pointedly.

I thought about it for a minute. It would be a far cry better than my apartment in Oakland and with five acres, Steve and I would have lots of room to play. Slowly, I nodded my head. "Alright. I could use a change of scenery."

Bob smiled. Before I could get back to the Bay Area, though, I would have to figure out how I was going to drive a stick shift with a cast on.

MAYAN TREASURE

PROLOGUE

It had taken her almost a year to find the right target and the right tool to use against him. Of the people she had to choose from, her target made the most sense. He was one of only two people called to fulfill a certain role, and of those two, he was the one called on the most often. Plus, he was a sentimental fool. She found it was easier for her to think of people in terms of being targets or tools – particularly people she had known for so long, people she had pretended to care about. She had known her target since she had gone to work for his and, at the time, her boss when she was only twenty years old. Using him like she was, she almost felt guilty. Almost.

Finding the tool to use against the target had been more difficult. Someone close enough, geographically speaking, that their meeting wouldn't seem out of the ordinary. Also, it had to be someone she could manipulate. In short, a man.

Janice "Jan" Cordova was stunning when she applied her makeup, but even without it, she was cute. The man who had once been her boss had spent nine years teaching her everything he knew. That included passing along his considerable skills in the martial arts. Training she had not given up on, despite the fracture in their relationship. Her on-going physical regiment had left her already petite body strong and in great shape. Put on a pair of yoga pants or a tight-fitting skirt and she turned heads. She was acutely aware of how men looked at her and she added that as yet one more skill in her repertoire.

She had found her tool on a dating website. Lonely men were the easiest to manipulate. A little online research and she knew that her tool's parents and her target went to church together. Plus, her tool had served in the military, specifically the same branch as her target. A perfect match.

Jan reached out to him, said all the right things and it wasn't long before he was doing her bidding. One meeting, a lingering kiss, and he was willing to do anything for her. She'd have her revenge on her former boss.

CHAPTER ONE

"**S**omeone is following us," Nez stated in the same monotone, matter-of-fact manner that he would use to comment on the weather.

I paused and looked down the tree-covered slope that we had been hiking up for the past hour. I couldn't see anything. "Break," I said, dropping my pack and pulling out my water bottle for a drink. Steve, my Australian Cattle Dog, laid down next to my pack. In the past year she had filled out considerably and had reached her full size at just over thirty pounds. She was panting heavily from all the running around she was doing, so I poured her some water into a bowl before taking a drink myself.

Anna Smith and Jerome Rivera, the other two members of my team present besides Eugene Nez, did the same. Nez left his pack on, his hawk-like gaze scanning the forest below us.

Nez and I had known each other since we were in the Navy together. Our careers had paralleled one another. While I had spent the first five years of my military career in the Marine Corps, Nez had spent his in the Navy. We had both left our active duty military service to go into law enforcement, him with a small sheriff's office in New Mexico and later as an investigator for the Bureau of Indian Affairs, me with a large department in the San Francisco Bay Area. We had met while on a deployment during our time in the Navy reserves.

Nez was as solid as they came. Unwavering in his loyalty and honest to a fault. When I realized that the assignments I was taking were getting too complicated for me to handle alone, I had called on some of my friends and acquaintances to help me out. Nez had covered my back on these little expeditions more than a few times. His prominent nose and strong facial features marked him as Native American, Navajo to be specific. He was 5'8" and heavy-set. He didn't look it, but the man was a beast. He was twice as strong as me and he could run for days.

About ten feet above me on the hill was Jerome. Jerome had been a police officer until an officer-involved shooting had left him with a post-traumatic stress injury that forced him into retirement. He had since sought treatment and many of the symptoms that had plagued him had subsided. When he wasn't working for me, Jerome ran his own MMA gym. He was also an accomplished combat marksman. He flipped the ball cap he was wearing around to keep his dark, curly mop of hair out of his eyes and sighted through the 4x magnification scope of his AR-15 rifle to get a better look at the area where Nez was staring. Tattoos covered his heavily muscled arms. "Got nothing, boss." He scanned downhill again and then, dropping the rifle from his cheek, looked at me and shrugged.

Like Jerome, I wasn't picking up anything, but then I was looking with my naked eye. Nez wasn't usually wrong about these things. "Radio back to home base and let them know we may have picked up a tail. Unconfirmed at this time."

Nez's facial expression didn't change as he looked at me and nodded his head. That he didn't argue told me that it was more a feeling than something concrete.

Anna was running the radio today. It worked off satellite communications and the bandwidth cost a pretty penny, but it was the only radio that worked this far up in the mountains of California.

Anna was one of my closest friends. Her thick, chestnut hair usually fell to about the middle of her back but today was tied up in an unruly pony tail. Anna and I had known each other since our days in the Navy as well. Back then, she had been a gunner's mate and could still field strip an M2HB .50 caliber machinegun with her eyes closed. Now she held a graduate degree in ecology as well as bachelor of science degrees in both biology and zoology; she also had a good working knowledge of geology, botany, and half a dozen other sciences. She was a good person to have around if for nothing more than her sheer breadth of knowledge.

I had three people back at home base: Andy Luna, Karl Williams, and the new kid, Carlos. Andy was our camp manager and he took care of most of the cooking and cleaning when we were in garrison. Karl was our field medic. He had been a corpsman in the Coast Guard and then an EMT in the civilian world. He had gone to school and earned his degree as a physician's assistant and currently worked in the ER at one of Albuquerque's hospitals. In the field and wounded, there was no better man to keep you alive until advanced life support arrived. I was always glad when he was able to take some time off to join me on these little outings.

Carlos was the kid that Andy brought in to start training as his replacement. Andy was pushing seventy and while he was still just as spry as when he was in his thirties, his wife was in the advanced stages of cancer and was having a harder and harder time getting around. Being gone, even for a few weeks, was putting a strain on both of them.

Anna keyed the radio and spoke, "Castle, this is Ranger, over."

"Ranger, Castle, over," Karl was on the other end of the mic.

"Castle, we may have picked up a tail, over. Unconfirmed at this time," Anna said, her southern accent clear even though she wasn't talking that loudly. She looked at the GPS device we all carried and gave our latitude and longitude and then ended her transmission with a "roger, out." I could almost see Karl on the other end of the radio shrugging. He'd log it, but there was nothing he could do about it from where he was at.

We had been three days out in the wilderness searching for a trail that started back in 1697. A Conquistador named Juan Julio de Sonya Ramirez together with a band of his followers made off with a sizable portion of Mayan treasure following the sacking of Nojpeten by Martin de Ursula Arismendi in February of that year. One of the items they made off with was a significant religious artifact – a sacrificial dagger of the Divine King that signified the king's right to rule the Mayan people and his ability to interpret the will of the gods.

Two weeks ago, Curtis Feldman, a Professor of Archeology with Harvard University who specialized in Mesoamerican civilizations and Paleo-Indian culture, had sent me the information about Juan Julio de Sonya Ramirez and the theft. The recent discovery of a shipwreck off the coast of Northern California had uncovered a well-preserved captain's log belonging to one Masey Sole, Captain of the *Fancy Star*, a pirate ship that sailed the Pacific in the late 1600's. The log showed that the *Fancy Star* had taken on passengers at a small port in Guatemala. The time frame roughly corresponded with the sacking of Nojpeten and supported Curtis's theory that instead of going east toward the Caribbean (a much easier journey home), due the Spanish occupation of that region, Ramirez instead fled west toward the Pacific.

If not for the recovery of the logbook, the theft would have been relegated to the mysteries of history and most likely forgotten. The passengers Sole had brought on board were forcibly disembarked for being unruly and fostering dissension among the crew. Using the rough sketch of the coastline that Sole had drawn into the log, Curtis had a cartographic friend of his estimate that Ramirez was put to shore near the mouth of the Klamath River in Northern California.

The trail would have gone cold at that point, but a discovery of a Mayan figurine in 1978 and another in 1985 had led us to our current location: the mountains above the Trinity River, a main tributary of the Klamath River. Both figurines had been turned over to the de Young Museum of Fine Art where they had remained forgotten until Curtis had accessed their data base a few weeks ago and found them in the de Young's inventory. A few high definition photos later and we had confirmation of the figurines' origins, and I had a dinner date with the lovely curator, Dr. Catherine "Cat" Merritt.

Based on rough estimates of where the figurines had been found, Curtis and I believed that Ramirez hid the treasure somewhere in the vicinity of the Trinity River and that years of fluctuating water flow had pushed those figurines downstream. For five days we had searched for a lead. I was about to call the whole expedition off when Nez, using a metal detector, had found a Mayan coin at the mouth of a gulley that originated higher up in the mountains. Since then, we had been working our way steadily uphill, setting camp in the evening hours when darkness forced us to stop for the night.

I looked at my watch. "We have about two more hours of daylight left. Let's push on and see if we can find a good spot to settle down for the night."

"What about the people following us?" Nez asked, tilting his chin back down the hill.

I glanced back in that direction and scanned the trees for movement. I saw nothing and shrugged. "Besides us, only Robert and Curtis know where we are or why we're here. Could just be some hikers."

Robert was our benefactor for these little expeditions. His full name was Robert Hansen III, a multi-billionaire venture capitalist who collected ancient artifacts and relics. He also kept his ear to the black market for such items and, when he could, ensured those items got back to their proper owners.

Robert, or Bob as I usually called him when it was just him and me, paid for most of the gear, food, and equipment we used, as well as a stipend of $250 a day plus expenses to each member of my team. He's the one who had given us our unofficial name, "The Adventurers' Club." In private conversations with him, I called him Bob, mostly because he hated it.

Nez's face remained as impassive and unreadable as it usually was. He said nothing. Readjusting his pack, he started hiking up the slope again.

I also stood and shouldered my pack. "Steve, with me." She immediately fell into position on my left side, tongue out and happy to be moving again. I often wondered what I had done for companionship before she had entered my life. Given my active lifestyle and these adventures, I required a hardy dog and she fit the bill. If anything, her energy surpassed my own.

Nez took the lead, followed by Jerome. I was bringing up the rear but quickly caught up to Anna. She turned her brown eyes toward me, the hazel flakes that were normally barely noticeable were clearly visible now. It was a tell she had that told me she was worried. "What's on your mind, sis?" It was a term I had started calling her when she had pinned on her anchor as a Chief Petty Officer in the Navy. The Navy's Chief Mess, made up of Chiefs, Senior Chiefs, and Master Chiefs, was considered the backbone of the US Navy. The power of the Mess was derived from its unity. We were brothers and sisters that relied on and supported our fellows and, when necessary, held each other to task when we stepped out of line. Anna and I had been close before we had served as Chief Petty Officers together, but that shared experience made that bond unbreakable.

"Whoever is following us has Nez nervous which makes me nervous," she said in her southern accent. Anna was originally born in Arkansas but had spent most of her life in North Carolina.

I glanced up ahead at Nez and Jerome, not sure how she could tell that Nez was nervous. "We'll find a defensible spot to camp for the night and set a watch," I told her, as we continued our hike.

Looking back down the hill I thought I noticed movement, but it was so fleeting, I couldn't tell if my eyes had really caught a motion or if my imagination was getting the better of me. Probably nothing more than a bird or small animal anyway.

CHAPTER TWO

Camp the night before had been a cold affair. No fire so we didn't give away our position. When I set that condition, no one had argued. We were all convinced now that we were being followed, even though not a one of us had proof to support that belief. Even Steve seemed more subdued; occasionally she paused to look back down the mountain, her ears up and nose raised in an attempt to catch a scent.

We heated water up over a small, one-burner, propane stove. It was enough to make a few cups of coffee and rehydrate the food packs we had. The food packs came from a company called Expeditionary Research Group. Some of ERG's more ingenious innovations included their stackable boxing system and the biodegradable packaging of their products. When the meal was done, we could throw the packaging in the fire and it would burn down to ash without harming the environment. We ate and talked quietly as the sun rose above the horizon. At this altitude, the nights were cold despite the time of year and we were all wearing jackets – Anna, Jerome, and Nez, in thin down jackets, and me in my usual bull-hide leather jacket.

When breakfast was over, we spent a few minutes repacking our gear and checking our weapons. Between the four of us, we had three handguns and two rifles. Nez was carrying an M9 Beretta 9mm and an M40 with a 10x fixed power scope. The M40 was based on the Remington Model 700 bolt action rifle adopted by the Marine Corps as their standard issue sniper rifle. Jerome and I were both carrying M11s, the military version of the Sig Sauer 9mm, and Jerome added his AR-15 with a 4x scope and a red dot. I wasn't entirely sure his rifle was considered legal in California, but as three of us were retired law enforcement, I didn't think any of the local police types would make a fuss about it.

When we were all ready, we lifted our packs and begin the hike again. I watched my team. They were getting tired as we moved into our fourth day of uphill hiking, following gullies and ravines ever higher in an attempt to locate the source of the figurines and the coin. The trees were starting to thin out and the climb was getting more technical. I estimated that by mid-day, we might have to start using some of the climbing gear we had brought.

It was just past 9:00 a.m. when Jerome spotted the rocky outcropping just barely sticking above a thick stand of trees. "Worth a look?" he asked, as we paused to study it.

The ascent was going to be a bear. The ravine leading to the rock formation was narrow and steep, but passable if we were willing to sweat a little. I nodded my agreement; it was worth checking out.

It took us an hour of picking our way across the rocks before we came across a small, mountain pond hidden in the shadows of the rock formation. It was chilly in the shade created by the surrounding rocks, but it was protected from the wind and there were sufficient dead trees and broken branches to provide fuel for a fire, as well as plenty of space to lay down our sleeping bags for the night. At this point, I was more concerned about the comfort of my team than I was about whoever was following us, which brought me to the most important aspect of setting this spot as a base camp to explore the formation above us: we had an unobstructed view of the trail we had followed to get up here – a perfect vantage point from which to set an over watch.

I took off my pack and leaned it against the rock wall. "Jerome and I will make the climb up to the rock formation. Anna, if you can be on belay?" Anna nodded her head. "Nez, if you'll take watch." Nez also nodded and, taking off his pack, grabbed his rifle and moved to the trail side of the alcove. Jerome started breaking out the climbing equipment we had dispersed through all our packs.

While Jerome laid out the gear we would need, I filled our water bottles from the pond using a compact filtration system designed by ERG. After our bottles were topped off, Jerome and I spent some time looking at a probable route up. We could probably do it without the gear but in the event one of us slipped, having it would keep us from serious harm.

"You want to lead, old man?" Jerome asked me, a smile on his face.

"Someone has to show you how it's done, junior," I said, returning his smile. In truth, I was the better climber and the one with the most experience. I pulled on my harness and threaded the rope through before starting the climb.

The first part of our ascent was easy enough. Hand and footholds were plentiful and there were sufficient spaces strong enough to place cams. Occasionally, we paused long enough to drill out a place for an anchor bolt.

We had gone about 100 feet up the rock formation when I saw the cave entrance. It was a little further up and to our left. It wasn't a huge entrance, about three feet in diameter. I pointed the opening out to Jerome and angled us that direction. Another ten minutes and we were entering the mouth. I took a moment to ease the tension in my forearms caused by the climb and to catch my breath.

Jerome shot me a grin. "Little climb and you're gasping for breath. When did you get so old?"

"Ten years ago and I'd hardly call it gasping," I said wryly.

"Like a goldfish out of water." He made a puckering face to mimic a fish gasping for breath and I shot him the bird, earning myself a deep-throated laugh from my younger friend.

Pulling out a flashlight, I pointed the beam deeper into the cave. The floor stayed even with the entrance for about ten feet and then angled upwards. I wished I had Anna up here so that she could tell us what type of cave we were in. The floor was swept free of any small debris, leaving only larger rocks.

I looked at my watch. We still had plenty of daylight. "Shall we push a little deeper and see what we can find?" I asked Jerome, who nodded his head.

Unhooking our harness, we made our way on hands and knees deeper in to the cave. This time, Jerome led the way.

The cave angled up a little steeper than I had originally thought. The floor was still smooth and now that I was on my hands and knees, I could feel the dampness of the place. A few times Jerome or I slipped, and with no handholds to grab on to, it inevitably led to us spending extra time regaining the ground we lost.

As we progressed deeper into the cave, the tunnel was becoming smaller, forcing us to now crawl along on our bellies. From in front of me, I could hear Jerome mumbling to himself. "Join me, he said. You'll get to see the world, he said. Asshole has me crawling around under god knows how many tons of dirt and rock above …." Jerome paused mid rant and stopped moving forward.

"What's up?" I asked as I closed the few feet between us. Jerome still hadn't said anything. I paused, slowing my breathing so that I could better hear. I thought maybe it was an animal but Jerome wasn't reaching for his side arm so if it was, it wasn't one he considered dangerous. "Jerome?" I asked again.

"Boss, you have to see this." There was a moment while he twisted over on to his back so he could see me. In his hand he was holding a gold coin. I wasn't an archeologist and I didn't have a lot of experience in Meso-American currency, but it looked like a Mayan coin.

"We found it," I said, a bit breathless.

CHAPTER THREE

Karl was on the radio back at base camp when the call came in from Jerod and his team in the field. "Castle, this is Ranger. Over."

"Go for Castle," Karl said into the radio mic.

There was a delay as the signal bounced off a satellite high above them and then transmitted back to the portable radio the field team was carrying. "We found it. Over." Even across the intervening miles, Karl could hear the smile in Jerod's voice.

"Roger that," Karl said, also smiling. "Go with coordinates. Over."

There were a few quick transmissions back and forth as Jerod relayed the latitude and longitude of the find and then repeated the location in grid coordinates. Tomorrow they would try to find a landing zone for a helicopter to set down and off-load the professionals and equipment to both secure and excavate the site.

Once Jerod had ended his transmission, Karl called Robert Hansen to let him know. It was Robert who would dispatch the archeologists, geologists, excavators, and security personnel necessary to properly document and collect the treasure they had found. There were other calls that had to be made as well. Calls to the Department of the Interior and the Department of Forestry to obtain the proper permits – all calls better made by Mr. Hansen's lawyers and public relations people.

After relaying all the information to Mr. Hansen, Karl went to the mess tent to tell Andy and Carlos. Andy was showing his young protégé the finer points of cooking in a camp when Karl walked in.

"It's all about the proper use of spices, son," Andy was telling him, looking up from the dish he was preparing for their evening dinner as Karl entered the canvas tent. Andy was about 5'6" and rail thin. He had long ago lost his hair and his head was cue ball bald. Add in oversized ears and a mustache so thin it was barely visible and Andy always reminded Karl of a cartoon character.

Carlos also looked in Karl's direction. Carlos was in his mid-twenties with coal dark hair that was just about 3" in length almost all the way around. After almost a week at the base camp he had stopped bothering to do anything more than run a comb through it at the beginning of the day. His dark brown eyes looked intelligent but wary and Karl had a hard time warming up to the kid. His tanned face was plain other than his attempt to grow a beard which, if Karl were to be honest with the kid, was a waste of time, so sparse was his facial hair.

Karl had had every intention of keeping a straight face, but he failed and a broad smile spread across the mocha complexion of his face. Like Nez, he was heavy-set and, like Nez, he was in deceptively better shape than he appeared. He had to be. They had been introduced to each other through Jerod and had become fast friends. Several times a year, when they weren't supporting Jerod, he and Nez would find some extreme climate to visit and spend a week surviving in it.

Andy's eyes widened. "They found it?"

"They did." If possible, Karl's smile widened.

Andy let loose a whoop and grabbed Carlos' hands and danced a little jig. Carlos' participation was less than enthusiastic. Karl's smile didn't drop but he did wonder if it was because, unlike full members of the Adventurers' Club, provisional members didn't get a bonus based on the find. The stipend they received for working one of the Club's operations wasn't bad, but the bonus was what made these trips worthwhile.

Andy let go of Carlos and walked over to Karl, his hand extended. Karl took Andy's extended hand in his own and then brought him in close for a quick hug. Andy didn't resist but, in truth, given their size difference, it wouldn't have mattered if he had. "This will help," Andy said in a tone just barely above a whisper, as he thought about the growing pile of medical bills for his wife's cancer treatments.

Karl understood. His youngest son had cancer, in remission now, but his medical insurance hadn't covered everything and he and his wife had to contend with mounting debt as a result. One of these little trips had helped cut that down to a more manageable level. Karl released his hug and took a step back still smiling.

The smile dropped a second later when he looked over Andy's right shoulder and saw Carlos holding a revolver that was pointed at the two of them. Andy noticed the immediate change in Karl's body language and turned around to look where Karl's gaze was locked. "What in the hell are you doing, son?" Andy asked incredulously.

The kid shrugged and pulled a satellite phone from his pocket. Whomever he was calling must have been on speed dial because Carlos hit one button and then held the phone up to his ear. They all stood there silently for a moment until someone picked up on the other end of the phone. "They found it. You can move in when you're ready."

CHAPTER FOUR

I pulled out the small bottle of whiskey I had been saving for this occasion and passed it around the campfire; each of the members of my team added a finger or two to their cups. In the protected space around the pond, the fire was providing adequate warmth to make the chill, nighttime air comfortable. Dinner had been a simple affair consisting of whatever dehydrated meal each of us had decided to bring.

Nez poured a little of the amber liquid into his cup and then went to stand watch over the trail leading up to our campsite. Outside the light of the fire, the landscape was nothing more than dark shadows and the vague outline of trees. It was a crisp, clear evening though, and the night sky was filled with millions of tiny points of lights. It was a dazzling display of the universe and one I never grew tired of.

Steve was laying on the ground next to me. Her head resting contentedly on her front paws, her ears up as she listened to the conversation around her. Idly, I reached out and scratched the blue merle fur along her neck and back, causing her eyes to close halfway as she relaxed.

Jerome asked me something which I didn't quite hear; I was about to ask him to repeat himself when Nez grunted in pain, followed half a second later by the crack of a firearm, a small caliber rifle by the sound of it.

We all started moving at once. Not missing a beat, Nez brought his M40 to his shoulder and, working the bolt action smoothly, fired three rounds in quick succession. Jerome snatched up his AR-15 and moved in a half crouch to cover the trailhead in the event someone tried to storm the camp. My own M11 cleared the holster. I held it at the low ready, prepared to come up on target if a hostile should appear.

At the sounds of the gunshots, Steve surged to her feet barking, the fur along her neck, back, and tail standing on end. I had done some training with her so she wasn't shying away from the sounds of guns firing, but she didn't like it either. Not that I blamed her – the heavier caliber M40 was loud and had left my ears ringing. I could only imagine how it affected her more sensitive hearing.

"Anna, radio," I said, even though she was already moving toward it. I glanced at Nez. He had ducked back behind the rocks for cover. Blood coursed down his right forearm. Other than the grunt when the round initially hit him, and the fact that the wound was visible, Nez gave no other indication that he had been injured. I went to grab the first aid kit to tend to Nez as Anna was picking up the receiver for the radio.

"Castle, this is Ranger. Need immediate assistance. Shots fired. Over," she said into the radio's microphone. The adrenaline coursing through her system had caused her voice to raise a few octaves. There was no immediate response so she tried again. "Castle, I say again, this is Ranger. Mayday, mayday, mayday. Shots fired. Need immediate assistance!" She was now yelling into the radio.

There was no response.

* * * * *

"I said, what in the hell are you doing?" Andy growled, his face and bald head turning beet red. This wasn't the first time Karl had seen his friend lose his temper. The last time, Jerod had to go bail the old man out of jail after he started a fight in a restaurant over some perceived slight.

"Andy, let's stay calm here," Karl said, as he tried to move where he could put himself in between Andy and the kid. "Carlos," Karl said, turning his attention to the kid, "whatever we have going on here, it isn't too late to alter your course."

Karl had managed to get close enough that he was now shoulder to shoulder with Andy. Carlos raised the revolver up an inch or two and shifted his aim to Karl. "Stop right there or I will shoot." He was hanging up the phone and returning it to his pocket.

Karl froze in place but Andy didn't. "Boy, you put that gun down right now or I am going give you an ass-whooping the likes of which you have never seen," he said, taking a step forward.

Carlos shifted the gun back to Andy. "I said stop!" The kid was clearly nervous. Sweat had beaded up on his forehead and his arm was starting to shake from the weight of the gun he was holding.

Karl edged forward another step. He had spent the last few years training in Brazilian Jiu-Jitsu and Krav Maga and was confident that, if he could close the distance between the two of them, he could wrest the revolver from Carlos's hands. Carlos shifted his aim back to Karl. "STOP!" His finger lighted on the trigger and his hand clenched, causing Karl to freeze.

"I'm only going to tell you one more time, kid, you drop that weapon or I swear to God I will kick your ass from here to next Sunday. I will literally stomp out your guts!" Andy's voice had raised to almost a roar. His fists were clenched at his sides and the veins along his neck and forehead were standing out.

"Andy," Karl said in a soft tone, trying to de-escalate the situation, "he has his finger on the trigger." From the other tent, Karl could hear the radio receiving but he couldn't make out the words. The tone of Anna's voice said they were having some problems as well. "One problem at a time," he whispered under his breath.

"I don't give a flying rat's ass where his finger is!" Andy took a stomping step forward, his boot making an audible thud as it hit the ground. "He puts that gun down or I kick his ass." Andy took another step.

The kid once again shifted his aim. Andy growled and then barked out, "Drop it! Now!" He said it with enough force that Carlos flinched and the gun went off with a loud boom. Carlos's eyes widened in surprise and his hand loosened on the weapon, almost dropping it.

Karl saw his opportunity and surged forward. For a large man, he was light on his feet. His Jiu-Jitsu instructor had told him that learning to ballroom dance would make him quicker and Karl had taken that advice to heart. He and his wife went every Saturday night. Karl's left hand went up, grabbing the kid's wrist. As he pushed the gun away from Andy, he tilted his shoulders away from the gun as well so that if there was another discharge, it would go wide.

Clear of the gun's barrel, Karl's right hand shot up and took control of the weapon, his fingers latching down on the cylinder so it couldn't rotate if Carlos squeezed the trigger again. Given his superior size and strength, there was little Carlos could do to stop the quick rotation of the weapon toward him as his wrist snapped audibly. Carlos cried out in pain and immediately grabbed his wrist and brought it into his chest as he fell to the ground whimpering.

Karl had the gun in hand now and pointed it at Carlos. "Andy, come check the kid and make sure he doesn't have any other weapons." Karl inhaled deeply and tried to calm the rapid beating of his heart.

From behind him, he heard Andy let out a wet sounding cough. Carlos was still laying on the floor crying and holding his wrist close to his body, so Karl hazarded a look in Andy's direction. "Oh shit," he breathed out. There was a blossoming stain of red on Andy's otherwise white shirt.

Years of training in the medical field kicked in. Carlos lay forgotten on the floor and Karl squatted down next to Andy and started assessing the damage that had been done. Karl stopped looking at Andy as his friend. That would bring emotion into play and this wasn't about feeling, it was about doing what was necessary to save Andy's life.

* * * * *

Jerome had replaced Nez watching over the trail leading to our encampment. Occasionally, he would see movement in the trees and would fire off a volley of rounds. I told him to conserve his ammo. We hadn't brought that much with us and with there being no answer back at Castle, I wasn't sure how long we'd be fending for ourselves out here, or how large a group had massed against us.

I finished bandaging Nez's arm. The round had entered just above the back of his wrist and exited his forearm near the elbow. While Nez's face remained impassive, I could tell the wound was hurting him. His face was pale and despite the coolness of the night, he was sweating. "Hang in there, brother," I told him. "We'll get hold of Karl or Andy here soon." I didn't tell him that my chief worry about their not answering was that they were also in trouble.

Anna was still trying to reach Karl or Andy via the radio. Steve was glued to my side, not leaving me either while I was bandaging Nez or as I rifled through my pack, looking for the one device we might be able to use to summon help – a cellular phone.

Pulling it out from near the bottom of my pack and removing it from the waterproof bag it was in, I powered it up and waited for it to see if, by some miracle, it would connect. Nothing. Without a clear line of sight to a cell phone tower, I had jack. "Shit!" I said emphatically.

I glanced up at where the cave entrance was. There were hand and footholds that I could use to climb above the altitude of the cave and into clearer space. We had a signal at base camp so there had to be a tower around there somewhere. Unless my mental map of the area was off, once I was above the tree line, I'd have a clear line of sight to Castle and, hopefully, a cell signal as well. There was a portion of the climb up, though, that I'd be exposed to incoming gunfire from our adversaries. That made me nervous, but I was willing to take the risk to do something to exfiltrate my team from the mess we were in.

I wondered how the men, or women, on the trail below our position knew we were here and what we were after. Outside my little team, Bob, and Curtis, I hadn't told anyone, and I was sure that none of those parties had either.

CHAPTER FIVE

Jan paced the floor of her hotel room nervously. She should have heard from Carlos by now. He was supposed to notify her that the treasure had been found, secure the two idiots at the base camp, and then call her back once he had established contact with Jerod and his team in the field. She had planned to use Andy Luna and Karl Williams as leverage against Jerod. Without that leverage, Jerod would hold out as long as he could. He had never responded well to being forced to do something.

She went over the plan in her head again. Recruit Carlos – he lived near Andy and had served in the Navy, which had immediately endeared him to the old fool. Wait until there was a mission and then have Carlos insert himself on that mission. That had taken awhile. Jerod was busy, but not so much so that he took a team with him every time he went out into the field. The first two steps, though, had gone reasonably well overall. No major snags.

The next hurdle was to wait until Jerod had found what he was looking for – in this case, the stolen treasure from Njopeten. Carlos was supposed to get the drop on Andy and Karl and notify her once they were restrained so she could let the team know they had some leverage to use. The team she had hired were pros – former military and security experts whose life in the shadows may have gotten them blackballed from their professions, but also made them ideal for this sort of illicit work. Once Jerod had found the treasure, they'd make their presence known and keep the team pinned down until her leverage was in play.

Once that was done, the rest was easy. Jerod wouldn't risk his friends if he could help it. Especially that bitch, Anna. If not for Anna, Jan wouldn't be in the predicament she found herself in. She had ingratiated herself with Jerod Gray, become his right hand, learned everything she could from him and thought that she had him to the point where he would make her his sole beneficiary in his will. Once that was finalized, it wouldn't have taken much for her to arrange an "accident." The man was foolhardy and often took risks he didn't need to take. No one would be surprised if he fell into a crevice or became lost in the wilderness, never to be seen again. In truth, she probably could have stepped back and let Darwinism run its course. She wasn't that patient, though.

When she had found out Jerod still had Anna listed as his only beneficiary, Jan became angry. All that time and effort for nothing. She shifted focus. Instead of going after Jerod's money, she decided to go after one of the treasures he was hunting. One with a large enough payout to set her up for a long while. Well, not just her – her and her three-year-old son. One solid score and she could take her son and leave her crappy boyfriend, her crappy family, and her crappy life behind and start fresh.

She had sent two thugs to St. Lucia where Jerod and a small team were diving for a sunken treasure ship. Jerod's team hit the motherlode, and Jan's two hired thieves had moved in. Both had ended up dead and eventually, Jerod had tracked them back to her. Always the self-righteous fool, he had thought that if he confronted her, she would give herself up. She hadn't, of course. What she had done was shoot Jerod – not fatally, unfortunately – and made her escape, but without her son.

Now she was a fugitive, forced to live a life always looking over her shoulder. A life where she couldn't see her son. Why? Because Anna Smith had been better at worming her way into Jerod's life. This time, Jan wouldn't fail. She had a solid plan and instead of the two amateurs she had hired for the St. Lucia job, she had professionals. All she had to do was wait for Carlos to complete his part.

* * * * *

I slid on the harness and prepared to hook myself on the line that Jerome and I had set up earlier that led up to the mouth of the cave. I had extra rope and cams to help me climb past the cave to the tree line. My hope was that, with the increased altitude and getting clear of the rock walls surrounding the small, glacier pond, I'd be able to reach out with the cell phone. My plan was to call the police first and then Bob. Based on our original plan, Bob would already have a team ready to push out once we had located the treasure. His team included men from his security detail. These weren't just regular security, either. Bob hired nothing but the best – Navy SEALs, Army Rangers, and Marines. Bob even had a man that I was convinced was probably a former officer of the CIA, his head of security, Josue Fernandez.

"Ready?" Anna asked me, once I was hooked in.

"Ready," I said, shooting her a smile over my shoulder.

"Be careful. You have a dog that would miss you terribly if something happened to you."

"Just the dog, eh." I responded with a chuckle.

"Well, and Nez. He'd be lost without you." From his position of cover near the trailhead, I heard Nez grunt – as close as I would probably get to any sort of acknowledgment that he would miss me if I was gone.

I laughed again, but I had butterflies in my stomach caused by my nerves and adrenaline. I took a couple of deep breaths and started the climb. For the most part, I was protected by the rock formations of the ravine leading up to the cave, but there was a stretch of about thirty feet where I'd be exposed to gunfire from below.

I took my time, ensuring I had the proper hand and footholds before advancing the next few feet. There was just enough ambient light from the moon and stars that I could see the outline of my hands, but not much else. The lack of light more than anything kept my pace to a crawl. I didn't want to rush, miss a handhold, and fall. Anna, being on belay, would catch me, but I could just as easily bang my head or break a bone. Moving slow and steady was the key. It was twenty minutes before I hit the beginning of the exposed area.

I found a spot where I could take a minute and loosen up my stiffening forearms and cramping hands. The exertion, particularly given this was the second time today that I had made this climb, left me breathing harder than normal. I took a moment longer to catch my breath before starting the climb again.

I inched out into the exposed area. The hair along the back of my neck stood on end and I could almost feel the cross hairs on my back. I estimated the distance from my position to the shooters' at around 800 to 900 yards. Just within the effective range of a high-powered rifle in the hands of a competent marksman. I pulled myself up another foot.

Reaching for the next handhold, my fingertips found the small crack in the rock that was just large enough to provide a secure hold. I reached out with my other hand. I heard the high-pitched whine of a bullet just a fraction of a second before the rock next to my face exploded. Fragments of stone and lead peppered the right side of my head and face, opening up a dozen small cuts. I flinched away too late, but by some miracle managed not to get anything in my eye.

"Fuck!" I said emphatically, and started climbing faster. A second round hit nearby but far enough away it didn't add to the minor damage already done by the first bullet. A third and fourth rounds did the same. I was scrambling now, finding the hand and footholds more by instinct than any sort of design.

I had only a few more feet to go when the impact of a round striking my left shoulder almost knocked me completely off my precarious perch. The immediate pain of blunt force from the projectile hitting me gave way to the sharp burning sting of the bullet having cut into my shoulder. I didn't dare stop moving forward or I'd make myself an easier target. It was either stop and I was as good as dead, or ignore the pain long enough to get back to a position of cover. It was an easy choice to make. It was an exercise of pure will to push the ache from my mind, but I pulled myself forward and out of the line of fire. If there were any more shots fired, I was concentrating too hard to hear them strike the rock wall beside me.

I did hear the answering bark of Jerome's AR and the louder crack of Nez's M40, unclear in that moment when they had begun returning fire as my focus had been on surviving. Auditory exclusion wasn't unusual in cases of extreme stress. Your body didn't need to hear to survive so it didn't waste any effort on that function. The result, sounds, even as loud as gunshots, were either muffled or went unheard.

Protected once more by the walls of the ravine, I planted my feet and took a couple of deep breaths. Instinctively, I reached up to feel the wound in my shoulder and winced. This was the second time that I had been shot in that shoulder. The first had been when I confronted Jan about the botched robbery attempt while a small team and I were in St. Lucia. I'd had a suspicion she was behind the robbery. The two thugs who had attacked me in my hotel room had been from Oakland where Jan had grown up and, more interestingly, they had attended the same school as her and at the same time. I'd thought it was worth asking her about it. I had no idea she would be willing to shoot me over it.

I finished checking the wound. I was bleeding but the round didn't seem to have hit an artery. Even if it had, I didn't have anything to stop it. An oversight on my part. I had known there was a possibility of getting shot but hadn't taken any action to mitigate that risk.

Pulling out the tactical folding knife I almost always carried with me, I cut a strip from the bottom of my shirt and used that to put pressure on the wound. I did my best to tie it tight but being able to only use one hand complicated that.

As patched up as I was going to get for now, I decided to pursue my original course of action and keep climbing. A few minutes later, I made the entrance to the cave. Ten minutes after that and I was in a spot that was relatively clear of obstacles. I pulled out the phone and looked at the signal bar.

* * * * *

Karl had cleared off the stainless steel table that Andy used for food preparation and that could double as a medical table in the event they ever needed it. Like now. He easily managed to lift Andy off the ground and placed him on the table. He wanted to immediately start working on him, but he knew he couldn't leave Carlos loose. The kid was still laying on the ground, his heavy crying having subsided to quieter sobs.

Quickly and efficiently, he snatched the kid off the ground, bound his right arm to his chest using gauze from their medical kit and then bound his torso with rope to one of the tent poles that was spiked into the ground. The whole process took him all of two minutes, but it was two minutes he could have been helping Andy, and that made him angry enough that he almost struck the kid just because of the delay.

Gaining control of his emotions, Karl went back to work on his friend. With sure hands, Karl cut the shirt away from the wound and got his first good look at it. The hole was about the size of a dime with pink, frothy blood around the wound. A clear indication of a sucking chest wound.

"I'm going to give you something for the pain. You hang in there, Andy, we'll get you patched up good as new," Karl said in a soft but reassuring tone. The kid was still crying and Karl had to fight the urge to shut him up in a harsh and definitive way.

Working quickly, Karl got an IV set up and pushed some morphine into the mix. It wouldn't take away the pain, but it would make it so that Andy didn't really care as much. Karl felt Andy's hand on his arm and he looked down at his friend.

"Make sure I get back to my wife," Andy said in a gasping voice.

"That's as much up to you as it is me, my friend," Karl told him.

"Well in that case, I'll be right as rain come morning," Andy said with a soft chuckle that turned into a coughing fit, causing more blood to pump from the wound. When the coughing stopped, Andy's eyes started to drift shut as the morphine kicked in.

Karl worked swiftly, setting up the monitor, identifying the exit wound, and cleaning both wounds as thoroughly as he could in the setting. Once the wounds were clean, he applied an occlusive dressing using medical grade plastic wrap and tape, making sure there was a space for air to escape out of the chest cavity. The whole process took him less than ten minutes.

Checking Andy's vitals, he found them strong enough. Karl would give it to the old man, he was tough as nails. Karl went over and cuffed Carlos upside the head, not hard, but it was a sign of his anger at the kid that he did it at all. "Listen up. I have to go call for help. You are to watch that monitor and if it starts to beep or drop, or make any noise other than what it is doing right now, you better scream for all you're worth to catch my attention. Understand?"

Carlos looked at the monitor and then nodded his head. His crying had subsided but tears still welled in his eyes.

"Good. I don't have time to deal with you trying to escape either, so try it, and I will simply shoot you in the leg. You understand that?" Karl placed the barrel of the revolver he had picked up against Carlos's leg for emphasis, causing the kid to try and pull back to little avail. Carlos nodded his head again, this time with a great deal more enthusiasm.

Karl didn't waste any more time. Quickly, he left the mess tent and went over to the tent where they had the radio set up. Picking up the mic, he talked hurriedly. "Ranger, this Castle, over."

There was silence initially so he repeated his transmission. A second later, Anna's voice came over the airwaves. "Castle, this is Ranger, over. Thank god. We're in deep out here." The stress in her voice came out clearly, even via the radio.

"Ranger, Castle. Same. Andy is down. Hurt bad. What's your sitrep?" Karl asked for their situation report. The adrenaline flowing through his body started to take its toll. His hands were shaky, and his heartbeat was too fast.

"Pinned down at our bivouac by unknown number of assailants. Nez is injured. None life threatening. Jerod's status is unknown," Anna said.

"Shit." Karl cursed under his breath, making sure not to key the mic when he said it. Anna didn't cuss and she didn't take kindly to those who did. She'd call him out on it even given the situation they were in. "Ranger, Castle. Good copy. Will call for help." He paused and took a deep breath. "Hang in there, Anna. Castle out."

Karl went to work. First he called the ranger station. They knew where the Adventurers' Club base camp was at. It would take them an hour to get a helicopter up in the air. First priority would be getting Andy to a hospital. After that, they'd try and get resources up to the team's location. Possible ETA, three hours. That was too much time.

Picking up the satellite phone they had on hand, Karl called Robert Hansen. Mr. Hansen would send help. Just then, he heard Carlos screaming for him to come and come quick. Pocketing the phone, Karl rushed into the mess tent.

Andy's blood pressure had dropped and his breathing was short and shallow. Karl knew what was going on but he checked him regardless. Bulging jugular vein in the neck and cyanosis, a bluing coloration of his lips and fingers. Tension pneumothorax, a buildup of air in the chest cavity. Grabbing the appropriate needle from his supplies, he removed the packaging and then prepared to relieve the pressure.

CHAPTER SIX

In place of the signal bars for the cell phone was the round circle with a line through it. I wanted to scream out my frustration but settled instead for a string of expletives that went on for a solid minute. I tried moving the phone to various positions in hopes of finding a signal, all to no avail. My head dropped and I exhaled loudly. There was still a chance we could get base camp on the radio, but I also believed that if they were going to answer, they would have, and in not doing so, gave an indication of a coordinated effort to cut us off from any help we could receive.

I thought Jan might be involved. This followed the same basic pattern as St. Lucia. Wait until the treasure had been found and then move in to steal it. The plan here, if base camp had been attacked as well, was more elaborate. I had found out almost too late what Jan's greed would drive her to do, so it wouldn't surprise me if she was behind this. She was smart and ruthless enough. My only question was how she had known now was the time to hit us. All fingers pointed to the kid, Carlos. Everyone else I had known for years and I was convinced none of them would betray me. Carolos was the unknown.

Sitting here moping about it wasn't going to solve anything. I started thinking about solutions and remembered what Anna had said earlier about her thoughts on how the cave was formed. She called the cave where we had found the treasure a corrosional cave – a cave formed almost entirely by water erosion from flowing streams. She had speculated that the stream that formed the cave was seasonal which explained why now, at the height of summer, there was no water running through it, and it likely remained that way until the spring when rain water and snow melt caused the stream to flow again. If that were the case, maybe there was an opening deeper in the cave that I could use to escape and then circle around behind our assailants.

It was worth a try. Plus, I wasn't keen on the idea of getting shot at again when I had to leave the cover of the rock walls to get back down to our campsite. Already my shoulder was throbbing in time with the beat of my heart and the pain was sufficient to make me queasy.

Making my way down from my perch above the cave, I entered the cool, dark interior. I flipped down the red lens on my flashlight and made my way deeper into the cave before switching to the brighter, white light. It had taken Jerome and me thirty minutes to get to the grotto in the cave where the treasure had been found. A lot of that had been spent collecting coins that had been washed into the main portion of the cave. I didn't waste time looking for more coins now. Those could be found by the team Bob had put together.

The going was easy to start out with, and it only took me a little over ten minutes to reach the grotto. After that things became a little tighter, and once I thought I had become stuck, almost causing me to panic. Calming myself, I exhaled and managed to slip through, barely. After that, the cave widened considerably, and shortly after that I exited an opening into another ravine that led from above the tree line.

I took a minute to survey my surroundings – as much as I could, anyway, given the darkness. From where I was, I thought I could see the reflection of the fire from our campsite. It was my only guide, so I put my faith in the idea that I was right and started making my way down the mountain.

* * * * *

Anna put down the radio mic and turned to update Jerome and Nez on Andy's status. As she did so, her eyes lighted on Steve. Steve's attention had been fixated in the direction that Jerod had gone in over an hour ago. She had been sitting perfectly still that entire time.

Anna noticed a slight shift in the breeze and Steve's head whipped around, her body following as she came to her feet and moved toward the edge of the pool. Letting out a small whine, her tail wagged slowly. Puzzled by the dog's behavior, Anna caught Nez's attention and asked for his insight.

"Jerod's on the move," Nez said simply and went back to watching the trail below their campsite.

Anna let go of a breath she didn't know she had been holding. She had been worried about Jerod since the gunfire earlier. They couldn't see him in the dark and she hadn't been sure if he was hurt or worse. If he was on the move now, though, that meant he was still alive and in at least reasonable condition. How he had managed to get on the other side of the camp, though, was a question she'd have to ask later.

* * * * *

It took me the better part of an hour to move down the mountain and past where I suspected our assailants had set their positions. I was being as quiet as I could but the rocks, dried twigs, and old pine needles made that nearly impossible. Now that I was behind the bad guys, I was being extra careful and each step was agonizingly slow. I had taken an inventory of the tools I had on hand – the M11 with 31 rounds, a tactical folding knife, and a flashlight. Not much, but it would have to do.

I came across the first guy almost by accident. A few more feet and I would have stepped on him. Had he not adjusted his body slightly, it would have been him ambushing me instead of the other way around, or at least mutual confusion.

The man had found a fallen log to use as both a prop for the AR-15 he was carrying and to provide cover from Nez and Jerome shooting back toward him. He was dressed all in black. Not the best choice for night operations. The dark material provided a decent outline of the man's body, now that I knew he was there. A camouflage pattern of dark grays would have been better at breaking up that outline.

His attention was fixed on the campsite above him. The glow of our fire cast shadows that danced on the rocks above. Occasionally, you could see the shadow of one of my friends as they crossed in front of the fire. Tactically, it wasn't the best set up, but the light cast by the fire would disrupt any night vision equipment these men had.

Carefully, I moved up, each step deliberately placed. I was within a few feet of him when a twig snapped and his head whipped around. I didn't give him time to contemplate what was happening. I surged forward, my left arm encircling his neck, cutting off the flow of blood to his brain by restricting the carotid artery. My right hand clamped tightly over his nose and mouth to keep him from yelling.

He pushed up hard with his legs, causing me to fall backward. I held tight to the lateral neck restraint I had him in as I hit the ground, my right elbow banging against a rock and a stick jabbing me sharply along the left side of my ribcage.

Smoothly and efficiently, I wrapped my legs around his waist; the heel of my boot hit his groin and what air the man had in his lungs exploded around my hand. Hooking my toes to the inside of his thighs, I extended my legs so that it stretched his body and made the neck restraint even tighter. Less than ten seconds later, his body went limp.

Quickly I rolled him off me. Contrary to what the movies show, the man wouldn't remain unconscious for very long. I had about thirty seconds to find something to bind him with. I found his pack and emptied the contents on the ground, finding some flex cuffs and a roll of duct tape. They had come prepared to take us prisoner.

Using the flex cuffs, I secured his hands behind his back and the roll of duct tape to keep his mouth closed and to bind his feet. He was starting to come to by the time I finished. He started to struggle but my hand pressed to his throat caused him to cease.

"Look," I whispered in his ear, my hand still pressed hard against his throat, "I don't have time for any guessing games. I'm going to ask you a question and I expect an honest answer." I took my hand off his throat and pulled my tactical folding knife, the blade making a clicking sound as it opened. Pressing the tip of the blade against his groin, I asked "How many of you are out here?" I started with ten and worked my way down to six before he shook his head yes.

"Good," I told him, "stay quiet and you'll live to see the sunrise." I took the knife away and closed it, putting it back in the sapper pocket of my pants. One down and five to go, if the guy was telling me the truth. I had a knife to his manhood so I had no reason to doubt him.

Before I moved on, I conducted a quick search of the man to ensure he had no other weapons and removed a handgun from a holster on his hip. The handgun and rifle I cleared of any rounds and then field stripped them both and scattered the parts.

After I was sure he wasn't still armed with anything he could use against me or use to escape, I paused, closed my eyes and focused on my ears. There was no indication that the brief scuffle had caught anyone's attention. Opening my eyes, I scanned the area carefully. About fifty yards to my left I saw a red light blink on and then off again. I'd found my next target.

Like the first, he had found a prop to rest his gun on, this time a rock, and like the last guy, I took him out with a carotid hold, cutting off the blood flow to his brain and inducing unconsciousness. He was quickly secured using the flex cuffs and tape and left struggling in vain against his bonds. After he was searched and his weapons disassembled, I tried to locate the next.

I was using a zig-zag search pattern and was just about to put my foot down when the ground shifted under me. "What the fuck, man?" said a rough, low voice.

I didn't hesitate, dropping to the ground with my left elbow leading. I was hoping to catch the back of his head or least one of the nerve clusters in his upper back. I failed to catch either but did manage to drop 200 pounds on top of him, knocking the air from his lungs. He was quick to recover though, and we rolled, trading short, weak blows back and forth as we jockeyed for position.

I ended up on top and was about to start laying down some serious hurt when a rifle encircled my chest and yanked me back with enough force that I felt my ribcage flex with the pressure. I was pulled back about five feet and the guy holding me started to squeeze harder.

Throwing my head back, I tried to connect with his nose but only succeeded in hitting him in the forehead. Unfortunately for me, his forehead was the stronger of the two bones and black specks danced across my vision. I was successful in getting him to loosen up his grip some. I pushed back my hips hard, creating enough space to allow me to take a step to my right and drive a hammer fist into that man's groin with my left fist.

With more space to maneuver, I pushed the rifle away from my chest and spun around, keeping hold of the rifle as I did so. The move crossed his arms allowing me to strip the rifle from his hands. I extended the rifle out as far as I could and then drove the buttstock back into his face. The man went down like a ton of bricks. He wasn't waking up in thirty seconds or less.

I brought the weapon up to my shoulder and flicked off the safety. I swept the area where I had last seen my second opponent. I found him easy enough, but he also had his rifle at his shoulder with the barrel pointed directly back at me.

"Drop the weapon!" I yelled, no longer worrying about stealth. The fight with the two guys would draw anyone in the area. Three on one, if the guy had been telling the truth, weren't great odds, but then I had taken out half their team and I was still standing. I didn't like my odds, but they were better than nothing.

"You drop yours!" The guy yelled back at me. We shouted back and forth for a moment. I thought I had won this round as well when the guy started to drop his weapon. Then I saw his smile at the same time I felt the cold barrel of a gun against the back of my head.

"Shit," I said under my breath, as I let the rifle I had been holding fall to the ground. My odds had changed from bad to worse and yet, I was still alive. All that remained to be seen was for how long.

"Bind his hands," a voice said from behind me. "We'll use him to bring the others out. It looks like the kid failed on his end."

I was sure "the kid" referred to Carlos. My hands were yanked roughly behind my back, letting me know that the third and final member of their team was here as well. Sharp pain shot through my shoulder, causing me to wince and suck in a quick breath through clinched teeth. I felt the flex cuffs go on. They were pulled tight enough my hands immediately started going numb. I was going to say something cliché like, "you won't get away with this," but it would have sounded corny. Better to just keep my mouth shut for now.

The third guy pulled me abruptly to my feet and turned me to face the man who had spoken. I assumed he was the leader. He was my height and heavy with muscle. I could make out only enough of his face to see a smattering of freckles across his face and a full beard. His hair was cut short to the scalp, similar to my own.

"So, you're Jerod Gray. Based on the way the bitch described you, I thought you'd be bigger," the man said, stepping up so that his face was inches from my own and I could smell the stench of his breath. "You and your team have given me a hard time. Two of my men are down." The anger in his voice seemed forced, like he was angry at the inconvenience of the situation more than he was angry that we had taken out two of his men.

For a moment, I tried to decide if the first guy I had choked out had lied to me about how many men had been in his team or not. Technically, it sounded like there had been eight to start but at the time I had questioned the man, there had been only six still standing.

In my own mind, I applauded Nez and Jerome. They were shooting blind, aiming for nothing more than muzzle flashes. I didn't have to guess who "the bitch" was. Based on the method of operation, I had been leaning toward Jan being behind this already.

I didn't see the fist that hit me solidly along the left side of my jaw. I definitely felt it. The power of it spun me halfway around, my feet getting tangled together so that I fell to the ground. It probably would have temporarily knocked me out if I hadn't landed on my injured shoulder. For a moment, the two pains battled it out. I almost wished the punch would have won out. Being unconscious was preferable to the pounding ache of the bullet wound in my shoulder. I felt the blood seeping from the injury.

I rolled so that I was facing the bearded man and to take some of the pressure off my shoulder. I was about to tell him to fuck off when the air was suddenly filled with an angry swishing noise, like someone swinging a stick forcibly through the air. I could only see two of the three men around me. The one who had bound my hands behind my back jumped as if he had been stung by a bee. The bearded man flinched and cursed, "What the hell?" He reached down to his chest and pulled out what looked like a dart. His brows furrowed together quizzically and then all three of the men dropped to the ground, unmoving.

I remained perfectly still as shadows detached themselves from trees, ten in total. Men who moved with a lethal grace, rifles raised, the lenses of their night vision goggles giving them an alien appearance.

"Any more of them?" one of the men asked in a quiet voice.

Recognizing the voice of Josue Fernandez, Bob's head of security, I sighed in relief.

EPILOGUE

The house Bob had given me sat in a nice part of Marin County, just across the Golden Gate Bridge from San Francisco, overlooking the town of San Rafael, though I couldn't see it through the trees that dotted the five-acre piece of property. I sat on the wrap-around porch, throwing the ball for Steve while I sipped on a scotch and smoked a cigar.

Anna, Karl, and Nez had all gone home. Andy had spent a week in the hospital before he was flown home. He had been provided the best of care, all compliments of Bob. I had likewise had surgery to repair the damage done to my shoulder. A sling held my left arm immobile.

At the end of the day, when the initial investigation was all completed by local law enforcement, the six men who had held us pinned down for most of that night went to jail. The rounds used by Josue's men were tranquilizer darts. Non-lethal, according to Josue, although I was sure that I saw them give one man a Noloxone shot, a drug that counteracted the effects of the drug contained in the darts.

Two more men were found – one clearly dead, the other just barely hanging on. He died in the hospital. Carlos had also gone to jail but had decided to cooperate. He told the police about Jan's plan to rob us of the treasure, how he was supposed to take Karl and Andy hostage so that they could be used as leverage to get me and my team out of our position.

Jan had fled the hotel she had been using as her base of operations. Within a week there'd be a warrant out for her arrest. I thought back to the time she had shot me. I hadn't gone to the police then, instead calling Bob who found me a surgeon who worked for cash with no questions asked. For a man on the straight and narrow, he knew people who clung to the shadows. Or maybe it wasn't Bob. If Josue had once worked for who I thought he had, he was more likely the one with the shady contacts.

The find was being excavated and the pieces they were removing were remarkable – enough so that it convinced Curtis Feldman, my friend from Harvard, to fly out as a consultant. One of the key pieces had been the sacrificial dagger of the Divine King. The Boston Museum of Fine Arts was already making a bid on it.

Overall, it had been a successful operation. Andy and I would make full recoveries. Andy had been clear, though, that this was his last adventure with the Club. His skills in logistics and in the kitchen would be missed.

I threw the ball once more and Steve took off after it. I polished off my scotch and put out my cigar. It was time to go in, pour myself another drink, and then spend some time reading before bed. I winced as I stood, the pain in my shoulder aggravated by the movement. I was reminded of something. Pain and discipline. That's how a girlfriend once described my life. I didn't necessarily believe in her assessment, but at the time, she knew me as well as anyone. Discipline was never something that was forced on me, it was simply expected. I grew up on a ranch and there were always things that needed doing and I did what needed to be done. Getting good grades in school, competing in sports, my eventual service in both the Marine Corps and the Navy and my 27-year career as a police officer all required discipline.

I was never sure what she meant by pain. Physical pain, in most instances, was temporary. Well, at least until you hit that point in your life when your body had a bad habit of reminding you of years of abuse. Emotional pain could last longer. I looked at the empty glass and was reminded that it could last much longer.

MURDER IN MONTEREY

CHAPTER ONE

I moved forward quickly, my left jab snapping out twice in rapid succession followed by a hard right, the impact of which echoed through the metal building. My form was almost perfect – the strikes rotated at just the right moment so that I hit with the first two knuckles of my fist. I was leaving the punch out there too long, though. Mentally, I reminded myself that I had to pull the punches back in just as fast as I snapped them out or I ran the risk of getting trapped or countered. I immediately let loose a strong-side roundhouse kick that plowed into the rib cage of my opponent.

I was about to hit the man-shaped heavy bag a dozen more times when I heard a voice exclaim behind me, "Je pensais que je vous rendrais en ssueur et que vous avez commence sans moi." I could hear the smile in that sweet French accent, even if I couldn't understand a word of what she said.

I turned around to see Cat watching me appreciatively. Catherine Merritt was, by any standard, beautiful. Dark brown eyes and long, dark hair, a perfectly symmetrical face and a body to die for. She was way out of my league and I knew it. Still, for some crazy reason she liked me, and we had been dating for a few months now.

Cat had been the curator for the de Young Art Museum in San Francisco. Shortly after she met me, she had left her job to go into business for herself, acquiring objects of art for those who could afford it. She had clients in Marin where I lived, so it hadn't been unusual for her to stop in and see me during the day and, since my trip up to the Trinity River area, I was almost always home as I allowed for yet another bullet wound to my left shoulder to heal thoroughly.

Steve, my Australian Cattle Dog, who had been busy sniffing at something she found interesting in a corner of the out building, gave an excited bark and ran up to Cat, tail wagging. I was worried for a moment that she might just be excited enough to jump up on Cat; given she was wearing a white skirt. That would have cost me a dry-cleaning bill at least. She didn't. Instead she gave Cat's outstretched hand a friendly lick, wagged her tail ferociously, and then returned to the corner she had been investigating since we came out here for my workout almost an hour ago.

"It is good to see that you are man enough to wear a skirt. Perhaps you could borrow one of my blouses and we can go to lunch together. Oui?" she said with a laugh.

I looked down at my attire. "It's not a skirt, my dear, it's a kilt. It allows me freedom of movement and, as a Scot, is perfectly acceptable for me to wear." I was wearing a sport kilt, a Marine Corps tartan comprised mostly of blue and green with some yellow and red. Much easier to get on and off then a standard kilt, and it did allow me the freedom to move. Other than the kilt, though, I was shirtless and wearing wrestling shoes. I kept meaning to get some floor mats for the little area of the outbuilding I had taken over to use as a gym but hadn't quite gotten around to it. The wrestling shoes allowed me to flex my toes back when delivering front kicks to the bag and protected my feet from the rough concrete that served as the foundation for the building. I was also wearing boxer briefs under the kilt. I enjoyed the freedom of movement, but I didn't need that much freedom.

"Oh, so I'm falling for a Scot? Here I thought you were Irish. What would papa say?" She stepped closer to me, seemingly unconcerned with the fact that I was covered in sweat.

I took a step forward as well and put my hands around her waist. "Aye, I have a wee bit of the Irish in me, but mostly, I'm Scottish." I tried to affect an accent that was somewhere between being Irish and Scottish, but mostly came out as simply pathetic. She laughed nonetheless, encircled her arms around my neck and gave me a long kiss.

When we finally broke contact, I was starting to think that I should wear a kilt all the time. Cat gave me a friendly grope, kissed me on the cheek and then broke away. "Come. I am here and I am famished. Let us go have lunch." She grabbed my hand and started pulling me toward the door. I followed, trailing slightly behind. I took in the view of her in a skirt and playfully implied that I preferred to skip right to dessert. She laughed again and we walked hand in hand toward the house.

I live on a five-acre lot in Marin County. The space was nice and the house was a modest, two-bedroom, one-bath older model. Built in the 1950's, it had been remodeled a few years before I moved in with a new kitchen and bathroom, and new windows, floors, and doors. It was perfect for just me and Steve and had the extra room for a guest or two when people visited.

Cat lived in San Francisco in a three-bedroom condo on the 21st floor of a very nice building. In getting to know her, I had found out that her father was an international attorney who had done quite well, climbing up to the level of a senior partner. Cat had been born in San Francisco, but her mom had passed when she was six and her father had fled the Bay Area to Australia. From there, they had lived in Istanbul, London, and Frankfurt, and eventually settled in Paris where her mother had been born. Kat finished her primary education there and attended college, earning dual graduate degrees in Art History and Public Policy with a focus on International Relations. She thought to follow in her father's footsteps some day and go to law school. She spoke four languages, including English, French, German, and Russian, as well as a smattering of Spanish and Portuguese. Like I said, way out of my league. She had returned to San Francisco after graduating college to visit her aunt and had fallen in love with the City, deciding to stay.

We entered my house through the back door. The place was, fortunately, clean. I had retired a few years ago from both the military reserves, and from the police force after a 27-year career. I had the time to do housework and the inclination to keep a tidy place – a byproduct of my days in the military and having a mom who was anal about keeping a clean house. Even closing in on eighty, my mom swept, mopped, and vacuumed every day. Most of the women in my life whom I had dated (or married) had been very appreciative about how well my mom had taught me.

As soon as we entered the house, Cat went straight to the cabinet where I kept Steve's treats and pulled a few out to share with the dog. "Not too many, you'll ruin her girlish figure," I said with a smile. "I'm going to head upstairs and take a shower." I gave her a wink.

"Shu, shu mon petit chou-chou. Let the girls have their time," she said, making a little dismissive motion with her hands, and I found myself suddenly grateful that Steve couldn't talk.

I bounded up the stairs, stripped off what few clothes I was wearing and hopped in the shower. It didn't take long to get cleaned up. When I stepped out of the shower and dried off, I wiped off the fogged-up mirror with the towel and looked at my reflection.

At 52, I didn't look as old as I was. Most people thought I was in my late thirties or early forties. I had a short, military-style haircut. The shortness hid the little bit of grey that was sprinkled along the temple and sides. Also, when short, my hair also appeared darker than it really was when it grew out.

My face was relatively free of wrinkles except around the eyes where you could see fine creases when I smiled. My eyes were brown sprinkled with little hazel flakes. My nose was crooked – a byproduct of my days as a fighter. I had a full beard and mustache that I kept trimmed close and they had a smattering of grey, red, brown, and blond. I wasn't in bad shape for a man in his fifties; I had broad shoulders and a relatively flat stomach, even if you couldn't see the abs underneath. I did have a slew of scars, though. A bullet had torn up my left shoulder, leaving a nasty scar from both the wound itself and the surgery to fix it. A newer scar, still pink and swollen, decorated my left deltoid – also done by a bullet, but what they would call more of a flesh wound. Various other scars from battles past were evident as well. A nearly vertical scar along my abdomen that had been made by a perp with knife. A third bullet wound on my right hip and a peppering of smaller scars along my right leg had been made by shrapnel from an IED and then subsequent small arms attack when I was stationed in Afghanistan. I had led an exciting life. Overall, not the best-looking guy in the world, but not hard to look at either – and women seemed to dig the scars. No idea why.

I finished drying off and returned to my bedroom to get dressed, putting on my standard hiking pants, hiking boots, and a button-down shirt with a t-shirt underneath. I added a spray of cologne. Just a little. I subscribed to the theory that cologne should be discovered, not announced. Fifteen minutes after going up the stairs to take my shower, I came back down.

Cat had moved from the kitchen to the living room and was sitting on the couch with her legs crossed which had caused her skirt to ride up along mid-thigh. She had very nice legs and the way she was seated showed them off to great effect. Steve was sitting on the couch next to her, looking for all the world like they were engaged in an intimate conversation.

Cat was speaking French so I couldn't understand what she was saying, but Steve seemed entirely attentive.

"Mmmhmm, my girls conspiring against me, I see," I said playfully.

"Oui. Steve and I were just gossiping about you," Cat said, smiling. She stood up, straightening her skirt as she did so.

I gave her a quick kiss. "Where would you like to go for lunch, my dear?"

"Hmmm, Sausalito?" She didn't need to say the name of the restaurant, it was one of our favorite spots.

"Works for me." I took her hand in mine and started for the door to the garage, grabbing my keys off a small table just to the left of the door.

Cat pulled up short. "Can we take my car, mon amour?" She drove a little Subaru BRZ sports car – much easier to maneuver in town than my truck. The Jeep, my other vehicle, was easy enough to drive, as long as there wasn't a lot of traffic or hills. That's when the stick shift could be a pain. But the Jeep had the doors off and was only sporting a bikini top. Fine for me with my short hair, but it was murder on Cat's unless she had time to put it back in a braid.

"Sure, love." We reversed direction and went out the back door and walked, still holding hands, to Cat's car. Steve trailed behind us. She was used to going with me everywhere I went, so she wasn't happy when I told her to stay. Cat's car had a back seat, but it wasn't very big. Plus I didn't want her to get dog hair all over the interior of the car. I could feel the condemnation in Steve's eyes as she returned to the porch. It was a look designed to make me feel guilty and it worked, even if I refused to let on.

"She has your number, mon amour, does she not?" Cat hugged my arm and looked up at me with sympathy.

I smiled. "Yes, she does."

It was a quick ride to Sausalito, taking almost as long to get through the little touristy downtown area as it did to get to Sausalito itself. The restaurant was on the main street, Bridgeway.

We parked the car on the street and walked up to the restaurant. The host greeted Cat like a long lost friend, speaking to her in French; he gave her a quick hug and they kissed each other's cheeks. He greeted me a little more formally but no less friendly. "Monsieur Grey, a pleasure to see you again."

I shook his extended hand. "Gregori. Good to see you as well." He took us immediately to a table. I remained standing until Cat was seated and then pulled out my chair to sit down. Without asking, Gregori brought Cat a glass of red wine and me a bourbon, neat, and he was nice enough to make it a double. We had eaten here more than a few times since we started dating.

We ordered our food and chatted while we ate, discussing our day. Well, mostly Cat's day, as mine was rather boring, consisting of me cleaning, working out, and taking Steve for a walk. Cat told me that she had to go to Monterey on Friday.

"For?" I inquired.

"Business, mon amour." She told me that there was a seller there with an original Salvador Dali painting who was willing to part with it, for the right price, and she had a buyer willing to pay that price. "It is a cute story, Jerod. The seller's grandmother was apparently quite the beauty and quite adventurous in her day, and she caught Salvador Dali's eye when he had sought refuge at the Hotel Del Monte. He gave her the painting as a show of appreciation and it has been with the family ever since. They did not know what they had until the seller's mother passed away and the painting was passed on to him."

"Friday, you say?" I asked.

"Oui."

"And when do you meet with the buyer?"

"Monday morning. Pourguoi demandez-vous? Why do you ask?"

"Thinking we should make a weekend of it. Once you handle your business, we can enjoy the rest of the weekend in Monterey. Go to Carmel, get a couple's massage, kayak the Bay. How does that sound?" I raised an eyebrow. "We can come back on Sunday evening."

Cat clapped her hands together excitedly. "Oh, mon petit chouchou, that sounds like a delightful weekend."

I grinned. "Excellent. I'll make the arrangements." She nodded. We finished lunch and returned to my house. We gave each other a long kiss goodbye and then she returned to work, while I returned to the very busy life of being a retiree, which mostly included throwing a ball for Steve.

CHAPTER TWO

C at was meeting with the seller at 9:00 a.m. It was a three-hour drive without traffic, and in the San Francisco Bay Area, there was always traffic. We wanted to make sure she got there in time to make her meeting, so we planned on leaving my house at 5:00 a.m. Early, even for me.

The alarm went off at 4:00. I didn't usually have to set an alarm to wake up. My internal body clock seemed to be permanently set to zero-dark thirty. Except, of course, when I needed to wake up, in which case I would often oversleep. Plus Cat had come over to spend the night. That meant less sleep, no matter how hard we tried to get to bed at a decent time.

I picked up my phone and swiped it to turn off the alarm. Cat hadn't even stirred. I set the phone back down and turned over to face her. She appeared so peaceful when she was sleeping that I didn't really want to wake her, but it wasn't me who had a meeting with a client. I reached over and stroked her face gently. She started to stir but still wasn't quite waking up. I leaned in and gave her a few gentle kisses on the face and then a longer one on the lips. That brought her awake as she reached her hand up and brought my face tighter to hers for a deeper kiss.

"That is the way to wake a girl, mon amour," she said, opening her eyes and smiling.

I smiled back. "Rise and shine, my dear. We have a road trip ahead of us."

She tried to bury her face in the pillow. "Do not remind me."

I hopped out of bed and called Steve. "Let's go, girl." Steve was almost as reluctant to get up as Cat, but she did, stretching dramatically as she got out of her bed on the floor. I started out the door and called back to Cat, "Five minutes or I'm stealing the shower from you." I heard a pillow hit the wall near the door and laughed.

Steve and I walked down the stairs and into the kitchen. I opened the back door so she could go out and then proceeded to make some coffee. Coffee was one of the habits I couldn't give up. That and bourbon, although since dating Cat I was drinking less of it, and if she slept over, I managed to fall asleep without a glass or two.

I heard the shower start upstairs. Cat was up. It would take her a minute. She didn't need much in the way of makeup but her hair was so long it took her a bit to wash and style it. I imagined she'd go with a single braid today.

The shower cut off about the same time the coffee was done brewing. I poured two cups. I liked my coffee black and as strong as I could get it. In Cat's cup, I added some cream and a teaspoon of sugar, then picked up both cups from the counter and made my way upstairs with Steve trailing behind me.

When I reached the top of the stairs, I could see that Cat had opened the bathroom door, presumably to let the steam out. She had dried off and wrapped the towel around her head but otherwise stood nude in front of the mirror. Not for the first time, I admired the curves of her body.

I came up behind her and set her cup of coffee on the counter where she could reach it. I pushed my body close to hers and give her a light kiss on the neck. I saw the goose bumps raise along her arms. "Keep that up, mon amour, and we will never leave the house in time to make it for my appointment," she chided.

I laughed and backed away. I set my coffee on the dresser in the bedroom and returned to the bathroom. Stripping off my shorts, I started the water and climbed in to wash myself off. It didn't take long. One thing I had picked up in the military was the ability to take a fast shower and still feel like I was completely clean.

Once I was done showering, I left Cat to her devices in the bathroom and I returned to the bedroom to get ready. By the time we were headed out the door, we were only running thirty minutes behind schedule. For Cat, that was pretty good.

The night before we had moved the Jeep out of the garage and parked Cat's Subaru inside next to my GMC truck. We walked out of the house and into the gravel driveway where the Jeep was parked. I had put the doors back on but left the back uncovered. I liked a little air flow but with the doors on, it would cut down on the wind and noise quite a bit. I opened the back door and Steve jumped in. She traveled with me everywhere unless there was absolutely no way for me to take her. Cat took the passenger seat and I jumped in to drive.

The Jeep was a 2008 Wrangler Unlimited 4-door. I had almost bought a Rubicon but for the price difference, I had been able to upgrade my Jeep with all the trimmings to make it a formable off-road rig. It had a two-inch lift, snorkel, winch, heavy duty axles, lockers and all the extras you'd need to give someone Jeep envy. My GMC Sierra king cab pickup was practical, but the Jeep was just plain fun.

Bags thrown in the back, we were on our way in short order. It was a three-hour drive to Monterey. Leaving now, we should be there by 8:30. Cat would be able to make her appointment with the seller and then we would have the rest of the day to explore. I was hoping that at this time of day, traffic wouldn't be too bad, and we could make it on time.

Winding our way down from my house to the freeway, we jumped on the 101 and headed south. I planned on taking 580 through Richmond and then 880 to Oakland in order to avoid the higher toll fee on the Golden Gate Bridge. Plus, I avoided cutting through San Francisco when I could. I spent more time over there now than I did before meeting Cat, but that was a testament to how much I liked her. I disliked driving in, or through, San Francisco, and avoided it when I could.

In the case of getting to Monterey, though, it was roughly the same distance to go down 880 as it was to take 101.

We had just hit freeway cruising speeds when Cat pulled out her iPhone and rifled through my glove compartment looking for the speaker adapter. She had told me she'd prepared a special playlist for our trip. Finding the adapter, she looked at me and gave me a dazzling grin. "Ready?" she asked.

"Sure, babe." I laughed. "What's on the menu?"

"Show tunes!"

I must have let the inward groan show on my face because she gave me a friendly punch to the shoulder and hit play. The first song was from a Broadway play. Cat immediately started mouthing the words to me and it wasn't long before I was singing the refrain and we were both laughing.

The trip down to Monterey went quickly. We eventually traded listening to show tunes for discussions on current events and arrived in Monterey by 8:15, enough time for me to grab a cup of coffee and her a tea from a local coffee shop and then we were driving up to her appointment. The seller's house was in Pacific Grove. We found the address readily enough and made our way up the long driveway to the house.

The driveway wound for a quarter of a mile under the shade of large trees. It was a beautiful property, well landscaped and the driveway was in good repair. There was a turnabout that ran in front of the house and around an ornate fountain – dry now, most likely because of the drought-like conditions that had plagued California for the last few years. The house itself was not large and if not for the size of the property itself, you'd be left with the impression the family had done well for themselves but weren't necessarily swimming in money.

I stopped the Jeep in front of the double doors and Cat exited, grabbing her briefcase as she did. She turned toward me and asked, "How do I look, mon amour?"

"Like a goddess," I responded with a smile.

Her grin was worth the compliment. She knocked on the door and waited a few seconds before it was opened and she disappeared inside.

I waited in the Jeep, drinking my coffee, absently petting Steve who decided that now was a good time for some attention, and listening to my favorite morning talk show on the radio. It was only around twenty minutes before Cat returned to the car. Before she left the house, she shook hands with a tall, thin man in a black suit. He looked to be about my age, maybe a little older. His pale skin and drawn features reminded me of Lurch from the Addams Family. Nonetheless, he seemed very cordial and he returned Cat's smile warmly.

Cat was carrying what had to be the painting in a parchment paper-wrapped package. When she was done saying her goodbyes, she started walking the few feet to the car. I got out to assist her in stowing the painting. We had both agreed that it wouldn't be good to leave it exposed to the elements in the back seat of the Jeep or run the risk that Steve would accidently damage it.

When I had made the modifications to the Jeep to extend its off-road capabilities, I had also had them expand and conceal a small storage area underneath the back floor mat. It had originally been there to hold the jack and a few tools. With the lift kit and bigger tires, though, I had to go with a larger jack that was mounted to the tail gate along with the spare tire. The storage area had been enlarged and had the additional benefit of being securable with a good locking system. My thought had been a place to conceal any weapons I might want to have with me, but it was also big enough to hold the painting.

This was a pleasure trip, so I didn't feel the need to bring an arsenal with me. The only weapon I currently had was a Sig Saur P238 that I carried in an inside-the-pants holster. The P238 was a 1911-inspired .380 ACP that was large enough to feel comfortable in my hand but small enough to be easily concealable under a t-shirt. One of the benefits of being a retired police officer was that I could still carry concealed, as long as I met my department's policy regarding qualifications. Easy enough for me to do, as the department was only about thirty minutes from my house.

I had retired a few years ago after a 27-year career – not quite maxing out my retirement benefits, but I'd had enough. Twenty-seven years in one of the most dangerous cities in the nation can take its toll. The politics of the city, the hostility toward law enforcement officers, and daily exposure to violence had left me feeling hollow. I had chosen to hang up my gun belt a little early so I could keep at least some of my sanity.

The painting secure in the concealed compartment, Cat and I headed back down the driveway.

I had rented us a room at the Navy Gateway Inn and Suites on the Navy Post Graduate School campus. Normally I would splurge a little for a weekend trip and get us a room at the Hilton, or maybe a little bed and breakfast somewhere, but rooms for the Navy Gateway in Monterey were located in the old Hotel Del Monte, the very same hotel that Salvador Dali had stayed in when he gave the painting Cat had just picked up to the seller's grandmother. It seemed appropriate. Check-in wasn't until after noon, though, so we had time to kill.

As we drove down the driveway, we passed an older model black sedan. I wasn't a car guy but it looked to be a mid-1960's model Chevy Malibu. It had been beautifully restored. The windows had been tinted so I couldn't see too much of the interior other than the two men sitting in the front seat. They never made eye contact and both were wearing black suits, white shirts, and thin, black ties similar to what the seller had been wearing. They looked somber.

"Friendly crowd," I heard Cat murmur next to me, the sarcasm evident in her tone of voice.

"Oh, those two? I'm sure they'd be the life of any party they showed up to." We both chuckled and continued on our way.

We headed down to Cannery Row and decided to check out the Monterey Bay Aquarium. It had been several years since I had visited the aquarium and Cat hadn't been there since she was a small child.

It didn't take us long to get there, but finding parking proved to be a headache. The streets were packed with people and any street side parking was only ninety minutes. I was sure we'd be longer than that. I tried a few parking lots off the main road, but when they turned out to be full as well, I went with a garage. It would cost me $30 to park for the day, but it also was only a few blocks from the aquarium.

The good thing about the garage, though, was that it provided shade for Steve. She'd be fine in the Jeep with the back open, a bowl of water if she got thirsty, and a chew toy to keep her occupied. While she wouldn't let anyone into the Jeep that she didn't know, she also wouldn't hassle anyone just walking by.

We walked down the Monterey Bay Coastal Trail to David Avenue, dodging bicyclists, kids, and dogs along the way. The aquarium was located at the corner of David Avenue and Cannery Row. We jumped in the line to purchase our tickets and surprisingly, the line moved quickly. We were inside within twenty minutes and immediately began exploring the exhibits.

CHAPTER THREE

Detective Ryan East received the call at 11:00 a.m. It was his first homicide as lead detective. Pacific Grove was a small community and had the lowest crime rate in the county. Homicides just didn't happen here. Nonetheless, he had gone to the appropriate classes and had lent his services to both the city and county of Monterey to put those classes to practical use.

He arrived on scene at 11:23, pulling his silver, unmarked Ford Crown Victoria into the long driveway and parking behind one of three marked patrol vehicles that were already on scene. Crime tape had been strung up in front of the door where a uniformed police officer stood guard.

Detective East went to the trunk of his vehicle and pulled out a set of surgical booties and some gloves, along with his evidence collection kit and a digital camera for pictures. He'd need a crime scene technician to come in to process most of the scene, but he'd look around first and see if there was anything obvious.

As Detective East pulled on the nitrile gloves, he looked at the uniformed officer. "Hey, John. What do we have?" John had been with the agency for about three years – a sharp kid with a good head on his shoulders.

John looked down at his note pad. "One male, 41 years old, positively identified by the complainant as Harold Tousher III, was found dead at the scene at about 10:52. Or at least that's what time the call came in to dispatch. The lady who cleans the house found him and reported she immediately dialed 911. Multiple stab wounds to the upper torso. The murder weapon hasn't been recovered yet. He's single, no children. Lived with his mom up until three months ago when she passed away." John put away his notebook. "That's all we have right now. Smitty and I were first on scene, followed by Sarge. We secured the area so as little evidence was disturbed as possible."

"Thanks, John. Do me a favor, would ya? Can you notify dispatch that I'll need the county Crime Scene Unit and the county coroner out here?" he asked politely.

John nodded. "Sure thing, Ryan." He immediately hopped on the radio and started notifying dispatch of the resources Ryan would need.

Ryan lifted the tape stretched across the front door and ducked under it to enter the foyer. Immediately he noted bloody footprints leading to the front door from an area further back in the house. At least one of the footprints seemed to be from a boot. Mostly likely Smitty's or the Sergeant's, although if Ryan had to guess, he'd say Smitty. Sergeant Graham was a wily veteran of law enforcement and too street savvy to step in blood if he could help it. By contrast, Smitty had only been on the department for less than a year, having just graduated from the field training program a little over a month ago. Rookies tended to be gung-ho, charging into a scene with guns out, ready to take on a bad guy. Preservation of evidence and not disturbing the scene too much came as after-thoughts.

The other footprints were made by a smooth-soled shoe. A dress shoe, perhaps. He snapped a few photos of the foyer and the bloody footprints and continued into the house.

He found Smitty and Sarge in a large living room area toward the back of the house. A sliding glass door leading to a large, well-appointed patio stood open along the far wall. Ryan looked around. To his right was an open kitchen and beyond that, just visible, a dining area. To his left, a smaller, den-like room. There appeared to have been a struggle in the living room. A chair was overturned and a lamp broken on the floor.

The body of Harold Touscher III lay sprawled on the living room floor. His shirt had been torn open and Ryan could see approximately six stab wounds to his chest and stomach area. A large pool of blood had spread out around him. The footprints lead right from the body. "These yours, Smitty?" Ryan asked, pointing to the booted prints.

"Yeah. Sorry, Detective. I had to check and see if he had a pulse and there was no way to do that without stepping in blood. There's so much of it."

Ryan nodded his head. "The human body does seem to hold a surprising amount." He scanned the room again, making mental notes of a few things. There didn't appear to be any blood on the sliding glass door, which meant that the killer probably didn't open it. Plus, the smooth footprints seemed to be scattered around the body, possibly from the struggle, and then led to the front door.

"Any idea who made these other prints?" Ryan asked.

"No, sir. Those were here when we arrived. The cleaning lady never made it past the hallway. As soon as she saw the body, she said she left the residence and called us."

"We opened the back door, Ryan. Damn smell of blood. Hate it. Needed to let some air in," Sergeant Graham piped in.

"No problem, Sarge." Even now that coppery smell permeated the air, but it wasn't unbearable. Ryan continued to snap pictures and make notes in his small notebook. His first homicide as lead investigator and he wanted to do it right, take his time. This would be all over the news by this evening. Murders just didn't happen in Pacific Grove. It was a quiet town. Other than the tourists who flocked to the area every year, nothing much went on here and Ryan would like to close this case as soon as possible.

Ryan walked into the den area. Here and there were some more of the bloody footprints left by the smooth-soled shoes. A large desk occupied a corner of the room and books lined shelves along the wall. A large, wood-burning fireplace was set into one wall. The room had been thoroughly rifled through. "Hey Smitty, ask the cleaning lady if she knows whether or not Mr. Touscher had a safe and if so, where it might be located."

"Ok," Ryan heard Smitty call back from the living room.

Ryan snapped photos of the room. On the desk, he noted a file with several bloody prints on it. Someone had tried to wipe the prints away. While smudged considerably, Ryan thought the crime scene technicians might be able to still pull a partial from the file once they arrived.

Using his gloved hand in order not to leave any prints of his own, Ryan opened the file and glanced at the contents. There were a number of email printouts from a ycmerritt@merrittacquisitions.com. He scanned through them quickly and got the gist of the content. Mr. Touscher was in the market to sell an original Salvador Dali painting he had inherited from his mother and Ms. Merritt was the broker. Despite the "y" at the front of the email address, she signed her emails with "Cat." In one email, it appeared that they had agreed to meet today at 9:00 a.m. That would have been about two hours before the body had been discovered. Ryan felt a little surge of excitement; he had a suspect.

CHAPTER FOUR

We finished up our tour of the Monterey Bay Aquarium around 1:00 p.m. and walked down the street to a nearby restaurant for a bite to eat. The place was a little crowded, but we managed to get a table fairly quickly. Sitting down, we opened our menus and perused their selections. I had made dinner reservations at a high-end steakhouse for this evening at 7:30, so I didn't want to fill up on lunch. I ordered a BLT, minus the mayo, and Cat got a salad. I had an aversion to condiments. Ketchup, mustard, or mayonnaise, would never grace my sandwiches if I had a say in the matter. Cat thought it was amusing and liked to tease me about it.

Lunch arrived and we ate slowly, discussing our plans for the rest of the day. We would go to the Navy Gateway Inn and check into our room and drop off the painting in a place that was more secure than the back of my Jeep. The Navy Gateway was located on a military base with ID-only access. Cat had just forked over a check for a considerable amount of money to purchase the painting, and it made her understandably nervous to have it simply locked in the back of a Jeep. She'd feel better having it in the room.

After we had checked in to the room and explored the old Hotel Del Monte, now called Herrmann Hall by the Navy, we'd head to the Dali 17 Museum. Neither Cat nor I had ever been, but it was supposed to contain the largest private collection of the artist's works. Seeing how Salvador Dali was the reason we were in Monterey to begin with, it seemed only fitting that we spend some time admiring his work.

When we had both finished lunch and paid the bill, Cat and I walked out on to Cannery Row and into the teeming mass of tourists here for their last hurrah before summer came to an unofficial end and all the kids headed back to school. Labor Day was right around the corner.

Making our way back to the Jeep, Steve greeted us with her usual excitement. Cat had saved a couple of pieces of chicken from her salad and shared those with Steve. For my part, I gave her a good ruffling of her neck fur but stayed out of the giving her people food part. I didn't like for Steve to beg and I spoiled her enough.

Steve properly greeted, Cat and I hopped in the Jeep and I started to make my way out of the parking garage, stopping at the kiosk to pay my $30 parking fee before pulling out onto Foam Street. I made my way to Lighthouse Avenue and then headed toward the Naval Post Graduate School.

It was a short ride and we arrived at the main gate within ten minutes. There were two Department of Defense police officers on duty who looked at my military ID and welcomed me on base. Herrmann Hall was easy enough to find, as it was the largest building in the immediate vicinity and clearly visible. Luckily there were also clear signs, and I followed those instead of trying to navigate my way there using the Hall as a visual reference. Like almost every other campus I had been on, the Naval Post Graduate School's road system followed no discernable pattern. It was like the roads were added as afterthoughts and you'd often turn onto a road thinking it was headed in the right direction, only to find yourself in a small courtyard behind a building.

Finding a place to park near the old Hotel Del Monte was easier than finding the hotel itself. We grabbed our bags, the painting, and Steve, and headed for the lobby. I did take a minute to put Steve on a leash, but instead of holding my end, I gave the leash to Steve who was happy enough to carry it in her mouth as we walked around. The grounds were well-maintained; there was a beautiful flower garden as well as a nearby pool. The pool looked like it had, at one point, been a swimming pool. Now it had been converted into more of a fountain with the pool itself roped off.

We entered a side door and came into a well-appointed reception hall complete with a fireplace and comfortable-looking couches and chairs where people could gather for quiet conversation. In my opinion, the only thing missing was a bar where you could order a good scotch to sip on while you talked.

The clerks at the registration desk were all pleasant and it didn't take them long to get us checked in and issue us our keys. The lady I was speaking with reminded me that dogs had to remain on a leash at all times while on base. I acknowledged her admonishment and pointed out that Steve was, in fact, on a leash. When I had reserved the room, I had looked at the post regulations regarding dogs. The dog had to be leashed, and the leash could not be more than eight feet in length. Nowhere in the regulation did it say I had to be holding said leash. Cat stifled a giggle while the lady at the desk just looked flabbergasted for a moment.

"Um, ok. Well, Senior Chief, I hope that you enjoy your stay." The lady handed me the keys to our room, wrote down the room number on a slip of paper and Cat, Steve, and I headed off, Steve's leash still firmly gripped between her teeth.

As we made our way to our room Cat asked, "The receptionist called you Senior Chief. What does that mean, mon amour?"

"That was my rank in the Navy before I retired."

"Is that as high as you could go?"

I laughed. "It's as high as I got. There is one enlisted rank above that and that's Master Chief. Master Chief wasn't in the cards for me, so I retired as a Senior Chief."

We found our room, slid the key card in the door and went inside. You could tell that the room had seen some use. It had that comfortable, worn feeling that old hotels sometimes acquired after decades of guests coming and going. There was a small living room area with two chairs, a couch, and a modern, flat screen TV. The bed was in an adjoining room and appeared to be comfortable. The bathroom was off the bedroom area and while small, it was functional. The room itself appeared clean. I expected nothing less from a Navy installation.

I tossed my bag on the couch and looked out the window. We had a good view of the flower garden and reflection pool. The room was a little stuffy and didn't seem to have any AC. It was probably not something people worried about in Monterey, where the average annual temperature was 56 degrees. Generally speaking, even if it got hot during the day, the wind blowing in off the cold Pacific Ocean cooled the area enough to make it comfortable at night. I opened the window to allow a little air to flow through.

Cat had taken her bag to the bedroom and set it down on a chair; she placed the painting behind the chair so that it was upright. Steve wandered the room, sniffing every corner and piece of furniture, ensuring that everything was safe.

"I think before we go to the museum, I will shower and change into something more comfortable." She was still wearing the business attire she had worn to her meeting – a practical grey pants suit and a dark blue blouse. It looked great on her but I could see why she'd want to change.

"Hmmm, yoga pants?" I inquired, trying to sound innocent. I failed. Cat shot me a withering glance, winked and then stuck out her tongue before shutting the bathroom door and turning on the shower.

I rapped my knuckles on the door to the bathroom to catch Cat's attention over the sound of the shower. "I'm going to take Steve out for a quick walk. Be back shortly." I heard her muffled acknowledgement.

I gathered up Steve's leash and allowed her to hold it in her mouth and then we left the room and went down the stairs and outside. While the grounds were all well-maintained, there seemed to be an abundant amount of geese and, as geese do, they left an abundant amount of geese shit everywhere. I managed to step around most of it but Steve had no such aversion. She'd need a quick bath before the night was over.

We took our time. I knew Cat. Her shower would be quick enough, but it would take her an hour before her hair was styled the way she wanted and she was ready to go again. We returned to the room about thirty minutes later to find Cat, her hair wrapped in a towel with another towel wrapped around her body, standing in front of the mirror applying some light make-up.

I took the opportunity to give Steve a quick bath and used one of the two remaining towels to dry her off. After her bath, I laid out her dog bed on the floor and she promptly curled up and went to sleep.

Cat had finished her makeup and was putting on a pair of jeans when her phone rang. She picked up and pressed the answer button. "Bonjour. Merritt Acquisitions, Cat speaking, how may I assist you?"

I couldn't hear the voice on the other side but I could read Cat's reaction to whatever it was that they said. She paled visibly and her hand started to shake. I got up from the couch where I had been sitting and went to her, placing my left hand in the small of her back. I didn't know what was wrong but I wanted her to know that I was there for her.

"Oui. I will be there as quickly as I can." She hung up and the phone slipped from her fingers and hit the ground. I guided her to a chair so she could sit.

"What's wrong?" I asked, concern in my voice.

"Monsieur Touscher, the gentleman I met with this morning, was found dead at his house. The police found out that he had an appointment with me and would like to talk to me. They asked if I could come down to the station."

"Aw, love, that's horrible." I thought for a second. "Finish getting ready and we can head down there right away."

Cat put on a white t-shirt, some ankle socks, and her tennis shoes, but she appeared to be in a bit of daze. For me, death was nothing new. I had been to countless homicide and natural death scenes over the course of my career in law enforcement. She and I were witnesses and could help the police establish a timeline. We also had seen the Chevy Malibu pull up as we were leaving. That car would stand out and might give the police another lead if they could find it.

Once she was ready, we walked down to the car with me holding her hand. Steve would stay in the room for now. I was sure we'd be back in time to let her out again before bed time.

The trip to the Pacific Grove Police Department only took about fifteen minutes. We pulled up and found a place to park and went in to the front counter. "Dr. Merritt to see Detective East, please," I told the desk officer, using her official title. On the way over, Cat had told me the name of the man we were supposed to meet.

The desk officer nodded, picked up a phone and dialed an extension. "Hey, Ryan, there is a Doctor Merritt here to see you, along with a gentleman." The officer was silent for a moment and then nodded. "I will let them know." He hung up the phone. "He'll be out in a moment."

They hadn't said much to Cat over the phone, just that Touscher had been found dead in his home. If they believed it had been of natural causes, I was thinking they would have divulged that information. As they hadn't, I had to presume they were investigating it as a homicide versus an unexplained death. Of course, I would have started it out as a homicide investigation even if the death appeared to be of natural causes and there were no known risk factors involved, such as heart disease or cancer.

Detective Ryan East came out of a door to the side of the desk officer. He was of average height, maybe 5'7" with dark brown hair. He looked to be in reasonably good shape but was wearing an ill-fitting, blue, pin-striped suit that probably came off a rack at JC Penny. The first rule of buying a suit was to have a good tailor. A good tailor can make even a cheap suit look ok.

I stepped forward and introduced myself as Dr. Grey and Cat as Dr. Merritt. It may seem petty, but police officers were a respectful group of people as a whole, and being a doctor gave you respectability. I was hoping it would ease any tension.

"I was only expecting Ms. Merritt." No pretense at pleasantries, so I knew he considered her a suspect. I felt a momentary twinge of anger. She was one of the sweetest people I knew and wouldn't hurt a fly if she didn't have to. That he thought she was a suspect seemed preposterous to me but, then again, I knew she didn't do it. Detective East didn't have that knowledge. He was trying to get to the truth of what happened, nothing more. I forced myself to relax.

"I took her to her appointment this morning and waited outside until it was concluded." I saw his eyes narrow. He looked at Cat and then back at me. At 120 pounds, Cat would have some difficulty overpowering Mr. Touscher. Me, on the other hand, at eighty pounds more, wouldn't find it as hard. I had just become his number one suspect. Joy.

"Let's find a room where we can talk. If you don't mind, I'd like to speak with you both separately." I nodded. He'd want to see if our stories matched up. Not conclusive, because we could have rehearsed our alibis beforehand, but the truth would be hard to maintain under scrutiny. We had nothing to hide, though, so we both agreed readily.

We were split up and put in different interview rooms. They asked if they could conduct a pat search prior to putting me in the room. I declined, but did disclose that I was a retired police officer and was armed. I voluntarily turned over my firearm. I didn't want anyone to be overly nervous talking to me.

I could see the camera in the interview room I was placed in and knew that it was already on. No reasonable expectation to privacy in a police interrogation room, but still, it rankled a little that they didn't even notify me. But this wasn't my first time being here. Unfortunately, I had been involved in two officer-involved shootings in my tenure as a police officer. Despite what the movies tell you, you are investigated as a potential criminal until proven otherwise. I had always felt the system, as it applied to law enforcement officers, was backwards. Guilty until proven innocent instead of the other way around.

I sat down and waited. A uniformed officer came by to ask me if I needed anything – a cup of coffee, or maybe some water. I declined, primarily because I didn't want to have to ask to use the restroom. Having to ask permission to leave the room would annoy me as much as being recorded involuntarily did.

I presumed that Detective East chose to interview Cat first. I sat in the room for nearly an hour before he came in, a yellow pad of paper in his hand.

He sat down across from me. He didn't waste a lot of time with building any sort of rapport but instead launched right into asking his questions. "Your name, sir?"

I didn't waste any time on being friendly back. "Jerod Grey."

"How long have you known Ms. Merritt?"

"A few months."

The questions and answers went back and forth like this for a few minutes until he had enough background to proceed. He inquired how we had ended up at Mr. Touscher's residence, when we had arrived and departed, and if I had noticed anything unusual.

For my part, I told the truth: that Cat was there to purchase a painting for a client of hers, and that we had arrived right at 9:00 a.m. and left by 9:20. I also told him what I could remember of the Chevy Malibu and the two occupants.

When he was done with most of his questions, he asked if the clothes I was wearing now were the same ones I had worn when I had gone to Mr. Touscher's. I told them they were. He asked if he could test them for blood residue. Knowing he would find nothing, I consented. The fact that he asked to test just for blood and not gunshot residue was telling. Touscher hadn't been shot. It wasn't long after they sprayed some luminol on my clothes that he walked me out to the lobby. Cat was waiting for me. She seemed annoyed. We were told we were free to go and Detective East started to walk away.

My anger finally got the better of me. "Detective East." Twenty-seven years of law enforcement, most of those in positions of leadership, a retired Senior Chief in the Navy, and my voice could ring with command when I wanted it to – and it did now. I could see every fiber in Detective East's body respond to that tone. He was a good police officer, conditioned to receiving and responding to orders.

"Yes, sir?" For the first time since we had walked into the Pacific Grove Police Department he looked apprehensive.

"We came down here voluntarily. We patiently answered your questions and consented to your tests. At the very least, you could do us the courtesy of saying thank you. If you find that too difficult, I'm fairly sure I could seek a little gratitude from your Chief of Police." My stare was ice.

He looked for a moment like he would bristle but then I saw his shoulders slump. "I'm sorry, sir. It has been a long day, and this is my first homicide case as lead."

It was more of an admission then I expected. "I've been there, Detective. Trying to stay human and adhere to those basic human traits of empathy and politeness are not only the right thing to do, but essential to your well-being. You lose touch with that and you've lost touch with your humanity. Good day, sir." I turned and walked away, taking Cat's hand in mine as I did so. I saw too much of myself in Detective Ryan East and I didn't want to look that close into the mirror.

* * * * *

Detective East watched the two doctors walk out of the station. He knew he had been somewhat rude to the two of them, but he also knew, almost as soon as he saw them, that they were not the ones responsible for Harold Touscher's death. He was hoping to wrap this case as quickly as possible. Now, he had to accept the fact that he still had a killer, or killers, out there. That bothered him more than he cared to admit.

The County Crime Scene Unit had processed the area but they wouldn't have any preliminary results back for a bit. Unfortunately, labs didn't work at the same speed as they did on TV. The coroner would have a cause of death here soon, though. Not that it would be any surprise. The only part Detective East didn't know was which stab wound was the fatal one.

Both Dr. Merritt and Dr. Grey had given him a lead – the black Chevy Malibu, mid-60's model. He had one of the police service technicians already running that information through both the DMV and the license plate reader databases to see if they got any hits for this area. He crossed his fingers and said a silent prayer that this would be wrapped up quickly with the responsible party in custody.

CHAPTER FIVE

As soon as Cat and I were seated in the car, she let loose a string of what I was sure were expletives in German. German was always a good language to curse in. It sounded much harsher in German than it did in, say, Spanish, or French. I let her annoyance run its course. "That man! He basically accused us of killing poor Mr. Touscher and he was very rude. Very rude, Jerod!"

I patted her leg and rubbed her knee with my hand in between shifting gears on the Jeep. "I know, babe. He was just doing his job. You heard him. It's his first homicide case as the lead detective. That's a lot of pressure."

"You are taking his side!?" Now those angry brown eyes were turned on me.

"No, babe. There was no excuse for his behavior, which is why I dressed him down a little. Just making allowances. I let him know how I felt and I will give him a chance to self-correct," I reassured her.

She closed her eyes and leaned her head back, letting out a big sigh as she did so. The storm had passed. I had seen Cat lose her temper before and it generally ran its course in a short amount of time.

The interviews had taken awhile and we were closing in on the time for our dinner reservation. I asked Cat if she was still up for dinner and a drink or two. She nodded.

We headed for the area back down by the aquarium. We'd be a little early at the steakhouse but we might still get a table. If not, they had a bar where we could have a drink while we waited.

This particular steakhouse was one of my favorite restaurants in Monterey and I had been going here since the late 80's. They had always had excellent steaks, good cocktails, and a friendly and attentive staff. It had been years since I had eaten there, though. I didn't make it down to Monterey too often.

I found a parking space about two blocks down from the restaurant and maneuvered the Jeep into place. I took Cat's hand in mine as we walked down the street toward the restaurant. She gave my arm a hug and laid her head on my shoulder for a moment. "I am sorry that I lost my temper, mon petit chou-chou."

I kissed her forehead. "No worries, babe."

We walked in to the restaurant and met with the maître d. He found us a table right away and we sat down and started looking at the menu. Our waiter stopped by with two waters and asked for our drink selections. Cat went with a Pinot Grigio while I ordered a Manhattan.

We chatted about nothing important while we ate our salads and then dinner. The ribeye I had was fantastic. Cat ordered the tuna and exclaimed that it was some of the best she had ever had. We finished eating dinner and ordered a dessert to share, key lime pie. By the end of dinner, we were laughing and Cat was fully relaxed again.

It was close to 9:00 p.m. when we walked out of the restaurant. I brought up the possibility of heading down to Cannery Row. A lot of the restaurants and bars down there would have live music on a Friday night. Cat thought about it for a minute and then gave me a kiss on the lips followed by a kiss on the neck. "I am sure we can find a way to make music of our own, mon amour." Her voice was low and sultry. It was enough to convince me we could skip Cannery Row and head back to our hotel room. Plus, Steve had been locked in the room for some time and could use a walk. We started walking back to the Jeep, holding hands.

We'd gone about halfway to the car when I felt like someone was watching us. I looked around and spotted the two guys almost immediately. Tall, thin, wearing black suits with narrow ties. I was almost immediately sure that they were the same two guys who had been in the Chevy Malibu.

Cat was holding my right hand. Unfortunately, that was also my gun hand. I didn't want to alarm her but I had to put myself in a better defensive position with access to my .380. "Hey, babe," I whispered under my breath, "we're going to stop and kiss for a second and then when we start walking again, I want you on my left side."

She could tell by the tone of my voice that something was wrong, but she didn't question it. We stopped, kissed momentarily and then began walking again, this time with her on my left. She leaned against my shoulder. "What is the matter, Jerod?"

"Two guys following us," I said, still whispering. "I think the two from this morning at Touscher's place." I felt her tense next to me. "Keep walking, until we get to the Jeep."

We were almost to the Jeep and I took out my keys and unlocked the doors with the remote. I kept a firm hold on Cat's hand as I stepped up to open the door for her. I was finally in a position that I could see behind us. The two guys had closed the distance and were less than fifteen feet away. One was carrying a fixed blade knife in his right hand, while the other, the taller of the two, was reaching into his jacket at the waist area.

I pulled Cat across my body so that I was now between her and the two men. "Run. Call the police." Cat immediately took off. She loved running for exercise and that served her well now.

The man with the knife immediately started to take off after her, trying to run past me. Sometimes the simplest methods are the best. I stuck out my foot and tripped him. He hit the ground with an audible grunt as the air expelled from his lungs. He'd be down for a least a second.

The taller man was faster on the draw then I had thought he would be. He was already bringing the weapon up on target. Unfortunately, that target was me. I didn't waste time trying to draw my own firearm. I would be reacting when I should be acting to take back the initiative. I surged forward, my left hand grabbing the gun and moving it to my right so that I was out of the line of fire. Good thing I did too, as the gun went off. I just hoped that the round didn't strike an innocent bystander.

I continued to drive forward, pushing the gun down and into his hip as I did so. I launched a series of strikes at his face and throat. The first two hit his nose, breaking it in a shower of blood. His eyes immediately started to water and swell. The next one hit him on the cheek and then the fourth in the mouth; I felt his teeth cut into my hand. It also cut into his lip. The last struck him in the larynx and he immediately started to gag and wheeze.

I stopped hitting him and, reaching under the gun with my right hand, yanked it out of his grip. Still trying to draw air in his lungs through his damaged throat, the man didn't put up much resistance to me stripping the gun from him. Just to be sure the fight with the taller one was over, I delivered a sweeping front kick to the man's groin. Like punting a football except the balls were plural. He collapsed on the ground with a choking whimper.

I spun around to find the other man just getting to his hands and knees, reaching for the knife that had fallen just a few feet away from him. I pointed the other man's gun at him. "Stay down on the ground, hand away from the knife, or I will shoot you." The man hesitated and then seemed to resign himself, lying down on the ground, arms outstretched.

I used the moment to pull my own gun. The one I taken off the taller subject didn't appear to be a bad firearm, a Ruger 9mm, but I didn't know how well it had been taken care of and whether or not it would fire if I pulled the trigger. Mine, I knew was reliable.

Glancing up the street, I saw Cat stopped about three blocks ahead. She was talking on the phone, her hands waving frantically as she did so. The cavalry would be coming soon. I kept both men at gunpoint until the Monterey Police arrived on scene. It took a bit of explaining to convince them that I wasn't a bad guy. After all, when they pulled up there were two men in suits on the ground and me hovering over them with a loaded handgun. When I was finally able to pull my police ID and badge out, they relaxed a little.

At some point while Cat and I were giving our statements, Detective East showed up. Monterey PD had found a '65 Chevy Malibu a few blocks away that matched the description we had provided. Luminol in the interior showed trace amounts of blood, and so did the knife that the shorter of the two men had been wielding. There were still tests to be conducted and evidence to be analyzed but Detective East was convinced he had the people responsible for Mr. Touscher's death.

The two suspects clammed up, invoking their right to remain silent and requesting a lawyer before they were interrogated.

It was almost midnight before we finished up with the police and were on our way to our hotel room. We were both exhausted and after a shower and taking Steve out for a walk, we were asleep as soon as our heads hit the pillows.

CHAPTER SIX

I sat on the back porch of my house and threw the ball for Steve. We had been at it for thirty minutes when my cell phone rang. It was Detective East. We had gotten to know each other a little better in the past few weeks since the incident in Monterey. He stayed in regular contact; I was positive that it had as much to do with making sure Cat and I would show up to the court dates as it did anything else. Nonetheless, we had struck up a casual friendship.

The two men had turned out to be Mr. Touscher's cousins, his mother's sister's sons. Their mother had been estranged from the family for years, apparently because she chose to hang out with the wrong crowd. Not to say the grandmother was any saint, as Cat and I had found out after we came back to the Bay Area and started digging into the history of the family. She had been somewhat adventuresome – an American intelligence agent during World War II. She had been a woman I would have loved to have met.

When she got tired of the life of adventure, she settled down, married and had three children. Her eldest, a son, had joined the Marines during Korea and ended up being killed in action. The second eldest, Harold Touscher III's mother, had been a homemaker who married into a family of moderate wealth. The youngest, the two suspects' mother, had gotten involved in drugs, gone to prison, and had two sons from two different fathers.

The two sons had been to their grandmother's house when they were young and the oldest (who turned out to be the shorter of the two) remembered the painting and the story behind it. He thought it was worth some money and they could have used some money. Their plan was to steal it, along with anything else they could take – at least that's what the police surmised.

Unfortunately, their luck was bad. Cat had purchased the painting just minutes before they planned to steal it. It was a simple case of bad timing but, in a rage, the shorter man had stabbed and killed Mr. Touscher. His brother rolled on him for a reduced sentence.

On top of all the hoopla involving the attempted theft of the painting, first from Mr. Touscher and then from Cat, Cat's buyer had backed out, and now she was the proud owner of an original Salvador Dali painting. It was one of the hazards of the job. The painting itself was hanging up above the fireplace in my living room as it didn't go with the décor of Cat's office or her condo – a reminder of our trip to Monterey and the brief adventure we had there.

I hung up the phone after Ryan was done talking about the next court date and when we were expected to be there. He'd issue subpoenas, but he liked to call before we received them. It was a nice gesture on his part. Opening the back door, I walked into the kitchen and, grabbing a bottle off the counter, poured myself a whiskey, neat. Sitting down on the couch, I looked at the painting and raised my glass in a silent salute. Steve crawled up next me and made herself comfortable.

I thought for a moment. I didn't mind risking my own life, and those of my friends who joined me on our little adventures did so knowing the risks. If anything ever happened to Cat, though, I'd never forgive myself. I lifted the glass to my lips and swallowed the whiskey in one go. Returning to the kitchen, I poured myself another and before returning to the living room, grabbed the bottle.

MANHUNT

PROLOGUE

It was the perfect day for a memorial service. The sky was a gray mass of clouds that made the morning feel more like dusk. Everyone was dressed in black, umbrellas up to thwart the steady rain that was falling. Beside me, Steve sat quietly but looked every bit as miserable as I felt. I glanced up at the soggy wreath that acted as the main centerpiece. "Rest in Peace, Yolanda Catherine Merritt." My girlfriend for the past six months. The nice thing about rain at a service like this – no one could see your tears.

She had died at 9:54 on Saturday, February 12th. Two days before Valentine's Day and two days after her best friend had found her lying, unresponsive, on the floor of her office. The doctors said that it was a tumor in her brain that caused a massive aneurism. Her father had flown her remains back to France where Cat would be buried alongside her mother. The memorial service was for her friends and family here in the States. There were some beautiful eulogies, I'm sure, but I had stopped paying attention.

I turned and left, Steve following beside me, her generally enthusiastic demeanor muted. The drive back over the bridge to my house in Marin County was done in silence; the only noise, the sound of raindrops beating on the soft-top of my Jeep and the mechanical swishing sound of the windshield wipers.

When we arrived back home, I changed out of the suit I was wearing, threw on my hiking pants and a khaki-colored long sleeve shirt, packed my canvas backpack and matching messenger satchel and we were on the road. I didn't know where Steve and I were going and, in all honesty, it didn't matter. I just needed to get away and Steve went where I went.

CHAPTER ONE

The phone next to my bed rang, startling me awake. The bright light of day had penetrated the shades in my bedroom and was glaringly bright. I squinted and threw my arm up to block some of the light. The phone continued with annoying persistence, jarring me from my alcohol-induced slumber.

I didn't normally drink as much as I had the evening before. It was my first time sleeping in my own bed in over a month. It was also the first time I had slept in the bed since Cat had died. I could still smell the faint jasmine scent of her shampoo on the pillow next to mine. That's when I started drinking and hadn't stopped until I passed out.

Fumbling around, I finally managed to pick up the receiver and bring it to my ear. "What?" I asked gruffly. The phone was old school with nothing digital to it, including a caller ID. I didn't know who was calling me and frankly, at that moment, it didn't really matter.

"Jerod! Thank God. I've been trying to reach you for days." It was Susan Hansen, wife of Robert Hansen III, my friend and part-time employer. Susan was thirty years junior to her husband and while many thought he had married her for her youth and beauty, she was one of the smartest people I knew. She also had an uncanny knack for planning three moves ahead of everyone else that made her seem almost prescient. It could be intimidating if you didn't know her.

"I've been out of cell phone range," I said lamely. I was sure I had been out of cell phone range for most of the past month, having spent it in Downieville, California, where cell phones couldn't reach. But I also hadn't charged my phone in all that time. I hadn't wanted to talk to anyone and I had made myself as unavailable as possible. "What's going on?"

"It's Robert," she said, worry in her voice. For a moment I panicked. Bob, as I liked to call him because it annoyed him, was in his mid-sixties and for a moment, I imagined he'd had a heart attack and died and that Susan was about to tell me I had lost someone else close to me. "He's missing."

I almost breathed a sigh of relief. Worrisome, but it wasn't being dead, so I relaxed a little. "Where was he last?" I asked.

"He was at the Empress in Victoria, British Columbia. He'd been in contact with a seller about some sort of book." Susan didn't share her husband's enthusiasm for ancient artifacts and relics. She did have a Master of Fine Arts degree from the Pratt Institute, one of the top art programs in the nation, but her taste ran more toward Monet and Rembrandt. "He was supposed to meet with the seller sometime yesterday and I haven't heard from him since."

Some of the fog from my sleep and alcohol-muddled mind was starting to clear. I sat up and rubbed my eyes, my back spasming with the movement. I clenched my teeth against the pain and looked at the clock, it was just past 5:00 p.m. Damn. I had way overslept. I looked around the room but didn't see Steve. "He take anyone with him?" I asked. I wanted to go look for my dog but the phone had a cord that wouldn't let the receiver extend more than six feet from the base.

"No. I wanted him to but he didn't think it would be dangerous." Her voice cracked at the end and a tiny sob escaped her. I had never seen Susan this worried.

"I'm sure he's fine. He's probably just out of cell range," I told her, trying to mollify her somewhat.

"Can you go look for him? Please? As a favor to me?" She had composed herself somewhat.

I didn't want to go. I wanted to continue to wallow in my misery. I took a deep breath. "Give me an hour to get my shit together and then I'll try and find the quickest flight from here to Victoria."

"You don't have to worry about a flight. I'll have a car pick you and your dog up in an hour and there will be a private jet waiting for you at San Francisco International Airport. I'll text you the company name and address." Three steps ahead. She knew I was going to say yes even before I did.

CHAPTER TWO

True to her word, a car picked Steve and I up exactly an hour after Susan and I got off the phone. I had found Steve down sleeping on the couch. There was a doggy door that she could go in and out of to do her business, but the last time she had eaten was the evening before. I felt like a heel, having drank so much that I neglected my dog. She was no worse for wear and happy to have me up. I spent a little time playing with her until the car service arrived.

The drive over to San Francisco took some time but when we arrived, I boarded the Cessna Citation X quickly and we were wheels up within thirty minutes of my arrival. The plane was luxurious. Leather chairs that were as comfortable as my recliner at home. The crew was small, consisting of the captain, his co-pilot and a flight attendant. Despite my scruffy appearance, they treated me like royalty. I hadn't shaved or received a haircut in the past month. My untrimmed beard was bushy and out of control and I hadn't done anything more with my hair, now a light brownish-blonde due to its length, than run a comb through it so that it was out of my eyes. With my leather jacket, khaki shirt, hiking pants, and boots, I looked like I belonged in the Outback of Australia versus on a private jet.

The flight was a little over two hours. The landing was smooth and Steve and I were off-loaded as quickly as we boarded. A quick trip through the Canadian Border Services Agency checkpoint, and I was met by another driver. He was an older gentleman, maybe about sixty, with a strong French-Canadian accent. His name was Pierre. He graciously took my backpack and placed it in the trunk of the newer model sedan he was driving. A few minutes later we were on our way to the Empress Hotel.

This time of year, the weather was cool but not cold. I rolled down the window so Steve could enjoy the wind after being cooped up in the plane for two hours. I could smell fresh rain and based on the wetness of the road, the storm had passed through not long ago. I made idle conversation with Pierre, asking about the local sights, weather and news.

Pierre turned out to be a wealth of information. Well-read regarding the local politics, he was more conservative than I would have expected from a Canadian. He also inquired about Bob which caught me off guard, although if I had thought about it, it shouldn't have surprised me. Bob believed in loyalty and he had probably been using the same car company and driver for years, or at least any time he visited Victoria. It's who Susan would call if she needed transportation services.

"How is Mr. Hansen, monsieur?" Pierre asked politely.

"I'm not sure. We haven't heard from him in several days and his wife is getting worried. Do you know if he is still at the Empress?"

"I do not, monsieur. He told me that he would be here for only a few days and that he would call when he was ready, but he never called for a ride. He did speak with my dispatcher, Benny, to inquire about renting an ATV."

His accent was thick, so I asked to clarify what he had said. "An all-terrain vehicle?"

"Oui, monsieur."

"Could you ask Benny to give me a call when he can, Pierre? I'd like to ask him what company he recommended."

"Of course, monsieur."

I handed Pierre a business card with my cell phone number on it and we continued with our small talk until we arrived at the

Empress Hotel. I took my backpack from Pierre and tipped him well in American currency, not having had time to convert any of my cash to Canadian dollars, and then I walked into the lobby of the Empress.

The lobby was gorgeously appointed with multiple columns and old Victorian-style upholstery on the furniture. I walked up to the front desk and told the clerk that I had a reservation. She quickly and efficiently looked me up on her computer. "Oh, you'll be staying in 330." That turned out to be the Bob Hope suite. While she was courteous before she had looked up my name, she was practically fawning over me now. My guess is that only big money clients stayed in the Bob Hope Suite. It also turned out to be the room Bob was staying in. I worried briefly that we would have to share a bed. That worry was put to rest as soon as I entered the room. The suite had two bedrooms.

I let Steve off her leash and set my backpack and messenger bag on the floor next to the door. Steve immediately started exploring the room. I let her do her thing. I paused where I was and took in the room. It was spacious, with comfortable-looking chairs and a couch done in a light shade of green in the living room area. A fireplace was against one wall. The curtains were open and the view to the waterfront was spectacular, even at night. There was a portrait of Bob Hope. I could see why Bob – both of them – would choose this room. It was nice.

The room itself was clean. The floors were freshly vacuumed and there was not a speck of dust anywhere I could see. I would have to ask the cleaning staff tomorrow when the last time they had seen Bob and if anything had appeared amiss in the suite after that.

Satisfied I wouldn't disturb anything that could be evidentiary in nature, I explored the living room and then each of the bedrooms. In one room, I found Bob's suitcase, clothes, and toiletries. If he left on his own accord, he apparently didn't plan to be gone for more than the day. His grooming products were stacked neatly on the bathroom counter along with his toothbrush, giving every indication that, wherever he had gone, he had intended to return.

There was a small writing desk in the room with a pad of paper on it. There was an indentation on the pad that led me to believe someone had written on it, but trying the old shading trick with a pen didn't reveal what it was. I finished searching the room and found nothing of interest.

While I had fed Steve on the plane, I hadn't eaten anything since the day before. I ordered room service and an Irish whiskey and then settled in for the night.

CHAPTER THREE

I was up without the need of an alarm by 5:00 a.m. I slipped on my pants, t-shirt, and shoes and took Steve out for a walk around the grounds. When we returned to the room, I ordered some breakfast and a pot of coffee from room service and hopped in the shower while I waited for delivery. I thought my shower was fast but I walked out of my room to find breakfast already set up. Props to the hotel staff. I fixed Steve some food and poured myself a cup of coffee and sat down to enjoy my meal.

I turned my thoughts to how I was going to find Bob. I only had two avenues to pursue: hope that the hotel staff had seen something that might help, or the car service dispatcher would call with the name of the ATV rental company he had recommended.

For all my years in law enforcement, I had spent precious little time in investigations. I did my time on patrol and then transferred to the Special Operations Division. We did surveillance operations on major players in the drug and crime business, conducted felony warrant service, and crashed street corners where drug sales ran rampant. Halfway through my five-year stint in SOD, I was picked up by SWAT as an operator. It was a collateral duty, a part-time position within the Department versus a full-time assignment, so I still worked in the SOD but there was overlap with SWAT and SOD operations.

After SOD, I went to the Intelligence Unit as an analyst where I made Sergeant. From there, I did a six-month stint in property crimes before being pulled for an Alcohol, Tobacco, and Firearms (ATF) task force that turned into a full-time position. By that time, I was a Team Leader on SWAT. After ATF, I went back to patrol and finally back to SOD where I finished up my career as a Lieutenant and as the SWAT Tactical Commander. Had I wanted to go to the missing person bureau, that option had always been open to me; it was just not something I had wanted to do. Now here I was, trying to track down my friend.

I sat in the room, drank coffee, watched the morning news, and played with Steve. Around 7:00 I received a call from Bob's executive assistant, Julie. The security team would be on the ground by noon. They were flying commercial, a red-eye from New York to Victoria. There would be five members and a team leader, giving me six extra sets of eyes and ears altogether. I thanked Julie for the information and hung up my cell phone.

Around 8:00 I figured the hotel staff would be clocked in and getting ready for their day. I hooked the leash to Steve's collar and handed her the loose end. I wasn't familiar with the leash law in Victoria, but most city ordinances read that a dog had to be leashed. They didn't say who had to be holding the leash and, in those rare instances, where someone ventured a comment, it was usually to say how cute it was that Steve was, in essence, walking herself.

Steve and I departed the hotel suite and headed down the hall in search of the cleaning crew and found two older ladies in their mid-sixties. They were at the end of the hallway near the stairwell setting up their carts before beginning the arduous task of cleaning rooms. I was in luck in that one of them had been working the day Bob had checked in and each day since. They were initially reluctant to speak with me. I was sure the Empress probably had policies to protect customer privacy, but after explaining that Bob was my friend and that we were both staying in the Bob Hope suite, they opened up a little. "Was there anything amiss in his room when you went to clean it that day?"

"No, sir. The typical. I made the bed and replaced the towels, removed any dirty dishes, tidied up and went about my day. The room hasn't been disturbed since."

I thanked them for their time and made a mental note to leave a bigger than usual tip for them before checkout. Steve and I made our way to the elevator and then downstairs to the lobby. We drew a few glances, mostly because of Steve carrying the end of her leash in her mouth, as happy as a dog could be.

Once we were in the lobby, I pulled out my cell phone and called Julie. She picked up on the first ring. "Hansen Investments, Mr. Hansen's office. How may I help you?"

"Julie, it's Jerod. Can you do me a favor and call the transportation service? My driver last night said that one of the dispatchers gave Robert the name and number to an ATV rental company. I need to find out who that company is. I believe he said the dispatcher's name was Benny." I used Bob's full first name. Calling him Bob had become our inside joke. When talking to his employees, though, I used his full name or simply referred to him as Mr. Hansen.

"Right away, sir. I will call you back when I have something." She hung up.

I pulled up a picture of Bob on my phone and started asking around. I finally found a doorman susceptible to being bribed and, for $60 in US currency, I was able to find out he had seen Bob get into a blue pickup truck a few days ago. He thought Bob had a day-pack with him but couldn't remember the name on the sign that graced the door of the truck.

So, Bob had been picked up. My guess would be by the ATV rental company. At least I now knew he had gone willingly. He hadn't taken anything with him, though, other than possibly a backpack. Unless Bob had extra toiletries in the backpack, I still thought he'd planned to return that same day.

Now, it was a matter of waiting: waiting for the security team to arrive, and waiting for Julie or the car company to call back, hopefully shortly. Steve and I occupied our time by wandering the hotel grounds. We didn't get far, Julie called back within ten minutes. "I have something. Victoria Wilderness Rentals. They rent gear like snowshoes, skis, and, more importantly, ATVs and snowmobiles. I'll text you the address and phone number."

I thanked her and then asked the doorman to get me a taxi. He picked up the phone and within a few minutes, a taxi pulled to the front of the hotel and the doorman pulled open the passenger side rear door so that I could take a seat. Once Steve and I was safely inside, he shut the door and the taxi started to pull away.

I gave my driver the address and then glanced at his license and cab operating permit. His name was Avi Sharma. I struck up a conversation with him and the thirty-minute drive to Victoria Wilderness Rentals went by quickly.

We pulled up to the company and I asked Avi to give me a few minutes. He explained that the meter would still be running and I answered that was ok. He nodded his agreement and Steve and I got out.

The office that the company operated out of was really no more than a shack. A single door made of slatted wood with crossbeams was the entrance and beside that was a small window. It was not the kind of company I would have thought Bob would do business with. Generally, he looked for businesses that looked more professional, so he must have been in a hurry or felt this was the best he could do. The windows didn't have curtains or blinds, but they were almost dirty enough not to need them. Scattered all around the area were ATVs, kayaks, snowmobiles, and a variety of other outdoor gear.

I entered the small office area and found it occupied by a man in his seventies. He was wearing coveralls and a black and white plaid shirt that had seen the wash more than a few times. He was overweight with a receding hairline that left almost the full front half of his head bald and shiny. He got up from his chair behind a short counter with some effort and used a cane to help him walk the few feet to where I was standing.

"John Wellington." He stuck out his hand in a friendly manner and I shook it.

"Jerod Grey."

"That's a fine looking dog you have there. Australian Cattle Dog?" He asked.

"She is." I replied, looking down at Steve who was sitting by my right leg.

"Had one as a kid. Good dogs. How can I help you, Mr. Grey? Interested in renting some equipment?"

"Perhaps. I'm looking for a man who possibly came through here a few days ago. Mid-sixties, about 5'6", 140 pounds with a full head of snow white hair. He's a friend of mine and we haven't heard from him since then. His wife is worried sick." I had seen the ring on the man's left hand. A wedding band. Throwing Susan in the mix might generate some sympathy.

"You'd be talking about Mr. Hansen?" The man did an impressive job of raising his eyebrow in a manner that would have made Mr. Spock proud. "Yeah, he came through here a few days ago. Rented an ATV and asked my son to take him out by River Jordan, about an hour west of here. Said he'd call when he was ready for a pick up. When we didn't hear from him for a day or two, I notified the Mounties."

This was at least a solid lead, although based on what he'd said, I had other concerns. Bob was not known for his skills as an outdoorsman. I had always told him that he'd go on an expedition with us when we placed basecamp at a five-star hotel. Now he was wandering around British Columbia on an ATV. I could foresee a dozen different outcomes to such a venture, none of them particularly pleasant. I asked John if he had a map of the area and he grabbed one from behind the counter.

We opened the map on the counter and he showed me where the town of River Jordan was. "What's out that way?"

"Not much. There's the town itself and a few campgrounds. There is, of course, the river, and lots of forest."

"Anything else?" Bob had told Susan he was going to meet with his contact. That contact must have picked a spot that Bob could find.

"There's survival cabins, spaced about five miles apart along the river. Just in case some city clown ends up getting caught in a late spring snowstorm, there is a place they can get out of the weather to stay warm and dry."

"Do you have a map with the cabins marked on them?"

"No sir, but they're pretty evenly spaced apart and easy enough to find if you follow the river."

"Thank you, Mr. Wellington. I appreciate the information. Do you have four ATVs I can rent?"

John smiled, "That I do, Mr. Grey. That I do." He grabbed some paperwork and started filling it out.

* * * * *

Steve and I went outside and paid Avi for his time, adding in another $20 for a tip. I notified Julie that I had found a lead and asked her to advise the security team of my location as soon as they touched down in Victoria. I also asked her to locate and rent the services of a helicopter. My plan was to have three guys go with me on the ATVs and the other three in the helicopter. The helicopter could cover far more ground along the river, but landing would be difficult with all the tree cover, so they could guide us in on the ATVs to investigate anything they saw from the air. Bob was not going to like the bill for this little adventure, but if he came home safely it would be worth it.

I chafed at the delay and Steve, picking up on my anxiousness, gave a little whine. I had been tempted to have John's son take me up to the drop-off point ahead of the team's arrival but knew patience would be the better course to follow, no matter how I felt about it in the moment.

The team arrived a little after 2:00 p.m., driving a black SUV with heavily tinted windows – standard security protocol, if you could get away with it. It made it difficult to see who, or how many people, were inside. The large SUV came to a stop and three of the four doors opened to disgorge the team.

The driver was someone I had worked with before. His name was Hector, a former Navy SEAL who had left the service after six deployments to ply his skills in the private security world. He'd been with the company for about two years now. Short, with a shaved head, he still looked fighting trim. None of them were carrying weapons but I could see the extra magazines tucked into the pockets of the tactical vest he was wearing. Canada wasn't known for being gun friendly but I trusted the team to know what they were doing. There were ways of obtaining permits to carry a weapon, but they weren't easy or cheap.

Exiting the front passenger side was the man I knew was the team leader. I hadn't met him in personally, but I had heard him. He was

6'5" and weighed about 300 pounds. He wasn't overweight per se, but you could see some of it was settling into his stomach region – the disadvantages of getting older. His name was Edward Nelson, a former full-time SWAT operator from Los Angeles. His normal tone of voice was about twice as loud as anyone else's, which is why I had heard him before, even though we had never met in person.

The other member was introduced to me as Adam. Adam had come from Marine Special Operations Command, better known as the Raiders or MARSOC. He looked to be about my age, maybe a few years younger, with a short, cropped, military-style haircut and a five o'clock shadow.

I shook each man's hand in turn and then started briefing them on my plan. As I did so, a helicopter flew overhead. The remaining three members of our team were on the Bell 206. John told me that on the helicopter was Mike, a corpsman who had served with the Marines in Fallujah, Orlando, also a former Navy SEAL, and Alfonso, a retired Army Ranger.

John's son was named James. He was a pleasant enough guy, if a little on the quiet side. The four ATVs were loaded on to a trailer that would be towed behind James's truck. Steve and I got in the front passenger side of the truck, after asking if James minded Steve riding with us; Edward and the team would follow in the Suburban. We left the small office behind and drove toward River Jordan. The helicopter went ahead of us and would refuel there. The Bell 206 only had a range of 325 nautical miles. That should be enough for our needs, but there was also no reason to push it if we were able to refuel along the way.

We arrived in the town of River Jordan at about 3:00 p.m. I was starting to worry that we'd lost too much daylight and would have to delay our search via ATV until tomorrow. We had maybe four hours of sunlight left before it got too dark. The ATVs had headlights, but they provided a narrow range of vision in the dark. The helicopter would be useless unless Edward and his team had brought a Forward Looking Infrared Device, better known as a FLIR. I hadn't seen what was in the Suburban, so I wasn't sure what equipment was available.

By 3:30 we were off-loading the ATVs. James was going through a standard safety brief regarding the operation of the equipment. No one was paying attention. The characteristics that made for good special operators – independence, intelligence, confidence, etc. – also made them difficult to manage. They only listened if they respected the person they were listening to and most of them knew as much about riding an ATV as James did.

Once James was done and on his way, the team broke out what equipment and weapons they had brought with them. Each man carried a Heckler and Koch MP5, a German-designed 9mm submachine gun that was compact, accurate, and easy to control when firing. To that they added Glock 19 pistols and various other pieces of equipment. Edward handed me a drop-down holster and a Glock of my own. I strapped the holster to my pants belt and placed the Glock in it, feeling the locking mechanism click to hold it in place.

The helicopter was overhead by the time we were underway and it scooted ahead to start scouting the river. I left Steve guarding the Suburban. We still had gear and weapons in the vehicle and people would be less likely to mess with it if there was a dog there protecting it. They spotted the first survival cabin almost immediately and guided us in. It turned out to be empty, as did the next two after that. It was the fourth cabin, about twenty miles up the river, that we found occupied. The helicopter crew reported light smoke coming from the chimney of the cabin.

When we were about 300 yards out, we pulled the ATVs off the trail and proceeded on foot. Edward hadn't brought a FLIR with him. The plan was to let Hector and Adam approach the cabin to scout it out. They'd let us know what they found. I wanted to find Bob, but I didn't want to scare the daylights out of a young couple out for a little romantic interlude.

Hector and Adam pushed out ahead and Edward and I trailed behind, stopping about 25 yards from the cabin. There was no indication anyone had heard or seen us.

We watched as Adam and Hector made their way around the cabin. I could see them trying to peak into the few windows. Each was covered with curtains, though, and they looked back at us and in an exaggerated way, shook their heads "no." They had gone separate directions around the cabin and met at the only door.

I watched as Hector pulled a piece of electronic equipment from his vest. It was a battery pack and small monitor for a camera. He then took out the camera portion and screwed that into the pack. He slid the small camera under the door and watched the monitor intently. Once he had pulled it back, he waved us over.

"I can see a body on the small bed but no one else. I can't tell if the person on the bed is male or female or if they are alive or not," he whispered.

Edward nodded. "I'll breach. You and Adam enter and clear. Copy?"

Both Adam and Hector acknowledged the hasty plan.

I stood up and allowed Edward to use me as a brace as he donkey-kicked the door. It wasn't a particularly strong door and it flew open, bouncing off the inner wall and started to swing shut again but Hector and Adam were already making their way through. A second later I heard both men call clear and Edward and I entered the cabin.

I saw Bob lying on the bed. He was pasty white and sweating with fever. I could see his right leg was braced. "Get the medic down here ASAP," Edward ordered, and Hector jumped on the radio to contact the helicopter.

I walked over to Bob. He had other scrapes and bruises on him, but it appeared the worst of his injuries was what I was sure was a broken leg. He had used two pieces of wood, no doubt fallen from a tree, and some duct tape to splint it. The pants leg was split and the lower part of his leg below the knee was red and swollen.

Edward came to my side and said that the helicopter pilot had found a clearing about a half a click from the cabin to put the Bell 206 down in and that he had sent Adam to retrieve Mike. They should be back here in about five minutes. While we were waiting, I did a cursory check to ensure Bob didn't have any other serious wounds we didn't initially see. I found nothing. Adam and John had split up to search the cabin but found nothing of interest other than Bob's backpack.

I broke out some water and wet Bob's lips with it. He stirred briefly, only to say, "Took you long enough." Then he passed out again.

CHAPTER FOUR

We transported Bob via the helicopter to the nearest hospital. I waited until we had arrived to contact Susan and tell her we had found her husband. I wanted to be able to tell her a little more than he had broken his leg and was unconscious before making that call. As soon as the doctor updated me on his condition, I pulled out the phone. He was dehydrated and the break had caused a fever, but other than that and a few scrapes, bumps and bruises, he was expected to make a full recovery. Susan sighed in relief and told me she'd be on her way to Victoria.

Bob didn't regain consciousness until the next morning. I had stayed in the waiting room. Getting Steve into the hospital had been difficult. There had been arguments but in the end, the compromise was that she could stay in the waiting room. I agreed to that before they could add on the stipulation that I had to be with her.

While I had stayed at the hospital through the night, I cut Edward and his team loose to go grab some hot chow and some sleep. They had caught a red-eye from New York and then had been up all day. I was sure they were exhausted and there was no reason for them to hang around the hospital. Plus, it was making the staff nervous.

Once Bob had regained consciousness I was allowed into the room to visit him. He was still a little out of it, but he had the presence of mind to shake my hand. "Glad you found me. I was starting to get worried."

A dozen things went through my head. What the hell was he doing out there by himself? How the hell did he break his leg? I wanted to call him a fool as well as a dozen other names, but I settled for saying that I was glad I had found him in time, too. The rest would come later.

When the awkward silence stretched on for too long, I asked him to tell me what had happened.

Bob explained, "Several weeks ago I received an email from an unidentified party regarding the desire to sell a tome that they claimed had been found in Iraq. They sent several pictures of the book and it looked to be in remarkable condition. Initially, I thought it was just a hoax. They were asking for $5000 for a book that could realistically be priceless. Out of curiosity, I forwarded the email and the pictures to Curtis."

Curtis Feldman was a mutual friend of Bob's and mine. He was a professor of archeology at Harvard and one of the foremost experts in ancient Mesoamerican civilizations. While the tome was found in Iraq, and therefore a little outside of Curtis's area, if he didn't know, he'd be able to point Bob to someone who did.

Bob went on, "Curtis called me within fifteen minutes, excited. He couldn't verify the authenticity of the book but it appeared to be Sumerian in origin, and based on the photos that had been taken, potentially contained the full Epic of Gilgamesh, a King of Uruk from around 2100 BC. If it was authentic, Curtis surmised it could potentially be one of the greatest finds this decade. If not, I was out $5000."

I interrupted for a moment. "How did you end up in Canada?"

"This is where the seller wanted to meet. He gave me a drop location where I could put the money and then retrieve the book." Bob blushed a little at that admission. He knew where I was going to go with this.

"So, you thought it would be a good idea to go out into the wilderness with $5000 – cash, I presume?" Bob nodded his head, so I continued. "Without backup. Did it occur to you this could be a set up? That there could have been people there to rob you?"

"It seemed a little elaborate for a robbery set up to have me fly all the way to Victoria. Plus, if the book hadn't been there, I would have moved on," he told me, missing my point about a set up for a robbery.

"How convenient to have the fly come to the web. Jesus, Bob, you could have been killed!" I knew my voice had raised in volume, I was on the verge of yelling. "Why didn't you just call me? Or at least have Josue assign a couple of his guys to you?"

"Don't patronize me, Jerod, and DO NOT CALL ME BOB! I would have called you if you hadn't been so busy feeling sorry for yourself. I understand it hurts, but you have a life to live and for Catherine's sake, you need to keep on living it." Now he was pissed too. Great.

I took a deep breath to calm myself. "Look, boss, I'm sorry. After losing her, I can't stand to lose another friend right now. Believe me when I say I'm acting out of concern for you. I'm sorry if it came across as patronizing. I have been distant and an asshole lately." I slumped into the chair next to his hospital bed. "How did you break your leg?" I asked, changing the subject. Bob visibly calmed down and then, at the question, blushed red with embarrassment. "I crashed the ATV," he mumbled.

I laughed. "This is what happens when you have people drive you around all the time, you forget how to drive yourself. Why didn't you call? No cell signal?"

"Not even a single bar." He slid his middle finger along his nose and I laughed again. "After the crash, I realized I had broken my leg. I splinted it up the best I could and dragged myself back to the cabin."

I nodded and gave him some kudos for toughing out the haul to the cabin. "I'm taking it you didn't get the book? The backpack you had still contained the $5000. Edward, the team leader your wife sent out, has it," I explained.

"Shit. Susan. I need to call her. She's going to be furious."

"I told her you were unconscious still but were expected to be ok. She's probably in the air by now. She'll see you when she gets here."

"Yeah, and no doubt after she's done ensuring herself that I'm going to be fine, she'll probably chew my ass." Bob exaggeratedly let his head fall to his chest in a gesture of defeat.

"Oh, you can pretty much count on that, my friend." I smiled, trying to be reassuring and failing miserably. "What's the next step, Bob? You want to pursue the book?"

"I just told you not to call me Bob." His glare was back.

"Oh, you were serious about that?" I feigned surprise.

"Yes, I was serious. Have been every time I have told you that for the last thousand times."

"Yeah, well, I'm a little hard-headed and set in my ways. Hard to teach an old dog new tricks." I said with a wink.

"I guess you're in good company then."

"Some of the best, my friend." I smiled.

Bob and I talked about what he wanted done from here. He still wanted to get his hands on the book. He was hoping that the seller would reach out to him again, but in the interim, he wanted to go on the offensive in tracking the seller down. I also got the location of where he was supposed to have met the seller. It was an old abandoned truck off a side path that split from the main trail about a mile past the cabin where we had found Bob. That was also where he had crashed the ATV. Apparently, there was quite a drop along that trail.

He forwarded me what information he had. Their communications had all been through email. I noticed one curiosity almost right off the bat. "These came to your internal work email account?" I inquired.

Bob looked confused for a moment. "Yes. Why is that relevant?" As soon as he asked the question, I could see his eyes light up with the answer. "I don't give my internal email address to anyone. It's strictly for inter-company business."

That means someone inside the company either sent the email or gave out the email address. I had concluded, for now at least, that the seller must be male. There was no evidence to support that conclusion, but it made it easier for me to talk about him if I had a gender specific pronoun to use. At least this information gave me a place to start. I doubted the email was anything but a dummy account, but I might be able to glean enough information from it to lead me to the right person to question regarding the seller, if I had some help. Computers weren't my thing. "I'll need to bring in some people to assist. To start, I'll need a computer guy."

"Whatever you need, Jerod. I'll give Julie approval rights and you can make your requests straight to her."

I nodded. "Thanks. I'll get right on this." I stood up from the chair. I reached over and touched his shoulder. "Glad you're ok, old man. Get some rest. You'll need your strength for when Susan gets here."

"Thanks, and thanks for the reminder," he responded. We both chuckled and I left the room and headed down the sterile hallway to the waiting room. Hospitals always had a particular smell to them. Like bleach and sorrow.

I entered the waiting room to find Steve sitting on one of the benches with her head in the lap of a beautiful young lady wearing hospital scrubs with a stethoscope draped around her shoulders. It was hard to tell how tall she was sitting down but my guess was about 5'5". She had straight, blond hair that fell to just below her shoulders, full lips, and the brightest blue eyes I had ever seen. If Steve had been a boy dog, I would have accused him of flirting. As it was, she was looking for all the world like she was in heaven as the lady scratched her head and talked to her in soft tones that Steve was obviously enjoying.

"Gone for a few minutes and the dog is cheating on me," I said as I walked up.

The young lady jumped. She had been so intent on petting Steve that she hadn't even heard me approach. She stood up and Steve gave me the doggy equivalent of a glare for interrupting her petting time. "I am so sorry. She was here all alone."

I laughed. "No worries. She seemed to be enjoying it."

The girl gave me a shy smile. "I'm pretty good with animals. I'm Stephanie." She held out her hand.

"Jerod. And the pup is Steve." Steve thumped her tail as I shook Stephanie's hand.

Stephanie looked confused for a moment. "Steve? I thought she was girl." She glanced down at Steve just to be sure.

"She is." I laughed. "I just liked the name."

"Oh. Well, it's cute." She leaned over and gave Steve's neck a good rub. "Pleasure to meet you, Steve."

She didn't sound convinced that it was cute but I didn't take offense. I had long ago accepted the fact that not everyone was going to get my sense of humor. "It was a pleasure to meet you, Stephanie. Steve and I have some work to do." I bowed my head a little in her direction and then called Steve to me. For Steve's part, she made an exaggerated effort to get out of the chair like she just couldn't be more exhausted. The dog could play for hours; I was certain that lying around all morning had not worn her out. She was putting on a show for Stephanie and hoping to garner some additional attention. It worked. Stephanie fawned over her until I got Steve rolling. We said our goodbyes one more time and then Steve and I walked out the door of the hospital and into the busy, mid-day traffic of Victoria.

I made a few phone calls. The first was to Avi. I needed a ride back to the hotel and if he was available, I'd rather use his cab company. He was, and had about a ten minute ETA. Next call was to Edward to let him know that I was leaving the hospital and to send over one of the guys to sit with Bob in case he needed anything. I also told him to bring Bob's phone and charger which we had found in his backpack, along with the $5000 and some minimal supplies. Now that Bob was conscious again, he was going to want to get back to work. I was pretty sure that being holed up in a survival cabin for several days without a cell phone signal was the longest he had ever been out of touch with the rest of the world. I also asked Edward to send two guys out to the drop site to see if maybe the book was still there, or if there was any clue that the seller had left behind that would lead us to his identity.

After that, I called my best friend from high school, Dan Thomasson. I considered him family now and was more apt to refer to him as my brother than as my friend. Dan was a computer geek, a top-notch programmer, and a hacker. Few people knew about his hacker background, but we had grown up together and pretty much knew everything about one another. That's what being friends for almost forty years will do for you. He worked for a hospital in Colorado Springs in the IT department. I had pulled him in on a few cases I had worked over the years and his talents with computers had proved more than useful. He picked up his office phone on the third ring. "IT Department, Dan speaking. How can I help you?" His voice was deep and often intimidated people on the phone. At 6'6", he was almost as intimidating in person.

"Hey, brother. Need your help."

"Hey. What you got for me and will it land me in jail?" He let out a deep chuckle. We were each adrenaline junkies in our own way. Mine manifested itself in being a cop or a Sailor or trekking through dark jungles. Dan's came by way of seeing how many security systems and firewalls he could bypass to get at someone's darkest web secrets without getting caught.

"I need to find out who an email address really belongs to. It came in on Bob's internal email server so either someone in the company sent it, or they gave it to the person who sent it. I can call Bob's executive assistant and we can get you set up with a backdoor to their server."

"Sounds easy enough. Forward me what you have, bro, and I'll get to work on it."

"You'll be compensated for your efforts, brother. Appreciate it."

"You're about to give me access to the internal server of one of the richest venture capitalists in the nation. Pretty sure I can arrange my own compensation." He laughed.

"No funny business or Bob will fry us both." I said it only partially teasingly.

Dan's voice affected a quality of innocence. "Wouldn't think of it. I'll let you know if I find anything."

We didn't bother with goodbyes, opting instead just to hang up.

Avi had pulled up and was waiting patiently while I finished up my call with Dan. Steve and I climbed into the cool interior of cab. "How are you, Avi? Empress Hotel, please."

Avi turned on the meter and we pulled away from the hospital. When we arrived, I paid my fare and tip. We had made small talk on the way over and the more I heard, the more I liked the man. He wasn't just smart, but had a good sense of humor, too. I dropped a few hints about what I did for a living now and he seemed interested. He was definitely a prospective recruit at some point in the future.

Steve and I walked through the lobby and headed to the third floor. Entering our suite, I took off my boots and sat down on the couch in the living room. I had been up most of the night waiting to hear Bob's prognosis. Now that I knew he was going to be ok, I needed some sleep. Plus, until Dan got back to me with something, I really had no direction in which to travel.

I called Julie and asked her to add Dan to the payroll and to forward him a copy of the standard contract we used when doing these little side jobs for Bob. A behind-the-scenes guy like Dan made more per day than one of the field agents. The field agents, though, had the opportunity to get a bonus based on what we recovered and whether it could be sold. During our last expedition, each member of the Adventurers' Club walked away with an extra $25k in addition to the $250 a day they received in salary. It actually was not as much as we had originally anticipated, but it generally made it worth the risk, even though that last excursion had come with a little too much risk that had landed two bad guys dead and a friend of mine, Andy, in the hospital with a gunshot wound. That didn't include the fact that I had also been shot. $25k didn't replace your peace of mind.

After my call to Julie, I laid down on the couch and took a long nap. I wasn't sure how long I was out. I woke to the sound of my phone ringing. It was Susan. She had landed and was on her way to the hospital and wanted to know if there was any change to Bob's status. I told her he was conscious and according to the doctors he would make a full recovery. I also told her to go easy on him. Her only response was a "hrummph."

When I had hung up the phone, I stood up from the couch and stretched, feeling the muscles in my back loosen just a little. I told Steve we could go for a walk after I showered. Steve seemed to agree to the plan and laid her head back down to wait until I was showered and had a fresh set of clothes on. I had only brought five days' worth of clothes and had worn three sets already. I was going to have figure out the laundry situation here shortly.

It was about a quarter to three before I was done with my shower and changed into a fresh set of clothes – not that it would look that way to the casual eye. I grabbed a clean pair of hiking pants and a plain black t-shirt – which is pretty much what I had worn the day before. I called Steve to me, grabbed her leash, and the two of us headed out for a nice walk around the Empress.

The stroll was relaxing as we made our way down along the waterfront. I found a place to grab some dinner and Steve and I sat in the outside patio area. While I waited on my food, I thought about what I might need to track down the tome's seller. I had gotten lucky with Bob. When I had called Julie and asked her to call the transportation company to get the information on the ATV rental, a simpler and more direct method would have been just to have her pull up his credit card statement and see where he had used it. I'm pretty sure you can't rent a vehicle of any sort without a credit card. I was making things harder on myself than I needed to, primarily because this wasn't my area of expertise.

This manhunt was going to be harder. All I had was a bogus email account and the possibility he was an employee, or knew an employee. Slim pickings. It was time to call in an expert. I picked up my phone and called Raymond Jimenez. Ray and I had served on an ATF task force together. He later left ATF and went to the US Marshals Service where he was quickly integrated into a fugitive task force. He had a talent for tracking people who didn't want to be found. He was also retired and had a son in college, so he'd be happy for the extra money. Plus, I'd be willing to bet that his wife, Marina, wanted him out of the house. He tended to get a bit neurotic when he wasn't kept occupied.

He picked up the phone within a few rings. "Hello?"

"Hi, Ray. It's Jerod. Did I catch you at a good time?"

"Depends on who you're asking. I'd say no, I was on the verge of convincing Marina that we needed a boat for the summer and your call interrupted my flow. But, and this is probably more important, your timely interjection also probably kept her from strangling me with my own tongue." I heard Marina's voice in the background; I couldn't quite make out the words but it sounded curt. "She said hi."

I laughed, "That didn't sound like hi to me."

"It wasn't. I just didn't want to embarrass her in front of you. My wife has a potty mouth." I heard a dull thump and Ray exclaimed "Ouch!" and then he chuckled. "No one believes me when I say she beats me. Now I have an eyewitness."

"All heard, nothing seen. You could have been beating yourself for all I know."

It was Ray's turn to laugh. "True. So, what's up? How have you been? What's the job?"

"I'm doing ok, brother. Thanks. You and the kids?"

"Good. Marina is still letting me twiddle my thumbs around the house while she goes out and earns a living that keeps me in the lifestyle to which I have become accustomed. My oldest is about to get married in a few months, if I don't kill her fiancé by then. The son is doing well in school, just needs to learn some money management skills and the youngest is too cute for her own good."

"Sounds like life is good for you. Glad to hear it, brother."

"That it is. So, what do you have for me?"

"I'm trying to track down an unsub (unknown subject) who sent Robert an email. I have a friend of mine that is working the internet side of the house but I could use someone on the ground side that can track down people. You're the best I know."

"You flatter me, Jerod, but you're also right, I am the best. This unsub dangerous? Any threats in the email, explicit or implied?"

"Unknown. He's only ever contacted Bob via email about purchasing an ancient book, but he hasn't done anything direct, no threats. He set a meeting with Bob in Victoria, British Columbia, but either didn't show or showed and wasn't able to complete the transaction because Bob crashed his ATV on the way to the meeting location," I explained.

"He ok?"

"He's fine. Are you up for a little manhunt? I don't know where it will take us or how long we'll be out but Roberty wants the guy found and if possible, to recover the book."

"I'm down. Let me talk to Marina and I'll call you back here soon." I thanked him and then we both hung up.

By the time I was done with my phone call, my food was delivered. I thanked the waiter and dug in. The food was excellent. The waiter brought me a second beer almost as soon as I finished my first.

I appreciated that. I finished up my meal and Steve and I just sat and relaxed while I finished my beer. I occasionally checked my phone to see if anyone had texted, even though I had the volume up so I could hear if they did. I was getting impatient again. I wanted Dan to call and tell me had tracked the guy to his exact location or for Ray to call and tell me he'd be joining me. I wanted to get to work. I had been moping about too long.

I finished my beer, paid my tab, and Steve and I walked back to the Empress. The room was cool and comfortable. I turned on the TV and switched on the local news. I made it through the weather forecast and a story looking for information regarding a fight that had broken out behind a bar in River Jordan, and then at some point, I nodded off.

CHAPTER FIVE

I woke to the sound of my phone ringing. I answered, trying to sound wide awake, but failing miserably. Ray laughed and asked if I had been asleep. "What is it, like 8:00 p.m.? Damn, man, you're getting old."

"Yeah, yeah. So? Coming along?" I asked.

"Yes, sir. Where should I meet you?"

"I've been thinking about that. How about we meet in Colorado Springs? It's centrally located depending on where we need to go from there. Plus, Dan is there and we can crash at my mom's place. She won't mind and would love the company. "

"Oh, think we can convince her to make chicken fried steak?" I laughed and said I would ask. I hung up with Ray and called my mom. As anticipated, she was excited and as soon as she heard Ray was coming as well, she told me she'd make chicken fried steak. I didn't even have to ask. It was one of my favorites as well. She also chewed my ass for not having called for the past month. It was a short and to the point one-way conversation.

After mom, I called Dan and told him the plan. He was still trying to track down the seller's electronic footprint. Dan did have access to Bob's company's server and was in the process of writing a program to search for the email address or anything close to it. I told him dinner would be at mom's tomorrow evening and to bring a bottle of the good stuff. He knew what I meant. The man bought more whiskey than I did. The only difference was I bought it to drink, while he held on to it. I think at last count he had 160-plus bottles.

After speaking with Dan, I called room service and requested a double bourbon, neat. While I waited, I tried to think if there was anyone else I would need on this adventure. No one came to mind. For the time being, it was a simple locate and recover. Well, simple from the perspective of not having any information that the seller had allies, or was dangerous. If that changed, I'd call in some reinforcements, but until then, my team would consist of Dan, Raymond, Steve, and me.

My drink arrived. I sipped contentedly as I watched the TV. Despite the naps, I started to get tired again and decided to call it a night once my glass was empty.

CHAPTER SIX

I caught an early flight to Colorado Springs the next morning. It cost a pretty penny, being last minute and because I was flying into the Springs. The Colorado Springs airport wasn't very big and there were very few direct flights. As a result, it was always more expensive to fly in to that airport than it was to fly into Denver International and make the hour or so drive south. There were two layovers, one in Seattle and one in Denver. Both were less than hour in length so I got into the airport about 3:00 p.m.

Before I left Victoria, I called Julie and had her turn on Ray's credit card and asked her to prepare a contract for him as well. When I touched down in Seattle, I called Ray and ensured he'd booked a flight. He had and would be landing a few hours after I touched down. I told him I would meet him at the airport. The flights went smoothly. I had to pay extra to have Steve fly in a carrier in the baggage hold. I didn't like doing that to her, even if she didn't seem to mind overly much. As long as she had her ball or a chew toy with her and a bed to lay on, she appeared content.

I walked out of the airport and saw my mom's familiar red Pontiac Aztec. I had never understood why she'd bought that car, but she loved it and it had served her well over the years. She was excited to see both me and Steve, so after a long hug, we got in the car and headed to cargo to pick Steve up, then we were off to her place which was less than fifteen minutes away.

My mom still looked good for being close to eighty years old. She was still spry and other than some arthritis in her knee that acted up when she spent too much time on her feet, she got around well.

We arrived at my mom's and pulled into the garage. I hadn't grown up in this house. I had grown up on a ranch near a small town about twenty miles outside of Colorado Springs. It was less of a town, really, than it was a blip on a map. Or, it used to be – I had heard it had grown in the intervening years. I hadn't been out there since I was a kid. When I ran off to join the Marine Corps and my sister graduated from high school, my dad and mom sold the ranch and bought a house in town. My mom had now been living there over 35 years. Even having not grown up in this house, it still had the feel of home to it.

We entered the family room through the door to the garage and Steve immediately went to say hi to my mom's two cats, Logan and Belle. Logan freaked out and ran upstairs, but Belle was curious enough to pause and sniff Steve before deciding the dog wasn't worth the effort and moved on to curl herself around my mom's feet.

I put my backpack down by the recliner that had been my dad's and thanked my mom for letting Raymond and I stay there until we had a direction to go in. She didn't ask exactly what we were doing. Years of me being in the military and times when I couldn't talk about a mission and where I was going or what I was doing had taught her not to pry too hard, but she knew enough to gather we'd be in and out within a few days. She walked up the stairs to the kitchen, opened the fridge and brought out two beers, a Michelob Ultra for herself and a Corona for me, popped off the tops and walked out to the backyard patio. I took the proffered beer and followed her out, having a seat on the bench she had out back.

"How are you doing, son?"

I didn't put on a show for my mom. She knew me too well. "I've been better, but this little job for Bob has been a nicer distraction than I thought it would be."

Mom nodded her head and reached an arm around me to give me a tight hug. "Sorry she's gone, but if you ever disappear again without calling for a month, I'll wring your neck." That was all she had to say on the matter.

We sat out on the back patio for the next hour and talked about a variety of things. How her health was, how my sister, her husband, and my nieces and nephew were doing. I inquired about my Aunt Georgia. She was my dad's sister and my favorite aunt, primarily because I had grown up with her and her kids always being around. I remembered my cousin Vickie taking me on my first Jeep ride when we all lived up in Kremmling, Colorado, and her brother Mike teaching me how to hit a baseball when I failed to make the high school baseball team. Mom said Aunt Georgia would be joining us for dinner.

After an hour, mom and I went back inside, our beers empty. Mom started preparing dinner and I grabbed the keys to her car and went to the airport to pick up Ray. He was just coming out of the terminal when I pulled up. Like me, he packed light – a backpack and a duffle bag his only two pieces of luggage. I got out to shake his hand and help him load the two bags into the back seat of the vehicle and then we were on our way.

Ray looked almost exactly the same as the last time I had seen him. About my height, a little overweight, his black hair was longer but not long enough to pull back into his customary ponytail. His arms were tattooed with tribal lines that stood out even against his swarthy skin.

As soon as we sat down in the vehicle, he looked over at me. "Well, you look like shit," he said, referring to my scruffy appearance. Bob and my mom had been too polite to comment.

I gave him a "fuck you" look which only made him laugh.

We arrived at mom's house within fifteen minutes. My mom gave him a hug and told him what room he'd be sleeping in so he could put his bags away. She gave me a stare that said I should do the same. I grabbed my backpack from beside my dad's chair and took it upstairs.

Dan arrived twenty minutes later, followed shortly by my aunt. We grabbed chairs from one of the spare bedrooms and then all sat around the dinner table. The steak looked fantastic, as did the mashed potatoes and green beans. I grabbed two Ultra Lights for my mom and my aunt and Coronas for everyone else except Dan. He had an allergy to the hops in beer so I fished out a small, single serving of Sutter Home wine that my mom had in the fridge and I poured that into a glass for him.

The chicken fried steak was every bit as good as I had remembered it. I had my mom's recipe but no matter how I tried, it never quite came out as good as hers. After dinner, Ray, Dan and I cleaned up and did the dishes then we grabbed our jackets and went out on the back patio to sip whiskey and smoke some cigars Dan had brought with him. We were out there until after midnight and by the time I hit the rack, I was pleasantly buzzed and slept well.

CHAPTER SEVEN

Tuesday turned out to be a quiet day. Ray and I helped my mom with some things around the house that she couldn't do for herself, including changing light bulbs in the ceiling fan in the living room and setting up the swamp cooler in her bedroom before the weather turned hot for the summer. I did a load of laundry in between chores and later that evening, we took mom out to dinner at a local Mexican restaurant.

Wednesday morning started out slow as well. Dan called around 9:00 a.m., though, and told me that he had isolated the seller's IP address and was running a search for locations where it had pinged off a wi-fi network. He said it would take anywhere from a few hours to a few days to complete the search.

He had also run all the employees in Bob's company against any who had called in sick or been on vacation during the time frame the seller was supposed to meet Bob in Victoria – made possible by the electronic payroll system Bob's company used. He came up with a list of half a dozen names. I had him forward those to Julie so she could provide whatever personal information their HR department was willing to give up. It was ultimately for Bob, so I'm sure they'd give up everything. Not sure of the legality of obtaining that information, but Bob also had a team of lawyers whose job it was to shield him from such liability.

Around 10:00, I received a call from Stephanie, the young nurse I'd met at the hospital in. Susan had given her my number and asked her to call me and let me know that Bob was going into surgery. Nothing too major; they thought maybe the break had damaged one of the arteries in his leg and that it was bleeding internally and causing additional swelling. I wasn't sure why Susan couldn't have called me herself to tell me that, but I detected her machinations in this, particularly when Stephanie asked me if she could save my number and call me back when Bob was out of surgery. She made a point of saying that she had called me from her personal cell and if I had any questions or just needed to talk, to feel free and call her. I agreed and once I hung up, saved her number as well. With that beautiful smile and blue eyes, it wasn't like I hadn't thought of her a time or two in past few days since we first met.

I pushed the thoughts from my mind. Cat had been dead for a little more than a month and I felt guilty for having such thoughts.

Julie emailed me the information from the personnel files around 11:00 a.m. They didn't contain anything useful that I could see. Two of the employees who had called in sick during that time had returned the next day. One was on vacation in Hawaii and another in Europe, both with family and both were actively posting to social media. Ray had a trick he could do to check the geolocation of the photos posted which confirmed they were exactly where they said they were.

Of the remaining two, one had allegedly had minor surgery and was out recovering. I used the home phone number listed in the personnel file to call and verify she was at home. Her daughter, maybe four or five years old, answered and one thing I've found is that kids that age are terrible liars. She said her mommy was sick and would be a minute getting to the phone. Once the employee was on the phone, I pretended to be a telemarketer and she hung up.

The last person had resigned to take a position with a rival company. A written report in her file indicated that they thought she had been engaged in corporate espionage, but Josue and his team had been unable to confirm it. Among the circumstantial evidence was the fact that she was driving a new BMW, had moved to a larger and more expensive apartment, and had upgraded her wardrobe. Not the spending habits of someone desperate for money. Plus, the $5k the seller was asking for the book wouldn't go very far with those expenses.

After a lunch of sandwiches, Ray and I were cleaning up branches from the trees in my mom's backyard when Dan called again. He had tracked the location where the first email had been sent. It was from a Red Roof Inn in Raleigh, North Carolina. Even better, that same computer had sent a series of emails to a Brenda Hendrix, who happened to be a junior member of the finance department for Hansen Investments, Bob's home office. We had our connection and I booked us a flight to New York for the next day, including airfare for Steve.

Stephanie called in the afternoon as well to tell me that Bob's surgery had gone smoothly and that they had located and repaired the arterial bleed. The conversation slowly turned to more personal matters and she expressed her condolences about Cat. I was sure that Susan had let that little bit of information leak out. I did find out that she was 33 years old and had gone to school at Alabama and then obtained her nursing degree from Dominican in San Raphael, California, not fifteen minutes from where I lived. She had grown up in Santa Cruz and then took the job in Canada after breaking up with her long-time boyfriend. I guess we all need to get away sometimes. We agreed to talk again soon and hung up.

That evening, we took mom out to dinner again; back at her house, we stayed up talking for a bit before making our way to bed. It would be about a seven-hour flight to New York, with a layover in Denver and one in Charlotte. We didn't have to be fully rested as we could sleep on the plane, but I didn't want to be exhausted, either.

CHAPTER EIGHT

My mom dropped us off at the airport at 5:00 a.m. She cried, as she usually did, over me leaving, and made me promise to call or text her as soon as we had arrived in New York. I promised that I would.

We had dropped Steve off at the cargo receiving warehouse for the airline. I had to show her papers proving she had her shots and was in good health for her to get on the plane. Everything went smoothly. Ray and I checked in and got our tickets. We'd be split up on our way to Denver, but after that we had a row to ourselves in first class for the other two legs of the trip. It was quick trip through airport security and then an hour wait for our plane to leave. We were in the air by 7:00 a.m.

The flight was relatively uneventful, landing in New York around 5:00 p.m. – too late to go to Bob's office and meet with Ms. Hendrix, but early enough that Julie was still at her desk. She had arranged a meeting for us tomorrow at 10:00 a.m. She had also made reservations for us at the Waldorf Astoria Hotel and for dinner at Delmonico's, as well as arranged for a limo to pick us up at the hotel and to shuttle us around tonight and tomorrow.

We walked out of the secure area of the airport and among the plethora of other drivers, we were finally able to find our ride. He was a middle-aged gentleman with greying hair holding a sign that said "Dr. J. Grey" on it. Yes, I am a doctor. I have a Doctorate in Education with a focus on educational leadership. It had been a personal goal and not one that I put to any practical use.

I walked up to the gentleman and introduced myself. He offered to take our bags but as both Ray and I were only carrying backpacks and one small carry-on each, we waved him off and told him we were fine. He led us to our limo.

We were able to get Steve and within a few minutes of picking her up, we were on our way to fight through the evening New York traffic. Our driver told us it would be about an hour to go from JFK to the Waldorf at this time of day. Ray and I settled in and I poured us a drink from the limo's bar while Steve curled up next to me for some much-needed petting.

We sipped the bourbon and talked about how we thought the interview should go tomorrow. Ray was the more experienced interrogator. I had watched him interview people from a witness to a street crime to hardened members of the drug cartels and he had a way of building a rapport and sense of trust that managed to get people to open up. We agreed he'd take the lead.

We arrived at the Waldorf Astoria and checked into our rooms. Julie had planned well as they were right next to each other. Once we had dropped off our bags, freshened up a little and I had a chance to give Steve a little walk, we rejoined the limo driver for the half hour drive to Delmonico's. Steve stayed behind, although I had every intention of taking her somewhere tomorrow where she could run off some excess energy.

Ray had never been to New York City before and was taking in the sights. I told him that after dinner we could go to O'Brien's in Times Square. It had been a while since I had been to a good Irish pub and New York had several of them.

While we were on our way to Delmonico's, I received a call from Stephanie. At Susan's request, she had reached out to update me on Bob's medical status. Truthfully, I was happy to hear from her and wished I could have stayed on the phone longer but I felt awkward talking in front of Ray. For his part, he pretended to feign disinterest but failed miserably. We only talked for a few moments but as soon as I hung up, Ray started to pose a question. I put up one finger in a signal for him to hold on a moment and called Susan.

Susan picked up the phone and answered like she didn't know who was calling. "Hello?"

I didn't waste time on any small talk. "What are you doing?"

Susan pretended innocence. "What do you mean, Jerod? I'm not trying to do anything other than take care of Robert."

"You keep having Stephanie call me – calls you could be making yourself. Not that I have minded talking to her, but I'm not in a place, nor do I have the time right now, to pursue a relationship with anyone."

"Oh, come on Jerod. She's beautiful. She's sweet. She liked that dog of yours."

"Steve." Susan wasn't a big fan of dogs, never had been. I was pretty sure there was a childhood tragedy there somewhere, but she hadn't seen fit to share that with me. She just barely tolerated Steve and only because of me.

"Yes, Steve. And once I arrived here, she started asking questions about you. She's interested. Why aren't you?"

I sighed. "It's complicated, Susan. It hasn't been that long since Cat passed. I'm not sure I'm ready."

"What's complicated about it, Jerod? She likes you, you like her. That's a good place to start."

I gave up. "Fine. I'll ask her out after I've completed this job for Robert. But you'll pay for the flight to Victoria, the dinner, and my hotel for the time I'm there, and in the interim, you'll stop playing matchmaker."

"Deal." Damn, I hadn't expected her to agree so readily. She obviously liked Stephanie, too.

"Deal." I hung up the phone before I talked myself into anything else.

"Well, that was interesting," Ray said.

I shot him a dirty look. "Don't ask." Ray raised his hands in surrender.

We arrived at Delmonico's and were seated within a few minutes. We ordered cocktails and then dinner and spent the evening catching up. It was pleasant to be out with a friend and having a good time. After dinner, we went to Times Square. Even at this time of night, the place was a beehive of activity. People thought Las Vegas was always active and it was, but it was a different kind of activity from NYC. You could have taken a scene from this evening, added daylight, and it otherwise wouldn't have changed. People coming to and from work, people out on the town enjoying the sights, party-goers eager for a good time. It seemed like this 24 hours a day.

We eventually ended up at O'Brien's, sampling a variety of Irish whiskies before we headed back to our hotel rooms to catch some needed sleep before our interview with Brenda Hendrix tomorrow.

CHAPTER NINE

I was up early and took Steve out for a long walk and found a park where she could run. I tossed the ball for her for nearly an hour before my arm grew too tired to continue and we headed back to the room. After a quick shower and a couple of cups of coffee to shake loose the cobwebs left over from last night's excesses, I met Ray down in the hotel lobby at 8:30. The limo was already waiting for us.

We arrived at Bob's office building in the financial district with plenty of time to get set up for the interview. We'd be using one of the smaller conference rooms a few floors below the executive suites. I grabbed some more coffee and told Ray that after the interview, we could catch some lunch or a late breakfast in the executive dining room. The chef there was superb.

Brenda was escorted into the conference room at exactly 10:00 a.m. She was tall, about 5'10" with heels on, slender, with long, dark hair and dark brown eyes. She looked anxious; I offered her some water, tea, or coffee, and she opted for water.

"Sorry if we made you nervous, Ms. Hendrix. You aren't in any trouble," I explained, after handing her a glass of water and making introductions.

"I wasn't sure." She had a soft voice and I saw Ray lean forward to catch what she had said.

"I can assure you that you aren't," Ray said. "Let me get right to the point. Mr. Grey and I work directly for Mr. Hansen. A few weeks ago, Mr. Hansen was contacted by a gentleman regarding the purchase of a book he claimed had come out of Iraq. Mr. Hansen is still interested in obtaining that book but we have lost contact with the gentleman. In our attempt to locate who he is, we discovered that he had sent you a few emails prior to reaching out to Mr. Hansen. We were hoping you could tell us more about this gentleman."

Brenda sighed and her shoulders slumped. "He's my brother."

Ray continued, and over the course of the next thirty minutes, we figured out that Brenda's brother was William Hendrix, better known as Bill. He had served four years in the Army and had done a tour in Iraq. We presumed that it was during that time he had come to be in possession of the tome. Taking antiquities from Iraq was a big no-no, though. The military hadn't done enough early in the war to crack down on antiquity theft, but when enough complaints had been lodged against military members, they had begun to come down hard on anyone taking home "souvenirs" that weren't bought legitimately. People were going to prison over this type of activity.

Bill had been out of the Army now for several years and according to his sister, he had recently fallen on hard times. He had needed money and mentioned the book in one of their infrequent phone calls. She had recalled rumors around the office that Bob consider himself a curator and had given her brother his email address to contact him about selling the book. She hadn't expected the cloak and dagger part of the equation, believing he had come in possession of the book legitimately.

We inquired why Victoria, and Brenda explained that her grandfather on her mother's side was Canadian and she and her brother used to go visit him every summer when they were kids. Her grandfather had lived in a little cabin near River Jordan. When her grandfather had passed away, the land had gone to the national forest service.

"When was the last time you heard from Bill?" Ray asked.

"Oh, it's been a few weeks. He contacted me to tell me he was visiting his girl in Raleigh and I haven't heard from him since. Not that unusual, though. He may call me only once every month or so."

Ray got what information he could regarding the girlfriend. Brenda didn't know much but she did have a name: Samantha McElroy. It was a place to start. She also gave us Bill's cell phone number and the last address she had for him which was also in Raleigh.

We wrote down every bit of information she was willing to provide and managed to get her to text us the most recent picture she had of her brother. He looked younger than his 28 years with short sandy brown hair and brown eyes like his sister's. He was a little scruffy in the picture, having not shaved in about a week, but was smiling as he snapped the photo, cheek to cheek with a young lady we assumed was Samantha.

When we were done, we thanked Brenda for her time and she left the conference room. As soon as she was gone, Ray kicked his chair back from the table and brought his hands up to his face. "It makes no fucking sense, Jerod. This boy is in Raleigh, North Carolina, and then travels all the way across the US and into Canada to trade a book for cash? Why the fuck wouldn't he just fly to New York, meet with Robert in a restaurant and do the deed there? Simpler, and there is just as much in the way anonymity in a city like this as there would be at a remote rendezvous location in the wilds of British Columbia."

I had to agree with him. It seemed to be over the top. Bob had felt similarly when I had pressed him about whether he had considered this whole mess to be a set-up for a robbery, feeling it was a bit elaborate for a robbery attempt. Something to consider, though: Bill was familiar with the drop location, having spent his summers there with his grandfather. Perhaps he had some misguided concept about Canadian extradition laws and felt that if he got caught with a stolen antiquity in Canada, the punishment wouldn't be as harsh. That might have some legitimacy to it. The military wasn't known for coddling prisoners. He would do hard time in a military prison if he were caught stateside and it could be shown he had acquired the tome illegally during his military service.

"Maybe he read too many spy novels as a kid, Ray. I don't know." I pushed my chair back as well and leaned back. "You're right, it doesn't make sense. This kid gets out of the Army, presumably with the tome in hand. A few years later, he gets hard up for cash, decides to sell. If he is hard up for money, it's quite a bit more expensive to travel from

North Carolina to British Columbia then to travel to New York City, or better yet, you're broke and have a wealthy buyer willing to pay hard cash for your merchandise, have him come to you. That's prudent."

"Maybe Raleigh is too hot for him," Ray mused. "Brenda doesn't have solid contact with her brother but she gets the impression he walks the line between being on the right or wrong side of the law much of the time. Maybe he finally crossed that line."

It was as good a theory as any, but didn't explain why he failed to choose somewhere closer. Again, Canada seemed as good a place as any to start over, and perhaps that was the intent – get the cash and start over. Too many unanswered questions and us spinning our wheels over the what-ifs was a waste of our time.

"Let's go grab some lunch in the executive dining room." I stood up.

Ray nodded his head and stood up as well. "And from there?"

I shrugged my shoulders a bit. "I say we head to Raleigh. The first email was sent from there and the girlfriend lives, or at least lived, there. His address is there."

Ray nodded his head slightly. "Sounds like a plan."

We took the elevator up to the top and got out on the floor with the executive suites. I stopped by Julie's desk to both say hello in person and to get her to book us a flight to Raleigh as soon as we could comfortably leave. Julie was the epitome of office efficiency. She also looked like a retired model. In her early sixties, she was still beautiful, with her dark blonde hair shot through with streaks of grey, regal features, and a body that would make a twenty-year-old jealous. She was wearing an off-white dress with delicate embroidery work that hugged her form and stopped at about mid-thigh. Her stockings were white and she was wearing two-inch heels that matched the dress. She was married to the same man she had met when she was in her early twenties. They had two kids who were both now married as well, and had kids of their own. Julie said she'd get right on the plane reservations.

The executive dining room was down the hall and to the right from Bob's office. The interior was decorated similarly to any small, trendy café, complete with tables and formally dressed wait staff. We sat down and were immediately greeted by our server. At our request, he brought water and iced tea and by the time they were settled on the table, Ray and I were ready to order. I went with a burger, medium well, with just lettuce, tomatoes, and onions. The server asked if I wanted to add ketchup or mayonnaise but had a slight quirk to his mouth when he did so. I hadn't seen him before, but no doubt someone in the kitchen had told him about my dislike of condiments, given the number of times I had eaten here. I told him no and then leaned back in my chair and shot the middle finger toward the kitchen. I heard chortling. "Please, do me the kindness of telling the chef he's an ass." I smiled politely and the waiter laughed. Ray ordered a chorizo omelet.

We enjoyed the reprieve while we ate our lunch and waited for Julie to make our reservations. We'd have to swing by the hotel and get our bags and Steve but I was hoping to get out this afternoon. We were on a trail now and I felt the need to push forward. Ray would be equally ready to keep going. It was the thrill of the chase. Old habits die hard.

Julie called by the time we were done eating. We had a 3:15 flight out of JFK to Raleigh, putting us in about 7:00 p.m. She had also rented us an SUV that we could pick up when we landed. The hotel was on us. She didn't want to rent rooms at a location that was on the opposite side of town from where our trail led us. Couldn't disagree with that.

The limo took us back to the Waldorf Astoria where we picked up our backpacks and Steve and checked out. We arrived at JFK by 1:45 and checked in to get our tickets, once again having to show the paperwork for Steve to fly. It was a bit of an inconvenience to have do it every time, but it was worth having Steve with me.

On our way to the airport, I called Dan and gave him the name of Bill Hendrix's girlfriend to see what he could dig up on her. He was able to find a last known address and a possible phone number. We would try the address first.

Getting through security took a bit; by the time we were through, our plane was boarding. We were flying first class again. I'd appreciate the leg room and the free cocktails. The flight attendant brought me a whiskey, neat, and Ray a beer. We sipped in companionable silence and settled in for the plane ride to North Carolina.

CHAPTER TEN

We arrived in Raleigh a little before 7:00 p.m. we walked off the plane with our bags in hand. It took about an hour before we had our SUV, a Jeep Grand Cherokee, and another thirty minutes before we had Steve and were headed away from the airport. Steve was riding in the back seat and our bags were in the rear cargo area. Ray was driving. I pulled up the address we had for Samantha McElroy on my cell phone and we started heading east on I-40 to I-440, following the directions provided by the map program on my phone.

We pulled up to the address at a little before 9:00. It was in a trailer park. The trailer itself was small, maybe a one-bedroom. A short flight of wooden stairs led to the only door facing the road. There was a light on inside. I stayed and watched the door and Ray took a walk around the exterior of the trailer and when he returned a second later, he indicated there was another door on the backside that he would cover. I nodded my agreement and then walked up the short flight of stairs, stopping on the second from the top so I wasn't right in front of the door when I knocked.

I tried to make my knock sound friendly, but it was quiet outside so it sounded louder to my ears than I had wanted. I heard a female voice call in from inside, "Who is it?" She sounded apprehensive but then again, I would as well if someone were knocking at my door at this time of night.

"Jerod Grey, ma'am. I'm looking for Bill Hendrix or Samantha McElroy." I heard the same voice curse and then a door open followed by Ray yelling that he had a runner. Ray had never been the fastest person in the world. I bounced off the stairs and ran around to the back side of the trailer in time to see Ray tackle a slight figure to the ground. In the dark, I couldn't have told you if it was female or male, but in my head, it was a female.

I caught up to the two of them as they wrestled on the ground. Ray was not having the easiest time controlling what did turn out to be a girl. She couldn't have weighed more than 110 pounds soaking wet; she was skinny as a rail with stringy red hair that seemed to be going in six directions at once.

"Calm down. We aren't here to hurt you," Ray was saying over and over. The girl responded by screaming. Crap.

I looked around a saw a few lights come on and a window curtain be pulled aside, but no one seemed to be taking an active interest. It was one of those kinds of neighborhoods where people kept to themselves so they weren't labeled a snitch. I had hated them as a cop. Now, it was working in my favor.

I knelt next to where Ray had the girl pinned to the ground. She was still fighting, trying to knee Ray's back. "Look, lady, we don't want to hurt you. I have some questions and I'm willing to pay for your time. How does $100 sound?"

That caught her attention. She stopped struggling. "A hundred bucks just to answer a question?"

"Questions. And yes, $100."

She immediately relaxed. Ray held on to her a moment more and then slowly released her. When she didn't make any attempt to run, I reached out and helped her to her feet. As a show of good faith, I pulled out my wallet and handed her two twenties. "You'll get the rest when we're done."

The girl nodded. "Go ahead then, ask."

She had a slight accent that reminded me of Anna, who had grown up about two hours from here. I needed to call her and apologize for being a jackass for the past month but pushed that thought to the back of my head for another time.

"Are you Samantha McElroy?"

"Who wants to know?" She jutted out her jaw.

"Like I said at the door when I knocked, I'm Jerod Grey. I work for a gentleman who is interested in acquiring a book that Bill had. This is my partner, Ray. Bill had scheduled a place and time to meet with my boss and never showed. We're trying to find out why." I left out the part where Bob had crashed his ATV, broken his leg and had never made it to the drop location.

Her shoulders slumped a little and she lost the defiant posture. "Yeah, I'm Sam. Bill never made it?" I could hear real worry in her voice.

"Would you like to go inside where we can talk at more length?" She nodded and led the way back to her trailer. We sat down in the small living room, Sam on the couch and me on a little chair across from it. Ray remained standing.

I asked the questions and for the most part, Sam responded. She was vague in some areas but told us that Bill had come across the book when he was on a tour in Iraq. His unit had cleared a small group of insurgents from a set of ruins between Basrah and Shu'aiba in southern Iraq.

During the firefight, a hand grenade had opened an entryway to a small chamber. There had been a few articles in there, including a sealed pot with the book inside. Bill had won the book later that week in a dice game and somehow managed to sneak it past Army customs and out of Iraq.

She told me that Bill had a gambling problem and had recently run up quite a debt. She didn't know to who, but some men had been by a few times in the past week looking for him which is why she ran. She thought the men were back, and this time would take it out on her.

Bill had held onto the book as a souvenir of his time in Iraq until recently, when he decided he might be able to sell it to get the money to pay back the gambling debt. That's why Bill had headed to Victoria. He thought he might be able to avoid the men long enough to sell the book and pay them back, and because he was familiar with the area, he figured if the men did show up, he could get away that much easier.

Ray and I listened as the story unfolded, asking clarifying questions as we felt necessary. Specifically, we wanted to know what she knew about the guy Bill owed money to. She just knew that they called him Rex or T-Rex and he operated out of a pool hall near Hillsborough. She'd never been there herself. He had a couple of bruisers named Hank and Roy. Country boys, big and beefy. They had roughed Bill up the last time they caught up to him and threatened to kill him if he didn't come up with the money soon. Rex had a reputation on the streets of making good on his promises, at least when those promises included violence.

When we felt we had learned everything we could, I paid her the other $60 and Ray and I returned to the Jeep. I searched for the nearest hotel on my phone and Ray started driving us toward the Holiday Inn in Midtown. We were both silent for a bit and then Ray said what I had also been thinking. "If we're looking for this kid, there's a good chance they are, too."

"Yes, sir," I replied.

"If they're the bruisers that the girl said, we should probably either bring in some back-up or acquire some guns. I'm more in favor of the guns."

"Yeah, I'll have Josue see what he can do." I picked up my phone and made the call, explaining to Josue what we needed. He said he'd get Riley on it. Riley was what they called a fixer. He solved problems, usually with less than legal methods. Not always, but as a rule fixers were only good guys because they worked for us versus the other guy. I thanked him and hung up as we were pulling into the parking lot at the Holiday Inn.

At the front desk, we were told that they didn't have two rooms, but they did have one with two beds. We took it. It was a Friday night, after all, and it wouldn't be easy to find a room anywhere. All we needed was a place to hole up until we could determine our next move.

Once we were in our room, Ray pulled up a menu in the hotel welcome binder and ordered us pizza from one of the local joints listed. I called Dan to see if he had anything of interest. Dan said that he had been tracing the IP address of the computer used across the country. Bill had apparently been driving. There had been pings at various motel wi-fi networks in Chicago, Minneapolis, and Bismarck, North Dakota – all the way across the country. He was working on locating a site in or around Victoria. That was Bill's destination so it seemed plausible that he might still be there.

Also plausible was that after he had failed to make the exchange with Bob, he had fled that area and headed back toward home, which meant he could be anywhere along the road. This is exactly why I never went into the missing person bureau. I put my hand to my forehead and rubbed for a moment.

"You good?" Ray asked.

"Yeah. Just wondered how you did this all those years. Tracking bad guys and always feeling like you were just a step behind."

Ray laughed. "Except we had a catch rate of 83% while I was a part of the fugitive task force. Eventually we caught up. It just takes patience."

"Mine's in short supply." My stomach grumbled. "Hope that pizza gets here soon. I'm going to take Steve out for a walk. Both of us could stand to stretch our legs."

Steve, hearing her name, stood up with tail wagging. I grabbed her leash but didn't bother to put it on. We walked out of the room and down the hallway to the exit. Steve was happy to be outside and immediately ran to a patch of green grass with a few trees on it. I pulled a plastic bag out of my pocket in case I needed to clean up after her and thought about what Ray and I were doing.

I walked around a corner and stopped as two men stepped out of the shadows. Steve was still playing around near the trees. It wasn't just that it was two men, it was their body language. They carried with them an air of menace. The men were big, both over six feet, and heavy, the smaller of the two topping out at least 250 pounds. They were wearing jeans, work boots, and flannel shirts. Big, beefy, country boys.

"You all must be Hank and Roy," I said, easing my right foot back while keeping my weight evenly distributed.

"Smart man. Where's the boy?" His voice was short and gruff.

"Are you Roy or are you Hank? Not that it really matters, you could be twins. For the sake of argument, I'll call you Red and Green based on the colors of your shirts."

"Smart mouth is more like it. My friend asked you politely, where is the boy? Don't answer, and I won't be so polite when I ask again," said Green.

"Well then, you're going to be disappointed in my response. I don't know where the boy is but was kind of hoping you did. The boy has something my boss wants, and through that transaction, the boy might be able to provide your boss with what he wants. Let's say we work cooperatively?" I still hadn't heard Steve anywhere near me but was hoping she'd come running soon. Dogs tended to intimidate people.

"Rough him up a little bit, Hank. Maybe that will help jog his memory some," said Red, who I now knew was Roy.

Hank started to walk forward, his hands clenched in fists and hanging low to his sides, leaving his head wide open – not that his head was going to be my initial target. Well, not the big head, anyway. I didn't move back but waited patiently until Hank closed the distance. As soon as he was within striking range, I exploded into action. To his credit, Hank reacted quicker than I would have given him credit for, seeing how big and out of shape he looked. Still, it wasn't quick enough to block the full force of the attack, and my sweeping front kick jarred heavily against the inside top of his legs, right in the groin. Hank made a gasping noise as he involuntarily doubled over at the waist.

My next attack came right on the heels of the last, driving three left knee strikes to his head area while simultaneously pulling his head down into the blows. The first hit with a satisfying crunch as his nose shattered. The next two had a wet, meaty sound to them. My last strike was a downward elbow to the brachial plexus in the left shoulder. The force of the blow held my entire body weight and would cause, hopefully, temporary paralysis to the left arm and tingling and a loss of sensation for a while longer.

I spun to my right and pushed Hank in the direction I had last seen Roy. Once again, I had misjudged the skill of my opponent. Hank hadn't had time to fully react, but Roy did. He had already moved wide and was closing the distance on me from my left. That big, beefy hand was flying through the air with a great deal of speed and power.

I managed to get my left arm up to absorb the brunt of the blow but it was still sufficient to knock me hard to the right. I stumbled, trying to catch my balance. Roy didn't give me the chance, using his right foot to push-kick me hard to the ground. I rolled, trying to put some space between me and Roy, and narrowly missed being stomped. As a consolation prize, though, Hank was still down hard and didn't look like he'd be bouncing back up right away. I heard a retching noise from his direction. I had been kicked in the groin before, and knew it had the tendency to cause your dinner to come back up again.

Roy stomped his foot down again and this time, instead of continuing to roll away, I switched directions and rolled into him, trapping his leg with my body. It tripped him up and he fell backwards, sticking out his arm to brace his fall. He was a big guy and had a lot of weight impacting on that wrist. I heard it snap and Roy cried out in pain. I had spent several years studying Judo and Hapkido. One of the very first lessons each art taught was learning how to fall, for specifically that reason. I didn't stop my forward momentum, though, and as Roy hit the ground, I rolled up his body.

When we were chest to chest with me on top, I drove two short, right knees into his rib cage and then followed with two elbow strikes to the left side of his head. They didn't contain a lot of power but were distracting enough for me to swing my right leg over his torso so I was now in a full mount position. I started raining down strikes to his face and head. One caught him on the left cheek, splitting it wide open, while another split his lower lip. Years of hitting punching bags and opponents and my knuckles were hard as rocks.

Roy started to push up and brought his right hand up to push me back, only to find that his broken right wrist made it painful to put any pressure on it. He cried out again but left his arm extended. I quickly grabbed the wrist and squeezed, causing more pain, and then swung my left leg out and around his extended right arm then leaned back, bringing the arm with me so that he was effectively arm barred. I didn't stop there, though; I lifted my hips so it put immense pressure on his right elbow, hyperextending it. For the third time, Roy cried out.

I rolled back and to my feet, shuffling back so there was distance between me and the two guys. Hank was working his way slowly to his feet. I was preparing to launch another attack when I saw a shadow racing low and fast across the ground. Steve to the rescue. Her jaws clicked together and she snapped at Hank's Achilles heel. I didn't think it was enough to tear it but it sure caught his attention as he hopped backwards two or three feet. Steve barked and growled and moved around the man, constantly snapping.

"You need to get your partner and get the fuck out of here before I get angry," I told Hank.

Hank raised his hands in a measure of contrition. "No problem. Just call off the dog." Steve was still harassing him with her quick jumps in and out, and her snapping at his heels was causing him to dance around.

"Steve to me." She immediately laid off her attack and came over to my side. Hank pulled Roy to his feet and the two of them stumbled away and out of view. I remained where I was for a moment until I could catch my breath and heard a car peel off and race away.

Assuring myself they were gone, I knelt and gave Steve a good scratch. "That was fun. Good girl. I think you might deserve a piece of pizza."

Steve and I made our way back to the room. I must have made quite a sight walking into the room like I was. My knuckles were skinned up, I had blood splattered on my pants and my left knee was soaked in it, I had a boot print on my left hip where Roy had kicked me, my shirt was torn from rolling around on the ground and despite my efforts to brush myself off, I was still covered in dirt and gravel.

Ray stopped halfway to putting a piece of pizza in his mouth. "What the hell happened to you? Tumble down the stairs?"

"I had the pleasure of meeting Roy and Hank," I said, more gruffly than I intended.

"The goons from that triceratops guy?" He finished bringing the pizza to his mouth and took a bite.

"T-Rex, and yes, one in the same."

"Well, we're not calling an ambulance so I'm guessing you won the first round." It was said as a statement but Ray included more than a little question in the words.

"Yeah. They won't be bothering us the rest of the night, but I do wonder how they knew we were here to begin with."

"Think we should change locations?" Ray took another bite.

"I'm thinking that would be prudent. I don't think we're in immediate danger. Give me a moment to wash up, change my clothes and eat, and then we can go from there." Ray nodded his agreement.

I grabbed my toiletry bag and headed to the bathroom. As soon as the door shut, I took the plastic bag out of the trashcan and stripped out of my clothes, carefully placing them in the bag. I didn't want blood from my pants all over the bathroom. That would raise suspicion and might earn a call to the police. Once my clothes were in the bag, I cranked on the hot water and jumped in the shower.

I always hated showering right after a fight. You discovered a dozen different minor scrapes and bruises you didn't know you had until the soap and water made them sting. It wasn't painful per se, just annoying. I scrubbed my body down and then rinsed off, cut the water and grabbed a towel to dry myself with. Less than ten minutes later I was changed and eating my first slice of pizza which I shared with Steve.

While we ate, Ray looked up hotel rooms on his phone and both of us speculated as to how Roy and Hank had come to be here at the Holiday Inn. We concluded that they had probably followed us over from Sam's place. It made the most sense. We had no connections to Bill, at least to their knowledge, but if I were trying to track down a person who owed my boss money, I'd stake out his girlfriend's house. They probably thought we had information that could lead them to Bill and had decided to test the waters. It would also fit in with their line of questions from when I ran into them in the parking lot.

Ray found two rooms at another location. It was a low-cost hotel, but it would suffice and if we could get there shortly, we'd probably cut down on the likelihood that Roy and Hank were calling for backup. This was the hotel where Bill had been when he sent the email to

Bob. It took us only a minute to pack our bags – one of the benefits of traveling light – and we were on our way. Housekeeping would open the door tomorrow to find the room empty and wouldn't think anything of it, assuming we had simply stayed the one night we paid for and moved on.

Getting over to the new hotel we employed a couple of tail countermeasures: sudden, unannounced turns, as well as a detour through a shopping center where Ray stopped at an all-night convenience store so I could pick up some laundry detergent. By the time we exited the back lot of the shopping center, we were pretty sure we weren't being followed.

We checked in at the front desk and headed up to our rooms. Unfortunately, we couldn't get side by side rooms. We gave false names, paid for the rooms in cash and threw in an extra $100 for the clerk to not ask too many questions. The guy probably made only slightly more than minimum wage so he was happy to take our money. Not having the rooms side by side wasn't ideal for security purposes, but we were feeling confident we could sleep through the night without any problems.

Before bed, I threw my clothes in the wash. I had bought some Shout to help with the blood stains. I wasn't overly concerned. I had a dozen more pair of pants at home. Unfortunately, I only had brought two pairs with me. If they were stained, I'd have to buy another pair along the way somewhere.

As I waited on my clothes, I thought about our next move. Dan hadn't come up with any leads on Bill around Victoria yet. Our best bet would be to return there and start pounding the pavement to see if we could find out where Bill had laid his head while he was there. It was always possible that he had a childhood friend in the area, too. We had his cell phone, but Dan had yet to see it ping off any of the cell towers. Smart kid, he was keeping it off. I'd do the same in his shoes if I had thugs like Hank and Roy looking for me, but it was making my job of tracking him down harder. Granted, that was the point, at least from his perspective, but I was one of the good guys. Bill should be more accommodating than that.

I finally decided that we needed more support, not necessarily with the field work but on the home front. I needed a tactical operations center (TOC) set up that could track Ray's and my movements, as well as someone we could check in and out with. This evening's confrontation could have just as easily gone against me and no one knew where we were, nor did we have any protocols in place in the event we didn't check in. A TOC could handle all that for us plus shoulder some of the logistics load, make plane reservations, track down hotel rooms, or whatever other resources we needed.

I called Dan and found that he was still awake, forgetting for a minute that he was two hours behind me time-wise. I told him what I needed. I had a warehouse there in Colorado Springs that could provide the workspace. I had purchased it a few years ago in the event I needed a place to store my personal belongings if I ever moved back home. It wasn't a huge space but it had a shower and small kitchen area on the second floor, along with a room large enough to hold a few bunk beds, a couch, and a TV if one was needed. The bottom floor was wide open, and one could set up a TOC complete with whiteboards, computers, and whatever else one thought necessary. Electricity and water were already available, but Dan would have to get some internet in there. I told him that mom had a set of keys to unlock the place.

Dan copied down everything that he would need and said he could probably get it set up by tomorrow afternoon, except for the internet capabilities. For that, he'd use a hotspot until an internet service provider could run the lines. It would be maybe two days before the TOC was fully operational. To provide extra personnel, I gave him the numbers to James Nickle and Zachery North. James and Zack were both techy kind of guys and could probably lend Dan a hand in setting everything up and then manning it after. I needed Dan to continue to work his magic in the shadowy world of hacking.

I hung up with Dan and checked my clothes in the dryer. They were done and the stain had come out for the most part, leaving the pants completely wearable. I folded them quickly and returned to my room where I called Ray and told him what I had done. Ray said he had been thinking we needed to expand our operation as well.

Tomorrow I would have to call Julie and tell her I needed two more contracts; after that, I would need to call Josue. I needed two things from him. First, I needed the fixer to be in Colorado with the rest of the group and only Josue could authorize that. I also needed him to do some legwork on the pool hall where T-Rex had set up shop. I wanted to know everything I could about the hall and the man who ran his business out of there.

By midnight, I was exhausted. A long flight to North Carolina, the fight, etc. – it all added up to wear and tear on the old body. I laid down in the lumpy bed and it was only a few minutes before I was out.

CHAPTER ELEVEN

My internal alarm clock went off just prior to 5:00 a.m. There was no coffee maker in the room so I grabbed Steve and we went out for a walk and to locate a cup. If I remembered correctly, the motel did little breakfast bags and usually had free coffee in the lobby. Day one and I was already violating the security protocols that Ray and I had discussed last night on the ride over – primarily that neither of us goes anywhere without the other. I had asked if that included walking Steve and was promptly told that it was walking Steve that had exposed me last night. It was hard to argue with that when my knuckles were still red and scraped up and my left arm was bruising from shoulder to elbow where I had absorbed Roy's blow. But it was 5:00 a.m., and now that I was awake, Steve's bladder wouldn't hold out for another hour until Ray was supposed to be up.

I stayed alert as I walked from my room to the lobby, checking corners before I walked around them and pausing in doorways to ensure the coast was clear. I was careful, thinking of how much grief I would get if Ray found out I had left the room without him going along. Imagine my surprise when I walked into the lobby and found Ray stuffing his face with a muffin and drinking a cup of coffee. He hadn't seen me come in; he was too busy watching the TV on the wall.

I cleared my throat. "Well, this would explain why you weren't in your room."

My voice was loud enough that it scared both him and the clerk. He coughed for a moment while he tried to clear the muffin from his throat. "Shit. I couldn't sleep. Figured I could stand watch here and that way if bad guys came in looking for us, old Mack over there could call you while I subdued them." He tried a smile.

"Mmmhmm. Good thing I decided to get coffee before I walked Steve. Now you can come along with me." I poured myself a cup from the pot, black. I used to like sugar and cream in my coffee and then one day, decided I didn't need that froufrou stuff anymore and started drinking it without. Now it was hard for me to have anything in my coffee, which explained why I seldom went to one of the big, franchise coffee shops. Why pay almost four dollars for a cup of coffee when I could get a cup at the corner market for half that?

Ray got up from the couch and refreshed his cup before we left together to walk Steve. "Good thing we talked about security protocols last night, eh?"

Ray blushed. "Look bro, I was just …"

I laughed at how flustered he looked. "I'm just fucking with you, brother. I had left my room and headed straight to the lobby. I was as surprised to see you as you were to see me. I couldn't help taking advantage of the situation a little, though."

A short laugh was Ray's only response.

Ray told me that he had talked to Mack, the clerk on duty at the front desk right now. He had been allowed to go through the guest register for the date that Bill had sent the email. There was not a William or Bill Hendrix listed. The kid had probably used a false name. Ray had showed him the picture we had of Bill, but it didn't jog any memories. It was worth a shot but ultimately it was also a dead end.

We finished walking Steve around the lot and agreed to meet back up at 6:30 to go get some real breakfast. No one else was going to be up yet. Josue didn't get into the office until 7:30 and Julie didn't usually show up until 8:00. For Dan, it was just after 3:00 a.m. I could call him, but he wouldn't be happy about it.

I took a quick shower and then gave Steve a fast bath. I didn't like to use people shampoo on her because it tended to dry out her skin, but we had been traveling for nigh on a week now and I didn't want her to get too ripe. After the shampoo job, I put some conditioner on her coat in the hope that if the shampoo did dry her skin out, the conditioner would help alleviate that. Plus, she'd be super soft which I would appreciate in those moments she decided she needed some dad time and would crawl up into my lap.

Packed up and checked out, Ray and I met back up at the Jeep at exactly 6:30 a.m. I used my phone and found a little mom-&-pop diner a few miles away and we headed over to get some chow. I paid attention to the vehicles behind us, but didn't see a tail. We made it to the diner without incident. Cracking the windows on the Jeep so Steve would be comfortable, Ray and I went inside.

The place wasn't too crowded this early on a Saturday morning and we found a booth where we could each keep an eye on one of the two entrances to the place. The diner looked like it was straight out of the 1950's, with black and white checkered floors, red and white booths and seats, and tables with stainless steel trim. We even had a little jukebox in our booth.

By the time that we finished breakfast and paid our bill, it was late enough I could start making a few phone calls. I dialed Josue's cell number and he picked up right away. I explained that I would like the fixer to go to Colorado Springs and meet up with Dan, James, and Zack. I thought if we had an irregular problem that required an immediate solution, he would best serve us by being at the TOC when it was set up. It would give Ray and me a one-stop shopping place for all our excursion needs. Josue agreed and said he'd have him on the first available flight today. I thanked him and give him the address to the warehouse and Dan's phone number, just in case.

I also told him I needed to have someone dig up all the information they could on T-Rex and the pool hall. I figured this would be a job right up the alley of a private investigator, and Bob's company kept several on retainer. I told him when he heard anything, to route it through the Tactical Operations Center. We'd get the information from them when we could. As we didn't yet have the TOC set up, that meant he'd have to call Dan. Poor Dan was going to be busy until the TOC was up and running fully.

When I was done talking with Josue, I called Julie and asked her to put James Nickle and Zachery North on the payroll and to route the contracts through, once again, Dan. He would tell her if both guys agreed to join in on this little adventure and if not, he would provide her the name of an alternative. All members of the Adventurers' Club had a list of other members and their skill sets.

There were only about thirty people in the Club but our range of skills was impressive. From Ray with his ability to track and find people to my friend Karl Williams who had been a corpsman for the Coast Guard and was now a Physician's Assistant. We had computer types like Dan, and communications specialists like James and Zach. But on top of their primary skills, everyone had secondary skills as well. For James, he was a certified dive instructor, and Zach raced cars. Karl was an avid hiker, mountain climber, and outdoor enthusiast while Ray was skilled in hand-to-hand combat and was an expert marksman. It gave us a well-rounded group of people to choose from, depending on the type of mission we were on.

With Julie and Josue called, it was time for Ray and me to plan what we were going to do next. We still didn't have a lead and I didn't expect to get one from Dan today. Our best bet would be to fly back to Colorado Springs and help with the TOC set up until something came in. Once again, we'd be centrally located.

I called the airline and booked us a flight out at 10:00 a.m. It was already after 8:00, so we headed for the airport. Another set of tickets, another security checkpoint, two more layovers, and we were touching down in Colorado Springs by noon. The time difference worked in our favor going back the other way.

We rented another Jeep Grand Cherokee, loaded our bags and Steve in, and headed to the warehouse located in the north part of Colorado Springs. We pulled up thirty minutes later and walked through the side door and into a beehive of activity. Dan had tables set up, and computers in various stages of assembly littered them. Zach was already there and was currently connecting cables to various pieces of communications gear. I could hear activity upstairs as well but had no idea who might be up there.

I greeted Dan, and he peeled away from connecting one of the computers long enough to say hi back. He gave me a brief update on what was going on so far.

"Zack has placed a satellite antenna on the top of the roof and is rigging the communications gear through that. I don't pretend to know all the details of what he's doing, but he's saying we should have satellite communications via the handhelds within the next few hours. I'm rigging three computer terminals that we can use. I already have a hotspot set up but it won't have enough bandwidth to run all the wi-fi devices we have. I called a friend of mine from the local internet provider. He's going to hook us up on the side." He saw the look on my face and made a calming motion with his hands.

"No, no, no. I'm not bootlegging internet service. It will all be legit as far as the company goes. Just the install will be done after hours. Quickest way we could get it done."

I nodded. "Fair enough. What's going on upstairs?"

"I put mom in charge of decorating the upstairs. If we're going to be here for days on end, I wanted to make it comfy." Dan smiled.

"My mom?" He nodded.

I walked up the wide, wooden staircase that led to the top floor. My mom was up there directing workers in the assembly of three sets of bunk beds. A couch and several chairs had already been assembled and set up in a way to create a somewhat separate space for a living room. The kitchen still looked the same but they had added a small dinette table with four chairs around it.

"Hi, mom."

My mom spun around, still spry for an older lady. "Hey, hon. What do you think?"

I nodded my head. "Looks good. Going to be a proper HQ by the time you're done." I laughed.

My mom had the upstairs well in hand and it wouldn't be long before it was a more than adequate living space. Bob wasn't going to like the bill for this one, but then again, even given what was being spent, it was barely even a blip on the radar screen of the money his company brought in every day. By comparison, it was like me spending a penny.

I returned downstairs and had Dan and Zach move the computers and communications equipment from the middle of the warehouse and over to one side where they were out of the way. This opened the space up and allowed for us to bring our vehicles inside. We could park three of them in the warehouse which cleared out the street a little and didn't attract as much attention.

Once the computers and communications equipment were moved over, I busied myself helping Zach out with the antenna array cables and set up. I was familiar with the gear we were using. When I had served in the Navy, I had been attached to the small boat squadrons under the Naval Expeditionary Combat Command. I had qualified up to patrol leader before I picked up my anchor and made Chief Petty Officer. From there, I was transferred over to the Headquarters Platoon and became a tactical watch officer – a fancy way of saying I talked on radios, or at least supervised the people who did. Headquarters Platoon was responsible for setting up and maintaining the communications array used by the boat units and land side security teams. I knew enough to get something set up but for all that knowledge, I quickly figured out that Zach was operating on a level far above mine and my willingness to help was just interfering with his plans.

I left the rest of the set up to Zach and went over to where Dan was working on the computer set-up. "I'm good. Don't need your help." He didn't even bother to look up from the keyboard and screen.

"You sure?" I asked.

"Oh yeah," he laughed. "I'm fine. You're getting restless and when you get restless, you tend to fiddle around in areas you aren't needed. Go upstairs, join Ray, talk to your mom. There are beers in the fridge and mom made some beef stew that you can heat up. If beer isn't enough, I'm sure if you poke around in the kitchen, you'll find a few bottles of something else."

I went upstairs and found my mom and Ray sitting and talking at the little kitchen table. Steve was curled up asleep on a rug in front of the kitchen sink. Ray was telling my mom about his kids and what they had been up to since she saw them last.

My mom said there was stew in the fridge and told me to fix myself a bowl. I opened the cabinet doors until I found the bowls, and then rifled through some drawers to find a serving spoon and a spoon to eat with. The cabinets had been fully stocked with pots, pans, and dishes. My mom had been very busy today. The workers were still finishing the bunk bed assembly but looked like they would be done within the next hour.

I spooned some stew into my bowl and threw the bowl in the microwave. When it was sufficiently heated up I grabbed a beer out of the refrigerator and sat down with Ray and my mom. We talked about inconsequential things while I ate. I went to get a second bowl and asked Ray and my mom if they wanted any. Both had already eaten.

By the time I had finished my second bowl of stew and my beer, my mom was signing the paperwork for the bunk bed assembly and the workers were packing up their tools and getting ready to go. Ray and I got up and helped my mom put sheets, pillows, and blankets on each of the bunks.

"We'll need to get a washer and dryer for here. I bought three extra pairs of sheets and some extra pillows and blankets in case someone needs them, but it will be better if we could just wash what we have here and then stow them away again until someone needs a fresh set," my mom stated.

"I don't think we have the hook ups for a washer and dryer here, mom, but we can eventually look at getting a plumber and electrician in to set it up. If we use the warehouse in the winter, we're also going to need to get this place insulated and some heating and AC going. These metal walls will become like an oven once summer sets in." My mom nodded and then grabbed a pen and paper from the kitchen counter and made a few notes. I think she was enjoying feeling useful.

"Jerod! You have a minute?" It was Dan, yelling up the stairs.

"Coming."

I walked down the stairs and saw that in the hour or so I had been eating and helping my mom, James Nickle and the fixer, Riley White, had both arrived. I greeted each in turn, shaking their hands.

Riley was a small guy, standing only about 5'5" with a thin build. He had an unruly mop of slightly curly, light brown hair, brown eyes, and looked like he hadn't shaved in a few days. Not that I could say anything as I involuntarily ran my hand over my untrimmed beard. He was wearing a khaki long-sleeve shirt and Dockers with what looked like trail shoes. As soon as we shook hands he said, "I have something to show you, Mr. Grey."

He took me over to a pelican case sitting on the tailgate of Dan's truck; the truck, our rented Jeep and my mom's bright red Pontiac Aztec had all been moved inside the warehouse. Undoing the latches, he raised the lid to reveal a small arsenal of firearms, each tucked neatly into its foam-padded cut-out inside the case. There was a short-barreled AR-15 that I was pretty sure wasn't legal in most states and could only be purchased if you were registered with the ATF. There was also an H&K MP-5, a short-barreled Remington 870 12-gauge shotgun, two GLOCKs, and two five shot Ruger LCR Model 5450 .357 caliber revolvers. He pointed to another case and said it held ammunition and extra magazines.

Ray looked at me. I knew what he was thinking. He was retired ATF and knew as well as I did that the rifle, at least, wasn't legal outside of maybe Nevada, or being a law enforcement officer. The shotgun, I was sure, was fine, as were the rest of the weapons. I shook my head almost imperceptibly. Riley had come here at our request and Ray and I had already discussed that a fixer tended to operate on the fringes of the law. We were retired law enforcement now, and even though that drive to do the right thing was always going to be there, Riley wasn't some gangbanger out for a revenge drive-by shooting. He was working for us. We needed weapons and he brought weapons.

I picked up one of the revolvers, opened the cylinder and gave it a cursory spin to check out how smooth it was. The weapon was clean and functional. It was also compact and had enough power in the round to make it an effective self-defense tool, which is all we really needed. Riley reached into a tan backpack, rifled around for a minute, and then brought out an inside-the-pants holster for the revolver. From the other case, he handed me five .357 rounds, and two speed loaders. I was old enough to remember how to use them. When I first joined the PD in the late 80's, my department-issued weapon was a Smith and Wesson 686 .357 revolver.

Ray picked up a GLOCK Model 19, compact 9mm. It was a bit larger than the revolver but held three times the rounds. Riley handed him three full magazines for the pistol as well as another inside-the-pants holster. I thanked him and added a gun safe to my mental list of things we needed. For now, the pelican cases would have to do. We'd also need smaller cases, as well as a hard-side suitcase to take the weapons with us on any commercial flight. I gave Riley specs for what I wanted. I also asked him to reach out to Josue to see how they had gotten weapons into Canada, just in case we had to return there.

Dan had wandered back over to his computers so Ray and I walked over to see if he had any updates. He didn't. His programs were still running, waiting to get a hit from the cell phone company or a wi-fi network. It seemed unusual that Bill hadn't at least reached out to his girlfriend to let her know that he was ok.

Ray looked thoughtful for a moment. "Hey, can you pull up the cell phone records for Samantha McElroy? Particularly interested in any calls from a number that has only cropped up in the last week or so. Maybe Bill got himself a burner phone."

"Good idea," Dan replied, and immediately started typing away at his keyboard. With just the hotspot, though, the program was running slow and the progress bar took an unusually long time to fill up. Dan said he'd let me know if he got anything.

With a lull in the action, I took the opportunity to take Steve for a walk and a little play time. She had been great over the last few days with various flights and stays at hotels. No doubt she was missing her time at home and chasing squirrels. Ray tagged along as backup. I didn't think it likely that Rex could have tracked us here but then again, we were breaking laws left and right to get a handle on where Bill was. No reason to believe Rex wasn't doing the same, although I'm sure he didn't have a Dan working on his side. Dan could not only get into some of these systems, he could get back out again without ever leaving a trace that he was there.

Ray, Steve and I stepped outside the warehouse and into the sunlight. It had turned out to be a beautiful day but as the afternoon crept into early evening, I could see storm clouds gathering above Pikes Peak. There would likely be some rain in an hour or so. It usually didn't rain long this time of year, but it would rain hard for that short period of time.

I hadn't bothered to leash Steve and as soon as we were outside, I threw the ball for her. She happily took off running to chase it down, only to bring it back at a slower pace and repeat the process all over again. Ray was watching the dog play, but he looked thoughtful.

"What's on your mind, brother?"

"Just thinking this is a lot of time and money to recover a book we don't even know is authentic."

"That it is. But if the book is authentic, it's worth a lot and would be considered one of the greatest finds in recent memory. I think we're banking on the chance it's the real deal."

"I hope that it is," Ray mused, "because if it isn't, I think I'm going to lay down some hurt on this Billy kid."

I laughed. "I'll be there cheering you on."

We played outside with Steve for about an hour until she was tired enough that she laid down when she came back to me, tongue fully out, panting to cool herself off. I picked up the ball and we went back inside. I went upstairs, Steve trailing behind me, and fixed her a bowl of water and some dinner. The rain hit ten minutes later and the noise it generated on the metal roof of the warehouse was almost painful. I needed to get this place insulated.

I ordered Chinese delivery for everyone and when it arrived, we all gathered in the kitchen area to eat and share some beers. Dan's internet installer would be here within half an hour. He had been delayed by the rain which had blown through with typical quickness. Once we had a decent internet connection, Dan's data mining program would work much faster and maybe we could get a hit from Sam's telephone records.

When the internet guy arrived, Dan broke away to go lend a hand getting the line and router installed. The rest of us sat upstairs and drank a few more beers while we exchanged stories. Zach had been an operational specialist in the Navy and had learned his way around communications gear and crypto there. James had been a communications specialist in the Army assigned to a joint operations command for a group of special forces units in both Afghanistan and the Horn of Africa. Riley had never spent time in the military, but he had been a government security contractor before they changed directions and went more into training than operations. He found he had a gift for finding things people needed and was trained by the company as a fixer. After he had done a few tours in Iraq, he decided to ply his skills on the open market and found that large corporations were willing to pay big money for a guy who had an unconventional approach to problem solving. He had been hired by Bob's company about three years ago and was enjoying his tenure.

Once dinner was over, my mom and I cleaned up and then we opened the large roll-up door so she could pull her vehicle out and head home. She promised to be back early the next day.

Dan's guy finished up the internet installation in about two hours. We paid him cash for the install and then gave him my credit card to charge the activation fee. He left shortly after and Dan set up the network. It wasn't long before he had a number that had called Sam several times a day for the past few weeks. It was pinging towers out of the Seattle area. Dan used the towers to triangulate an area where the calls could be coming from. Unfortunately, there were about a dozen hotels in the area. We did, however, have a description of Bill's vehicle. This was going to be about old-fashioned police work and hitting the pavement. The good news was that it didn't look like he had moved from the area in the past few days.

I hopped online and booked Ray and me a flight out for the next day – not as early as I wanted, but the earliest flight was already booked. We'd leave here at 10:30 a.m. and get into Seattle at around 1:30 p.m. – early enough to start checking hotel parking lots for Bill's car.

Riley had gone out and purchased two cases and a small, carry-on suitcase with a hard shell. I decided I didn't want to push my luck with the flight and opted to leave Steve here. My mom would take good care of her while we were out working.

We hit the rack around 11:00. It took me a bit to fall asleep. It didn't help that half the guys in the room snored. It brought back memories of barracks life.

CHAPTER TWELVE

I was up by 5:00 a.m. and hopped in the shower. God bless my mother who had thought to stock towels and washrags. There was even a clothes hamper for the used towels. We needed a washing machine and dryer, or a laundry service. I'd have Dan look into it after this operation was done.

Once I was showered, I put on a pot of coffee and took Steve out for a walk. I'd miss having her with me over the next few days, but spending some time with Grandma would be good for her. Steve would be spoiled. We walked around the industrial complex where the warehouse was located. Our closest neighbors appeared to be a metal fabricator, a mechanics shop, and an appliance repair shop.

I was thinking more and more about a headquarters for the Adventurers' Club. The warehouse, with some fixing up, would be an ideal spot. Centrally located relative to the rest of the country, it also had everything we needed. Several military bases were found here, including Fort Carson, and there were lots of outdoor shops. I could have Expeditionary Research Group, a company that we used to supply food, water, and equipment for our adventures, ship out some of the food unit boxes and various other supplies that we could have on hand here to send out anywhere we needed them. That would give us two locations, once you factored in the metal building located on my property in Marin. We'd have the West Coast and Midwest covered.

I also thought about adding some full-time staff, though that would require Bob's approval. I might be able to front some supplies if I dipped into my savings account, but I couldn't carry someone on salary for more than a year or so. Plus there were all those details like insurance and retirement benefits that I wouldn't have a clue about. Once Bill had been located and the book recovered, maybe it was worth exploring further. So far, I had been lucky in that the people I needed to pull off these ventures had been available. Dan, for instance, had the option of telecommuting for his work. That might not always be the case.

Steve and I made our way back to the warehouse and walked in to find everyone pretty much up and moving around: some waiting on the shower, and a few more debating over how much coffee to put in the filter to brew another pot. Apparently, the pot I made didn't survive first impact with five grown men all needing their caffeine fix.

Mom showed up around 7:00 with two dozen eggs and two packages of bacon, a toaster, and some bread. She also brought orange juice. As a collective, we cooked breakfast and then sat down to eat. It reminded me of a slightly rowdy family gathering. We talked, joked, made fun of each other, and generally had a good time. Mom seemed at home, making people pick their towels up and put them in the hamper, make their beds, and wash their dishes. She confessed to me later that she missed those days when all our friends – mine and my sister's – were over during the weekends and that the house had always seemed alive and full of energy. I gave her a hug and kiss on the cheek. My mom had always put up with our craziness.

At 8:00, Ray and I took off for the airport. Steve gave a little whiney bark to see me go without her, but while it tore at me, I knew she'd be better off staying with my mom this time.

We arrived at the airport and checked in. We declared our firearms, having taken only the GLOCK and the revolver and leaving the others behind. This prompted an inspection by TSA, but this was Colorado, a haven for sport hunting; they were used to guns and the TSA agent was quick and professional as he inspected the guns and the containers they were locked in. With everything in order, we checked that bag, got our tickets, and proceeded through security.

Our plane was twenty minutes delayed taking off due to rain in Seattle, but the captain said it was supposed to clear sometime this morning and that it shouldn't interfere with us landing. I had booked us first class seats and Ray and I each enjoyed a Bloody Mary prior to take off.

We landed without problem, picked up our guns from baggage claim, and then hit the rental counter to pick up an SUV. As soon as we were clear of the airport, we found a little place to turn off the roadway and cracked open the suitcase so we could arm up. Firearms and extra ammo in place, we sought out the strip where most of the phone calls to Sam had originated from. It wasn't a small area we had to cover and there were about a dozen hotels. Still, we thought we could do it in an afternoon and then maybe another run through tomorrow morning, just in case we missed him during the day.

Ray was driving and with the help of a GPS program, we negotiated our way through light Seattle traffic. When we arrived at the first hotel, I pulled up the picture Dan had downloaded from Bill's Facebook page – it was better than the one Bill's girlfriend had texted us – and read off the license plate from Bill's vehicle so we could both search the parking lot. I thought it was better to park the SUV and walk. We were more likely to pay attention while walking. I was reminded of something a Navy Chief had once told me: slow is smooth, smooth is fast. If we took our time now, it meant we might locate the guy that much faster.

We did four hotel parking lots in this manner and then found the truck at the fifth. At the front desk, Ray flashed his retirement badge and asked for Bill Hendrix's room. He told the clerk he might also be listed under William. The clerk barely looked at the badge. Flashing it quickly was usually sufficient but on rare occasion, Ray said you'd get a sharp clerk and they'd scrutinize the badge and ID. It was clearly marked "retired" so it wouldn't help either of us. This guy, though, wasn't so sharp, and he gave us Bill's room number right away.

We went to the second floor, room 207, and knocked; the door wasn't latched and it swung open a bit. That was always an ominous sign. Ray and I stepped back from the door and took positions on either side, drawing our weapons in the process.

I signaled to Ray that we'd go on the count of three. The doorknob was on my side so I'd push open the door and Ray would make entry first, clearing the hard corner. I'd follow right after, clearing my side. We'd both done this dozens of times before with each other and with others. Old habits die hard.

I counted down three on my fingers and pushed the door open. Ray entered almost immediately. I stepped across and into the room and worked my side until it was clear. We found Bill lying on the floor on the side of the bed closest to the exterior wall. His face was severely bruised, with one eye swelling shut and his jaw distended, indicating it was most likely broken or dislocated. Ray immediately pulled out his phone and called 911. I bent down to check on Bill and found him still breathing, though it sounded a little wet, like he was breathing through a soaked towel.

I took a quick look around the room and found it had been tossed. The contents of Bill's wallet were laying on the bed, minus any cash. There was also a wooden box that was lying open on the floor at the foot of the bed. My guess was that it had held the book. It was empty now. Nonetheless, I did a quick search of the room, hoping to find the tome. No such luck.

"Damn it. Looks like T-Rex got to him first," I mumbled under my breath.

"Or someone else. No sign of the tome?" Ray asked, once he'd hung up the phone.

"Nope. Police and medical in route?"

"Yes, sir." The sound of sirens could be heard from way off. "That should be the cavalry now."

"Fuck," I said emphatically. We were going to be tied up giving statements in an investigation for some time, which was just giving Rex's men a head start on us. Based on the condition of the room and Bill, I would have bet hard money that they hadn't left more than thirty minutes prior to our arrival.

"You said that there was a security team that had come out to Victoria. They wouldn't happen to still be there, would they?"

"No. Could have used them, too."

We looked at each other helplessly. As much as we'd like to just bail and get hot on the trail of whoever had presumably taken the book, we couldn't. We'd stay around to cooperate with the police. We might get lucky and be able to leverage local law enforcement in our search. Plus, we didn't know who, exactly, we were looking for. The kid could have simply hidden the book, or it could be Roy and Hank, both of whom I could identify, or it could be some other goons. We'd need to get what information we could from Bill.

I called in to Zach and James at the TOC to let them know what we had found and to see if Dan could pull up any of the plane flights going from Seattle back to Raleigh to check if a Roy or Hank were on any of them. It was a long shot, but Dan had pulled off miracles before. I used the radio system that Zach and James had put so much effort into setting up and was surprised when they responded back. The sound quality was a bit digitalized but otherwise they came in loud and clear. Kudos to them.

After that, we were mired in law enforcement officers and EMTs. The officers quickly and efficiently took our statements. We explained that the kid had gotten himself in some trouble with a loan shark in North Carolina and that it was most likely that man who had either put the beat down on Bill or had sent someone to do it. I gave the police descriptions of Hank and Roy. We didn't have a lot on T-Rex yet, including an actual name, but I promised that if any information came up, I'd share. Our story was that the kid's sister worked for our boss and out of concern, he had sent us out to check on Bill. It was a weak story, but we were cut quite a bit of slack, being retired law enforcement ourselves.

It was an hour before we were clear of the scene and back in the SUV. I called Dan, via the phone this time, to see what he had been able to do. He explained he'd have to hack into not just one airline's database but all of them, and that would take more than a little time. By the time he could pull it off, they'd be a week or more in Raleigh.

I called Josue next and asked him if the private detective had been able to come up with anything on T-Rex. He asked for an hour and said he'd get back to me. I couldn't say no. Some things just can't be rushed. Once I hung up the phone with Josue, I called Bill's sister and his girlfriend. I figured they would want to know that we had found him and what condition he had been found in. They were both upset, and I promised that I'd update them as soon as I had any additional information.

Ray was driving and started to head to the hospital. It made the most sense. If we wanted to know what had happened to the book, we were going to have to talk to Bill. Depending on what condition he was in, we probably wouldn't be able to speak with him today, but we were going to try. It would be pointless to fly all the way to the other side of the country, only to find out Bill had hidden the book somewhere in Seattle. The flip side was the longer we dallied, the more likely that Rex would get his hands on the book and either sell it or destroy it. I didn't think he would destroy it. If he took it, then he knew it had value, at least to Bob. He might try to reach out and make a deal himself. It just depended on how much Bill told them before he was knocked unconscious.

We found the hospital and parked in the lot and walked over to the emergency room. The charging nurse was friendly and free with the information to the best of her ability. It helped that we were able to provide her some details regarding the patient, including his date of birth, address, and next of kin. I had never garnered from either Brenda or our research on Bill whether or not their parents were still alive, but I figured even if Brenda wasn't technically his next of kin, she could direct the hospital on who to call.

The charging nurse couldn't tell us much. She said they were taking Bill for x-rays and an MRI and then directed us to the waiting room. We went and had a seat. It was several hours before a doctor came out and asked if we were the two gentlemen who were in touch with Bill's sister. When I said we were, he explained that his MRI had come back negative for any bleeding in the brain but that he did have a minor concussion. He said Bill's jaw was broken, along with several ribs and a few fingers.

"If there are no complications from the head trauma, he'll be fine. We'll probably keep him for observation overnight and then he'll be released to go home," the doctor said.

"Thank you, sir. Do you think we might be able to see him before we go?" I asked.

"Of course." The doctor led the way. When we reached a nursing station, the doctor pointed further down the hallway and said, "Room A21. It will be on your left."

We made our way down to room A21 and walked in to find Bill propped up in his bed. He had an IV going and a heart rate monitor, but otherwise he seemed to be comfortable. That changed as soon as he saw us walk through the door. His heart rate went up and his breathing became quick and shallow.

Ray was quicker to pick up on his distress than I was. "No, no. Calm down, kid. We aren't here to hurt you. We work for Mr. Hansen, the man you contacted to sell the book. We've talked to your sister and Sam to let them know you're here and we just wanted to check and see how you're doing and ask a few questions."

Ray had to repeat it one more time before Bill started to relax a little. I remained quiet and stood by the door. Ray was working his magic, approaching Bill slowly and introducing himself. "Hi, I'm Ray. This is my partner, Jerod. How you feeling?"

Bill tried to answer but his jaw was apparently wired shut and still very swollen, so all we got was a mumbled, "Ok."

"Good, good. You feel up to answering a few questions for us? We're still interested in acquiring the book and we're still willing to pay you for it if we can find out where it is."

Bill looked hesitant for a moment and then nodded his head.

"Good, good. We're the two men that found you in the room and called the ambulance for you. Do you remember any of that?"

Bill shook his head no.

"You were pretty beat up, my friend," Ray said sympathetically. "The people who beat you up, did T-Rex send them?"

Bill nodded his head enthusiastically but then moaned in pain as the motion jarred his jaw.

"Easy, kid. Easy. Don't want you hurting yourself further. Did they ask you about the book?"

I saw what Ray was doing. Yes or no questions alleviated the need for any verbal answers and saved the kid from having to talk too much. It also made it easier to lie. I had always found that asking open-ended questions during an interview forced someone to think about their answers and lies were easier to pick up on. In this instance, though, yes or no responses were the best we were going to get.

Bill nodded his head again.

Ray mimicked the motion, nodding his head as well to build rapport with Bill. That was another common trick of the trade, so to speak. Mimicking the body language of the subject helped build comfort. People did it automatically when they felt connected with someone. Ray made it look natural and it very well could have been; the kid had a likable face, despite the bruises and swelling. Kind of the boy-next-door look with his light brown hair, pale complexion, and smattering of freckles. You felt sorry for him in his current condition.

"Did you have the book with you when they found you in your room?"

Bill looked ashamed, his face turned red and he looked down.

"It's ok, Bill. They were some big guys. No one could have done better. Did they take the book?"

Bill nodded almost imperceptibly.

"It's alright. At least we know who has the book. Did they know you were trying to sell it to Mr. Hansen?"

Bill nodded again.

"Ok. Well, Mr. Hansen had already made a deal with you and someone else stealing the book isn't going to change that. As soon as we have it in hand, we'll let your sister know and she can put us back in touch with you. Is that ok?"

Bill nodded.

"Good, good. Ok, Bill, you rest up and get to feeling better. Jerod here is going to give you a card and if you need anything, you let us know, ok?"

Bill gave one more nod and, after handing him one of my cards, we walked out of the room and back down the hall. We were silent for a bit, and then Ray turned his head toward me. "Back to Raleigh?"

"Yes, sir."

We left the hospital and climbed into the Chevy. I contacted the TOC via our portable radio and advised them we would need a flight to North Carolina. Either Zack or James, it was hard to tell over the radio, responded back acknowledging our status and request.

It was about 7:30 p.m. and we hadn't eaten anything since earlier this morning. I navigated us to a good restaurant I had eaten at before when I had been in Seattle. They had good BBQ and they had a small batch bourbon that was better than their food – my kind of place. We arrived just before 8:00 and waited twenty minutes to get a table before sitting down.

Our waitress was at our table quickly with water and menus. I ordered a bourbon, neat, and Ray ordered a beer from the on-tap selection. While we were waiting to order dinner, the radio squawked, "Boy Scout, this is Homeport. Guardian has delivered a package. Request landline contact with Homeport. Over."

I responded back, "Homeport, Boy Scout. Roger. Out."

Ray looked at me quizzically and raised an eyebrow. "Boy Scout?"

"Long story." I hid my discomfort by taking a sip of my whiskey. Anyone who was ever in the military understood that your call sign wasn't chosen by you, it was selected by your fellow shipmates/Marines/soldiers, etc. Mine had been selected after a series of incidents that started when I was deployed to Dubai.

The first incident was when Anna, my best friend who was also deployed with me, was on one of the remote towers and asked if I had a magazine or something she could read while she was out there. Specifically, she wanted a National Geographic. Coincidentally, I had just received a care package from my mom that happened to contain a National Geographic. Anna couldn't believe the coincidence and had accused me of being a boy scout, always ready.

The second incident had to do with one of the guys on my boat, a Boatswain's Mate First Class named Josh. He was looking for a new battery for his flashlight. It was one of those that required a special battery, versus a standard double A. I just happened to have grabbed a pack of them the last time I was at the store and handed one over. He had also said I was like a boy scout.

The last incident, though, is what sealed the deal. We all shared apartments and I was staying at the Coral Dubai Deira Hotel with three other guys. One day a young lady came to the door and asked if one of my roommates was home. They had struck up a friendship and she was dropping off some food for us all to eat. I was alone in the apartment. I had met her several times before and we had sat and talked a few of those times. She was attractive, slender, with deep brown eyes, and luxurious, thick black hair. From Turkey, she was the Director of Operations for a shipping company. She asked for a tour of the apartment. I tried to keep it quick but when I showed her my room, she sat on the bed and invited me to join her. I panicked, told her I was married (which I was at the time) and asked her to leave. She had shaken her head sadly and called me a boy scout. My mistake was in telling that story to the guys I worked with. From that point forward, my call sign was Boy Scout.

I relayed the story to Ray, who laughed out loud. "I see."

I tipped my glass to him and took another drink.

Our food arrived and we continued our small talk through dinner. We ordered another round of drinks. About an hour in, we received another transmission from the TOC. "Boy Scout, this is Homeport. Flight scheduled for 10:30 pm. Looks like you're taking the redeye. Over."

The radio attracted the attention of a few people near us but I ignored them. "Boy Scout, roger, out."

We only had about an hour to get to the airport, get checked in, and get on our plane. I'd call Dan to get the information that Josue had sent over when we landed in Raleigh. We paid our bill and left. Fortunately, we were close to the airport and it didn't take long to get the SUV turned back in and catch the shuttle to the airport. We made our gate with about fifteen minutes to spare. It was going to be a long flight. I ordered a double Jameson and after finishing that, settled in to sleep. The flight wasn't full and we had been able to get first class seats, even booking last minute. Worked for me.

CHAPTER THIRTEEN

We landed at around 8:30 a.m., picked up our checked luggage with our weapons from baggage claim, grabbed a rental vehicle and went to find a hotel room. While I wouldn't have considered us rested, we weren't dog-tired either, having been able to sleep most of the way through our flight. What we did need were showers and a fresh change of clothes – something I was getting light on again.

We ended up with a two-bedroom suite. I took the upstairs loft. The living room area was sufficient for us to work out of. I contacted the TOC and let them know our location and asked for them to forward whatever information Josue had gathered from the private detective. It was considerable.

To start, the pool hall was owned by Rex's grandfather. The grandfather, Elias Johnson, now in his late eighties, had bought the pool hall when he retired from the army in 1961. He had served in both World War II and Korea. He had married shortly after retirement and had one son, Obadiah, Rex's father.

Obadiah had followed in his father's footsteps and joined the Army at eighteen. He was killed in action ten years later during the Gulf War. Rex, whose actual name was Regis Phillip Johnson, had been five years old at the time. His mother had developed a drug habit and he was left to roam the streets from an early age. In and out of juvenile hall, he caught his first case at eighteen and did a year in jail for assault. Now 25, police records indicated that he had been detained several times on violations ranging from money laundering, theft, and loan sharking to dealing drugs, assault with a deadly weapon and an attempted homicide. No arrests, though.

Rex had started managing the pool hall for his grandfather a few years ago. The pool hall made a perfect cover for his loan sharking and money laundering. It was an all-cash business which made auditing a nightmare for a forensic accountant. It was rumored that he dealt drugs, primarily methamphetamines, from the pool hall as well, but the private detective hadn't been able to confirm it.

Staff at the retirement home where the grandfather was living had told the private detective that Elias and Rex didn't get along. During one of Rex's infrequent visits they had overheard them arguing about selling the pool hall. Elias was in favor of it and could use the extra money to live out the remainder of his life in some comfort. As it was now, his retirement from the military and his social security just barely covered the expenses of the retirement home and baseline sustenance. Any time a realtor had come along, though, Rex had scared them off.

There were some additional details, including Rex's home address, photos of his vehicles and their license plate numbers, known associates such as Roy and Hank, most of whom had been identified by at least a name. The apartment where Rex lived and the utility bills were all in the name of a female, Julia Hodges. Julia was presumably his girlfriend but the private detective hadn't been able to track her down. One of the two vehicles that Rex drove, an older model BMW, was also in her name. The other car, a newer Chevy Camaro, was in the grandfather's name, most likely without his consent.

As I read through the report provided by the private detective and scanned the supporting documents such as copies of birth and marriage certificates, photos of the utility bills, etc., I started to formulate a plan. I would need to consult with a legal authority, though. I wanted this to be clean, and to make it so would mean getting attorneys involved. I had a love/hate relationship with attorneys as a rule. Most politicians were attorneys and they passed laws that could only be interpreted by other attorneys. It was a self-supporting system.

Bill had found himself in Rex's debt when he had been hustled at the pool hall. Bill had thought he had been on fire, sinking balls all night long and winning decent sums of money. Then the table had turned and, in one game, Bill had found himself owing Rex $1000. Bill didn't have that kind of money on him, just the few hundred that he had already won. Rex had allowed him to finance the remainder at an exorbitant interest rate and when Bill refused, they had given him a taste of what reneging on that debt would cost him. Bill had been giving him all the money he could since then, and still the amount owed kept going up until it was at $5000; that's when Bill had decided to try to sell the souvenir he had brought back from Iraq.

His sister had heard the stories about Bob's attempts at recovering stolen artifacts and shared those stories with Bill in a kind of "look what my quirky boss does" kind of way. Bill knew the book was old and thought maybe it was worth enough to pay off the debt so he could go on with his life, buy his girl a ring, get married and live a decent life. Except Bob had gotten involved in the ATV accident and didn't show up with the money, and then Hank and Roy had caught up to him, thinking he was trying to skip out on the debt. It was a case of bad decisions followed by bad luck, and now Rex had the book that my boss wanted.

I called Josue and got the name of the PI they had used here in Raleigh and then I contacted him directly. I needed to know if Rex was still in possession of the tome and if he was, I needed him tailed, just in case he found a buyer. The fee for services on such short notice was high, but the PI was also on retainer for the company, so he said he'd drop whatever cases he had and get right on it.

After that, I called the retirement home where Elias was living and inquired if they had visiting hours. They didn't, except for those on 24-hour care. Most of their residents lived in small cottages and could receive visitors at any time of day. My next two calls were to Bob's staff attorney to get a recommendation for a real estate attorney in the area, and to the TOC to outline my plan to Dan.

Ray listened intently while I explained to Dan what I was going to do. In the end, they both thought it was too complicated. Legal, but complicated, whereas their much simpler plan – to break in and simply steal the book – was illegal, but easy. I listened to their arguments but in the end, I thought my way would put an end to Rex's business once and for all. First, though, I needed a real estate attorney.

It took an hour before the staff attorney got back to me with a name. I called the law office he had recommended right away and to the staff attorney's credit, he had already phoned ahead so the office was expecting me. They scheduled an appointment for a consultation the next day.

My last call was to Bob. He had been cleared from the hospital and was recuperating at his spacious home in Harrington County, New York. Susan picked up the phone. I spoke with her long enough to gather that Bob was already driving her crazy with the need to be busy. She figured if their marriage could survive until the end of the week, she'd give him her ok to go back to work at the office. When she was done venting to me, she handed Bob the phone. As quickly as he picked up, I knew he had heard everything she told me. He had to have been standing or sitting right next to her.

"Jerod. How are things going?" No preamble, he was getting antsy.

"Good, we think we know where the book is and I have a plan for getting it back, but it will take some time. Two weeks, maybe a little longer, to do it right."

"Ok. What's the plan?" I told him my thoughts.

When I was done, Bob was quiet for a moment and then said, "Sounds complicated. Can't we just steal the book back?"

Bob couldn't see me but I was shaking my head. "It's no secret that you're trying to get the book.; at this point, Rex knows it, too. I expected him to reach out to you with an offer to sell the book but that hasn't happened yet. If we break in and steal it, and then you turn it over to the proper people, it's going to be obvious we stole it. Follow me?"

Again, he was quiet for a moment before responding. "I see what you're saying, Jerod." He sighed and I had no doubt that he had already thought about the same things. "Ok. Let's make this happen then."

We said our goodbyes and then I turned to Ray. "We have the green light."

"Ok. What's our next step?"

With that, I started laying out my plan in more detail.

CHAPTER FOURTEEN

We were parked in a blacked-out SUV behind a line of law enforcement vehicles that included several SUVs of their own, about six marked patrol cars, and an armored vehicle containing the Raleigh SWAT Team. We had been sitting there for several hours, waiting for Rex to show up at the pool hall. There were teams set up to hit his apartment as well as two other locations. It was a coordinated operation and one Ray and I were instrumental in setting up.

After getting the green light from Bob to proceed, I had met the next day with a real estate attorney. My plan? To buy the pool hall from the grandfather, set up surveillance cameras on the interior to gather evidence of Rex's activities, and then to turn that evidence over to local law enforcement. I had developed a relationship with one of the narcotics officers, Jim Eirey, on the Raleigh Police Department. By purchasing the pool hall, it wasn't trespassing if I or someone working with me entered the premises.

It hadn't taken much to convince the grandfather to sell. I had offered a more than reasonable price for the business. Not excessive, necessarily, but over market value. Escrow closed within three days and the grandfather provided me with his key, the code to the alarm, and the combination to the safe that could be found in the back office. It was one of the old school safes that stood about five feet high, weighed around 500 pounds and was bolted into the cement floor.

The day after I took legal possession of the pool hall I had security technicians enter the building after everyone had left. Cameras had been set up. What was nice was that there was already a camera system installed along with signs that said, "This Premises is Under Video Surveillance." Rex wouldn't be able to claim that he had been videoed illegally.

It took not quite two weeks to obtain the evidence necessary for Detective Eirey to put together a search warrant. Combined with the surveillance conducted by the private detective, Jim was able to get warrants for the apartment and the other two locations. We wouldn't be allowed entry to the pool hall until it was cleared by the SWAT team; to ensure we didn't jump the gun, so to speak, they had assigned us a babysitter, a young officer by the name of Tyler Walton.

Tyler was driving the SUV and Ray was riding shotgun. We both had that pre-operation nervousness that never seemed to go away, no matter how many you had done. We also both dealt with it in our own ways. Ray was in an animated conversation with Tyler while I sat quietly in the back and ran through all the possibilities in my head. My many years as a Tactical Commander meant that I ran through everything that could go wrong and was trouble-shooting pre-planned responses.

Over Tyler's radio I heard the scout team advise that Rex was on site. There was a moment of silence and then the Raleigh SWAT commander gave the go signal and we were rolling, trailing the police vehicles by a good margin. I can't say I blamed Tyler for hanging back. Even though Ray and I were both veterans of law enforcement who had done probably close to some thousand operations between the two of us, it didn't look good on your record if you got a civilian hurt.

We pulled up to the pool hall just as the breacher popped the door open and the team flowed in. I heard a Flash Sound Diversionary Device go off with a loud boom and yelling for someone to get on the ground. According to the radio traffic, there should only be four people inside: Rex, Hank, Roy, and the bartender who had opened the hall. Minutes went by and then I heard the team leader announce over the radio that the location was clear and they would be starting their secondary search. The secondary search was generally more detailed and a bit slower. It was fifteen minutes before we received the all-clear signal.

Ray and I exited the vehicle along with Tyler. I had traded in my standard t-shirt, hiking pants, and boots for a high-end Italian suit. Ray was wearing a suit, as well. Both of us were armed, but the suits had been tailored to hide that fact.

We walked into the pool hall with Tyler leading the way. I met with the team leader, an older sergeant who had been on the force for just over twenty years. He had the look down pat. Short, iron grey hair cut in a military-style flat top, a square jaw and heavy brow that framed cold blue eyes. His arms were as big as my thighs. For all that he looked like an action figure, he was a nice guy with a dry sense of humor. I shook his hand.

"Looked good, Sarge. How many detained?"

"Four. Good intel. Eirey should be here in just a second with his evidence team and they'll start their search."

I nodded. "Any word on the other three target locations?"

"It will be a minute. They'll be routing that info through the lieutenant."

I nodded again. "Thanks again, Sarge."

Ray and I stepped off to the side to allow the cops to do their job. Once Jim arrived, he told us that the other three locations were clear and that they would start doing those searches shortly. He also told us that on the cursory search of the back office they had found a sizable quantity of meth.

Jim had the four suspects seated off to one side where they were out of the way and under guard by a couple of uniformed cops. The search team had set up sections, numbered them, and started their search. Jim gave us the all clear to talk to the suspects.

It was my first good look at Regis Johnson. I saw immediately why he had earned the nickname T-Rex. When I stood upright, my arms naturally hung about six inches below my waist. Rex's arms ended at his waist, making them unusually short, like a T-Rex. I suppressed the smile that was trying to creep up on my lips.

Roy was sitting to Rex's left, his right arm in a cast from his hand to his shoulder. You could still see some bruising from where I had struck him. Hank was sitting to Rex's right, head hung low. All three of them were handcuffed, though Roy, with his cast, was handcuffed to the chair. Roy and Hank reacted immediately to our approach, trying to pull back out of reach. I thought about yelling "boo" but decided against it. The fourth guy was sitting next to Hank. He was also handcuffed and had his head hanging low.

I set my briefcase on the table and opened it, pulling out some paperwork. "Roy. Hank. Mr. Johnson," I said, making eye contact with each one. "I'm Jerod Grey, the new owner of this establishment. These are your termination papers." I set the papers on the table where Jim had also set a copy of the search warrant. "Additionally, these are restraining orders. Once you are escorted by the officers out of my pool hall, you are not to return to within 100 yards of it for the next five years."

Hank and Roy looked wide-eyed. Rex's eyes narrowed. "What do you mean, you're the new owner? This is my place." His face was getting flush.

"Point of correction, Mr. Johnson, this place belonged to your grandfather and I purchased it from him. Now it is mine."

"You can't do that!" He started to stand up but the officer behind him put his hand on Rex's shoulder, forcing him back down to the seat.

I raised an eyebrow. "Can't? I have a team of lawyers who would argue otherwise. I assure you, it's all legal. I also suspect you'll be too busy trying to stay out of jail to worry about this place."

Jim walked up at that moment. The timing couldn't have been better. "We got the safe open and found additional drugs inside, along with about $30,000 in cash. I'm sorry, but we'll have to seize the cash."

I turned slightly to face the detective. "Not a problem. It's most likely from the sales of the drugs, anyway." Jim nodded his agreement.

I turned back to Rex. "Any questions can be directed to my attorney. His card is with the paperwork." Ray and I walked away.

It took several hours for them to finish the search and by the time they were done, they had recovered several pounds of meth, over

$35,000 in cash, and a small amount of other drugs including some cocaine and marijuana – most likely for personal use, but Jim told us they'd be booking them for possession for sales. When Jim was done with them, the vice squad was going to take a crack at getting them for the loan sharking. Roy or Hank would roll for either a reduction in sentencing or immunity, I was sure of that. Rex was going to do five to ten years easy.

When the cops were done and the place cleared out, Ray and I had the place to ourselves. We hung a "Closed Until Further Notice" sign up on the front door and then locked it. I looked around. The place was large, with about fifteen pool tables evenly spaced around a centrally located bar. Overall, it wasn't in the best of shape and would require a lot of work.

Off the bar was a kitchen, although the place hadn't been cleared to serve food by the Health Department in years. A door to one side of the bar led to two offices and a stairway at the back of the bar led to a large basement area where the alcohol was stored.

Ray and I made our way to the offices. We found the safe, still open from when the cops had done their search. On the top shelf of the safe was the tome. It looked a little worse for wear from when Bill had originally sent the picture, but was still in reasonable shape, given its age and the way it had been handled by both Bill and Rex and his boys.

I pulled the book from the shelf and looked at it for a moment before placing it in my briefcase. I had no idea if it was authentic or not, but it had the feel of something out of antiquity.

We left the pool hall shortly after. Tyler and his SUV had left with the rest of the officers. We walked around the corner and got into the vehicle we had rented several weeks ago and pre-staged a block or two away. As soon as we were in the car, I called Bob. He picked up on the first ring. "We have it."

"Outstanding. See you tomorrow." He hung up.

EPILOGUE

We had all gathered back in Colorado Springs at what was now called HQ – Dan, James, Zach, Ray, Riley, my mom, Steve and myself. Steve had been so excited to see me that it took almost an hour before she was calm enough that I could pet her without her going completely nuts.

At some point while we were in North Carolina, they had upgraded the kitchen area of the warehouse with granite countertops, a new sink and faucet, new appliances and cabinets. They had even added a larger dining table. Somehow, I had been talked into making dinner. It turned out to be a lot more work than I had thought. I wasn't used to cooking for seven people. Still, with my mom's help, we pulled it off.

They had also cleaned up the communications set-up so that it looked more professional, almost like the dispatch stations I remembered from the few times I had been to the comms center when I was a cop. The satellite set-up had worked well, allowing us on-going communications with HQ from Seattle to Raleigh. Better yet, Zach could print out a chronological log of all our activities from the time he started recording them in the computer. It helped support the receipts we had to turn in to Bob to cover the expenses charged to the credit cards. I was considering more and more whether I could justify keeping a few full-time employees on the payroll for the Adventurers' Club. At the moment, we didn't have enough work to do, but I could start the process of legitimizing the Club, file for a taxpayer ID number, business license, and so on. It was worth considering.

As predicted, Roy had rolled on Rex and helped the vice squad understand how the books were set up. Rex had done the cops a favor by keeping detailed records of his loansharking; all they had needed was the key, compliments of Roy.

Roy had also provided another tidbit of information that the cops had not been looking for. The alleged girlfriend whose name was on Rex's apartment, along with one of his cars, was dead. She had owed Rex money and was threatening to leave him; he killed her and Hank and Roy had helped dispose of the body. Roy had led them right to it. Rex was now facing homicide charges as well. He wouldn't see the light of day outside a prison for twenty years or more.

I had hired an architect to help me refurbish the pool hall. I wanted to turn it into an authentic Irish pub. Bob had initially resisted the idea and wanted to sell it right away, but when I explained that I had used my own money to buy the pool hall, our conversation turned from selling the place to him becoming a silent partner. The purchase had pretty much wiped out my savings, so my choices were to either mortgage my house or get Bob to front the cash for the renovation. Bob convinced me a home equity line of credit wasn't the route I wanted to go. It was hard to argue with the man, he had made billions.

Of course, there were a number of things that had to be done before the renovation was complete, and primary among those was hiring a manager for the pub. If I could find the right manager, I could delegate a lot of those duties: overseeing the renovation, hiring bartenders, a chef, and wait staff, buying the supplies we would need, etc. I had already started my recruiting and hiring efforts.

The tome had been turned over to Bob who had sent it to Curtis at Harvard, but not before he had an expert make copies of the pages in the book so that he could keep an authentic reproduction. In truth, Harvard would probably do the same before sending the tome back to Iraq. After all, it belonged to that country. Harvard had verified that the tome was authentic and the archaeology world was abuzz with the find. A genuine Sumerian text, thousands of years old.

Bill had been released from the hospital. No solid food for a long while but he would make a full recovery. Bob had cut him a check for $10,000 for bringing the book to his attention – a finder's fee. We also kept his name out of any discussions on how we had found the tome. While ultimately the tome would end up in the right hands, he could have still faced charges for bringing it out of the country of origin. We understood that the international community took the theft of antiquities very seriously, but in the end, we all agreed that we wanted to give this kid a chance. That was one of the nice things about being a civilian – I didn't have to enforce the law without bias. Sometimes, I could help someone out instead of put them behind bars.

Dinner was laid out on the table and we all gathered around to take our seats. I pulled a bottle of Irish whiskey from the small store of liquor Dan had laid in and filled the glasses of those who wanted some. For the rest, I poured wine or popped the top on a beer for them.

When dinner was over, Dan and I stood outside the warehouse sipping bourbon and smoking cigars. It was a beautiful spring night, the temperature comfortably cool and the night air smelling of the rainstorm that had passed through earlier. Our conversation had drifted into silence as my thoughts turned to Cat and then to Stephanie.

"You're always going to miss her, brother," Dan said, when the silence had stretched on for too long.

"I know. Was just wondering when the right time to move on is," I replied.

"I think you decide that. If it feels right, you go for it. If it doesn't, you don't. Pretty simple."

It was that simple, but also, it wasn't. Nothing ever was when emotions were involved. I would admit to myself that I had taken an instant liking to Stephanie and, according to Susan, she felt the same about me. So why did I feel guilty?

In the end, I decided that I was mostly worried about people's perceptions – someone judging me because my girlfriend had been dead for just over a month. I smiled and tilted my glass in Dan's direction. He looked confused but didn't ask why I had smiled.

I put the glass to my lips and drained it in one swallow. Since when did I worry about what people thought of me?

THE ADVENTURERS' CLUB

CHAPTER ONE

I had spent two weeks in Africa with my best friend, Anna Smith. It had been an amazing trip. I had often thought that I should have been a biologist. Maybe. I was also somewhat of an adrenaline junkie and chasing bad guys, whether it was through the streets of the city where I worked as a cop or across the arid lands of Iraq or Afghanistan for the military, had been more than fulfilling. Being amongst the animals of the Serengeti during the great migration, however, had been awe-inspiring.

I had arrived back in the San Francisco Bay Area late last night and had gone to bed almost as soon as I had arrived home, taking time only to brush my teeth and take a quick shower before crawling into my bed. I had slept like a baby, not even needing my usual bourbon to help me get there – the power of time zone changes and a twenty-plus-hour travel day.

Despite the lateness of when I arrived home, I still woke up early. It was 5:24 a.m. when I looked at my phone. I considered rolling over and trying to catch a few more minutes of shuteye but also knew it would be impossible. It had been two weeks since I had seen Steve and my friend, Jerome Riviera, was supposed to drop her off early this morning before he went to work at the gym he owned. I was excited to see my dog.

I got up and took another shower, even though it had only been about four hours since the last one. While we'd had a decent set-up at the research camp in Africa, the showers had all been military style, or what we affectionately called a combat shower. In essence, it was get yourself wet, turn off the water, lather up, and then rinse. In and out in less than five minutes. While effective for keeping yourself relatively sanitary, you never felt like you were completely clean. Add to that the long travel day, and it felt good to climb under the heavy stream of a hot shower again.

After my shower, I threw the clothes I had brought back with me from Africa into the washing machine. Like me, the clothes had not been given a serious cleaning over the past couple weeks.

Laundry in, I went downstairs and fixed breakfast. I'd need to go to the grocery store before the day was done or I wouldn't have anything to eat for dinner. I had a few basics in the fridge and cabinets but needed some standard items like bread and milk. I'd add that to my list of things to do.

While I cooked some eggs, I called back east to talk to the general contractor who was working on renovating the pool hall I had bought. My plan was to turn it into an Irish pub. It had been a long-term goal of mine to own my own pub, and when the opportunity presented itself to purchase a property that would fit the bill, and take a loan shark and drug dealer out of commission in the process, I had jumped on it.

My contractor gave me a run-down on our progress. The renovation of the public room was going well, but I had asked him to add in some extras, including remodeling the basement area where the liquor was usually stored. I had the large metal building on my property here in California to store supplies for the Adventurers' Club's expeditions on the West Coast and the warehouse in Colorado Springs for expeditions in the Midwest, but I needed something equivalent on the East Coast. That's what the contractor was working on now and he wasn't sure the pub's basement would have sufficient room for my needs; he was encouraging me to purchase a building just behind the old pool hall that he could renovate into what I wanted.

I was interested, but that was extra money to buy the building and to convert it and it was money I didn't have, particularly after making a large donation to the research group in Africa. As it was, Bob was footing the bill for the renovations of the pub and I wasn't going to ask him for more capital. I told him to do what he could. Even if we couldn't store a large amount of supplies there, it would be better and cheaper than having everything shipped to the East Coast from California or Colorado.

After my call, I ate my breakfast and started washing dishes. There was a knock at the front door. Thinking it was Jerome and Steve, I yelled for them to come in, turned off the water and dried my hands. Dishes could wait, I was ready to see Steve.

Smiling, I started walking toward the front door. Jerome normally pulled all the way around and came in through the back door. That should have been my clue that something was wrong but in my excitement to see Steve, I didn't pause to think it through. I was almost to the door when I heard the distinctive sound of a shotgun racking a shell into the chamber. Once you've heard it, it's a sound you never forget.

I reacted instinctively, leaping to my right and into the living room where there was some furniture to provide concealment and maybe a little cover. I also had a 9mm handgun in a holster under the coffee table. I wouldn't say that I'm paranoid but I do like to be prepared.

The shotgun went off, blowing a large chunk of my door off in the process. The sound was louder than I remembered. Could be that my hearing was already damaged when the patrol boat I was on was involved in a firefight with an Iranian attack boat near Dubai. I had been forced to fire a .50 caliber, heavy machine gun without the benefit of hearing protection. The result was that my hearing had been damaged, or damaged further, and I had ringing and a sensitivity to loud noises which, at the moment, included a twelve gauge being fired less than ten feet from me.

The shotgun racked and fired again, taking more of my door off in the process. I scrambled on my hands and knees toward the coffee table and ripped the gun from the holster it was secured in on the underside. I flipped over to my back and aimed my handgun in the direction of the door. I was holding a Sig Saur P226 with sixteen rounds, fifteen in the magazine and one in the chamber.

It sounded like the front door was kicked open and I heard the clack of boots stepping on to the hardwood floor in the entryway. Unfortunately, I also heard the back door swing open and bang against the wall and someone enter in from that direction. Seemed I had multiple visitors.

I was on my back between the coffee table and the couch. The couch would provide me some concealment from the person in the kitchen, but I was clearly visible to the person coming in through the front door. The only advantage I had was that most people wouldn't be looking for me at floor level and they didn't yet know I was armed. I fired two rounds through the short wall that separated the front door from the living room and was rewarded by cursing. A man, judging by the sound of the voice.

I pushed myself up off the floor and headed for the stairs at a sprint. For good measure, I fired two rounds into the kitchen as well, and once again heard cursing. They now knew I was armed and would proceed with more caution.

I was almost to the top of the stairs when out of the corner of my eye I saw a man wearing all black come around the short wall leading from the front door. He must have racked the shotgun again when I was firing the handgun, or shortly after, because he aimed it in my direction and pulled the trigger. I didn't wait to hear the loud boom but leapt the last two stairs and hit the top landing in a roll.

The shotgun went off, ripping away part of the stair railing and putting multiple holes in the wall. I had been hoping they were amateurs and would be using bird shot. No such luck. I had seen enough impacts from a 12-gauge round to know they were using 00-buck. Nothing made you stand up and say hello like nine .32 caliber lead pellets coming at you from downrange. In my favor, though, was that I had made the top of the stairs and not been shot in the process. I didn't plan to pause at this moment to celebrate my good fortune, but I was sure that later I'd break out a 21-year-old scotch and have a toast to luck's good graces.

I ducked into the spare bedroom where the door jamb would offer some cover and aimed my weapon toward the stairs. I had the advantage of high ground now and they wouldn't be able to approach without exposing themselves. And at least as important – if I ran out of ammo in this weapon, I had another pistol and a rifle in my bedroom. My only hope was that they weren't smart enough to realize they could fire through the floor. That would make my day considerably more complicated. For now, though, they didn't know exactly where I was at.

My cell phone was downstairs on the kitchen counter. I did have a landline phone but it was also in my bedroom and I didn't want to give up the advantage I had with my position. I decided to bluff. "I've called the police," I yelled.

Again, I heard cursing and then footsteps through the hallway from the kitchen to the living room. I saw a sliver of a body come into my view and fired a round. This time I was awarded with a cry of pain. One hit for the good guys, but now they knew where I was.

I back stepped to my bedroom. Keeping my eyes on the doorway, I opened the closet and took out the rifle, a modified AR-15 that wouldn't be entirely legal in the state of California if not for the fact that I had been a police officer and member of the military. I tucked the handgun into my waistband and then pulled the charging handle back on the rifle to put a round in the chamber and flicked off the safety.

Still keeping my eyes on the door, I picked up the phone and dialed 911. I was put on hold waiting for a dispatcher to pick up. Now it was my turn to curse. I tossed the handset on the bed, leaving the phone line open. If there was more shooting, the sheriff's department would figure it out quick enough and the landline was tied to my address, so they'd know where to send the troops.

I stayed behind the bed with the rifle pointed toward the stairs. There were only two ways up here and that was either via the stairs or through the window from the roof of the porch. I hazarded a moment's distraction to peek out the window, making sure I wasn't going to have a surprise visitor come through that way. It was clear, for now. If needed, I could bail out that way.

Faintly, because the phone was on the other side of the bed, I heard a female voice say, "911, what's your emergency?"

"There are at least two armed intruders in my house. I need the police now!" I spoke louder than I wanted to, partially because I had people trying to kill me for whatever reason, and partially because the phone was lying on the bed about five feet from me and I wanted to make sure the dispatcher could hear me.

The female voice started asking questions. Descriptions, weapons. I did say back that at least one had a shotgun, but that I hadn't really seen them well enough to provide a description other than the one with the shotgun was wearing all black. Seemed to be the color of choice for bad guys.

I must have been loud enough for the bad guys to get a general idea of where I was at upstairs. Rounds started popping through the floor between the end of the bed and the closet, six total from a handgun, and based on the distinct sound of multiple cartridges hitting the ground all at once, my guess was a revolver that was now being reloaded.

I collapsed to the floor between the bed and the outside wall and groaned like I had been hit. From my position on the floor I could see under the bed and into the hallway where the stairs came up. I wasn't above a bluff if it meant keeping my life and right now, we were at a stalemate until the police arrived. I couldn't go downstairs and they couldn't come up. I still had the window as an escape option, but if it was me, I would have brought at least one other guy whose job was to maintain the perimeter. Two more would be ideal because then you could stick them on opposite corners of the house and maintain a full 360-degrees on the exterior.

There were muffled voices from downstairs followed by six more shots coming through the floor in about the same spot as the last ones. Made sense – if I had been hit once in that location and had collapsed to the ground, a few more shots might finish the job. I clamped my teeth down to keep from cursing and waited. There was the sound of cartridges hitting the ground again and the notable sound of a revolver cylinder clicking back into place. Way off in the distance I heard sirens and prayed they were coming for me. I couldn't hear the dispatcher on the phone but assumed she had stopped asking questions and started listening.

Down on the ground, my vantage point had changed considerably. I didn't have the view down the stairs like I'd had from the kneeling position. My first glimpse of anyone coming up the stairs was going to be seeing the top of his head rise above the top stair. I cautioned myself to patience and waited. I heard the creak of weight being placed on the third stair from the bottom. I had been meaning to fix that for about a year but just had never found the time. Or, I probably had the time, but couldn't find the motivation to fix it. Now I was thinking maybe I should just leave it be.

Adrenalin was coursing through my system. I had once heard it explained that there were three basic parts to the brain. The frontal cortex was where all our cognitive processes took place like our ability to reason, solve problems, and carry on a conversation. The back portion handled automatic functions like our heart beating and digestion. And then there was the mid-brain. The mid-brain was where all our survival responses derived from. It was likened to a puppy, all action and energy – but also like a puppy, it lacked discipline. To exert some discipline, you had to exercise conscious control over an automatic function, like breathing. The technique I used was called combat breathing. I had done it so many times over the years that I didn't have to think about it overly much. Breath in for a four count, hold for a four count, exhale for a four count, hold for a four count, and repeat. I didn't do it more than once or twice, but it did help keep the jitters caused by the adrenaline to a manageable level.

The sirens could still be heard far off in the distance. I couldn't tell if they were getting closer or not, but I did hear a vehicle pulling on to the gravel driveway that ran around to the back of the house where the kitchen and back door were. I was hoping it wasn't Jerome. He'd be walking into a shit show. Like me, he was a retired police officer. Unlike me, he didn't normally go around with a firearm on his person. It was normally in his gym bag. The car came to a stop and the engine went off.

The two guys, closer to me now that they were on the stairs, said something to each other. Between the whispers and slight ringing in my ears from the gun fire, I couldn't make out what they were saying, but I did hear them go back down the stairs and then the sounds of their footsteps went quickly across the downstairs floor.

I gave it a second and then slowly stood up, sweeping the stairwell with the rifle. I glanced out the window and saw Jerome's old white Saturn sedan parked. I could see Steve standing in the driver's seat and could just make out her barking through the closed window. I didn't see Jerome anywhere.

I crept my way to the bedroom door, keeping my rifle up and ready. I took one deep breath and then fast walked down the stairs, rifle up and moving to clear what space I could see. I picked up movement to my left and swung the rifle around. Jerome was coming out of the kitchen, gun out. Sensing my movement, he swung the handgun my way. "BLUE! BLUE! BLUE!" I yelled. Our signal that I was a friendly.

Jerome came down off target and I did the same. "Rest of the downstairs is clear. Saw two guys flee out the front door and get into a black van. What the fuck, bro? You haven't even been home for 24 hours yet."

I shrugged my shoulders. "I don't know, man." I looked around the living room. My front door was toast, bullet holes in the walls, and the few paintings I had were taken off the walls and the backs torn off them. The Salvador Dali painting that Cat had left for me was still hanging up, though. "My homeowner's insurance is going to love this."

"FREEZE! SHERIFF'S DEPARTMENT! DROP THE WEAPONS!" Jerome and I both almost reacted instinctively to come up on target. That would have gotten us both shot. We dropped our weapons to the floor. Well, more like threw them, so that there was a lot of space between them and us. I didn't want an amped-up cop thinking I was reaching for it. I still had the problem of the 9mm in my waistband but as long as I kept my hands up, everything should be fine.

"I'm the one who called. My name is Jerod Grey. I'm a retired police officer." The deputy didn't seem to care. We were ordered to the ground and, when a few more officers arrived, we were handcuffed.

It took about thirty minutes before the cops had the gist of the story and had located our police identification cards that said who we were. Combined with my driver's license that listed this as my home address, the sergeant in charge of the scene finally took the cuffs off and allowed me a short reunion with Steve. Like usual when she hadn't seen me in a while, she was excited to the point of being unable to sit still if I even glanced in her direction.

A crime scene technician arrived, followed by a man and woman, both in suits, who turned out to be the felony assault detectives. Jerome and I were both interviewed and gave our stories. The new digital age upon us, the statements weren't written but instead were recorded. It made it easier. When the detective asked if I knew of anyone who would want me dead, both Jerome and I laughed.

The female detective, I think she said her last name was Stattler, gave us a wry look. "Care to expound on that further, Mr. Grey?"

I ran down the past twelve or so months, starting with the woman who I used to think of as my daughter and ending with T-Rex and his gang. It had been a busy year. Detective Stattler looked at me like I had lost my mind, but when she looked at Jerome for some support, he shrugged his shoulders and confirmed that it was all true.

The crime scene technicians and the detectives finally finished up after a few hours. Jerome was allowed to go after he had given his statement. He had a business to run and my little conflict this morning meant he was losing money, as he hadn't been able to open the gym. After shaking his hand and telling him thank you for backing me up, I told him to send me a bill. He wouldn't, of course.

After Jerome left, Steve and I sat down on the couch while the police went about their business of taking photographs and collecting evidence. Steve was content to lie next to me as long as I was petting her. We hadn't seen each other in two weeks. It would be a week or more before she would leave my side.

One by one, the law enforcement personnel started to leave. Detective Stattler was one of the last to go. She was polite but all business. I got the distinct impression that she didn't appreciate me engaging in a firefight within her jurisdiction. If I wasn't being hard-headed, I would have told her that this whole ordeal had left me less than happy, too. I had managed to live here for a while without being overly concerned with security, but that was going to have to change. I couldn't have people just showing up on my property and trying to kill me. It set a bad precedent.

Once Detective Stattler left, I got up and walked around to survey the damage. Most of it was superficial. I would have to get a contractor out to fix all the drywall and repair the stairwell railings.

I walked into the kitchen and saw a young lady sitting on the bench in the breakfast nook. She appeared to be in her mid-to-late twenties, with short, curly black hair and dark skin. She was rifling through an accordion file with what appeared to be mounds of paperwork. Steve, who hadn't left my side since she and I were reunited, sat down next to me, ears up, and head cocked to one side in curiosity.

"Uh, hello?" I said.

"Hello. I'm Zuleyka Perez. Mr. Hansen sent me."

She was precise, almost clipped, in her inflection. "Ok. He say why?"

"Yes. Over the past few months we have been in the process of creating a non-profit organization. He donated $20 million to get it started. We still have a lot of work to do and it is my job to assist you in this endeavor."

"Twenty million? Jesus, that's a lot of money."

"Actually, it is only .35% of his overall assets."

I sat down on the bench opposite her. "And exactly what is this non-profit supposed to do?"

"Its primary mission will be to locate and recover lost artifacts and return those artifacts to their rightful owners and to facilitate the growth of knowledge."

"He's turned the Adventurers' Club into a non-profit? Like a full-on 501(c)(3) non-profit?" It had been an idea I had toyed with off and on for the past year but nothing I had considered seriously.

"Well, not yet, Mr. Grey, but that is the goal. He has provided the funding and me. The rest is up to you."

"I think I understand. Excuse me for a moment." I got up from the table and grabbed my cell phone off the kitchen counter. As I walked to the living room, I dialed Bob's private line. He picked up after three rings.

"Robert, there's a girl in my house who says she was sent by you and that I'm now the head of a non-profit. Why is that?"

"You called me Robert. Are you angry?" His voice was neutral.

"No. I'm not angry, Robert. I've had somewhat of a rough morning and now I have a lady here with an armful of paperwork. I just want to know why?"

"Now you have called me Robert twice. Three times and I'm summoned forth, I believe. You are referring to Ms. Perez. She's there to assist you in creating a non-profit. It doesn't happen on its own. The government, problematic as it is, likes paperwork, and you hate doing it. I hired someone who thinks paperwork makes the world go around to help you."

"But why, Bob? This was just an idea I had that I discussed with you. I didn't intend to make it happen. At least not yet."

"You procrastinated, Jerod. It's a good idea and it helps me solve a financial dilemma in that I use my own money to fund these expeditions and company resources to support them. The former I have no issue with, but the latter puts me in a bind with the shareholders. They don't like expenses that do not in return earn them a profit. By creating a non-profit bolstered by my donation, I can separate the latter from the for-profit side.

"Also, it gives you more autonomy. You no longer have to ask my permission to initiate an operation, have credit cards turned on, or generate contracts. All of that will be handled in-house with your operations staff."

"Operations staff?"

"Well, when and if you hire them."

I thought about it for a minute. Bob was usually right on these things. He hadn't managed to build a multi-billion dollar company without at least some instinct for how things should work. Plus, I could see the ethical problem of using his company's assets to support the Adventurers' Club's expeditions. I wouldn't say they hadn't been profitable, but it wasn't what Hansen Investment Corporation did as a part of their business model. They bought companies, streamlined them, and then sold them for a profit – or held on to them if they were making a good profit already.

"Dammit, Bob. I was enjoying my retirement."

"You were languishing in a general malaise over the death of your girlfriend. Not that I blame you, my friend, but grief has had its time."

I thought about it for a second. I had been grieving for Cat, but I also felt that I had shaken that off, for the most part, and even started to date a little again. Of course, Susan, Bob's wife, had strongarmed me into the date. Nonetheless, I had gone, and even had fun that weekend, and I was looking forward to her coming down to my place soon.

"Fine, Bob. I'll give it a shot, but if it starts cutting too deeply into my ability to just have fun, I'll resign and you can find someone else."

"Technically, the method of selecting your successor has yet to be determined. You haven't written the by-laws yet."

"Now you're just being a smart ass." I heard him chuckle a little and then he hung up. I took the phone away from my ear and stared at it for a moment before putting it in my pocket and walking back into the kitchen. Ms. Perez was sitting there exactly as I had left her.

I returned to the bench opposite hers. There was an awkward silence as we took each other's measure. I broke the silence first. "So, you're the girl who does the paperwork."

Not missing a beat, she responded, "I'm the woman who assists you with the paperwork."

"There's a difference?"

"A very big difference."

We stared at each other for a minute. I'd give her credit, there were a lot of people who wouldn't hold my gaze for long. "I didn't ask for you to be here. As far as I'm concerned, you can leave."

"You didn't, and yet here I am. Mr. Hansen asked me to help you and he promised me a decent salary in return. I could use the financial stability of a steady, decent paycheck."

"Sounds like a personal problem, Ms. Perez."

"Sounds like your problem, Mr. Grey. I am the first of the Adventurers' Club's full-time employees and until it's decided otherwise, you are the presumptive head of the Adventurers' Club. If you fire me, it will be without cause and it will open you up to civil liability."

My eyes narrowed. Her eyes did likewise. I leaned forward, and she mimicked me and did so as well. It was like facing a younger version of myself. I was getting nowhere trying to intimidate her and she knew it. We were at a stalemate. I let the silence draw out a little longer. When

I thought that it had gone on long enough and she hadn't blinked or backed down, I broke it. "Ok, then. Let's get to work."

Her whole demeanor changed. "Excellent. Can I call you boss? I hear a lot of people call you boss?"

"No. You can call me Mr. Grey or, if you prefer, Dr. Grey."

"Ok, boss," she said without missing a beat. I almost smiled, thinking of Bob and how much he hated being called that name. I didn't hate being called boss and she was right, a lot of people did, particularly those that had served on my tactical patrol boats when I was in the Navy.

Zuleyka Perez laid out her credentials for me. She had graduated from San Jose State University with a degree in business and then from UC Berkeley with her MBA. She was 27 and had focused most of her efforts on managing non-profits and had met Bob through his wife, Susan. Susan was the benefactor for a number of different charitable organizations, one of which Zuleyka had been a part of. They had met at an event several years ago and then she met Bob about six months ago.

According to her, after Bob and I had discussed the possibility of making the Adventurers' Club a more formal organization, he had reached out to Zuleyka and asked her to be a part of the team that would be instrumental in creating the non-profit. She also said that Bob had been clear that I hated paperwork. He knew me well.

Zuleyka had grown up in Oakland and, as the oldest daughter to a single mother, she had to learn to work early and she had been continuously employed since she was fourteen. While her mother may not have been particularly successful in life, she had instilled in her daughter a strong work ethic and a drive to do something positive with her life. She was bubbling with ideas on how the Adventurers' Club could be utilized: helping to bring much needed supplies to areas ravaged by natural disaster, working with impoverished youth to show them alternatives to life on the streets by taking them to museums and archaeological sites, and investigating natural phenomena, to name a few of the dozen ideas that sprang into her mind. I could tell she had a creative side as well as a pragmatic business-minded side. I was starting to warm up to her.

She would need a place to work. I had an office in the basement of the house, but it was really kind of dreary with just four cinder block walls, an old metal desk with my desktop computer, bookshelves lined with books and an old oak table that I used as a workbench. For now, I would let her use the dining room until we could work out a more long-term solution.

Turned out she and Bob had already started planning. One of Hansen Investments' subsidiaries provided portable offices and a representative would be by today to survey a site to place one. All I had to do was to sign the authorization to spend money on the project. I was back to being annoyed, though not with Zuleyka so much as with Bob. He had obviously been working on this with her for a bit now and had failed to discuss it with me. In his defense, though, I probably would have dragged my feet getting started on all of this. I was retired and this sounded an awful lot like work to me.

I showed Zuleyka to the dining room and told her the space was hers to utilize until I had determined whether I wanted to put a portable office on my property. It wasn't like I didn't have the room. The house itself wasn't too big – two bedrooms and a bathroom upstairs and a living room, dining room, and decent-sized kitchen on the first floor, plus the basement office. I had an attached two-car garage that was big enough to hold my Jeep with its two-inch lift kit and a full-sized GMC Sierra king cab pickup with the standard Z71 off-road package. There was also the large metal building, 15,000 square feet worth, where a lot of the supplies we used for our adventurers were stored. In addition to the food unit boxes and tent boxes provided by Expeditionary Research Group, the outbuilding is where the Toyota Land Cruiser, ATVs, snowmobiles, and a variety of other pieces of gear and equipment were stored. It also had a bunkhouse and bathroom for when I had more people here than I had room for in my house.

With all that, though, I had five acres of land around the house and it was more than enough room for a portable office. Several of them, in fact. Damn, this was going to happen.

After showing her the table where she could set up a place to work, I gave her a tour of the house and the property. She noted the damage done by this morning's scuffle. "I overheard the police talking. Were there really men here trying to kill you?"

I looked around the living room at some of the paintings that had been torn off the wall and pulled from their frames. "They didn't seem averse to me being dead, but I'm not sure that was their primary goal, either. I may have just been in the way. Question is, did they find what they were looking for, and if not, will they be back to either finish the job or continue their search?"

Zuleyka got a wry look on her face. "Well, Mr. Hansen did say you were exciting to be around. I just thought he meant the normal kind of excitement that comes from your expeditions. I didn't realize he meant cloak-and-dagger, fighting-for-your-life kind of excitement."

"It's kind of fifty-fifty."

CHAPTER TWO

It had been over two weeks since the attack on my house and there had been no further occurrences. It probably helped that I'd hired a private security firm to provide around-the-clock, on-site services until the new security system was installed. In addition to cameras and motion sensors, I had upgraded the windows on the bottom floor with nearly indestructible polycarbonate plastic and had the frames reinforced. Likewise, the doors were steel core in steel frames with some of the best locks money could buy. Someone who was determined, or who had military or SWAT training, could still get through, but with the addition of steel shutters that could be closed with the push of a button, the house was now practically a fortress. It had also drained what little I had left in my savings account.

The guys who had come in to complete the repairs and security upgrades went about their work as unobtrusively as possible, but after two weeks I was ready to have my house back to myself. The final touch was turning the basement into a safe room and that was still a few weeks from completion. I'd have to deal with the intrusion until then.

Things were likewise progressing with the Adventurers' Club (a Non-Profit Organization). That last part was an official portion of our title. Apparently there was already an Adventurers' Club registered out there, so we had to add in the extra part to avoid copyright issues or conflicts.

Zuleyka and I had completed all the necessary paperwork and filed it with both the state and federal governments. It could take anywhere from two to twelve months before the IRS granted approval for the 501(c)(3) status. We had the paperwork reviewed by an attorney who specialized in tax law and he said everything appeared in order. He had posed questions that he thought the IRS might ask so that we could be sure to have the answers before the package was submitted.

I had split the administration of the Adventurers' Club into two sections: Operations and Personnel Support. Operations was responsible for the planning and execution of any of our expeditions. We were in the process of trying to hire an Operations Chief to oversee that section. Under that position would be a logistics specialist who would make sure we had the supplies and equipment we needed for any operation, as well as arrange transportation, billeting, and deal with the expedition budget.

On the Personnel Support side, we had hired Dan Thomasson to be the Personnel Chief. Dan and I had known each other for over forty years and he was more of a brother to me than a friend. He'd jumped at the opportunity and would be here in a few days. Under him would fall all the administrative duties including human resource management, finance, and IT functions. Dan was a whiz with the computers so he could handle the IT portion himself. HR and finance, though, were beyond our capabilities. Finance was going to be headed up by Zuleyka. She had proven herself more than capable over the past few weeks and I had to call Bob and give a roundabout apology for my initial reaction to her showing up at my house. Finance included allocation for operations, receiving and managing donations, the annual budget, and taxes.

Our HR specialist was an old friend of mine from the Navy. Rosalia Gutierrez had retired as a Master Chief from the reserves (something she had never let me forget, as I had only attained the rank of Senior Chief). She had her work cut out for her from day one: human resources and dealing with government codes to make sure we weren't in violation of any state or federal laws. On top of that, she had to secure benefits packages for each employee, document and categorize the skills of each of the thirty-some-odd people who were "official" members of the Adventurers' Club, and deal with payroll. We could offer her some help in that we already had a list of people – including their general skill sets – that was distributed to each member of the Club. She just had to make it more official. Rosa had started working last week and currently occupied the other half of the dining room table that was acting as her and Zuleyka's workspace.

For physical structures, the concrete slabs for the portables to sit on had already been poured and the necessary utilities run to them and prepared for hookup. The modular offices would be delivered within the next day or so. We had chosen one 8'x28' building that would serve as my office and conference room, along with two 14'x66' buildings with two private offices and a bathroom in each, plus additional space for workstations and a communications center.

In addition to the Operations Chief, Personnel Support Chief, Finance Director, Human Resources Director and me as the Executive Director, we had decided to hire three additional people as full-time employees. The first was an office manager – someone who could maintain our work spaces, field calls when we were out of the office, and basically make sure we were all communicating properly. Another was a Public Information Officer. That was Zuleyka's idea. We needed someone to manage our press so our name got out there, coordinate fund-raising, and act as spokesperson for the Club. Finally, the last position was my recommendation: I wanted a researcher – someone who was actively pursuing work for us to do. Up until now, we had mostly waited for work to come to us.

Things were moving quickly. It helped that Bob ultimately owned the company that provided the modular buildings and that the general contractor and I had served in the Marine Corps together. It meant everyone bent over backwards to make this all happen. I was impressed.

CHAPTER THREE

A couple minutes before 5:00 a.m. my internal alarm woke me up. Zuleyka, or Z, as I had taken to calling her, would be in around 7:00 and Rosalia by 8:00. The construction crews would be here by 9:00; that gave me two hours of personal time and two hours to work before the house became too crowded. I leveraged myself out of bed and stifled a groan as my back protested the movement. First order of business was to let Steve out and to put on a pot of coffee.

Steve had just started sleeping back in her bed. This was something that happened any time we were separated for more than a few days. She became clingy and wouldn't leave my side, just in case I disappeared again. That meant she also felt compelled to sleep in my bed with me until she was convinced I was staying put.

Steve stood up from her bed, stretched and let out a big yawn, and then came up to me, tail wagging, for her early morning scratches. There were worse ways of waking up in the morning than to have someone simply happy just to see you up, but there weren't many better. I gave her a few extra scratches and then headed downstairs with Steve trailing behind me.

When I got to the kitchen, I flipped on the lights and then grabbed a small Motorola two-way radio that was sitting on the counter and let the security team know that I was up and was about to let the dog out. This was the system we had come up with when, after their first day on the job, I had walked out onto my back porch and startled one of the guards to the point where he drew his gun on me. I'm an understanding kind of guy but I don't like weapons pointed in my direction. We calmed the situation down quickly, but we did decide that to avoid future confusion, I'd just radio them once I was awake and moving.

I opened the back door and turned on the porch light. It would be another 30 to 45 minutes before the sun was up. Once Steve was out taking care of her business, I started the coffee and then fixed Steve some food.

Putting the dog food on the floor next to her water bowl, I headed upstairs to shower and put on clothes other than the t-shirt and shorts I was wearing. After the shower, I grabbed a cup of coffee and went out on the back porch to play with Steve.

By the time breakfast was done and the dishes washed, I only had about half an hour left before Z came in for work. I spent the time cleaning what parts of the house I could. It was hard to sweep and mop every day when you had construction workers in and out every five minutes.

I walked into the living room and looked around to see if there was anything that could be done that wouldn't be undone within a few minutes of the construction crew showing up. For the most part, the living room was tidy. The work to repair the bullet holes and the damage done when my two assailants had torn a few paintings down had been completed a few days ago. Plastic still covered the furniture to keep it from getting paint or too much dust on it. The only thing that I could see was that the floor needed to be cleaned, but that wouldn't happen until all the work was done.

I started to head upstairs when the Salvador Dali painting caught my eye. It was the only one the two men had not torn from the wall and removed from its frame. I presumed they were men. They both sounded like men, although I suppose it's possible that one, or both, could have been women with masculine voices. Two weeks and the cops didn't have a lead yet. Detective Stattler was heading up the investigation. She had gone through and verified that all the people who I thought wouldn't mind seeing me dead – the two Touscher cousins, and Rex and his crew – were all still behind bars. Jan was the only one unaccounted for, but they suspected that she had fled the country and gone to Mexico. None of the others would be getting out any time soon, each being held for homicides they'd committed.

Still, the painting was itching at the back of my mind. I was about to go pull it off the wall when I heard the back door open. Steve gave out an excited bark so I knew it wasn't anyone to worry about. A second later I heard Zuleyka's voice calling Steve a good girl. I temporarily forgot the painting and headed for the kitchen.

Zuleyka came in with her usual whirlwind of activity and a stack of paperwork that never seemed to grow smaller. If anything, it looked bigger than it had when we first started working on this project. "Good morning, boss. Anything new and exciting?"

"You mean since you left work yesterday at 8:00 p.m.? No, in the intervening eleven hours, nothing new has happened." I laughed. "Good morning, Z. What's on the agenda today?"

I followed her to the dining room that she was using as a makeshift office. Hopefully by this time next week, the offices would be done and I could have my house back. Not that I minded all that much. It was nice having people around and, in the bustle of activity surrounding getting the Adventurers' Club turned into something more formal, the weeks had flown by.

"Let's see," she said, pulling out a notepad and thumbing through the pages. "We have a pre-installation meeting with the modular company's manager today at 9:00. He said it should only take about thirty minutes for him to make sure he knew exactly how we want them set up, but I gave him an hour just in case. At 10:00 a.m. we have an interview for PIO. That will take an hour. Lunch after that and then two more interviews at 1:00 and 2:00 p.m. for PIO and Office Manager. I really like the lady applying for officer manager. She has the experience and she's pleasant. At 3:30 we're meeting with Rosalia to go over some of the benefits packages. That should finish off our day."

"So, a light day then." Zuleyka rolled her eyes at me.

I flashed a smile. "I will leave you to your work. Coffee pot is on and still has some coffee left. I'd get yours before Rosa gets in. She drinks coffee like most people drink water. I'm going to take Steve for a walk and then work out."

"Rough being the boss."

"That it is." I laughed.

I called Steve and we headed out the back door. The nice thing about having five acres was that we could walk a little trail through the trees on the property and Steve could get some exercise in by running ahead and playing with the squirrels who tormented her by scurrying up the trees out of her reach. If the squirrels wouldn't play, she always had a ball or a stick with her that I threw for her. Unless it was raining, it was a part of our morning and evening ritual.

It was almost 8:00 before I got back to the house. Rosa was already seated on her side of the dining table and was furiously typing away at a computer keyboard. I changed into my workout clothes and after a quick session, showered and changed into something more appropriate for the workday. For me, that consisted of hiking pants and a t-shirt.

When I went back downstairs, Z was waiting in the kitchen. Our 9:00 a.m. appointment was already here and she told me I was running late, giving me a reproachful look in the process.

The project manager for the modular offices was friendly and thorough and he walked us through how they were going to place the buildings in relation to each other. The overall effect would be to create a courtyard-like area between the buildings. Zuleyka was already planning out the courtyard, including tables for people to eat lunch at, trees or umbrellas for shade, and bushes at the open end of the courtyard to give it more privacy. We were on five acres in the foothills of Marin County; I didn't think privacy was an issue, but did agree that a courtyard area would be nice.

The meeting with the project manager lasted about 45 minutes and because I had been running behind that morning, it meant our 10:00 a.m. interviewee was already waiting for us. Rosalia, as our Human Resources Director, joined us for the interview. I liked the applicant, Joanna Walton. She was fluent in Spanish, knew the ins and outs of social media and more importantly, how to use that social media to generate brand name recognition. She had also spent some time as a spokesperson for a dot-com company and had done on-air interviews. For her part, she liked the flexibility that we offered. She and her wife were trying to start a family and that flexibility and our proposed benefits package would be beneficial to that endeavor.

I was ready to hire her on the spot, but we had one more interview that afternoon and then we would all sit down and decide.

We had a working lunch on the back porch of the house. Z went over our finance report and gave me a list of expenses that had to be approved before she could request checks. Rosa gave us a synopsis of the benefits packages we'd be discussing later in the afternoon so we'd have time to review them before our meeting. Business out of the way, we sat and ate our lunches and talked about how our weekends had been.

The afternoon was spent making phone calls, conducting interviews and, my all-time favorite, reviewing and signing paperwork. There seemed to be no end to it. But by 6:00 p.m., we had decided to hire Ms. Walton as our PIO and Ms. Nadia Bello as our office manager. Ms. Bello was quiet but efficient, a gnostic Christian whose family had fled Muslim persecution in Sudan. She was fluent in Sudanese Arabic and Bejawi, had an arranged marriage to a man who still lived in the Sudan, and had one son, Najir, who was now two.

My plan was to make this a family-friendly work environment and, to that end, our policies included allowing parents to bring their children to work. I didn't think we would be so busy that it would detract from getting the work done, but if it did, we'd consider changing the policy then or, more likely, just addressing the individual. Considering now that most of my staff were women, including the Finance Director, Human Resources Director, PIO, and Office Manager, all of whom, except for Rosalia, were of an age where they were starting, could start, or had started a family, it made sense to be flexible in this regard.

To be fair, though, the policy also applied to men, but at least for the moment, the only two men who were full-time staff were Dan and I and both of us were later in years and more than likely not having children at this point. Not that it wasn't possible. The lady I had been seeing was just 33 years old and she wanted to have children. If things continued to work out for us, it was still possible I could be a father.

While Rosa and Zuleyka finished up their work for the day, I made spaghetti for all of us. Nothing fancy, mind you. Some spicy sausage and a jar of sauce were the extent of my spaghetti-making skills, but with a little garlic bread, it was a filling meal for the three of us.

While eating dinner, we finished the conversation we had started earlier in the day regarding benefits packages. Debating the pluses and minuses of each plan, we finally settled on one that would cost the employee some money out of pocket but would offer better coverage for medical and dental.

When dinner was done, Rosa and Zuleyka collected their personal belongings and straightened out their work space while I did the dishes and cleaned up the kitchen. It was almost 7:00 p.m.

Once they had left for the night, I took Steve out for our evening walk. The two security guards were out and about, too. During the day, they mostly monitored the traffic coming in and out. In the evening, they patrolled the property. I talked with them for a bit while throwing a ball for Steve. They were both young and fresh out of the military, trying to decide what to do with the rest of their lives. One kid wanted to be a cop and the other was taking some classes at a local junior college until he decided what to major in.

I continued my walk with Steve and we were back in the house by 8:00. I poured myself a bourbon and sat down to watch some news. I was trying to pay attention to the TV, but my eyes kept going to the Dali painting. Finally, my curiosity got to me and I got up out of my recliner and pulled the painting from the wall, much more gently then the two men who had stormed into my house had done with the other paintings.

I looked at the painting in greater detail. According to what Cat had told me, the painting was a variation on a Metamorphosis of Narcissus, maybe a later version of the famous painting that he created in 1937. The Spanish surrealist had given the painting to a young, adventurous young lady while he was staying in Monterey, California. Cat had purchased the painting from that lady's grandson and was going to sell it to a client of hers; when the deal had fallen through, she ended up with the painting and out the large sum of money she had spent to buy it. Not fitting the décor of either her office or her condo in San Francisco, she had left it with me. Apparently, I had no décor, so you could throw anything on my walls and it would 'fit.' When she passed, her father let me keep it, rather than sell it as a part of her estate.

I flipped the painting over and looked at the back. It had been expertly framed, but the back was covered in a thick paper. To remove the painting from the frame, you'd have to cut away the paper. I laid the painting on the coffee table and pulled out my knife. Making a small, careful incision in the paper, I lifted the cut portion of the paper to see if anything was inside.

I was not disappointed. Inside the painting were several age-yellowed pages that appeared to have been torn from a journal. Carefully, I removed the pages until I was sure no more were inside and then I hung the painting back up on the wall.

Gathering up the pages, I took them to the kitchen where I'd have better light and laid them out on the small table in the breakfast nook. Each was scribed in a neat, flowing hand and, fortunately, in English. Unless I missed my mark, I would say the writer was female and most likely the lady to whom Dali had given the painting. I read through the pages. They weren't numbered so I had to guess at their order, but once I thought I had them correctly laid out, they told a story. I just didn't know what the story was.

I went back to the living room and grabbed my glass, refilled it with bourbon and returned to the kitchen, and sitting down in the breakfast nook, I started reading through the pages. Each entry was dated, and some had locations given by address like the entry that read "333 Wonderview Avenue #221." Others were just descriptions of locations. Six pages in total, each having several entries. I sipped my bourbon and tried to puzzle out why she would hide these pages in a painting.

The first entry was dated May 4, 1969, and it read, "Your journey starts here, follow the path." Unlike the rest of the dates, this one seemed to be out of order. I picked it as the first page because of the inscription next to the date and because the dates on the other entries were in closer chronological order. The next was September 2, 1941 and the entry was "Night in a Surreal Forest, Bali Room." After that date was an entry for September 14, 1941 that read "The Fahnestocks, Kamasan, third time."

I couldn't make any sense of it. These were pages torn from a book and I had to wonder if there wasn't more information in the book itself, like these were a table of contents of sorts and so they didn't give anything more than just enough information to jog a memory. The Fahnestocks entry was followed by "October 8, 1941 – Salli, Betty, and Rita" and "January 10, 1942 – Town Hall, sold-out crowd."

I continued to look through the pages for another thirty minutes. I knew that I wasn't going to get anywhere just staring at them, but I was also hoping that maybe I could puzzle out their meaning. I gathered up the pages and took them to the dining room. Since my home office was under renovation to become the panic room, we were all using the dining table as a work station, although I used it less than Z and Rosa.

I sat down and fired up my laptop. While the computer went through its start-up process, I snapped photos of the notebook pages with my cell phone and emailed them to both of my accounts. If this is what the two men had been looking for, it would be prudent to have multiple copies.

Once the computer was up, I opened the internet browser and typed in the first date and clicked on the webpage titled, "What Happened On May 4, 1969." There wasn't much there. The Montreal Canadiens swept the St. Louis Blues in four games, Sandra Haynie won the LPGA Shreveport Kiwanis Club Golf Invitational, and Charles Gordon's "No Place to be Somebody" premiered in New York City. Nothing of serious interest.

I went back to the search engine and added "Monterey" to the search criteria. I received an entry about the Grateful Dead playing at the Monterey Performing Arts Center and some things about Fort Ord. I scanned further down and saw a name I recognized. It was an obituary for Harold D. Touscher III, born May 4, 1969. Touscher was the man who had sold Cat the painting – the painting that had belonged to his grandmother. The pages were meant for him, or at least that's what I surmised.

Entering the date and other information for the next line, I was rewarded with a slew of webpages regarding Salvador Dali's gala at the Bali Room at the Hotel Del Monte. That fit in with the story I had been told regarding Harold Touscher's grandmother having been given the painting by Salvador Dali. I felt like I was on the right track now.

I typed in the information for the next entry and came up with nothing useful. I removed "Kamasan" and just went with the date and

"Fahnestock." There was a link near the bottom of the page for the "Fahnestock South Sea Collection." My first thought was that it was possibly a painting collection, my logic being that Salvador Dali was a surrealist painter and maybe some of his paintings were kept in the South Sea Collection.

It turned out to be more than that. It was a collection of audio recordings, film footage, photographs, and the accompanying manuscripts assembled by two brothers, Bruce and Sheridan Fahnestock, during their expeditions to Oceania and Southeast Asia in 1940 and 1941. Their journey took them to Bali, which is also where I found a reference to Kamasan. Turned out it's a city in Bali with some cultural significance, although I didn't dig in deep on what that significance was. It was starting to get late.

I looked at the clock and realized it was almost midnight. I looked around for Steve and found her asleep on the couch in the living room. I didn't normally let her up on the furniture but when she was miffed at me, no doubt because I had spent the last few hours doing research on this and taking notes, she crawled up on the couch in defiance – a subtle reminder that if I didn't give her the attention she wanted, she'd do her own thing.

"Come on, girl. Let's go outside one more time and then we'll go to bed."

Steve raised her head and then slowly stretched her way off the couch. We headed for the back door. I grabbed the two-way radio off the kitchen counter and told the two security guys that I'd be coming out with Steve. Once they acknowledged, Steve and I stepped out.

Steve ran off into the darkness and I sat down on one of the several chairs that were on the porch. It was a beautiful night. There were things about California that I disliked: the high taxes, the politics, and the crowds, but there were only a few states that could match California for its beauty. The coast line, the Sierras, the redwoods, and so on. The other major benefit, at least in the San Francisco Bay Area, was the weather. It would get hot during the daytime, but it was only a few times a year that it got hot enough at night to need air conditioning. Right now, it was a perfect temperature.

While I waited for Steve to finish her business, I thought about the notebook pages and the three entries I felt I understood. I could somewhat follow the logic of going from the Bali Room at the Hotel Del Monte in Monterey to Bali itself, although I wished I had more of explanation for why. It seemed whimsical, and maybe it was. I was presuming it was Harold Touscher's grandmother and if I was correct, she could have only been in her early twenties at the time. I wanted to find out more about her but that would have to wait for a few days. We had a packed schedule with the delivery of the modular buildings, the plumbing and electrical hook-ups, and the delivery and set up of the office furniture, and all that while we continued with interviews.

Dan would be in on Wednesday and he could take over sitting in on the interviews with Rosa and I could turn my attention to recruiting someone for the position of Operations Chief. When we first started advertising the openings, there had been plenty of people drop applications for the other positions, but we'd received only a few for operations. It took a particular skill set, one that you would find only in the military and law enforcement, and none of the people who had applied so far had that skill set. I was going to have to reach out to my friends in the Navy Chief's Mess and those in police work and generate some names to call.

Steve broke my thoughts by dropping a ball on my lap. "Want to play some, eh, girl?" I reached down and ruffled her neck fur and then picked up the ball and threw it for her. I didn't worry about her losing the ball in the dark. I swore she could track her ball across an ocean if she needed to.

We continued to play for another ten to fifteen minutes before going back inside the house. I shut and locked the back door, checked the downstairs windows and front door to ensure they were all secure, and then radioed the security guards that I was in for the night.

Shutting off the lights as I made my way upstairs, I brushed my teeth and then climbed into bed. The bourbon I'd had while doing research on the computer was enough to make me feel relaxed and it wasn't long before I was sound asleep.

CHAPTER FOUR

I was up by 4:30 a.m. no worse for wear, given I only had a little more than four hours of sleep. Throwing on a pair of shorts, an old t-shirt and my running shoes, Steve and I headed downstairs. I almost forgot to notify security that I was headed out the back door but recalled it in time to avoid another embarrassing moment with them. I could just imagine how they would react if some figure went running by in the dark.

Steve and I stepped out onto the back porch and she ran off to do her business while I stretched muscles tight from a night's sleep and warmed up some. When she came back, she and I started off up the driveway for a morning run. I hated running but it was good cardio, and given the amount I hiked or found myself in awkward situations where running might be required, I did it two times a week, whether I hated it or not.

I had courses marked off going either direction on the road once I was out of my driveway. I could either run downhill to start by going to the right, or run uphill first if I went left. Today, I decided to get the uphill run done first and went left. Steve didn't care one way or the other. She was an Australian Cattle Dog and they were known for their incredible endurance. I had seen her hike all day, chasing squirrels and rabbits and then still want to play for hours once we arrived back at our base camp. I had to force her to sit still or she very well might literally run herself to exhaustion.

We did a three-mile circuit, taking a moment from the run up the hill around the halfway point to do three sets of pull-ups on a tree branch well suited to the purpose, plus some push-ups and crunches, before heading back down the hill. It wasn't a fast run, maybe only around a ten-minute mile pace, but it was enough to cause me to break a sweat and to get my heart rate up. By the time we arrived back at the house, it was almost 5:30.

I fed Steve, put on a pot of coffee and then headed upstairs to shower and get dressed. By 6:00 I was coming back down to the kitchen dressed in my typical t-shirt, hiking pants, and the boots that Bob had sent me not long ago. They were hand-crafted leather with a toe cap and some subtle broguing. They were a little heavier than the hiking boots I had been wearing, but they were holding up beautifully, and the more I wore them, the more comfortable they were. When Bob had asked me for my opinion, I had given them five full stars and he invested in the start-up company that was making them.

Pouring myself a cup of coffee, I heated up some water on the stove and made myself some oatmeal and ate a banana. Not a fancy breakfast, but enough to see me through the morning. As I ate, I looked through yesterday's mail. Most of it was either junk mail or addressed to the Adventurers' Club. There was also a letter from my friend, Curtis, who was a professor at Harvard. I opened it.

The letter started with Curtis' typical formal greeting and then cut right to the chase. He had two graduate students who were taking some time off from school to work on their theses and to gain some practical skills in research application in the field. He had heard about the Adventurers' Club going formal and that I was looking for a researcher and wondered if I would be interested in talking to them. The letter also contained the two kids' curriculum vitaes and some documentation regarding a grant they could operate under while they worked for me that would offset some of the cost to the Club.

I called Curtis. The nice thing about being on the West Coast was that it was anywhere from one to three hours later everywhere else. It was almost 9:00 Eastern Time and I didn't run the risk of calling Curtis too early. We talked about the two kids, a man and a woman, both good students who excelled at research. They both sounded like they would work well with my operational concept for the Adventurers' Club. I told Curtis to give them Rosalia's number and to work out arrangements with her to fly out here for an interview and that we would cover the plane ticket and accommodations while they were here. Curtis thanked me for giving his students the opportunity and we hung up the phone with the promise to catch up soon.

The possibility of having someone to do research was almost as exciting to me as having the Adventurers' Club fully operational. I thought about the notebook pages I had found in the painting. Someone with more computer and research skills then I had could probably have found out considerably more in half the time it took me last night to research just three of the entries. Not that I was a slouch at academic pursuits. I had earned a Doctorate, after all, which had required I do extensive amounts of research to complete. But sitting at a desk behind a computer was not my thing.

Zuleyka walked through the door at about a quarter to seven. She had her hands full of accordion files and paperwork. I had yet to grasp her filing system but whatever it was, it seemed to work for her. I got up from the breakfast table to give her a hand.

"Mornin', boss."

"Good morning, Z. What's on the agenda today?"

She handed off a stack of files and we walked to the dining room. "Well, we have one interview but not until after lunch. Besides that, relatively easy day. Tomorrow will be busy, though. The modulars are supposed to be delivered in the morning and the office furniture in the afternoon. The contractor will also have the electrical and plumbing hooked up and we all get to move in." She sounded excited. Not that I blamed her, working at the dining room table wasn't ideal. Even as big a table as it was, with the three of us using it for office space it could get crowded.

"Sounds good. What's the interview for?"

"Logistics Specialist. You might like him. Former Army guy, ran a motor pool and a supply division. When I talked to him on the phone, he seemed to know what he was doing."

I nodded my head. I suspected that logistics would be the most boring position we had. There would be some things that needed to be done as a matter of routine, but it wasn't until we were on a mission that the role would be crucial.

"Anything for this morning?"

"No, sir."

"Ok, then. I need to get the Jeep serviced so I'll probably do that this morning and then maybe swing by the barber for a haircut."

"You barely have any hair now, boss," Z said, raising an eyebrow at my close-cut hair.

"What? It's almost long enough to braid." I tried to grab a hold of some of the hair on the side to demonstrate just how long it was getting and failed. It was short. I still wanted a fresh haircut.

"Oh, don't forget to make sure Dan has a ride from the airport. I left his flight information on a sticky note by your computer," she said, as if suddenly remembering.

"Already done, Z. Thanks."

She set all her paperwork down and I set the pile of files she had handed over to me next to them, taking a moment to ensure the stack was as neat as I could make it. "Awesome. Ok, boss, I'll see you later then."

I felt like I was being rushed out, but I was also sure that she wanted to get to work and if I stuck around and didn't have anything to keep me occupied, I'd talk her ear off. I gave her a quick nod, called for Steve and then headed out to the garage. I pushed the automatic garage opener. As the door went up, I unlocked the Jeep and got Steve situated in the back. She had her place by the window with a dog bed big enough for her to lay on and to keep her from getting dog hair all over the back seat.

Backing the Jeep out of the garage, I headed down the driveway and then toward 101 north. The oil changer I used was in Novato, about fifteen minutes up the freeway. There was a carwash right next door so maybe after I had the service done, I could also get the Jeep washed.

As I made the final turn to get on the freeway, I noticed the small, black sedan behind me. It was a typical car, not unusual to find in any city. Maybe I was just being paranoid, but I made a mental note of the license plate number – not that I thought anyone could blame me after my house was broken into, people tried to shoot me, and the place was torn up. As a result, I was now in the process of turning my house into a fortress complete with video monitoring and a state of the art of alarm system. It annoyed me. I enjoyed my peace and quiet and didn't like the idea that the peace had been disturbed. It wasn't my first gunfight. Not even my first gunfight within the past year. This was, however, the first one where I had been attacked in my own house.

I looked in the rearview mirror. The black sedan was still there. I could see at least two occupants but couldn't really provide a description on either due to the tint on the front window. I pulled on to the freeway and accelerated, shifting gears on the Jeep's manual transmission to get up to freeway speed as quickly as possible. We entered on a slight incline and I was hoping the 3.7L V-6 on the Jeep would take the hill faster than the little four-cylinder engine on the sedan and I could put some distance between us just in case. I left the Jeep in fourth gear a little longer than usual to give me the power necessary to accelerate up the hill and then as soon as I hit the crest, I shifted into fifth and hit the gas.

The distance between me and the sedan widened. Steve must have picked up on my mood because she gave a little whine from the back seat. The distance widened a little more, but the sedan was now moving faster, and it could maneuver through traffic a little better than the Jeep and was closing the space between us.

At the next off-ramp, I cut across two lanes of traffic, earning me a horn honk and a guy giving me the finger as I did so. It wasn't graceful, but it worked. The sedan couldn't get over and it zipped past the off-ramp as I exited.

I continued on surface streets to the oil changer. It took considerably longer but I also didn't see the sedan reappear. Again, I could have just been being paranoid. It made no sense to me to follow me anywhere. If it were the same people, and they were after the pages from the notebook, it wouldn't be logical for me to have those pages on me when I could leave them at the house, and that's assuming they believed I had found them.

It could be that it would have been a kidnap attempt. But if they had done their homework, they would know I was a retired police officer and retired military and that more than likely, I was armed. Not wise to try and kidnap a trained and armed man. It would be much easier to kidnap one of my associates. I'd target either Z or Rosa. Maybe I should hire security for the two of them, too?

Despite my reservations that I was just being paranoid, my gut told me I wasn't. I pulled my Bluetooth out of my pocket and stuck it in my ear and then, once it was connected, called the detective who had investigated the Harold Touscher murder, Ryan East. He picked up after a few rings.

"Pacific Grove Police Department, Detective East speaking. How may I assist you?"

"Ryan, it's Jerod. I may have something of interest to you related to the Harold Touscher case."

"Good morning, Jerod. That case is closed. The cousins are in custody and currently sitting in county waiting for trial," he said in a matter-of-fact manner.

I ran down the events of a few weeks ago when I was attacked in my house. I told him about the painting and the notebook pages and added that I believed that when I left my house today, I had been followed. I gave him the plate number of the vehicle.

"Probably shouldn't be doing this but I can see how the two could be connected." I heard typing on a computer keyboard. "Comes back as a 2010 Toyota registered to a rental car company." He casually mentioned the name of the rental car company and said that he would follow up on it as soon as he processed the dozen cases he had pending. It was summer, and no matter how nice the Monterey Bay area was, tourists always came with problems. I thanked him for his time and hung up the phone.

I pulled into the service center, still distracted. The young lady who was my service representative went through a list of recommended services, including flushing my coolant system and servicing the differentials. I agreed to each, signed the paperwork they had and then kicked back in the Jeep while they did their jobs. I was still thinking when she brought over my air filter to show me. My first thought was,

"Yes, it's dirty. It's doing its job." Instead I focused for a second on what she was saying and then agreed to let them change the filter, too.

Maybe it wasn't just the pages they were after. Cat and I had been the last to see Mr. Touscher alive before he was murdered by his cousins. Perhaps they thought I knew something they wanted to know. I had waited in the car, though, while Cat went in to meet with Mr. Touscher and to purchase the painting. I started racking my brain, trying to recall every bit of the conversation Cat and I had after she came back out.

Nothing stood out. We were excited to get our weekend started and had headed back to the Navy Post Graduate School and the old Del Monte Hotel that was now a part of the Navy Gateway Inn and Suites. It was the same location where Salvador Dali had held his gala to raise money for artists displaced by the war in Europe.

My thoughts were interrupted by the service representative. She asked me to start the Jeep and then went through a series of checks to ensure that my headlights, brake lights, and turn signals all worked. Declaring my vehicle safe, she had me sign the credit card receipt and then guided me out of the vehicle bay.

I pulled out, drove down the street and turned into a shopping center across the street. Time for a haircut. It was still early so there wasn't much in the way of a wait. Within fifteen minutes, I was seated in the chair. Once the haircut was complete, I went to a small diner nearby with outdoor seating so Steve could sit with me. While I ate, I shared small bits of my bacon with her and used my phone to try to find more information on Harold Touscher's grandmother. It wasn't easy. I knew, based on the story that Cat had told me, that the Touschers themselves had been moderately wealthy. I also knew the grandmother had three children. Her son had died while serving in the military. Her middle daughter, Harold's mother, had married, and the youngest daughter had run with the wrong crowd. I didn't know if the youngest was still alive or not and quite frankly, I didn't have enough information on the family to determine any of their maiden names. I was getting frustrated.

It was almost 10:00 before I finished breakfast and Steve and I were back in the car. I decided to take Steve to a dog park for a bit before heading home. I had also reached the conclusion that Zuleyka and Rosalia needed better security until this matter was resolved. Dan would be staying with me for the time being until he was settled and had time to find a place of his own and none of the other people had started work with us yet. If the bad guys were going to target someone other than me, it seemed most likely that they would select someone that they might have seen consistently coming and going from my house, someone who was obviously not a part of the construction crews.

I called up Rosa and told her to contact the security company. I explained why and that it was just a precaution. If I was wrong, no harm done, and if I was right, she and Z would have additional protection when they weren't at the property. She wasn't happy with the idea. She had retired as a Master Chief from the Navy and she didn't like the thought of putting her security in the hands of anyone but herself. Still, she agreed to do it.

I had also decided it was time to be more proactive in figuring out what these men wanted. I pulled into the dog park and Steve and I walked over to the gate leading to the large enclosure. There were three dogs with their owners playing in the area. As soon as I opened the gate, Steve was through it and off to check out the other dogs. She'd be preoccupied for at least the next ten to twenty minutes and then she'd want to play ball. I found a seat on a bench, politely greeted the other dog owners, and then set Steve's chewed up tennis ball on the ground by my feet.

Pulling out my cell phone, I called a friend of mine who specialized in reconnaissance missions. Rob McGregor and I had served in the Marine Corps at roughly the same time. Our basic training dates had been only a week apart and we had spent time on the same bases. For all that, we had never once run into each other while we served. It wasn't until a few years after I got out of the Corps that I met Rob when he came to work for my department as a police officer and I served as his Field Training Officer. From there, we became fast friends. He had been Force Recon while in the Corps and his skill set had quickly earned him a spot on the SWAT team.

Unfortunately for Rob, he also had a penchant for finding trouble. Multiple use of force incidents, a few of them fatal. They were all clean, but that many incidents in a city as liberal as the one I worked in and the administration got nervous. They moved him inside, but then a complaint had been filed and Rob was fired. He had fought it in court and won. After a big settlement, though, Rob resigned and went into business for himself as a private detective. He was good at it, too, and if he wasn't too busy, he was just the guy I'd like to have lending me a hand on this.

The phone rang and Rob picked up. "MFR Investigations."

"Hey, Rob, it's Jerod. How are you?"

"Hey, buddy. Doing good. Yourself?"

"Can't complain. I don't want to take up a lot of your time, but I may have a job for you if you're not overly busy. Time sensitive, though."

"Never too busy to help out a friend. How about we meet at the pub in Point Richmond? Say at around 1800 hours. I'll let you buy me dinner."

I laughed. "Only if you buy me a beer."

"Deal. See you then." Rob hung up the phone.

I looked up to check on Steve and found her romping around with the other dogs. Her tongue was rolling out the side of her mouth and she looked like she was grinning and having a perfectly good time. It was late enough now that I decided to call Stephanie and see how she was doing. I wasn't sure what shift she had worked the day before, so I tried to avoid calling her too early as she might have just gone to bed. The life of a nurse. It went straight to voicemail, but I received a text message from her a few minutes later that said she was working day shift and that she'd call me around 3:00 p.m. when she got off. She was supposed to fly down this weekend.

I responded back and then contented myself with watching Steve play with the other dogs. When she grew tired of that, I threw the ball for her until she was completely tired and then we loaded back into the Jeep and headed home.

I took the long route. Instead of coming up from the freeway, I went around the hill and came down from the top side. It wasn't a direct trip and had a lot of turns down narrow streets, but it would be unexpected, and it would also make it easier for me to spot a tail. The military always taught as a part of its anti-terrorism plan to utilize alternating routes to and from your place of work and your residence. Some time ago, I had planned alternate routes to my house but I seldom used them. I had retired from the military not long after I had retired from law enforcement and I'd stopped worrying about protecting myself from being the target of terrorists. Now, though, I was glad for the training.

As I pulled into the driveway, I could see the construction workers going about their business. The two security guards who patrolled the property were at the beginning of the driveway and greeted me with a wave as a drove in.

Opening the garage door, I pulled the Jeep into its parking space and killed the engine. I paused before getting out, closing my eyes to take in the feel of the place. Everything felt normal. Well, as normal as it could be with construction guys and security guards running around. There was a comfortable rhythm to the flow of the workers.

Satisfied, I exited the Jeep and then opened the back door for Steve to get out. I closed the garage door and walked into the house. I could see Z and Rosa busy working in the dining room. The general contractor was in the living room holding a set of plans and going over them with the lady who would be installing the security system and cameras.

He nodded to me when I walked into the house. I greeted him back and made my way to the dining table. Z looked up from her computer. "Hey, boss."

"Hey, Z. Rosa. How are things going this morning?"

Rosalia also took a moment to look up from her computer. "Good. I think we have our benefits plan locked in. Everything should be in their system by Thursday and we should be able to start signing in. Benefits will kick in two weeks from now and for anyone hired after that, it should be immediate upon enrollment. Also, I called the security company. They'll have guards here when we are ready to leave for the evening. Just need to give them about a thirty-minute lead time."

"Excellent. Things are moving along. Thanks, ladies."

They both said "you're welcome" at almost the same time.

I moved to my spot on the table and opened my laptop and powered it up. Once I was logged in, I checked my emails and responded back to those that required it. Joanna Walton, our new Public Information Officer, would start working on a website as one of her first projects. In addition to the website, she would set up business emails for all of us, but for the time being I continued to use my personal email address.

When I was done with my emails, I pulled up a search engine and typed in the next entry on the pages that I had pulled from the painting last night. "October 8, 1941 – Salli, Betty, and Rita." My initial search turned up nothing of any significance – some local death and marriage records and a link to a website about Rita Hayworth, none of which I figured had anything to do with the entry.

I tried again, this time just using the date. I came back with hits about this being the first day of the Nazi invasion of Russia. Interesting and historical, and I spent a few minutes reading through some of the information provided, but it didn't strike me as being related to the entry, either. I then tried just searching for "Salli, Betty, and Rita." Still nothing of value. I hadn't even been at this ten minutes yet, and I was already getting frustrated.

I gave up on that entry for the time being and moved on to the next. "January 10, 1942 – Town Hall, sold-out crowd." I was rewarded by a return that I at least thought fit the pattern. The Fahnestocks gave a talk at the Town Hall in NYC in January 1942. It didn't list an exact date, but it did say they played to a sold-out crowd.

Jotting down some notes, I looked at what I had so far. I still didn't know the name of Harold Touscher's grandmother – something I would like to know, with the possibly misguided belief that it would help me in understanding the story before me. In September 1941, she attended the gala put on by Salvador Dali at the Bali Room located in the Hotel Del Monte in Monterey. From there, she went to Bali, the island in the Dutch East Indies. I was still trying to figure out what the October 8, 1941, entry was about. The last one I had looked at was in New York City but tied back to the Fahnestocks. That was in January of 1942.

I looked at the next entry. "October 20, 1942 – Leonora and Renato, Mexico City." I typed that into the search engine and saw a webpage for Leonora Carrington, an English-born surrealist artist who ended up marrying Renato Leduc. Leonora's work was shown at the Art of This Century Gallery in Manhattan when the gallery opened on October 20, 1942. The gallery had also displayed the works of Salvador Dali.

I was starting to paint a picture in my head about how this story was unfolding. Each prior entry tied back to the others. I was missing the information in between those timelines but I was starting to get an idea of how she traveled. I admit to being fascinated and I wanted to see how the story would end, but I also had work to do.

Forcing myself to put the pages aside, I concentrated on work for the next few hours. I had never been a good administrator. Don't get me wrong, I was decent at it, but it also drove me crazy. I wanted to be on the move, not stuck behind a desk for hours on end. Around 12:30, I got up and stretched and then went to the kitchen to fix myself some lunch.

Pulling out some bread and salami from the refrigerator, I made myself a sandwich and, grabbing a bottle of water, I headed outside to the porch, Steve following behind me with a ball in her mouth. I was pretty sure she hated me being stuck behind a desk, too. I ate my sandwich in relative peace and tossed the ball for Steve.

Tonight, I had my meeting with Rob, and tomorrow was the installation of the modulars and the delivery of the office furniture. Once a building was in place, the plumbers and electricians would start hooking up the utilities. It was going to have to be a well-choreographed dance. Dan was also coming in tomorrow and I would have to bring him up to speed and get him settled. Many of the decisions that had been made fell under his division and while he hadn't been here to actively participate in the process, we had been keeping him up to date, and when we could, conference-call him on the phone.

Thursday would be a busy day as we settled in to our new offices, but I could carve out some time for Steve and me to go on a hike. Thursday evening Z wanted to hold a BBQ in the courtyard area that would be formed by the layout of the modular buildings. Joanna and Nadia were also invited.

Stephanie would be flying in on Friday. Bob, Susan and the boys would also be flying in but would be staying at the Mark Hopkins in

San Francisco. I had already planned to take Stephanie out to dinner that night to the Buckeye Roadhouse in Sausalito. On Saturday night, Stephanie and I would be meeting Bob and Susan at the Marine Memorial Hotel for a fund-raising event supporting the Museum Grant Fund. Bob thought it would a great way for me to meet people who might also be willing to donate to the Adventurers' Club, which reminded me that I would need to go pick up my tuxedo from the dry cleaner in the next few days.

I threw the ball for Steve a few more times until I saw a beautiful 1967 Ford Mustang in arcadian blue pull up the driveway. It appeared to be all original. I probably had my mouth open with drool coming out. Whoever this was had just parked my dream car in my driveway.

I stood up and started walking toward the vehicle. A young man got out. He was maybe 5'5" with a stocky build. Jet black hair, brown eyes, and darker skin marked him as most likely Hispanic in origin. He was professionally dressed in a suit and tie. This must be the applicant for Logistics Specialist.

"Beautiful car you have, sir." I nodded in the direction of the Mustang, even though there was only Z's slightly beat up 2003 BMW 325i and Rosa's newer model Honda Accord sitting in the driveway near it. I obviously wasn't referring to one of those vehicles.

"Thank you. I did the restoration myself. Took me awhile." He turned toward the car and rubbed his hand over the roof affectionately.

"You did a fantastic job. I'm Jerod Grey." I extended my hand.

Extending his hand as well, he gave me a firm handshake. "Isiah Hernandez. I'm here for a job interview."

"I was hoping you'd say that," I said, smiling. "Come on up to the porch and let's have a seat for a few minutes."

We climbed up the short stairs to the back porch and I took a seat on one of several chairs I had out here for those times I liked to come out here and relax, smoke a cigar, have a whiskey, or just talk with my friends. "My people tell me that you served in the Army."

"I did, sir. Six years. Worked in the motor pool, supply, and the armory during that time. I already knew my way around a car engine, but I learned diesel engines as well. Also figured out how to do inventory and stocking and – in the armory – how to break down, clean, and repair weapons. The Army treated me well."

I nodded. "Why did you get out?"

"Family, sir. I have a wife and two kids, and I realized the kids were growing up way too fast and I was gone way too much. I didn't want to miss out on it."

"I can understand that. In my thirty years in the Navy and Marine Corps, I was deployed eight times."

"That's a lot, sir."

"That it is." I stood up and Isiah did likewise. "Let me show you around so you can get a feel for what I'll be asking of you."

"Lead the way, sir."

I took him over to where the modular buildings were going to be and explained that one of his duties would be to ensure we had all the necessary office materials on hand to do our work. I also showed him the warehouse and the equipment he would be maintaining, including the ATVs, off-road motorcycles, and snowmobiles. Pointing out the stock of expedition supplies we had on hand, I added that inventory, inspection, and re-order would also be his responsibility.

Isiah nodded as I talked, asking questions where it was pertinent, particularly when it came to travel. I told him I had an additional warehouse in Colorado and was in the process of considering one in Raleigh, North Carolina. It would mean he would occasionally have to travel to maintain those locations. That was a concern of mine since he'd said he had left the Army to spend more time with his family. Not that taking two to three days to go to Colorado to inventory and reorder supplies was that long of a trip, but when we were on mission, he could be out in the field for several weeks. He didn't seem to mind, though, and said that it was being gone for thirteen months at a time that had been hard on his family. A few days or a few weeks would be more than doable.

"Excellent. Let's go inside and meet the others. Rosa can go over pay and benefits with you and if you're interested, I think you'd be a good fit for the Club."

"Thank you, sir." He shook my hand again, more enthusiastically than the first time, and we turned back toward the house.

Stepping into the kitchen and around two of the construction guys that were working, I led him to the dining room and introduced him to Rosa and Z. I pulled Rosa off to the side and told her that I liked the guy and unless she noticed something, I wanted to hire him.

"No formal interview?" She looked quizzical.

"I interviewed him but even if I hadn't, you should see his car. A man who can maintain a car like that is a man I don't mind handling my equipment."

I watched Rosa's face go completely blank and then the corner of her mouth started to twitch. I furrowed my brow trying to judge the cause of her behavior and then realized what I had said. "Not like that, you perv." Rosa broke out laughing.

"I won't tell Stephanie that you don't mind having men handle your equipment." She laughed more.

"Keep it up and I'm going to file a complaint with HR." She continued to laugh but turned and went back in to the dining room.

I shook my head and walked back out on to the porch with Steve. All the key personnel were almost in place. I just needed to fill the Operations Chief position and hire a researcher. I'd follow up with Rosa to see if Curtis' students had called her yet. I'd also start reaching out to my brothers and sisters in the Chief's Mess to see if anyone with the right skills needed a job. My law enforcement partners didn't have the same level of organization as the Mess, but I could probably put the word out to a few people. There was an informal organization of retired and current police officers that met once a month. Maybe they knew someone who would be interested.

It had been a very busy few weeks. I didn't see that we had much else that absolutely had to be done today and as I knew tomorrow was going to be a long one, I wanted to get Z and Rosa out of here early for a change. I stood up, tossed the ball for Steve one more time, and walked into the house.

I was just walking into the dining room as Isiah shook Rosa's hand and turned to leave. "So, you take the job?"

Isiah smiled. "I did, sir. Thank you for the opportunity."

"My pleasure, and you can call me Jerod." We shook hands again.

"That one," he said, pointing at Zuleyka, "said to call you 'boss.'"

"I wouldn't listen to that one. If I had a shit list, she'd occupy the top spot."

"I heard that," Z said, not looking up from her computer screen. Isiah and I both laughed and then he thanked me again and left.

"Hey, you two finish up what you're doing and then get out of here. Go enjoy an evening at home or something."

Rosa finished labeling a file and placed some paperwork inside of it. "That would be a nice change."

"So, make it happen," I said with a smile.

Despite my attempts to get them out sooner, they didn't leave until about 4:30 – which was still early for them, though, so I considered it a win.

As the construction crew started cleaning up and getting ready to go home for the night as well, I fed Steve and went upstairs to shower before I headed to Point Richmond to meet with Rob. I had decided to take the Land Cruiser. It hadn't been driven in a while, and because it had been stored in the warehouse, I thought there was less of a chance that the people who had ransacked my house had seen it.

I pulled a fresh pair of hiking pants out of the closet and threw on a t-shirt. The house was quiet when I returned downstairs, Steve trailing behind me. I grabbed the portable radio off the kitchen counter and turned it on. I saw the battery was getting low and would throw it on the charger before I left. I told the security guards I'd be out for a few hours and let them know I'd be taking Steve with me. The pub didn't have outdoor seating, but Steve would be content in the car as long as the windows were down and she had some water. It was warm outside but not overly hot.

I grabbed one of Steve's dog beds out of the garage and then we walked over to the warehouse. I went through the side door and then hit the button to raise the large rollup door. As I waited for the door to go fully up, I got Steve loaded into the Land Cruiser and started it up.

Everything seemed to be running fine. I pulled out of the warehouse and then got out to close the rollup door. Locking up the warehouse, I jumped back in the Land Cruiser and Steve and I headed down the road to the freeway.

Keeping my eyes open, I did see a black sedan parked off one of the side streets about a quarter mile from my house. I could just see two occupants as I passed and, for safety's sake, I kept my eye on the rearview mirror to see if they were going to follow. They didn't. I was grateful, though it would have confirmed I wasn't being entirely paranoid.

I jumped on the 101 South and then over to the 580 and across the bridge. Even with the evening commute and heavy traffic on the bridge, it only took me twenty minutes to get there.

Finding a parking space proved to be more difficult than navigating evening rush hour. I finally found one a few blocks away from the pub. I rolled down the windows and made sure Steve had some water and a chew toy and walked the couple of blocks to the pub. The place was already crowded but I had called ahead, and they found me a table within ten minutes. By the time I sat down, it was five after. I checked my phone and saw a text from Rob saying he had gotten caught in traffic and was running about fifteen minutes late.

I texted him back that I'd see him when he got here and ordered an Irish whiskey, neat, and a glass of water from my server. When she brought my drinks to the table, she also brought two menus.

I was perusing the menu and trying to remember what I had ordered the last time I was here when Rob walked in. With a full, Grizzly Adams-style beard and a full head of hair, I didn't recognize him, and I was about to tell him the seat was taken when he gave a big smile and said, "Jerod Grey. Good to see you."

"Rob?"

"Yeah. Didn't recognize me with all this hair, did you?" He laughed.

I laughed as well. "To be honest, no, I didn't. How are you?"

"Good, good." He picked up his menu and started looking it over. The server brought him a glass of water and took down his drink order, also an Irish whiskey, this one on the rocks.

We did a quick catch-up while we waited for the server to return and take our food order.

Our orders in, I explained to him the events of the past few weeks with the attack in my house and the belief that I might be being tailed. "I need you to poke around the neighborhood some and see if you can flush these guys out. If we figure out where they're staging, maybe we can sic the county on them and get them off my ass. Plus, I'd really like to know why they targeted me." I didn't tell him about the notebook pages that I found in the painting. Motive was important to me, but for Rob, it was about tracking these guys down and getting the deputy sheriff to both stop them and identify them. The police scrutiny would hopefully get them to back off.

Rob said he'd get right on it. "Most of my jobs are during the daytime so I have my evenings free for now. Maybe I'll take a run through the neighborhood tonight. What's your address again?"

I gave him the address plus some details regarding the car that I thought had followed me, including the license plate number. "The morning of the break-in, though, a partner of mine had stopped by the house and saw the men fleeing in a blacked-out van. Realistically, the sedan could have just been coincidence. That is the most direct route to the freeway."

"Except you don't believe in coincidence," countered Rob.

"True."

By the time we were done eating and had finished our second round of drinks, it was about half past seven. I paid for the dinners and Rob picked up the drinks. As we walked out the door I told him, "Let me know what you find and send me the bill."

"You got it, boss."

We shook hands and went our separate ways. As I walked up to the Toyota, Steve gave an excited bark and started wagging her tail fiercely. "Good to see you too, girl." I got in the driver's side and took a moment to give her a good back scratch before I had her return to her bed in the back seat and headed home.

As we got closer to my house, I looked down the street where I had seen a black sedan earlier. There was no sign of it now. I was hoping

Rob would come up with something, I'd just have to be patient. Pulling into the driveway, I saw the two security guards making their rounds. They waved and met me over by the warehouse. As I stepped out of the Land Cruiser, one of the guards approached me. "Mark, how are you tonight?" I asked.

"Good, Mr. Grey. We think someone has been hiding over by the copse of trees on the east side of the property. There's a place there that looks worn down, like someone was standing on it, and there are a few cigarette butts on the ground. Could be one of the construction guys goes over to have a smoke when he can but thought you should know."

"Thanks, Mark. I'll look into it in the morning." I knew the contractor frowned on smoking on the job. He didn't outright ban it, but he didn't like finding cigarette butts lying around the job site. I was more concerned with the fire hazard. California had been experiencing a drought for some time and the leaves and twigs that covered the ground by the trees were dry as tinder. I'd ask the contractor to help me police it by creating a smoke pit where they could curb their nicotine fit and have a can or something to put their smokes out in.

I finished putting the Land Cruiser away and gave Steve some time to stretch her legs after being in the car for several hours. Naturally, we had to play some more fetch. She never seemed to tire of it. When she had burned off some extra energy, we returned to the house and I let the guards know via the radio that we were in for the night. It was almost 9:00 p.m. I fixed myself a bourbon and sat down in my recliner to watch a little TV before bed.

CHAPTER FOUR

I woke up at 4:29 a.m, just a minute before my alarm clock went off. I was proud of myself. Generally, I woke up an hour or more before the alarm. I popped out of bed and then grimaced as my back reminded me it didn't like sudden movements first thing in the morning. I paused a moment to give the spasm time to relax and then grabbed a pair of sweat pants and a t-shirt.

Steve crawled out of bed, stretched and gave a big doggy yawn and then we both headed down the stairs.

I pulled the radio off the charger, turned it on and advised the security guards I was up and about and would be letting Steve out for her morning ritual. The guards acknowledged, and I flipped on the porch light and opened the door for Steve. There had been a doggy door there before, but they had done away with it during the security upgrades to the house.

Today was going to be a long day with the delivery of the modular offices and the office furniture and I wasn't sure if I'd find time for lunch or not, so I planned to make a hearty breakfast, starting – as always – with a pot of coffee.

When I was done eating, I did the dishes and stacked them on the counter to dry and then went upstairs to shower and get dressed.

It was just a little after six in the morning when I came back down to find Zuleyka already doing some work at the dining room table. "Morning, Z."

She looked up from her computer screen. "Good morning, boss."

"We ready for the day?"

"I'm ready to have an actual office to work in. Not that I haven't enjoyed using your dining table as a desk, but I'd really like to have an actual desk to work at and filing cabinets to help me keep organized."

I looked at the cluster of paperwork spread all over one half of the dining table and raised an eyebrow. "I can see your point, Z." She stuck her tongue out at me, causing me to laugh. "Real mature, Ms. Perez."

I heard the radio from the dining room but couldn't understand what the guard said. Returning to the kitchen, I picked up the radio and asked them to repeat their last traffic. The guard came back and said that the trucks with the modular offices were here. I thanked him, yelled at Z that our offices had arrived, and headed out the back door.

The guards had let the trucks proceed down the driveway, modulars in tow. I was more excited than I thought I would be. When I first brought up the idea of formalizing the Club to Bob, I wasn't so much dragging my feet as I just wasn't sure where to start. Now that we had filed the paperwork for the non-profit, hired people, and now had our offices arriving, it was starting to feel very real. More importantly, I felt we could do some real good in the world by saving pieces of our past. It was sometimes tedious, sometimes dangerous, but overall very rewarding work.

Steve barked at the trucks as they drove by. Following them was the Ford pickup driven by the project manager. He stopped near me and climbed out of the truck. "Delivery day, Mr. Grey," he said with a smile.

"That it is, sir."

"It will take a few hours to get them set up and leveled, but once we get one set, you can start with the electrical and plumbing hook-ups and moving furniture in if it's here."

"Copy that. Thank you." I shook his hand and he hopped back in the pick-up and drove off.

I walked back in the house and told Z the news. She didn't look willing to wait and started picking up her files and papers.

Rosalia came in at 7:00 and, like Z, started picking up her things and getting prepped to move into her new office. I guess we were all ready to have actual offices. With everything picked up, we all just sat around the table, drank coffee and waited until the first building was set. The project manager came in with a few of the construction workers and let us know the first modular was ready for move in. The way Zuleyka and Rosalia hopped out of their chairs and grabbed their belongings, I figured that they had decided that those offices were theirs. I told the general contractor that they could start tying in the electrical and plumbing and then the three of us walked out to see the new office.

Luckily it turned out to be one of the two larger buildings. We walked up the flight of metal stairs they had set up and got our first look at the office. It was a decent-sized space. There was an office on either end with the bathroom closer to the office on the left. The center area was open. This is where Joanna, the communications center (once the equipment arrived), and our researcher would have their desks and workspace. Zuleyka took the office to the left and Rosa the one to the right. I chuckled. The office furniture wasn't even here yet, so they didn't have desks or filing cabinets to set up. They were just empty offices.

By the time the modular that contained my office and the conference room was set and leveled, the furniture delivery company was there and assembling and moving the desks and chairs into place. The last modular would be the offices for Dan and whoever we hired to be our Operations Chief, as well as desks for Isiah and Nadia. Phone installation and internet lines would go in tomorrow. Dan would be hooking up all the computers, setting up our network and establishing our wi-fi.

It was after noon before my office furniture was in place. I walked into the space. I had a large, oval-shaped conference table with nine chairs around it. I planned to have a multi-media projector with a retractable screen and a computer hooked up in here. I thought it would professionalize any mission briefs we did and provide a better platform for documents to be shared during meetings. There were also three bookshelves. Of all the furniture that had been ordered, this was my only input. With the basement being converted to a safe room, I had lost the bookshelves where I stored my reference library. I needed a new place to store all my books. I had 680 of them at last count, covering topics from psychology to law enforcement practice to archeology.

I walked into my new office. I had a nice, large desk, two chairs and a black leather couch. Against the back wall were more shelves and cabinets. I returned to the house and started hauling boxes that held items that used to be in the basement out to my new office. The first thing I did was set up a bed for Steve near my desk. After that, I stocked books on shelves in the conference room, organizing them as I did so. I saved some of my more frequently referenced books to put on the shelves in my office. I brought a decanter that Anna had given me along with four crystal old-fashioned glasses and sat those on the shelf behind my desk. I'd buy a good scotch to go in the decanter later this week.

My computer went on the desk and I moved it around until I found a place where it would be functional for me to use while not blocking my view of anyone sitting in the chairs in front of my desk. I hung pictures on the walls that I had taken of some of our recoveries, as well as my degrees. The last thing I placed was a glass name plate that my ex-wife had given me. It had "Dr. Jerod Grey" etched into the glass with the Marine Corps eagle, globe and anchor on one side. She had given it to me when I graduated with my EdD.

I was just finishing up when the lights came on. The electricity was hooked up. I walked out to survey the rest of the installation in time to see a black SUV pull into the driveway. Dan had arrived. I headed over to the car.

Dan was taking his bags from the driver as I walked up. He was a big guy, standing 6'6" and weighing in at over 300 pounds. He was dressed in a manner that reminded me of an old Englishman on safari: a white straw hat with a wide brim, a denim colored shirt, and light beige khaki pants and blue boat shoes. It looked comfortable.

We gave each other a quick man-hug. "Good to see you, brother," I said when we broke apart.

"You too, brother." He smiled.

I grabbed one of his bags and led him into the house and up the stairs to the spare bedroom. I didn't expect he'd be here more than a few weeks. As a part of the incentive package we had to lure the right talent, we included a relocation bonus. He had the money necessary to pay first and last as well as a deposit on an apartment, even at Bay Area rental prices. He just had to find an apartment. Of course, he also had to buy a car. He had sold his truck prior to coming out so he wouldn't have to worry about driving it all the way from Colorado to California.

We got him settled and then I showed him to his office. He looked around and nodded his head in approval. "Not bad," he said.

"The computer lines and wi-fi network will be up tomorrow. We can go to Best Buy tomorrow to get computers, printers, and whatever else you think we'll need and you can get them up and running," I said.

"Sounds good, brother."

"Ready to meet the rest of the crew?" I inquired.

"Sure."

I took him over and introduced him to Zuleyka and Rosalia. Rosa ushered him into her office, so he could fill out all the paperwork necessary for employment. W-4s, benefits paperwork, direct deposit information, and so on. He'd be busy for a bit.

I left him in Rosa's care and went out to spend some time with Steve. The office furniture crews had set up three picnic tables in the center courtyard area. The nice thing about the tables was that they each had an umbrella to provide some protection from the sun. I sat at one and threw the ball for Steve. Before she got too tired, though, I got up and we went for a walk around the property.

I checked out the area where the security team had advised someone had stood for a time, smoking cigarettes. It took me a minute, but I found it. I looked at the butts on the ground and made note of the brand. Steve started sniffing around a tree about five feet from where I was standing and then started to whine. Figuring it was a squirrel, I didn't pay her much mind. The squirrels on the property were always tormenting her, and vice versa.

I stood up from my examination of the ground and was going to look around some more when I heard someone whisper my name. I wasn't sure at first, but when it came again I started scanning the area.

"Up here. In the tree. Your damn dog is going to blow my cover."

I recognized the voice. "Rob?"

"Yeah."

I didn't see him up in the tree until he moved. The camouflage he was using was almost perfect, even the bright light of the day. He looked like a part of the tree.

"What the fuck are you doing up there?"

"I think someone has been watching the house from here so I staked it out, but hey, I need your security guys to stand down. If they keep coming over here tonight, they'll spoil the site."

I shook my head. "I'll tell them. How long have you been up there?"

"I don't know. Since sunrise this morning. What time is it?"

I told him. It had been over ten hours. "Jesus, man. You're nuts."

Rob laughed. "Gets the job done, though. Pass along the word, will you?"

"Sure, bro. Hey, how many times have the guards been over and not seen you?"

"Six or seven times."

"Damn." I wondered if they were missing other things, then reminded myself that I hadn't seen Rob, either.

I called Steve to me and we walked away. I'd leave Rob to his methods.

Steve and I finished our walk and returned to the offices. By this time, all the modular offices were in place and leveled, the electricity and plumbing hooked up, and the office furniture assembled and moved into place. I stood at the open end of the courtyard and looked at our newly installed offices. It had taken a lot of work to get us here, but we finally had a legitimate organization. I'd have to get something nice for Z for all her hard work. This wouldn't have been possible without her. Same for Rosalia.

I'd have to do some shopping. Tomorrow was our BBQ. I'd do

the presentation then. The engraved name glass name plate from my ex-wife gave me an idea. I'd just have to find a place that could create an award in a short period of time. No doubt the short turnaround would cost me, but I figured it was small price to pay to recognize an employee for their hard work.

Dan, Rosalia, and Zuleyka were still working on setting up their offices. I called a local Chinese restaurant and ordered us all some food for delivery and when it arrived, convinced them all to come out and join me in eating. After a long day of work, it was a much-needed break. We talked, told a few stories, and had some good laughs. Z was a gifted storyteller. I had learned over the weeks we had worked together that she had a talent for numbers, but that grammar and proper English were not strong areas for her. As a nickname, I had started calling her "Spellcheck." Sometimes I swore she simply made up words that she thought fit. As a result, I hadn't considered that she might be able to tell a story.

When dinner was done, I picked up the empty containers and plates and tossed them in the trash. Zuleyka and Rosalia finished up the few things they wanted to do to decorate their offices and then they left for the day. Tomorrow wouldn't be as busy, even though the two graduate students Curtis had recommended would be coming by for interviews.

Once they were gone, Dan and I poured ourselves each a glass of whiskey, grabbed cigars from my humidor and retired to the back porch for a drink and smoke. We talked about what work we'd like to do with the organization. Like Z, Dan thought education would be a good sideline to our adventurers. Not only would we have stories to tell, but we could use those stories to illustrate solid lessons on preserving our past.

I agreed that education would be a good secondary focus. I also wanted to provide some humanitarian relief to people in need. Given the skill sets of the people we had available on our extended team, we could get food and medicine to people in remote locations and hard-to-reach areas hit by earthquakes or floods. We discussed the possibilities over the course of multiple glasses of whiskey and long into the night. It was 11:30 before we retired to our beds.

CHAPTER FIVE

The BBQ had gone well. Dan, Zuleyka, Rosalia, Isiah, Nadia, Joanna, and the two students, Adam Green and Tiffany Peterson, had all joined us. Isiah had brought his wife and kids and Joanna had brought her wife and Nadia her son. I was starting to feel us gel as a family.

We had quite the spread of food, and we ate, talked, and drank late into the night. I presented Z and Rosa with their awards and thanked them for all their hard work and gave them Friday off. Everyone else we would see come Monday morning.

We ended up hiring both Adam and Tiffany. The grant they received covered an allowance for food and housing, meaning I didn't feel like I had to pay them as much to cover the extra expense of living in the San Francisco Bay Area; that meant I could cut the salary in half and afford to pay for both. We still didn't have an Operations Chief, but I felt confident that my recruiting efforts would yield us someone in the next week or two.

Stephanie had flown in on Friday afternoon – another reason I wanted everyone off work, so I wouldn't be distracted. We had a great dinner and while the conversation sometimes turned to more serious matters, mostly we laughed. I hadn't felt that relaxed in a long while. It had been a wonderful evening. I couldn't deny the attraction

I felt toward her. She was a perfect combination of common sense, intelligence, sweetness and beauty.

Bob and Susan had also flown into San Francisco. While they were staying in San Francisco, they had taken a ride over the bridge to come tour the Adventurers' Club's new offices earlier in the day. It wasn't quite like the suite of executive offices his company occupied, but he gave his stamp of approval nonetheless.

Now we were getting ready for the Museum Grant Fund Gala. Stephanie was in the bathroom showering which freed up my room for me to get ready. Because Dan was staying here for the time being, I had given up my room for Stephanie to stay in and had slept on the couch. Even though she had flown down here for a few days, this was only our fourth date. We were taking it slow. It had been a mutual, unspoken agreement. She had attended nursing school just ten minutes away from my house at Dominican, but a bad breakup had required a fresh start and she had taken a job in Victoria and moved there. For me, it hadn't been that long since Cat died.

I continued getting dressed and was in the process of adjusting my bow tie when Stephanie walked into the room. She was wearing a dark blue evening gown that looked splendid on her and contrasted nicely with her pale, smooth skin. It also brought out the blue in her eyes so that they were almost luminescent. Her makeup was light – a bit of color to her cheeks and lips appeared to be all. I was a man, so while I really didn't understand how makeup worked, I had to say that the effect was perfect. She was stunning.

I finished adjusting my bow tie and then went over and gave her a kiss on the cheek. I didn't want to smear her lipstick. Not yet, at least. "You look gorgeous," I said, giving her a genuine smile.

"You don't look half bad yourself, Mr. Grey." She smiled back.

I turned and opened one of the drawers in my dresser and pulled out a Graff jewelry box. "Susan sent this over for you to wear." I opened the box to reveal a beautifully crafted sapphire necklace. The stones were large, and Susan had been correct when she said it would match the color of Stephanie's dress.

"Oh my god, that looks beautiful, and expensive. I'm going to be a nervous wreck wearing that." Stephanie reached out gingerly and touched the necklace.

"No doubt it is expensive. I don't know a lot about jewelry, but I do know that Graff is up there with Tiffany and Cartier."

"You're not helping."

I laughed and motioned for her to turn around, so I could put on the necklace. "I assure you, it is also insured. Nothing is going to happen to the necklace, but on the very outside chance it does, it's covered." I did the clasp and then turned her around so she could see herself in the dresser's mirror. "Perfect," I said, "and the necklace doesn't look half bad either." I gave her a wink in the mirror's reflection.

She turned back around and give me a gentle kiss and then wiped off the tiny remnant of lipstick she had left behind on my cheek. "You are sweet, Jerod."

"Your limo is here," I heard Dan yell from downstairs.

"Be down in a moment," I yelled back. I turned back to Stephanie. "I'll give you a moment to finish getting ready and I will meet you downstairs."

I left the bedroom and walked downstairs with Steve trailing behind me. She'd be bummed that she couldn't go with us, but she'd be home with Dan for the night and he'd keep her occupied.

Dan was sitting on the couch watching TV. A half-eaten bowl of popcorn was on the coffee table. I had finally been able to take the plastic off the furniture. The last bit of work to be done was on the panic room and they'd be done with that next week. I was looking forward to having my house back and being able to give it a thorough cleaning.

Dan looked over when I came down the stairs. "Looking good, brother."

"Thank you, sir. Wish we could have managed to get a ticket for you, as well."

"I would have had to rent a tuxedo, and this does not strike me as the rented tux kind of crowd."

He was right, of course, but I was also sure we could have bought him a tuxedo. I had bought mine on a whim a few years ago, and for no reason other than I thought every man should own a tux for those formal occasions when it was required.

When I had told Anna about the purchase, she had questioned why. My explanation had been along the lines of, "What if the President of the United States calls me up today and says, 'Mr. Grey, we have a mission of vital importance to the safety and stability of our country and the only person who can accomplish this mission is you. All you need to bring is your keen wit and a tuxedo.' What if I don't own a tux, Anna? Do I just let our great country slip into chaos? I think not." She had called me a fool. Amazingly, though, literally an hour after purchasing it, I'd received a call from a friend of mine that I sit with on the Board of Directors with for a non-profit that helps military widows. She asked me to attend a ball in Houston. Black tie, tux required. The next day, I received an invitation to the Black and Blue Ball in Sacramento, also black tie. The tuxedo had already paid for itself in not having to rent one.

I went and stood behind the couch. I didn't want to sit down on it; while I did a good job of keeping the dog hair off it, and did my best to keep Steve off, she still felt entitled to use it as a bed on occasion during the day and I didn't want dog hair on my tux.

"When you let Steve out this evening, don't forget to notify security. They get jumpy. Also, she can have a treat around 2000 hours, but only one. She'll beg for more and look pathetic. Don't cave."

Dan gave me a thumbs-up. "You're like a nervous parent afraid to leave your kid at home with the babysitter for an evening. We'll be fine. Go have fun."

I gave him the finger.

"I saw that," he said.

"How the hell did you see that?"

"I could have eyes in the back of my head, or it could be that I can see your reflection in the TV." Dan pointed at the TV where I could see a pretty good reflection of myself. Dan smiled and waved. I laughed.

Stephanie came down the stairs a few seconds later and I marveled again at how good she looked in a dress. Up to now, we had been mostly casual, with me wearing my typical t-shirt and hiking pants and her in yoga pants and tennis shoes. She had left the necklace on. Even Dan let out a low, appreciative whistle.

"Ready, my dear?"

"I am, sir," she replied, taking the arm I proffered.

I led her to the limo. The driver was waiting patiently outside and opened the car door for us as we approached. I allowed Stephanie to enter and get situated then I went to the other side. We were on our way a minute later.

The drive over to the City was far more relaxing when you weren't the one driving. I sat back and enjoyed the views from the Golden Gate. The trip to the Marine Memorial Club and Hotel was only around thirty minutes, depending on traffic. I had planned it so we would arrive sometime after the start of the cocktail hour, but before the middle of it. I didn't want to be too early, but I also didn't want to miss cocktail hour. Susan would expect me to mingle and meet people. As she explained it, these were the very same people who might be willing to donate to the Adventurers' Club later down the road when the non-profit was approved by the IRS, and it was better to start getting our name out there now, rather than later. This was her area of expertise, so I planned on following her advice.

We pulled up to the Marine Memorial Club and Hotel at 5:20 – perfect timing. With Stephanie holding my arm, we found the ballroom for the gala with little difficulty. People in formal evening wear lingered outside the ballroom, drinking champagne, martinis, or wine in equal measure. I located the bar and ordered myself a Manhattan and Stephanie a glass of wine.

Handing Stephanie her drink, I looked around to find Bob and Susan, but in a crowd numbering well over two hundred, I didn't think I'd spot them. I was looking for Bob's signature white hair but in this group, white hair was as common as any other color. For the first time in a long while, I felt like I was a part of the younger generation.

It was Stephanie who found them. They were standing near the entrance to the ballroom talking with a small group of people. Stephanie and I started to walk over.

Susan spotted us about thirty feet from the group and waved us over. Stephanie and Susan greeted each other like longtime friends. I gave Susan a chaste hug and a slight kiss on the cheek and then shook Bob's hand.

"Robert, good to see you," I said. I wouldn't call him Bob in public. It was our private joke and in a public setting, he was either Robert or Mr. Hansen, depending on who else was around.

"Likewise, Jerod." I had known Bob for a while now and was picking up on some residual annoyance. His eyes were tight, showing the fine wrinkles at the corner, and his smile was forced. It wasn't directed at me, though. We had just seen each other this afternoon and everything had been fine then. Nothing I had done in the intervening hours would have caused him to be even remotely angry. Susan seemed fine. She was busy talking and cooing over Stephanie and introducing her to the three other women in the group.

"Jerod, let me introduce you to Charles Bellington. Charles, this is Dr. Jerod Grey." I shook Charles's hand. It was soft and clammy. Charles was maybe a decade Bob's senior. He wasn't very tall, maybe 5'6", and he was carrying more than a little extra weight around his mid-section. His tuxedo was a light satiny gray, with tails. Like Bob, his hair was white, but where Bob still had a full head of hair, Charles' was receding, accentuated by the fact that it was slicked back. His face was a road map of fine wrinkles and heavy jowls. He reminded me a bit of Winston Churchill.

"Dr. Grey. A pleasure to finally meet you." Like his handshake, his voice almost immediately set me on edge. It was a combination of oily and condescending all at once. I was guessing that Charles was the source of Bob's annoyance. "I have heard about your exploits from mutual acquaintances of ours. You lead quite the exciting life."

"Really? I wasn't aware we had any mutual acquaintances, Mr. Bellington. Other than Robert, of course."

He made a dismissive noise. "Please, call me Charles." Another man was standing slightly to Charles's side. He was taller than Charles, just shy of my six-foot height but considerably heavier than me. His hair was dark and cut close to the skin to hide the fact that he was balding. He was clean shaven, apart from a pencil-style mustache. His complexion was darker than Zuleyka's caramel skin. "Let me introduce you to my colleague, Dr. Grey. This is Dr. Chandler LeBlanc. Dr. LeBlanc is my resident archaeologist. Like Robert, I'm a collector of antiquities. Dr. LeBlanc assists me with those acquisitions."

I shook Chandler's hand. "Pleasure to meet you, Doctor."

"Likewise, Doctor." His voice was devoid of emotion and he tilted his chin up slightly so that it appeared he was looking down his nose at me.

I could feel a tension here that I didn't quite understand. Susan, always perceptive to social cues, interrupted. "I don't mean to intrude, gentlemen, but I see some other friends that I would like to introduce to Robert and Jerod, so if you don't mind, I'm going to steal them away for a moment." She didn't really give Dr. LeBlanc or Mr. Bellington a choice in the matter as she grabbed our arms and started guiding us away.

I took a sip of my Manhattan and then transferred it to my left hand, so I could take Stephanie's arm with my right. Bob was walking beside me to my left. Out of the corner of my mouth I whispered, "What the hell was that about?"

Robert shook his head. "I have no idea. I've never cared for the man or his business practices, but this had a different feel to it."

"You two can discuss it later when we are alone, but for now, put on your smiles, we are working the crowd," Susan said in a voice almost as low as Bob's and mine had been. Stephanie gave my arm a reassuring squeeze.

The ballroom opened, and everyone started to file in to find their seats. Our table was on the left side, near the middle but closer to the wall. I looked around the room and found to my relief that Bellington and LeBlanc were seated on the opposite side. They had been joined by two other men, both of whom looked like the heavy muscle a mob boss might keep around, except instead of being Italian, the two men looked to be Samoan or Tongan. I took a seat that gave me the best view of the room and allowed me to see the table where Bellington and LeBlanc were sitting. There wasn't anything specific I could point to that was putting me on edge with those two, but my gut said something wasn't right and I listened to my gut. I was also lamenting the fact that I wasn't armed. It was a charity event and I hadn't thought a gun would be appropriate for such a venue.

The table seated eight and we were eventually joined by two other couples, both older, and pleasant people. Dwayne and Doris, and Tom and Darlene. Dwayne had retired from the banking industry some time back and Tom and Darlene owned a garbage company. Apparently, there was a lot of money in garbage. Given the amount of waste Americans generated, I shouldn't have been surprised.

A server came by and poured water in each glass. When he got to me, he stumbled a little and water spilt on the table. The server was quick with his towel and soaked up what he could. It was a minute later that I noticed the small note that had been left behind. "Meet me at the bar at the back of the room." No signature.

I palmed the note and excused myself from the table, gave Stephanie a quick kiss on the cheek and told her I'd be right back. I worked my way through the crowd to the back bar and then stood in line to order a drink. When I was next in line, I heard someone whisper my name. I scanned around. There was a server standing by a table along the wall picking up empty glasses and putting them on his tray. I almost glossed over him but had a moment of recognition. The hair was shorter, the beard was gone, but it was definitely Rob.

I gave an almost imperceptible nod of my head, ordered a whiskey, neat, and once it was poured, went to stand by the table, trying to appear interested in the crowd filing in. "What are you doing here?" I whispered out of the corner of my mouth.

"Working."

"Hey bro, if money is tight, you should have just said something. I would have paid an upfront retainer fee."

"Not like that, asshole. I'm working on your case. "I must have looked confused and Rob was a good judge of body language because he immediately followed up with, "You and yours aren't in any danger that I know of. I followed two guys here. One of them was the one who has been surveilling your property from the tree line."

"Hmmm. Who are they?"

Rob turned around and scanned the room. "The two meatheads with the two men you were talking to earlier. The Penguin and the Professor."

"The Penguin?"

"He reminded me of the villain from the comic books."

"Ah. Mr. Bellington and Dr. LeBlanc. The muscle that's with them, the two Samoan-looking guys?"

"That would be them," Rob replied.

"Roger that. Good to know. Let's meet tomorrow, say 1200 hours at the burrito shop in San Raphael."

"The one with the great mole sauce?" I nodded. "See you then." Rob peeled off carrying a tray full of glasses. He looked like he had done it before.

My first instinct was to go over and confront the two men. These were possibly the same guys who had broken into my house and shot at me. I was, understandably in my opinion, pissed. I didn't know what their game was, though, and if I let on I knew now, it might ruin Rob's chances of finding out more.

I tossed down the rest of my drink and returned to my table. As soon as I sat down, Stephanie put her hand on my arm and asked if everything was ok. Bob could also sense my tension and looked at me questioningly. I told them both that everything was fine and that I'd explain later.

The rest of the evening went by quietly, or at least as quietly as possible in a room filled with 200-plus people. Dinner was served. There was a keynote speaker whose speech was about the importance of museums to the preservation of our art and our past. I recognized his name and eventually realized I had a book on one of my shelves that he had authored. There was an auction and Bob won the bid on an 18th century brass helmet mask for the Oduda Ritual of the Benin Empire. He paid a hefty sum for it, but it was all in the name of charity.

I kept my eye on Mr. Bellington, Dr. LeBlanc and their two companions. I was still itching for a confrontation of some sort. I had noticed that one of the men was favoring his right arm and imagined that it was the result of our gunfight. I knew I had hit one during the exchange of gunfire.

Rob stopped by our table once or twice during the evening to refill water glasses or clear used dishes. On the last pass, he covertly dropped a wallet in my lap. I pretended not to notice and when the rest of the table was distracted by a heated bidding war for a painting on display, I took a moment to look at the contents of the wallet. The driver's license was in the name of Papahi Akauola with an address in Fairfield.

I committed the address to memory then closed the wallet without further inspection. I figured Rob had probably already been through its contents and would fill me in tomorrow when we had lunch. Stephanie would be headed down to Santa Cruz early in the morning to visit her family and would return early evening Monday, so lunch with Rob wouldn't be taking away any time from the two of us.

I looked around and saw Papahi standing with Dr. LeBlanc near the bar on the other side of the room. It took me a moment to be sure it was him. The two men were similar in size and appearance and while I wouldn't say they were twins, they looked like they could be brothers.

I asked Stephanie, Bob, and Susan if they wanted anything else to drink. Stephanie was still nursing a glass of wine and Susan had switched to water. Bob requested an Old Fashioned made with rye. I went to the bar and, when it was my turn, ordered Bob's drink along with my usual.

Drinks in hand, I returned to my table to drop off the Old Fashioned and then told them I had found a wallet and would be back as soon as I returned it to its rightful owner.

Looking up to confirm that Dr. LeBlanc and Papahi were still at the bar, I made a beeline toward them. Papahi picked me up about three quarters of the way across the ballroom. He twitched, his hand reaching for the inside of his jacket. LeBlanc put a calming hand on his arm, but the motion was all the confirmation I needed that he was armed. Maybe not a direct confrontation today. Even if I was also armed, I wouldn't want to engage in a gun battle with 200-plus innocent bystanders. Instead, I put on a smile.

"Excuse me, sir," I said, holding up the wallet. "I believe you dropped this."

Papahi's hand came away from his jacket and he automatically patted the back pocket where his wallet would normally be. "Uh, thank you," he said, taking the wallet from my hand.

Now that I was closer, I could just make out the outline of the gun inside his jacket. It appeared, based on the shape of the butt of the weapon, to be a large frame revolver. "You're a little twitchy there. What are you carrying? A .357?" I smiled and Papahi looked distinctly uncomfortable. He was a good two inches taller than me and outweighed me by around a hundred pounds. His knuckles were battered, and he had a jagged scar down the right side of his neck from, if I had to guess, a beer bottle. Papahi was a street brawler and he had a street brawler's instinct for smelling trouble. He just wasn't sure of the exact nature of that trouble.

"Oh, don't worry. I'm not a cop any more. I was just curious. You should see my tailor. He can adjust your tux so the gun doesn't show at all." I turned to face LeBlanc. "Doctor, good to see you again."

"Likewise, Mr. Grey," he said with a bored smile.

I ignored the lack of use of my honorific. "It's unfortunate that men in our line of work should require security, isn't it? My home was recently broken into, forcing me to hire security for my property."

"That's a shame, Mr. Grey. It is unfortunate. I hope nothing of value was taken."

"Nothing was, thank you. Just two idiots fumbling around in the dark, not knowing what they were doing. Still, it was an inconvenience." I watched Papahi's reaction as I said "idiots" and saw a tightening of the eyes and a slight clinch of his jaws. Now I was convinced he was one of the people who had raided my house, or at least he knew who those people were. I still hadn't been able to determine why, exactly, they had broken in. Yes, I suspected it had to do with the notebook pages found in the painting, but I didn't know what those pages led to.

"Glad to hear that, Mr. Grey. Now, if you'll excuse us, we must return to our table. Good evening."

"You too, Mr. LeBlanc." With all the innuendo and tension in our brief exchange, calling him "Mister" was the first I had seen LeBlanc start to get angry.

"It's Dr. LeBlanc," he said, his voice now a little deeper and more menacing.

A man with a weak ego – this could be fun. I smiled. "My apologies." I turned and walked away.

* * * * *

Bob and I sat in the living room area of his suite and sipped a decent twelve-year-old scotch we had purchased from the hotel bar before going up to his room. Stephanie and Susan were sitting at the dining table in quiet conversation. It was now almost 11:00 p.m. and Stephanie and I would be headed back to Marin County soon.

"You think LeBlanc is involved in the break-in at your house?" Bob asked again.

"I do, or at least his two men were. Everything fits but a motive. Two guys, and LeBlanc has two meatheads as muscle. One of them, the one we haven't identified, is favoring his right arm. I shot one of the assailants. Papahi is carrying a revolver, and a revolver was used during the break in. More specifically, a .357 magnum. Also, I'm pretty sure it was the one with the shotgun that I hit. The one with the revolver was in the kitchen area." I ran down my logic for him a second time. This wasn't unusual. Bob generally liked to hear a theory several times, each time trying to poke new holes in it until he was convinced.

"It could all be coincidence."

"Except I don't believe in coincidence. They're the guys, Bob, I'm sure of it." I took a sip of the scotch.

"Don't call me Bob."

I smiled. "Now we just have to figure out what those pages mean." I had told him about finding the torn-out notebook pages in the painting and what I thought the entries I had been able to research had referred to.

"Well, it's your show to run now. Still, I'd like to know, if you'll call me when you have something to share."

"Will do." I polished off the rest of the scotch in my glass and then looked in Stephanie's direction. "You about ready to go?"

Stephanie turned to face me. "Anytime you are."

We both said our goodbyes and then I texted the limo to meet us out front.

At this time of night, there was very little in the way of traffic and we arrived back at my place just a little after midnight. Stephanie and I changed into more comfortable clothes and we sat in my room and talked for several hours. We fell asleep around 3:00 a.m. with Stephanie's head laying on my chest.

CHAPTER SIX

We slept later than either of us intended, not getting up and out of bed until almost 10:00 a.m. It was the latest and longest I had slept in quite a while. Despite the late night, I felt refreshed. Dan had let Steve out that morning and fed her. He had also left a note saying he'd be out looking for an apartment and a car.

It had been my intention to drive him, but my guess was he'd become impatient waiting for us to wake up and gone out on his own. I called security on the radio and asked what time he had left, and they replied that it had been at around 8:00 a.m. I'd text him when Stephanie left to see if he wanted to join Rob and me for lunch. I could help him apartment search from there.

While Stephanie showered and got ready, I made a pot of coffee and fixed us a quick breakfast. We sat in the nook and talked until we had finished eating. I gave her a kiss goodbye and then she was out the door and on her way to Santa Cruz. I had lent her the truck, so she didn't have to worry about renting a car. It was bigger than the vehicle she normally drove, but she didn't know how to drive a stick shift, so the Jeep was out. I could have lent her the Toyota but that belonged to the Adventurers' Club now. She'd be back to my place by tomorrow evening.

I washed the dishes and then called Dan. His phone went to voicemail, but he texted back and said he was with a sales representative buying a car and should be done in about an hour. He'd call me back then. I texted him back and said to meet me at the restaurant at noon. "Ok," was his only reply.

I showered and dressed and then took Steve out for a quick walk around the property. I had maybe thirty minutes before lunch, but it would only take me about ten minutes to get to downtown San Rafael. The burrito shop was one of my favorite Mexican restaurants. They had seven different mole sauces to choose from and each of them was as good as the others.

After a quick walk, I loaded Steve up into the back seat of the Jeep and we headed down the hill to the restaurant. I got lucky and found a parking space right in front of the restaurant where I could see Steve. The place wasn't too crowded, and I was able to get seated at a table for four.

This time when Rob appeared I knew it was him, even though he had once again changed his appearance. This time he was sporting a long, gray ponytail, a medium-length gray beard and was wearing a Grateful Dead t-shirt, cotton pants, and sandals. He sat down across from me.

"Jerod," he said by way of greeting.

"Rob," I responded. "What the hell is with the disguises?"

"If I'm conducting counter-surveillance on them, what makes you think that they aren't conducting counter-surveillance on you? That lady over there," he said, indicating a woman sitting at a corner table by herself, "you think she's here just to eat?"

I looked over to where the lady was sitting in time to see her glance away. I was usually pretty good at picking up tails but if she had been following me, I hadn't seen her. I looked back at Rob and he was smiling so I knew then that he was just messing with me. Still, he had made his point.

"Duly noted," I conceded.

Dan showed up and joined us at our table. I introduced him to Rob and we caught him up to speed on what we were working on.

Rob gave a brief synopsis of the past few days. He had staked out the location on my property they had been conducting surveillance from, and when the man we had later identified as Papahi Akauola showed up, Rob had been about to take him down when he decided instead to follow him. Papahi had left before 4:00 a.m. and hiked down the hill to his car, the black sedan that had followed me when I went to Novato. Rob didn't have a vehicle nearby and couldn't follow.

During the day, Rob pre-staged a car near where Papahi had parked the night before. "People are creatures of habit," he explained. "He had been getting away with parking there for at least the previous few days, so he had no reason to believe that he would get caught if he parked there again." Dan and I both nodded at his logic.

That day Rob had also contacted the rental car company and had been able to obtain a name and address. They had used a female to rent the car. That wasn't uncommon among the criminal element, as Rob and I had both discovered when we were police officers. Her name was Sela Koloi. Rob had yet to figure out her relationship to Papahi, but he did discover that the other man was Papahi's brother, Kaivao Akauola.

Using a public records database, Rob had found a possible address for Kaivao and staked the place out. That had been yesterday. Around 5:00 p.m., Kaivao and Papahi had left Kaivao's residence and had driven over to the City where they met up with Mr. Bellington and Dr. LeBlanc at the fundraiser. Rob had stolen a server uniform and then simply blended in with the rest of the servers. With the number of people there, no one took notice of the extra body. He had been surprised to see me there.

For my part, I told them both about the notebook pages I had found in the Salvador Dali painting Cat had purchased from Harold Touscher and my theories on their origins. Collectively, though, none of us could determine the importance of the pages and why someone would go to such lengths to steal them. They were compelling, and I wanted to know the story behind them, but I was also sure I wasn't willing to kill to get that story.

Dan looked thoughtful for a moment. "Tomorrow, the Adventurers' Club will be fully operational. I say we take this on as our first official job. There's a mystery here and with the right spin, it could generate some attention that would get the Club and our mission out there in the spotlight."

I thought about it for a moment and then nodded in agreement. "Care to help me put together a brief for our staff meeting tomorrow?" Dan said he would.

Our strategizing was interrupted by the waiter bringing us our food. I looked at the carne asada burrito smothered in mole poblano sauce and temporarily put thoughts of mysteries and shadowy figures out of my mind and concentrated on one of the true joys in life: good food and good company.

CHAPTER SEVEN

Papahi and Kaivao Akauola stood before Chandler LeBlanc's desk, staring out the windows at a sweeping view of San Francisco. The desk was massive, almost eight feet in length and four feet wide; it was made of mahogany polished to a deep, rich shine. The office was scaled to match the desk, covering almost as much square footage as Kaivao's house in Fairfield. Massive bookshelves lined one wall, stacked with texts of all sort and various pieces of ancient art.

The other wall had some of Dr. LeBlanc's more precious pieces protected by glass cases. Here and there, the head of an exotic animal or the instruments of war of bygone civilizations decorated the walls.

"Last night was an unmitigated disaster, thanks to your incompetence," LeBlanc was saying. "Grey now knows who you are and if he is not already in possession of the lost pages, and from what I have heard about the man, he will not rest until he knows why you broke into his home. With the security guards and his new security system, we will not get another opportunity to retrieve those pages."

Kaivao shifted his feet uncomfortably but Papahi continued to stare out the window, his face impassive.

LeBlanc leaned back in his chair and rubbed his face with his hand. "Well, there are other ways to get the painting and we can hope that the pages are still in it. If not, it is going to make locating the pieces of Wodan's Key more difficult." He turned his chair so that he was now looking out the windows as well. "Find me Maryanne Bishop and bring her to me."

Papahi turned and started walking toward the exit, his younger brother following behind him. He was reaching for the doorknob when LeBlanc's voice stopped him.

"Oh, and Papahi, don't fail me again. I do not tolerate incompetence." Papahi ground his jaws together but said only, "Yes, sir." He simply opened the door and left.

Chandler LeBlanc continued to stare out the window even after the brothers had departed. This was a quest his father had started seventy years ago and Chandler fully intended to complete it by recovering Wodan's Key and finding the vault that key opened.

THE END

If you enjoyed this book, please read my other titles:

"Wodan's Key: A Me, the World and a Dog Named Steve Adventure"

"The Undying: A Me, the World, and a Dog Named Steve Adventure"

"Copy Cat: A Marcus Maddox Mystery"

"L.E.O.: The True Stories of Lieutenant Wayne Cotes"

And Coming Soon

"The Serenity Stone: A Me, the World, and a Dog Named Steve Adventure"

CPSIA information can be obtained
at www.ICGtesting.com
Printed in the USA
JSHW032114110921
18635JS00001B/3